Albatross

the scent of honeysuckle

Jeff B Grant

Published by Besonian
Copyright © Jeff B Grant

ISBN: 0993332803
ISBN-13: 978-0-9933328-0-7

DEDICATION

To my father, whom I recall only dimly when I was a very young child, and whose absence from the remainder of my life has been the inspiration for this book.

ACKNOWLEDGMENTS

My thanks - if 'thanks' are sufficient - to Anita, without whose enduring love and care, many things, including this book, would never have come to fruition. My thanks also to my children and my stepchildren who, by being there, have helped motivate my writing. My thanks also to my lovely sister Carol, of whose existence I got to know only a very few years ago. And in memoriam, to my dear stepmother Agnes, now departed this vale of tears. Finally, to my long-time friend Kevin, whose own forays into self-publishing have been an incentive for me to do the same.

Jeff B Grant

Jeff was born in the city of Leicester in the UK. He was educated at Bedford Modern School and at Strode's School in the county of Surrey, before going on to study English Language and Literature at Saint Edmund Hall, Oxford. After graduating he worked for several years as a Producer and then Director of television and cinema commercials in London. One of his early directing credits was for the 1973 Public Information Film, "Dark and Lonely Water". This was voted the UK's 4th favourite Public Information Film of all time, and is still garnering comments on YouTube today as the scariest of all Public Information Films broadcast on UK television.

Jeff then moved on to writing and directing films for organisations such as the Post Office, British Oxygen Company, Ford Motor Company, the BBC, etc. During his time in the film industry Jeff worked all over the UK, in mainland Europe, several African countries, India, Hong Kong, Japan, Australia, the USA and the Caribbean. He received many international awards for both directing and writing.

Jeff left the film industry during the recession of the mid-nineties. He moved out of London into the country and took a long look at himself and at life. He eventually moved back to London where he now lives and writes. He enjoys playing the piano, tinkering with computers, watching and listening to birds, taking photographs of the world around him, practising yoga, spending time with his partner, family and friends, and eating hot Indian food.

I walk a path between trees after rain.
I hear birdsong
And weep inside for something lost.

1.

I leave the light on at night, and lie on my back. That way I can keep an eye on the small black hole in the ceiling – there, just above the door. The home of two geckos – I presume that's what they are. I saw them last night. Man and wife. They emerged from the darkness very slowly, warily - then remained there upside down, still as stones. They're harmless, I'm told. But nocturnal, and apt to lose their grip in the night. What sleep I get is shallow and short-lived.

The mattress on my bed is thin. Through it, I feel the bedsprings. There is no spring left in them. The floor and the walls are bare concrete. I have nowhere to wash. There is a small cupboard fixed to one wall. It's where I keep my toothbrush. I've run out of toothpaste. The one wooden chair has a broken leg and lies useless on the concrete floor. By the bed, there is a small wooden table.

I have been in this place three weeks. It may be more. Things have got confused. Youssef said he would be back today. He wasn't. But he'll turn up. Maybe tomorrow. I trust him. I doubt he'll return with anything to add to the little we've managed to put together - I'm not holding my breath. I had offered to go with him. His response was to the effect that it would cramp his style. I didn't ask him to elaborate. This has all cost me dear in both time and money. The latter is not a problem. But I'm running out of the former.

The occupant of the next room forces open his creaking door yet one more time and urinates luxuriously against the outside wall in the darkness. That's where I do it. It's the best place. It's that, or the fly-infested privy across the courtyard which hasn't been cleaned since Mafeking was relieved. It's not a place to visit in the dark.

I'm calling time on all this. When Youssef returns we will leave the others and set out on the ball-breaker of a journey back to the capital. Fifteen hours down a plumb line of a road in forty-five degrees. But at the other end there'll be a shower. There'll be soap. A real bed. I haven't slept in a real bed for a long time. I can't sleep in this place anyway - geckos or no geckos. The air-con unit under the window grinds away with a whining, cyclical note that sets my teeth on edge. I've told them about it. They say they'll see to it. But nothing happens. Something about a problem with getting parts from Europe – France? Turning it off is not an option. I'd suffocate. I borrowed Youssef's electric razor and shaved my beard off. That helped. The heat made it itch. Without it I feel naked. But I'm getting used to it. I trim the stubble once, occasionally twice a week.

Where am I? Who am I? I knew, once. I was the king. The talker-king. I knew all things. There was no subject on earth or in the heavens about which I did not have an opinion. I had an opinion for this, an opinion for that and should some matter arise about which I had no opinion I'd pretty soon come up with one. They needed to know, you see. They needed to know. And whatever came out of my mouth they believed, and so knew – sort of. They would gaze at me like children at a party watching the conjurer. And inside, all I had for them was pity. Not the pity that comes from compassion but that dark pity – which isn't really pity at all but the offshoot of some corrupt conviction that one is superior. I looked past them, seeing only my own reflection.

I take up the little dog-eared black and white photograph and gaze at it yet again. He could be anybody; yet I know he's of me, mine. As I put it down again on the rough table by the bed, lines from a Chinese poem are in my mind.

'Let me go down next year with the spring waters
And search for you to the end of the white clouds in the East.'

2.

It had been an ordinary day. Ellen liked ordinary days. You could potter more or less amiably through them. Then, as evening drew on, put your feet up knowing there was a fair chance you'd have a decent night's sleep. She looked at the clock. Poured herself a small whisky. She added just a drop of still spring water. Those who knew said it brought out the bouquet. Ellen liked to do things properly.

She yawned. Then felt a twinge of unease. There was an outside chance she might have forgotten to tell him she'd be staying on here in the country tonight. If so, he might just be on his way to London, expecting to join her there. But as she thought about it, she decided it was hardly the sort of thing she would forget. And in any case, as he wasn't answering his mobile phone, there was little she could do about it.

She rang it once more but again it went straight through to his voicemail. No doubt he had switched it off before giving his talk then forgotten to switch it back on again afterwards. In the days when she had thought she might make a difference, she'd suggested that at times like that he didn't switch it off but simply set it to 'Vibrate' or even 'Silent'. But he objected to having it 'jumping around in his pocket' on 'Vibrate', and he wouldn't put it on 'Silent' because how then would he know it had rung? Barney and technology didn't mix. Their one desktop computer sat in the study here, gathering dust. Their friends spoke casually of ordering things 'online'. The modern world was passing them by.

She sipped her whisky. Then got up to draw the curtains. Dusk was settling over the garden. The shrubs were black hulks now, their lovely autumn colours in abeyance till morning. Between the hills to the east, the lights of Ludlow were coming on, twinkling through a slight haze. Already a sliver of pale moon hung amidst the silhouetted branches of the big beech and a robin somewhere piped the last of his day's song. She closed the world off and sat down again. Stretched her legs and closed her eyes. The whisky warmed her. It had been a nice, ordinary day.

3.

The afternoon was grey with a low, heavy overcast. The sea was calm but with an oily, sullen swell. What breath of wind there was wafted inland a penetrating drizzle. On the low wall near the very end of the breakwater a man sat alone. He aroused the interest of two fishermen who were packing up their lines and tackle. He was getting on in years, hatless, wearing a suit, collar and tie and expensive black overcoat. His shoes were well-polished black brogues. His clothes were soaking wet. On the wall by his side was an expensive black leather briefcase with a gold clasp. He sat forward, elbows on his knees, his eyes on the ground. What remained of his hair was plastered by the rain to his forehead and face. The fishermen passed him on their back way to the shore. Each tried to catch his eye, but he didn't look up. They continued on.

They called in at the chandler's shop to ask the man who ran it if he'd noticed the man at the end of the breakwater. Yes, he said, he's been there most of the afternoon. They wondered if they should notify someone – the police perhaps. Or the council. But they decided it was most likely he just wanted to be alone.

It was dusk when the man in the chandler's shop closed for the day. Before he left for home he took a walk to the end of the breakwater. The man had gone.

4.

It was an afternoon in early Spring when the man came to ask questions. Ellen was nervous. Although he was there at her instigation, she had, even so, a sense of being party to a betrayal. He flicked through the pages of his notebook. She hadn't expected in this day and age a man with a notebook and pencil. Nor a man in his sixties. Yet he seemed spry and sharp enough.

The afternoon sun shifted shadows across the deep pile carpet. She felt uncomfortably hot, got up from her chair and opened a window. The long curtains moved idly in the sudden draught. She sat down again opposite him and arranged her skirt with fingers which bore the early signs of arthritis.

He cleared his throat. "So," he said, "what sort of time – roughly – was this? Can you remember?"

She could. It was burned into her brain. "Three minutes past four in the afternoon. He said the sun was going down and it was starting to get cold."

"And that is the big garden - " - the man turned and pointed out the rear window - " - at the back of the house? He came in from there?"

"Yes." She shifted a little in her chair. "The walled garden. He quite often sat out there on his own. When there was some sun anyway."

He consulted his notes.

She watched. Was he married? Were he and his wife still together? He wore a ring. That of course didn't mean they were. Or even that he was still married. What did it mean? Little. All you could be sure of was that he was wearing a ring. A gold one. Or at least one that looked gold. And he was overweight. If he had a wife how did she feel about that? Did she notice? Or was she too tied up in her own concerns, her own anxieties? Life is short. You hear its running footsteps.

He ran a hand through what remained of his hair – as though that took the edge off some awkwardness. "How did he – er - how did your husband describe this person?"

She spoke almost mechanically, as though verbalizing something that had gone around in her head many times, rehearsed but unspoken. "A young man. Probably in his late twenties or early thirties. He had almost shoulder-length dark hair and wore a black overcoat. And a red scarf even though it was warm for mid-October. He was sitting on the wooden bench at the far side of the rose garden by the philadelphus - close to the gate that leads out to the meadow and the river."

"What sort of distance was there between your husband and this person?"

"They were on opposite sides of the garden." She shrugged. "Thirty or forty yards, maybe."

"Did your husband challenge him – call out to him?"

"He said he was too shocked – even though he'd seen him before. 'Shaken' was the actual word he - "

"He'd seen him before?" He was surprised.

"Yes."

"Once? More than once?"

"Once."

"Where?"

"The same place. On that bench. Wearing the same clothes."

His eyes narrowed. "And did he challenge him?"

She turned away. Beyond the window, early leaves stirred in the wind. She felt a need to forestall any suspicion of her husband's timidity. She turned back to him and said, "By the time he'd gathered himself together enough to call out the man had disappeared."

"Where did he 'disappear' to?"

"There's a beech hedge – a rather tall one. You have only to take a step or two from where he was sitting to be hidden by it."

"I presume your husband went after him?"

"He said he did."

"And - what?"

"There was nobody. Nobody behind the hedge, nobody on the pathway, nobody in the herb garden, nobody on the lawn. Nobody."

His pencil squeaked across the paper. "Had he managed to get a sight of the man's face?"

She looked down and picked at an imaginary loose thread on her skirt. "He said not." She paused. "It was one of those late autumn days when once the sun goes down it gets cold and slightly misty. Things can be deceptive in that light." She sensed an awkwardness. "Maybe you've noticed."

He stopped writing and looked up. "In the weeks or months prior to this incident had you noticed any change in his behaviour?"

"What sort of change?"

"Was he as he always had been with you for example? Did he appear preoccupied, distant? That sort of thing."

"He had probably been a bit stressed. But then he quite often was. His work is – well – I'm sure you understand."

"Had he seemed perhaps more so than usual?"

She shrugged. "Perhaps. If so, it would be something to do with work. He seldom talked about his work."

"You spoke of a gate - " - he flicked over the pages of his notebook - " - in the rear wall. Could this person have gained entrance that way to the garden?"

"He could. But it was locked. It's always locked unless there's some specific reason for it not to be. If Peter's here for example. He's the gardener. And he wasn't here that day."

"Are there any other ways out of that garden?"

"Through the house. That's all. Through the kitchen."

"And you yourself were in the kitchen at that time?"

"I was."

His pencil squeaked. How often do people write with pencils these days? His shoes were well-polished but old. Too old really, and polished beyond their useful life. Perhaps he wasn't very well-off. He seemed to be writing for ever.

Eventually he looked up. "You say your husband said he'd been 'shaken' by what he saw."

"When he came into the kitchen he was quite pale. I thought at first he was ill."

He scribbled a final note. Closed the book with a flourish and said he thought that was all for the time being. Thanking her, he stood up.

She eased herself with some difficulty out of her chair.

"Oh - one other thing." He slipped his notebook back into his briefcase. "How would you describe your husband?"

She looked puzzled.

"What sort of a man would you say he is?"

"A nice man. A conventional man – in a proper sort of way. Adores Mozart. No frills. Kind." She smiled. "A man who remembers my birthday."

"I see. Thank you." He went to leave.

She lay a hand on his arm. "This is between you and me - and absolutely nobody else. That is understood? There are people not so much interested in the truth as in what capital they may make from it."

"You have my word."

They shook hands. She saw him out, then sat again in the armchair and listened to the sound of his car as it faded along the lane. The sudden emptiness of the room pressed in on her. She felt if she reached out she might actually touch it.

5.

The black Jaguar threw water up from the road as it swung wildly into the forecourt and slithered to a stop on the gravel. Heavy rain driven by a strong wind, lashed the bonnet and windscreen. The two occupants conducted a hurried conversation behind the sweeping wipers. The man emerged, pulled his jacket up over his head and sprinted the short distance to the office.

The woman flipped down the vanity mirror, checked her appearance, then flipped the mirror back up again.

Room 410 was the last in a long, down-at-heel row. There were parking spaces in front of each. Rainwater filled the potholes in the asphalt. The only other vehicle was a battered Ford pickup in front of 409. The Jaguar rocked and splashed into its parking space. There was a lot of laughter from the steamed-up interior before both occupants tumbled from it and ran through the rain each clutching a briefcase. His lank, thinning hair trailed across his forehead in the wind. He flicked it impatiently back as he fumbled with the key in the lock. She held tight onto his arm and giggled.

"Can't get it in the hole," he said.

She shrieked with brief laughter before clamping a hand over her mouth.

The door of 410 slammed behind them.

In the window of the next room a corner of the curtain was lifted, then allowed to fall back again.

Steam rose from the bonnet of the Jaguar as it cooled in the wind and the rain.

6.

Barnaby Marechal looked up from his book. Red brick houses flashing past. One or two with their front steps polished bright red. 'Red raddle' – was that what they called it? Long rear gardens with washing flapping, garden sheds, a pigeon loft. A corner shop, a knot of women with pushchairs, talking. A bus full of faces bound for a place he'd once vaguely heard of. A shadowy world still half-remembered.

The train crashed through the girders of a metal bridge spanning a wide, empty, sluggish river far below, mud banks on either side, tidal, a thin, discoloured mist hanging low over it. Past a run-down industrial estate. In the carpark of one of the units, rubbish piled high in its own back yard, a man – early thirties perhaps, smartly-dressed, medium height with dark hair - walked towards a shiny black car. Nervously juggling a briefcase and car keys, he struggled out of his jacket. Barney watched until a factory wall wiped the view.

He went back to his book. The words floated up and past him like flecks of dust in the wind. The weight of this thing grew by the day, forcing him into an ever-narrowing slice of the here and now. With a flick of the wrist he shut his book. He closed his eyes, sat back and took a deep breath. He exhaled slowly, trying to believe what he had once read about the outgoing breath dismissing all that has been. If only. He saw the house in Halifax. The green front door. The roses in the garden. He'd never got the measure of roses. Perhaps he'd never really tried. The clickety-clacking of the wheels of the pushchair on the uneven pavements.

He sat up straight again. Set himself to mull over the last twenty-four hours. Lunch today with the usual band of ill-assorted dignitaries – how could one local authority summon up that many people of 'dignity'? - had gone well enough. He'd played the part so many times he knew it by heart and back again. Hands had been shaken, drinks drunk, smiles smiled, compliments and airy promises exchanged. Tout le monde had gone away claiming to have got "so much" out of it. So he had done his job. OK, fine.

His performance the previous evening however had been disappointing. His talk had veered off-centre and he had not been able to pull it back. It was unlike him. He was a natural communicator. Audiences warmed to him. He charmed them. It was said he could give a veneer of meaning to the utterly meaningless. A priceless skill in politics. But last night the magic had not happened. The talk had been edgy, the charm consciously applied.

His audience had irritated him. Audiences these days did. A self-important gaggle of small-town businessmen and women, sycophantic and dressed for the kill. In days gone by he would have licked his lips. He would cajole, amuse, impress, infuriate then placate them, make them think a little, shock them, then make them laugh out loud. He would take them up hill and down dale and they would follow - captivated, admiring.

But last evening, his irritation had been such that he'd had difficulty concealing it. At least, he hoped he'd concealed it. Either way, at the end of his talk, there they were, drinks in hand, eager to press the flesh and flash their comely smiles. How shallow and predictable the whole circus. And he the ringmaster. There came into his mind the young man back there getting into his company car. What pressures of money and targets and all the sweaty struggle for supremacy and to make ends meet was the poor lad under? And for what? This?

The train was slowing down past drab housing estates, rows of small shops, past a faux-doric supermarket surrounded by cars nuzzling it like piglets at a sow. A man walked a white dog by a stream in a park. A purple wall of Victorian brick slid across the window. From a diagonal crack across its surface, some sort of shrub waved its thin branches. How does a thing like that eke out a life from solid brick?

A long, sweeping platform and name-board - 'Wigan'. Ah - Wigan. 'The Road to Wigan Pier'. Read once, so long ago he'd forgotten almost everything about it. Wigan. A name he'd ever seen, rightly or wrongly, as iconic of the industrial north. Now no doubt a bloodless remnant of its past glories. 'Oh Maggie, what have we done to England?' The Floyd. Where are they now? Vanished. Like Wigan's glory. England's glory. All our glory.

Two men in thick overcoats, loaded with cases and laptops, struggled past him towards the exit. The train juddered to a stop. The sudden cessation of movement was disorienting. On the cinema screen of the window people glided past - pushchairs, suitcases, backpacks. Men, women, mothers with children, students, lone men, suited men, wide-shouldered career women, babies in arms, toddlers – so very many of those little people with their glowing cheeks and expectant eyes, newcomers to these cut-price shores. A feeling of huge pointlessness was on him. Then without knowing why, without the slightest preconsideration, he too found himself on the move. On his feet, slipping his book into his jacket pocket, pulling down his overnight case from the rack. He hurried to the end of the coach, and jumped down onto the platform just as the automatic door closed behind him. The chill of autumn hit him. The low sun made him squint.

People were pulling wheeled suitcases and hauling tardy youngsters along behind them, flowing around him as a stream bubbles around a boulder. Then the accelerating drumbeat of the train wheels vibrating the platform beneath his feet, the coach windows blinding him in the autumn sun. The backwash from the last coach flicked his trousers cold against his calves. He watched the train snaking away down the tracks – taking with it his world. There it went - ever smaller until the last remnant of the final coach and the little red light that clung to it was lost behind distant trees bearing the auburn, red and yellowing leaves of Autumn. Gone.

What, in God's name, had he done?

He sat on a cold metal seat on the station forecourt. Gusts of wind chased newspaper and fast-food cartons across the asphalt like urban tumbleweed. The small car park was almost empty of cars. On the main road he could see buses and people. A banner across a shop window – 'Payday Advances'. People in cheap clothes. A man stared at him like he had no right to be there. Perhaps he hadn't. He looked down at himself - Savile Row suit, Crombie coat. Church's shoes. Patek Philippe wristwatch. Louis Vuitton overnight case. He felt vulnerable. A cab appeared. He climbed into the rear seat and said the first thing that came into his head. "A hotel please."

"Which one?"

"Any one."

"What – a place to stay, like? Or do you – well – you know?" The man's Lancashire accent came as a surprise.

"A place to stay. What else would I want with a hotel?"

The man shrugged. "You're the boss." The cab pulled away.

He stared from the window. Wigan was a disappointment. Where were the mill chimneys, the colliery winding gear and other remnants of the gritty industrial north?

"Up here on business then, are you?"

He mumbled some half-intelligible reply. It seemed to satisfy. The man said no more.

He took from his pocket his mobile phone. Checked it was still switched off. Then slipped it back into his pocket. He looked out of the window again. Saw the odd half-timbered building. Not what he would have expected.

The cab pulled onto a tree-encircled forecourt. The Balmoral Hotel.

"Grand place, this," said the driver. "They'll see you alright."

Wide steps led up to an ornate entrance. Revolving doors with well-polished wood and highly-shone brass handrails. He paid the driver and thanked him. He got out, went up the steps. A chalked notice board announced that the Balmoral Hotel was today proud host to a conference of local businessmen and women. He put his nose to the glass of the revolving doors. The lobby was a crush of wide-shouldered suits, showy frocks with cleavage and jewellery, glasses in hand. Bustling, guffawing, pontificating.

He went back down the steps.

He walked. Just walked. For a long time, his mind empty. His overnight bag grew heavy. The shadows lengthened and the autumn air turned cold. As dusk was turning to night he found himself in a street of run-down, rambling, Victorian houses. One of them was the 'Welcome Hotel'.

He was nervous. His palms and fingers were sweating, making it difficult to get a grip on the casing of his mobile phone. Then with a sudden, sharp, snapping sound it seemed to spring off almost of its own accord. He peered curiously into the phone's innards. That thing – that red thing was the sim card. He was sure of that. But how to get it out? Press with the fingertip. The finger was too big. Press, then slide. The sweaty tip wouldn't grip it. But then, by edging a fingernail in around the edge, he eased it out.

He placed it carefully into his wallet. Then put the body of the phone in his overnight case, open on the bed. He was pleased with himself. It seemed important to have done that.

He sat back and studied his surroundings. The windows needed cleaning. There was a tear in one of the net curtains. The hangers in the rickety wardrobe were the wire things you get from dry-cleaning outfits. There were black marks on the threadbare carpet. Odd stains on the wallpaper above the bed. There was a faint and strangely unpleasant odour – like a cocktail of stale food and dust.

He was hungry. It was dark outside in the empty street. He wasn't going to eat in the hotel dining room. The last thing he wanted was some eager face bearing down on him, bent on either glad-handing him or telling him what a mess they were making of the country. Though he doubted there were many staying in a place like this who took any interest in the news or politics, it was a risk he daren't take. Nor dare he take that same – and probably much greater – risk in any decent restaurant in the town. He picked up the telephone and asked Reception to put him through to Room Service.

"Through to what?" She sounded hardly out of school.

"Room Service."

Long pause. "I don't think we have one of them."

Barney frowned. "I beg your pardon?"

"I said I don't think we have a room service."

"No room service?" He was instantly and profoundly irritated. "What is a guest supposed to do if they want to take dinner in their room?"

"I don't know."

"Why is there no room service?"

Pause. "I don't think there's any call for one."

He put the phone down.

He looked in his overnight bag. Two bananas which he'd taken from the fruit trolley at lunchtime, and a packet of biscuits Ellen must have put in. On the dressing table by the window there was a cheap electric kettle, some tea bags and a few of those tiny plastic tubs of milk. He'd survive.

That night, in a dream, he saw the man. On the wooden seat on the far side of the rose garden. He caught sight of him through the now almost bare branches of the philadelphus. The black coat, and the long red scarf trailing almost to the gravel path. He called out to him, but his shouts were whispers. The man stood up. His face was turned the other way. He tried to run to him, but his feet were lead. When he stood at last by the seat, the man was gone. He could hear the river in the meadow the other side of the high garden wall as it rippled gently across the line of boulders.

He shot upright in bed. His heart was pounding, his hot body running with perspiration. His pyjama jacket clung to him, cold, wet. He pulled it off and threw it to the floor. Sat back, closed his eyes.

He struggled out of bed, filled the plastic kettle with water and switched it on. He was cold and had no dressing gown. He put on his cast-off shirt. He felt foolish waiting for the kettle to boil wearing only a shirt. Outside in the street, beyond the torn curtain, a red neon sign flickered. Its light turned the film of dust on the windows pink and flooded the room red like a desert whorehouse. He was too old, too used to five-star hotels. He made himself a cup of tea then stood looking out of the window. A clock struck the half-hour. He sipped. The night was cloudless. A lemon-silk powdering of moonlight lay over the jumbled, silent rooftops.

Was Ellen asleep?

Don't go there.

Was she? And dreaming? Or just lying in bed unable to sleep, wondering, worrying?

Tell her, then. Ring her and tell her.

Tell her what?

The truth.

It's not just the boy.

She wouldn't need to know the rest.

The rest's almost as much a part of it.

Let's think of it like this then. As it stands, the situation's recoverable. You've a single night's absence to explain away – that's all. Too many glasses of vino at lunch. Decided to stay on another night but fell asleep in the afternoon. 'And do you know what, I didn't open my eyes again till this morning!'

Then what?

Then finito. Over and done with.

Six months on, I'd be back here. Or at some other flyblown hotel jumping through the same hoops. I can't not feel what I'm feeling. I've spent most of my life trying.

You really should have thought of this a long time ago.

A police siren threads its way through the city. Barney shivers, sips his tea. It warms him. But he is still cold.

Just a thought - have you considered the possibility that Ellen herself might quite take to the idea?

He puts the empty cup to one side. The moon hangs precariously off the edge of a roof.

Ellen is not a children person.

Are you?

I hear his cries in the night when there are no cries to hear.

The lights of a car sweep briefly across the frayed curtains, chasing shadows around the walls like cavorting grotesques.

I gave up trying to sleep. Took my notebook from my briefcase. I wrote -

'Let's be clear. Do this, and -

a - it's the end of my career.

b - it's the end of my marriage, in any meaningful sense.

c – it's going to hurt others.

d – it could all come to nothing.'

I am sixty-five. I am not a brave man but I have to deal with this. It is crowding out my ability to live. I sense I've trespassed against some fundamental law of the universe.

7.

By morning he was ravenous. He ate the bananas and the biscuits. The sun was shining and the day looked inviting. He opened the window. The torn curtain flapped in the clear, fresh air. It was still early and there were few people about. His eye was caught by a sudden movement. He experienced a wave of almost childlike pleasure at the sight of a canal boat, its Romany-style decoration brilliant in the low morning sun, threading its way silently between distant buildings. Sitting on its roof was a large black dog. Perhaps it thought it was the captain of the ship. And maybe it was.

He sat down on the bed. Decision time. If he were to go on with this he would have do something about his appearance. And do it now. Not that he could do a lot - he had with him only the few overnight clothes Ellen had packed. But something had to be possible. Not shaving would be a start. A beard makes one look older, changes the shape of a face. He'd never grown a beard. He'd heard they itched. He lay out on the bed the clothes he had with him. Wearing only his underwear and socks, he stood before the cheap wall mirror. He would effect what change he could.

One clean light-blue shirt – classic and timeless. He put that on. OK. The only trousers were his suit trousers. He put them on. The only footwear were the John Church brogues. He put them on. But already he was back to the middle-class executive. The trousers needed to be replaced with jeans, the brogues with trainers. Barnaby Marechal in jeans and trainers! How would he cope? A conditioned reflex sent his hand out for his tie. No. Leave the neck open. He did, but felt half-dressed.

Ellen, careful soul, had also included a thick, dark-grey sweater – autumn, she'd said, was on us. The evenings could be cold. He put that on over his blue shirt, then eased the collar of the shirt out so that it sat outside the sweater. That took the edge off the executive.

His hair. Although not a lot of it left, what remained was too well-cut. It needed to be longer. Maybe even a little messy. A bit arty. That would take time. Meanwhile he'd have to just keep it – sort of – untidy. He pushed his fingers into it and ruffled it up. It was too short to ruffle much. Men put some sort of pomade, Brylcreem or something, on their hair these days. And forced it into waves and odd shapes. That might be worth trying. He could of course dye it some other colour. That seemed a step too far. Though it might not seem so at a later date.

The overall effect wasn't convincing. The John Church shoes, the Savile Row trousers and the Fenwicks sweater – he looked like an off-duty middle-class executive who'd forgotten to brush his hair.

But then a brainwave. Always, at this time of the year, he carried with him a pair of sunglasses. If one is driving, the low sunlight of October and early November can play havoc with one's vision. He fished them out of his briefcase, settled them on his nose. With just the tips of his fingers he adjusted them so they sat nicely. There. Back a touch. Now – he was getting somewhere. He looked all around, up and down. The world was too dark for comfort, but he supposed it was a question of getting used to that.

He took a few steps back from the mirror. It was a start. He was beginning to look a little unlike Barnaby Marechal MP. When the trousers and shoes had become jeans and trainers; when his hair and beard had grown to a reasonable length, those in SW1 would be hard pressed to know who he was. A black leather jacket would not go amiss. And what about a hat? Maybe even that.

Without actually having made a decision, this thing seemed to be happening. He would not stop it.

He looked at his watch. Only half-eight. Should he risk the dining room and breakfast? He had to start somewhere. He checked himself again in the mirror. OK. Then stepped out into the corridor, locked his door and in the semi-darkness brought on by his sunglasses, set off uncertainly towards the lift. He guessed he looked something of a poser. But these days posers abound.

8.

In the sixties, Halifax to Northampton by car was a long journey. The main roads were often narrow and densely overcrowded. Many of them wandered in leisurely fashion around the countryside, following, more or less, the outlines of medieval fields and the borders of ancient farming communities. On the way, give or take the odd bypass, you had to negotiate the congested main streets of any number of small towns and villages. A short length of the UK's first motorway – the M1 – had by then been built, but even though we could have used it for part of our journey, Stella proclaimed it too busy and too fast a road on which to take a baby. The logic escaped me.

Our car – a pre-WW2 Morris Eight that had seen better days – had no heater. On cold winter days, in order to be comfortable, you wore a sweater and wrapped a blanket around your knees. Dad had tried his best to persuade us to accept his cast-off Rover - expensive, middle-class, built like a tank and as warm as toast in cold weather. He was much enamoured of the idea of our swanning around the north of England in a practical example of his munificence. And sure, I'd look the man in that thing Dad, and we'd have the locals wondering at our affluence. But Dad - I need to be the provider for myself and my own. As you were.

Dad accused me, on that account, of being a closet socialist. I couldn't make sense of that, and if Dad could, then it made me wonder what he knew of Socialism. Or, his magnanimity spurned by his only son, had he said it simply out of pique? Either way, he turned the spotlight on cousin Melanie. She lived on her own in Birmingham and was reputed to prefer girlfriends to boyfriends. As far as I knew he hadn't seen her in years. In the event, she was no more interested than I. A car, to her, was a metal box with a wheel at each corner, the sole function of which was to get one from A to B. Which her elderly Austin Seven did well enough most of the time, and with a petrol consumption a fraction of that of the Rover.

In the end, he gave it to Toc H. On the condition however, that they either sold or raffled it, then did with the proceeds whatever they normally did with proceeds. Both they and he were happy. Reeling at his philanthropy, they rubbed their hands, and he came away with face mostly saved.

The run-up to Christmas that year was bitterly cold. That was in the days when the winters were cold and the summers warm – that, at least, is how I remember them. The journey from Halifax to Northampton was purgatory. I sat in the front on my own. Stella sat in the back with baby Matt beside her in his carry cot. Stella and I had blankets wrapped around us. Matt was tucked in and swaddled like a tiny mummy. A mile or two from Endell Street he puked. He was a poor passenger in cars. I pulled into a pub car park. The pub had shut for the afternoon – they did in those days. The landlord wasn't pleased to have someone banging on his door out of hours. Nor was he inclined to help, until his wife looked over his shoulder and asked what was going on. At that, he sullenly agreed to let me take a bowl of hot water to wash the vomit off the blankets. But feeling somewhat upstaged by his wife, he attempted to claw back some authority by instructing me to leave the empty bowl on the step outside the door when we'd done with it. With which he shut the door with a crash and shot the bolts. Stella washed the sick off the blankets. I took the bowl back, emptied its unsavoury contents down a drain and placed it on the step outside the door. Then scribbled a note on a piece of paper from my pocket and left it in the bowl – 'Please piss in here.'

Some fifty miles further south, on a stretch of the A1, Matt filled his nappy. Then cried. The road at that point was dual carriageway so we couldn't stop. We had to drive best part of five miles to the next lay-by with Matt's crying getting louder and both front windows down to fend off asphyxiation.

Stella's patience had been thin before we started out. So had mine. Things had not been good between us for some while. By the time we arrived in Northampton both of us had had enough. I was angry with her and she with me. I was angry with Matt, poor little scrap. I was angry with my mother for having manipulated us – or me particularly - into spending the holiday with them. I was angry with the world because it wasn't going my way. And now there was Christmas and four days with my parents to get through.

My mother came from Hungary. Her name was Agnes. I've seen photographs of her, taken about the time she and Dad met. In those days she was seriously beautiful. And even in her early middle-age, as she was that Christmas, she still turned heads. But she was not easy to be with. She had become disillusioned and resentful. I don't criticize her for it. Given the hand life had dealt her, which of us could be sure we would have done better?

In 1937, aged eighteen, with little money and perhaps half a dozen words of English, she had turned up one day in England from Budapest, carrying a small leather suitcase. In it was all she possessed - a change of clothes, a photograph of her parents on their wedding day, and a little wooden doll made for her by her father when she was a child. It had been arranged she would stay with a distant male relative on her mother's side, a man referred to as Uncle Arpad. He had a house in Peterborough and had lived in England most of his adult life. Agnes had never met him.

The foresight of her Jewish parents almost certainly saved her life. Despite Hungary's being an Axis power, they'd cherished few illusions about what was likely to come their way – and if theirs, then hers too – as the darkness spread across Europe. During her first year in England, she received from them a few letters. They told her little. They were short and hastily scribbled. The last was little more than a note. It was in an almost illegible scrawl, and signed only by her father. There were no more. She never heard from or of her parents again.

With little money and less English she was dependent and vulnerable. For a while, she had a torrid time, eking out a scant existence and fending off Uncle Arpad's ageing advances. But Agnes Horvat was nobody's pushover. She soon had a working grip on the language. She found herself a job in a one-time clothing factory that had been requisitioned to manufacture parts for anti-aircraft guns. That factory was owned by my paternal grandfather. My Dad, then in his twenties, was his new, ambitious general manager.

By the time Agnes and Dad got together she had been in England two years. Within six months, they were married. Within a further six, I was born. I suspect I was the main – perhaps the only – reason for their marriage. That was how things were in those days. Their union was hardly ever a meeting of minds, and by that Christmas it was little more than a joint acquiescence in cohabitation.

Dad was a workaholic. He came from money and he made money. His two brothers, both quite a lot older than himself, owned and ran a high class boot and shoe manufacturing business. Then Dad himself, shortly after the war, started up on his own, manufacturing textiles. By the early nineteen fifties we were already living in some luxury on the outskirts of Northampton. Dad had inherited the family nous.

He was never called up. He suffered from a form of mild epilepsy. That, at least, was the story - though I personally was never around when he had an attack. Maybe his nous extended into other areas as well.

9.

It was late afternoon and dark as we drove up to the wrought-iron gates of 'Greenholme'. They opened automatically. Mother and Dad were very proud of their electric gates – a novelty indeed in those times. I turned the car into the gravel drive. The house looked like it was on fire - a yellow glow from every single window, including that in the downstairs toilet. The words 'Merry Christmas' in lights of many colours were strung all across the frontage. Attached to the front door, a huge wreath of holly. The crown of thorns. The crucifixion – a man hung on nails. I could never understand Christmas, or how Christians with their pain, misery and hand-wringing have so mangled that poor man's legacy. Already angry, I brought the little car to a stop and switched off the engine.

The front door of the house was flung open and Mother hurtled out at a run. She was wearing a paper hat which, to keep in place, she clutched tightly to her head. That was obviously meant to symbolize the happy family Christmas to come. She looked grotesque. Mother was not a paper hat sort of person. The gin was already at work.

Stella and I clambered wearily out. Mother threw her arms around me and enveloped me in her bosom. Then she held me away at arms' length and gazed searchingly at me as though to make sure Stella hadn't wrought some awful damage on me since we'd last met. That moment stayed with me. It is there in my memory now, as clear as it was all those years ago. Her head is just a couple of feet from mine and angled a little to one side, her lovely black hair pouring over her shoulders. And in her eyes, for one fleeting moment, there appears an unguarded vulnerability I have never before seen – or perhaps noticed. And with the colours from the battery of lights around us falling sidelong across her still beautiful features, the skin of her face reminded me for a split second, of a butterfly's wing. I felt afraid for her fragility. I wanted to gather her up in my arms and shield her – though from what I had no idea. But Mother wouldn't have wanted that. So I kept my arms to myself and looked around for Dad who was nowhere to be seen.

She turned to Stella, pecked her dutifully on the cheek and asked briefly how she was and how was the journey. And just as she was then about to bear down clucking and a-goo-goo-ing on Matt in his carry cot in the back seat, I hauled him out and slammed the door with my foot. Stella gestured towards the house, issuing at the same time a warning that Matt would get cold on his chest if we didn't hurry inside. With Matt in my arms I made my way behind the two women into the wide hallway. It was decorated with all the usual senseless Christmas gew-gaws. From a radio somewhere came the vacuous tinkling of a Christmas carol. And suddenly Dad, singing to the radio in a tuneless baritone, appeared with a tray of glasses and a bottle of champagne. He too was wearing a paper hat. This was going to live up to all my expectations.

Once we'd clinked glasses and toasted ourselves and the coming jollities, Dad turned his attention to Matt who was still in my arms, now half-asleep with his head on my shoulder. Dad was not a natural with children. Pressed into their orbit he would oscillate between a rather gauche attempt to appear part of their world, and an avuncular authoritarianism which bordered on the threatening. But today he'd had a glass or two and was untypically affectionate and playful. He put his arms out like rods before him, and plucked Matt from me as you would a cat stuck in a tree.

Stella, talking with Mother, watched from the corner of her eye. I watched her from the corner of mine. This, I recognized as a countdown to intervention. Ten, nine, eight -

"Dad!" She pounced. "Please."

"What?" said Dad, bouncing the giggling Matt up and down.

"Don't - please." She reached out and took the bemused little chap away from him. "I don't want him over-excited." She turned to Mother and asked where we were sleeping so she could get him to bed.

"Bed??" Mother was no doting grandparent, but there were things people in families did, and things people in families did not do. "You surely," she protested, "are not putting that poor little angel down before we all eat dinner?"

"He's had a very long journey, Mother-in-law. He's been sick on the way and if you haven't already noticed, he's filled his nappy. All he needs now is his bottle and bed." Stella was starting as she meant to go on.

Mother's face was thunderous. Muttering some dark Hungarian imprecation, she headed for the stairs. Stella followed. Matt's little face, just starting to crumple, peered at me over her shoulder as they retreated.

Dad looked at me. I looked at Dad. We both shrugged. He topped up my glass. Then his own. We raised them. He smiled. "Here's to Christmas," he said.

There was no one event, no one moment, action or conversation that I could single out as typifying that Christmas. It was a protracted period of more or less continual tension. I doubt my parents actually enjoyed it either, whatever gloss Mother may have chosen to put on it afterwards. There was the occasional moment of levity, laughter sparked off more often than not by something Matt did, or by some strange, mixed-up word that spluttered out of his mouth. Occasionally Dad would tell us all a joke – he could tell them well – or he would recount some humorous anecdote from his experiences at work.

But both women were incapable of keeping their feelings for each other more than half-hidden. Mother resented Stella's presence in the family. It was that simple, and nothing was going to change it. She made little secret of the fact she considered Stella's family low on the social scale. But Mother, I'm convinced, would have resented any woman of whatever social class. She was the woman, the mother, the Matriarch. No family could have two.

Stella, in her own quiet, insidious way was equally unbending. If this refugee from Eastern Europe was going to go on subtly savaging her, her family and the way she brought up her child, she would do it at a heavy price. Both of them were so bound up in achieving ascendancy in this pointless feud they were blind to the fact that they were not the only ones who paid. I spent the entire holiday with my stomach knotted. And what long term effect it may have had on poor Matt - who could possibly calculate? I can recall no warmth, no simple joy in being together as a family - which I imagined is what one hoped and expected to feel at times like that. Dad alone had the right idea. He breezed insouciantly along, amiably plastered throughout.

When the time came to leave, the relief I had expected to flood over me failed to materialize. Instead I felt profoundly depressed. Each of the two women in my life was presenting me with an ultimatum – betray the other; or betray her. I was confused and angry. As we drove back to Halifax in heavy post-Christmas traffic, something was hurting. I kept telling myself – it will pass. This too will pass. It's life.

Things had never been good between my parents. They seemed incapable of relating to each other in any meaningful way. The house of my childhood was forever imbued with a shadowy portent of conflict. It was never a question of 'if' – only 'when' it would break out. Its reach never extended directly to me. But its rumblings were unavoidable and destabilising. Sometimes, as a small boy lying in my bed at night, I listened, in the grip of a formless dread, to raised voices muffled by closed doors. At mealtimes, desperate to get down from the table and run away, I sat through silences so thick I could sometimes hardly breathe. With no sibling to turn to, it was just them and me. I was at the mercy of their dysfunction.

At eighteen I managed to secure a place to read Philosophy, Politics and Economics at Trinity College in Oxford. During my three years there, I returned to the family house in Northampton on as few occasions as possible. I felt guilty. But I preferred the homes and families of my friends. On the few occasions I did go back it was clear that their marriage was, in all but name, over. Mother seemed to be psychologically falling apart, and Dad appeared to be drifting through the catastrophe with bland indifference. As always with him, work came first.

On top of that – and no doubt one of the consequences of it – they were both putting away alcohol in quantities that frankly scared me. I remonstrated with each in turn. Dad reminded me that he'd been drinking all his life, that it was part of his physical, emotional make-up and to stop now, or even cut down to any significant degree, would do him more harm than good. Mother, three sheets to the wind even when I spoke to her, said in reply that she would relate to me a wise old Hungarian fable. But as she recounted it entirely in her native tongue – of which I understood about three words – she could have saved her breath.

I dreaded the evenings. The second Dad was in the house and his coat off he'd ferret out the gin bottle which likely enough had already been opened by Mother. He would then disappear with his briefcase and full glass into his study - to work on documents from the office, he said - while Mother would sit watching television, sipping her gin and every now and then dodging back to the kitchen to check on the progress of dinner.

By the time we sat down to eat – anything up to an hour later than arranged - both would be inebriated to some degree. On the table between them would be a freshly-opened bottle of red wine. Dad would pour a small amount into his own glass, swirl it around, sniff it, then taste. He would pour first Mother, then himself a full glass. "Cheers," he would say, raising his glass to her. Her response would be anything from a simple "Cheers" in return, to "Bottoms up" (which always drew from her a giggle), to some Hungarian phrase which neither Dad nor myself understood but which I sensed – and half-hoped - was some unspeakable profanity.

As they started on their food, they would spend some time in a ritual questioning of each other about their day. Neither seemed particularly interested in the responses. For the remainder of the meal, apart from the odd request to pass this or that, the only sound would be that of cutlery on plates. On a good day, that was how the meal would continue, to the point where one of them would wipe their lips with their napkin, say a brief, "Excuse me," and leave for the study or for the television.

On a bad day the silent period would be broken by one or other of them querying, in an accusatory tone, something the other had or had not done, said or had not said. Thereafter it needed only one out-of-place word or gesture from the other to trigger the explosion. After one such dinner, which took place on one of the very rare occasions that I was at home from Oxford for the whole weekend, I vowed never again to have dinner alone with them.

By the time we sat down to eat, both of them were ominously flushed. We got through half the main course in what just about passed for peace. But then, sensing some minor transgression on Dad's part – the nature of which quite passed me by – Mother turned on him. A red button had been pressed. She was like a Valkyrie. It was as if all the anger, pain and fear of her tortured early years was being hauled up in gouts and hurled across the table at him. He showed little surprise. Nor did he at first respond, just sat looking fixedly down at what remained of his meal, prodding at it with his knife and fork. But the skin of his face grew ever tighter. Mother's voice got ever higher, her train of thought ever more muddled. She pulled in words and phrases from her native tongue, turning the whole tirade into a mass auditory assault in which meaning was quite lost to effect. It was a diva performance.

Dad just sat and took it. Until the moment when it seemed he felt she'd crossed a line. He banged his knife and fork with a great crash down on the table. I thought he was going to get up and hit her. Instead he just started shouting back, leaning across the table, occasionally waving his napkin or his cutlery furiously in her face. And there they were, two middle-aged children, all dignity gone, shouting each other down. It was outlandish, grotesque. Had it not been my own parents it might just have been funny.

It came to a sudden end. Dad simply fell completely silent. As Mother ranted on, he folded his napkin and lay it gently down beside his plate. Unhurriedly refilled his glass. Then stood up, slid his chair back, and without a word, went from the room. I was waiting for the door to be slammed with an ear-splitting crash. But there was just the merest of clicks as the latch went home.

Only then did Mother stop. I gazed at her across the table in the sudden silence. Her beauty had vanished, supplanted by an ugliness which desolated me. Her face was red, her eyes protruded, her whole organism seemed disfigured with toxins. She banged both fists down on the table, one after the other in a short cannonade, folded at the waist and fell forward onto the table, her head resting on her arms.

I stood up, left the dining-room and made my way up the stairs. I remember little else of that dreadful evening except throwing myself on the bed in my room and attempting to smother my own sobs. My mother and my father had become in their middle-age a Duo of Death, as poisonous to those around them as to their own selves. I wanted to get out of the house and as far away from the pair of them as possible.

10.

'Darling Ellen,
Hello.'
Just 'Hello'? I've dropped out of her life. And all I say is 'Hello'? What else should I say? - 'Good morning'? It might not be morning when she reads it. If ever I send it. 'Good day'? But I don't ever say, 'Good day'. I don't say, 'Hi'. And it seems to need more than just nothing. So let's leave it at, 'Hello'.
'Darling Ellen,
Hello.'

First - I'm well. I haven't been kidnapped or taken hostage or in any way hurt. In fact, nothing bad at all has happened to me. I'm dreadfully sorry for what this must be putting you through.

I don't really know how to start this.'

And that's a fact. I get up and look out the window. Wigan is busy now, and about its business. I am very ill at ease. I jump at the slightest unexpected sound – a car backfires in the street outside, footsteps along the corridor. Nobody who has ever known me could possibly have the least idea where I am. Even so, I am in constant fear of the telephone ringing, of a knock on the door.

The implications of this thing are unthinkable. Even so, I think of them.

Money. That's going to be the problem. Holes in walls, cheques - out. Anything involving my name - out. No cashing bonds, no selling shares. Just a few hundred quid cash on me. Where is it going to come from?

He picked up the croissant he'd taken from the dining room at breakfast. Sat down to eat it. He looked again at the few lines on the paper. People were about to get hurt; everything he had worked for and built up was about to have its foundations pulled away. He was staring into an abyss.

'I really don't know how to start this.' Beside the paper, his pen. With leaden fingers, he picked it up.

'I don't know when I'll send it or even if I'll send it. But assuming I do, then when you're reading this please try and remember that however hard it may be to believe it at this moment, I do love you.'

He stared at those last four words. Leave them in? Take them out? Everybody uses them. What do they mean? The truth would be better expressed by saying that he had, during the course of their relationship, loved her. But he left it as it was.

'In all the time we've been together, there is something I should have told you and never did. One day – I wonder if you remember this - way back in those weeks just before we were married, we went shopping at Liberty's. (You bought that hat you took with you when we went to La Palma). On the way back to the house in Turney Road we sat for a while in Brockwell Park. It was a hot day and there was honeysuckle in the hedge near where we sat. You called my attention to its scent in the air.

'We were discussing the plans for the wedding, when I said that before the actual day came there was something I really had to tell you. You looked apprehensive. I suppose it had sounded a bit dramatic. Do you remember this? Then you said to me – you almost whispered it in fact, "What? What is it you have to tell me?" But as you said it, I saw the uncertainty in your eyes. I hesitated, fearful of what you might think of me once you knew. You might even change your mind about the wedding. Even so, it had to be done. But then, when I finally managed to open my mouth to tell you, you reached up and put a finger to my lips. You smiled and said, "No, my Barney. No. I love you. Don't tell me anything. Just marry me." And I did. I married you and I never, ever told you.

'Ellen, I have a son. His name is Matthew. I have not seen or heard of him for over thirty years. Nor have I, in all that time, made any attempt to contact him. I have no idea where he is – or even if he's alive. The last time I saw him he was a child of three. And yes, I was married at the time. And you didn't know that either. When I was a younger man, driven by ambition, the guilt and the regret was not so difficult. But when I met you and felt for you as I did, the reality started to come home. It weighed ever more heavily on me. When we decided to marry, I knew then I could keep it to myself no longer. Hence that day in Brockwell Park. But you put your finger on my lips and silenced me.

'I told myself I'd put it right after the wedding when we were settled. But still I put it off. The more I put it off, the more difficult it became. The time came when I started to think that if I ever did tell you, you'd leave me. Eventually it seemed my only option was to make a decision to never, ever, under any circumstances say anything – then for all practical purposes, he would cease to exist, even to me.

'But that's not the way it works. I think about him, I dream about him – he is the man in the garden. There have been many times recently when I have found it difficult to do my work. My life without him is not the life I was meant to live. I have to try and find him. I hope you understand, but I can't blame you if you don't. I have been no father to him. Yet he is mine and I am his: he may be missing me as I am missing him. He meant more to me than I ever knew. Please try and understand.

With love,

Your Barney xxx'

I sat back, read it over. It made uncomfortable reading. Even a long-abandoned son seemed hardly sufficient reason for leaving one's wife, ditching one's whole life and disappearing. Was I perhaps finding something attractive in the prospect of vanishing? Of starting all over again with a completely virgin slate on which I can write just and only what I like? A man with no baggage.

I read it again.

No. Ring her! I've decided. Put all this back in the cupboard. The lunchtime drinks had gone on – they do. She understands all that. I missed the train, etc.,etc., blah, blah, blah.

But - there are roads in life from which, once you've set off down them, there is no turning back. Wherever Ellen is at the moment - London or Ludlow - she will already be seriously concerned. She has probably rung Frank Lippincote and Frank has probably been onto the Chamber of Commerce at which I gave my talk. The police will have been notified. Various people in various places will already be wondering and gossiping. My office at Westminster will be a hotbed of goggle-eyed speculation. Workwise it will stumble. But only for a day or two. Then things will resume just as they were before. We are all of us, in the end, as wind across water.

No, I cannot go on as I was. With each evasion a little more of one's real self is pared away. And I've pared away more than my fair share in my life. The wheels of this thing, whatever it turns out to be, are already turning.

He stood before the mirror. It had those ugly brown spots in its corners – damp spots, mildew or something. Open-neck shirt worn rather untidily beneath jumper, along with shades and ruffled-up hair. It still didn't go with Savile Row trousers and John Church brogues. But already it was hardly Barnaby Marechal M.P. Until his hair and beard had matured, a carefully considered shopping expedition should take care of the rest.

He planned to get hair gel, jeans and a jacket. Perhaps some trainers. Certainly some other shoes. Each of these items would have to be bought in a separate shop. He must not hang around in any one place. Whatever he had to say to people such as shopkeepers should be as brief as possible. His middle-class southern accent would be instantly noticed and remembered.

Once he was satisfied with his purchases, he would leave Wigan and make his way to some other town. It didn't matter where, but he had to move on from here. He had spent over an hour the previous evening wandering around in full Barnaby Marechal mode. Any one of the hundreds he must have passed in the streets might, if pressed, recall seeing him.

He was surprised and quite taken with his own shrewdness. He had a twinge of what felt suspiciously like excitement. He checked out of the 'Welcome Hotel' and took a cab to the North Western rail station where he'd jumped off the train the day before. He sat back in the cab.

Look out of the window. Don't get your face too close to the glass. What goes on in this town? People in cheap clothes. Cheap shops, boarded-up shops, an amusement arcade, betting shops, women in headscarves pushing tots in pushchairs, men in vans smoking, drumming their fingers on the wheel at the lights, youths on street corners. And me, in this cab. What had I been doing? Did I once seriously persuade myself I represented people like these?

He booked his two cases and his classic-fit Crombie in at the Left Luggage. Then set off in the direction of a sign which pointed to the 'Town Centre'. He stopped and looked in the window of a Red Cross charity shop. He had never been inside a charity shop. He imagined they did well in places like this. They would take a suit, wouldn't they? And his shoes. That would off-load in one go his outward signs of affluence. He would do that on his way back.

A little further along was a newsagents-cum-general-store-cum-off-licence. He hesitated, then stepped inside. What a cornucopia! An Aladdin's cave. Cheap and cheerful goods overflowed the shelves, obstructed the floor, hung from hooks on the walls. Toothpaste, toilet cleaners, cake decorations, plastic dustbins, batteries, condoms, buckets, saucepans, ladies' tights, strong beer in six-packs, children's colouring books, curtain rings. Bewildering. And quite exciting. What, he wondered, would Ellen make of it? Ellen however, was a Fortnums woman. He bought a jar of hair gel and moved on.

He found a public toilet. It smelled of urine, disinfectant blocks and stale cigarette smoke. He braced himself, went into a cubicle and locked the door. There was no mirror so he was forced to do his first hair gel application blind. He pushed three tentative fingers into the cold jelly and excavated a blob. Rubbed it into his hair which collapsed into a slippery mess. He tried to knead it into some sort of shape. What shape? A wave? A roll? There wasn't enough hair to do much with anyway. And without a mirror how would the beginner judge? He settled for a general prodding of it with the ends of his fingers.

With an ear to the door, he waited until he was fairly sure there was no-one else around, then emerged to check the result. Above the one hand basin was a dented metal mirror. He looked in it and peered at himself between the scrawled red letters of 'Fuck the Pope'. He looked ridiculous. The gel had plastered the little hair he had all around his head, like gloss paint. With the dark glasses he looked like a close-up of a fly. He was about to dodge back into the cubicle and try again, when he heard voices. He adopted what he hoped was an expression of calm nonchalance, resigned himself to looking bizarre and headed for the exit. He passed a father and young son coming in. Neither gave him a second glance.

He continued on towards the city centre. Nobody took any notice of him. His confidence grew. He wandered in and out of shops. Local commercial radio pounded out a wall of drivel. He bought a pair of blue jeans. The material was paper-thin. The shop assistant was surprised he didn't want to try them on. "No problem," he said. "They're my size. I'm standard." He went into another public toilet and put them on. They were tight round the waist, loose and floppy everywhere else. He pushed his elegant suit trousers into the clear plastic bag which had contained the jeans, left the cubicle and strode back out into the street.

He came to a skip full of builders' rubbish. Added the plastic bag containing his suit trousers to the pile. Someone might spot it. Wear the trousers. Or sell them. He walked on.

At a stall in a street market he picked up a pair of trainers and a long, loose-fitting canvas jacket with more zip-up pockets than anyone could ever seriously need. He put it on over his sweater. It hung almost to his knees. Then took off his Church's brogues and with some difficulty, pulled the trainers on. They gave off an unpleasant, even slightly offensive odour. "They look grand on you, love," said the stallholder, a big woman with a snake's head tattooed on her upper arm. "I'll wear them now," he said. She produced a blue plastic bag, and giving him a very curious look, slipped his brogues inside. "Thank you," he said, taking the bag and walking away. The cheap trainers cramped the big toe on one foot and tilted the other foot outwards, straining the ankle. If he ever got used to them it would surely be at the expense of his feet.

His reflection in a shop window brought him to a sudden stop. He saw an old man. Unshaven, wearing standard, cheap, ill-fitting clothes. The shades, their quality counting for nothing at this distance, looked like a brave attempt to pass himself off as his own person, a one-off, elderly maverick. But he was just another old man - fragile, muggable. That the transition had been that quick, that the risk of misreading him was now that great gave him an unpleasant jolt. 'This isn't me! I don't really look like this.' But he did, and they all passed him by without a second glance. Gone now was Barnaby Marechal, M.P., M.A.(Oxon).

Uneasy, and with his burgeoning self-confidence set back a notch or two, he continued on towards the train station. Despite the obvious success of the physical transformation he had wrought, he began to be troubled yet again by the entreaties of his conscience - if conscience is what it was - and forced to go once more through the rigmarole rehearsed already a hundred times - Ellen, and should he have done such-and-such, or what if he did some other thing, then would she, or wouldn't she, and if this and not that, should she, should he and what if and what not?

He passed an old-fashioned 'Gentlemen's Outfitters'. Then stopped, frowned, went back and looked in the window. A display of hats. Quality hats. He'd never worn hats. But he had long half-entertained a notion that well-chosen, quality headgear on a man projected self-esteem, a certain dignity. And there, in the centre of the display, on a dummy male head of surreally handsome proportions, was a flat cap in shiny black leather. Set at a nice, cheeky angle, it looked good. It had character. And he had now the freedom to wear just what he liked.

He went into the shop. Pointed to the hat in the window, and said to the rather elderly male assistant who approached him and sized him up with unconcealed disapproval, "One of those please." But even as the words left his mouth he knew he was in trouble.

Taken aback by the diction and accent of this ageing ragamuffin, the man moderated his approach a little. "Head size, sir? What's your head size?"

Barney had no idea. And he couldn't be trying on different sizes of hat with this man standing chatting to him and scrutinizing the effect. Get this over with. But all he could think of in answer was, "Standard size. Medium." It wasn't going to do. This man wasn't going to just take the hat from the window and give it to him. He was old school.

The man gave an ingratiating chuckle. "I'll need to be a bit more precise than that, sir," he said, and smiled as he reached for a tape measure.

Barney was trapped. What a very foolish idea this had been.

"If you wouldn't mind then sir." The tape measure encircled his cranium. The man's eyes were inches from his own face. Thank goodness for the dark glasses. The tape measure was removed.

"Right sir," said the man. "We've a selection of caps. I'll go and bring you one or two so you can - "

"No. That one. I want that one. Or one exactly the same. Please."

"Well, we've a variety of styles sir, and you might just find something there that tickles your fancy and - "

But Barney had caught sight of a full-length mirror. Staring back at him was a crackpot, a circus freak. What inane farce was he making of his life? What to do? Turn round and get out? A sudden inspiration. He looked down at his wristwatch. "Ye gods!" he exclaimed. "Look at the time. I have a train to catch in five minutes. Just give me the hat, eh? Quickly as you can."

"Well - er -" The man scratched his head. "I'll need to try it on you sir, to make quite sure - "

"You measured me. I trust you."

"Nay, I can't let you take a hat away sir, without even - "

"If it doesn't fit, I'll not be back to trouble you. I live a very long way away." He jabbed a finger at his watch. "Look at the time! It's that - or no hat. Which?"

The man bit his lip.

"Please."

The man turned and made his way to the shelving.

"How much?" Barney called out.

It was expensive. Barney threw enough cash down on the counter to cover it.

The man came back with a cardboard box and was about to open it when Barney took it from him. "There's the money. Thank you. Don't worry about the change." Tucking the box under his arm he hurried out of the shop.

The man watched him leave. Scratched his head. Frowned. Then looked down at the money on the counter. There was virtually half as much again as he'd asked for. He hurried to the door, yanked it open, looked up and down the street. But whoever he was, the strange individual had already been swallowed up among the shoppers.

He closed the door, and went back to take a closer look at the money. It crossed his mind that maybe he'd been the victim of some sort of scam. But the money looked genuine enough.

Barney walked quickly and kept going. He slowed down only when he thought he'd put a safe enough distance between himself and the hat shop. What a cock-up. That man would remember him for the rest of his life. Probably dine out for months on the story. And he might even contact the police. Thank God he'd gone in there after he'd camouflaged himself in all the cheap stuff. But apart from the splendid hat, the good thing that had come out of it was the discovery that his old, old ability to fudge in tight corners had not quite deserted him. It might come in handy again some time.

He turned a corner into a narrow side street of little old Victorian terraced houses, their front doors and sitting room windows fronting the pavement. He stopped, looked around, then took the black leather cap out of its box. It caught the sun. It was rather beautiful. He set it carefully on his head. A woman in pink curlers watched from an upstairs window. He adjusted it till it felt comfortable. Then pressed it gently to his head. That brought the hair gel into clammy contact with his balding skull. But the cap fitted well. The man had known his business. Barney peered at his reflection in someone's front window. The hat looked cool. As for the rest of the ensemble – he guessed he looked as good or as ridiculous as anyone else wearing what he was wearing.

He collapsed the cardboard box, walked back to the main road and continued on towards the North Western train station. Down a side alley he spotted some commercial waste bins. He lobbed the flattened box into one of them. And at the same time realized with a nasty jolt that he had left the plastic bag containing his brogues in the hat shop. He shrugged. He wasn't going back.

At the left luggage he retrieved his overnight case, briefcase and his classic Crombie. Standing in the cramped station concourse and getting the heavy coat on over the long canvas jacket, which he was wearing over his thick woollen sweater, which he had on over his shirt, worn over his singlet was not easy. He was watched by a small boy who eyed his contortions with a curiously apprehensive deadpan. Barney turned away and continued facing a wall. He could feel the boy's eyes still on him. The nosy little squirt would no doubt recall him with enthusiasm if he were ever asked.

He buttoned up his coat. Picked up his cases and set off towards the ticket office. He was soon perspiring freely. He was trussed up like a Christmas turkey. What if the hair gel melted - leaked out under his leather cap? Then black dye from the new hat streaked his face and forehead? And now his unshaven stubble was starting to itch. He felt utterly inadequate. He cleared his throat before asking the woman in the ticket office the destination of the next train due in.

She looked up from her scratchcard. "Up? Down?"

"Pardon?"

"Which direction? Up or down?"

He struggled to figure out which was which. He gave up. "Doesn't matter."

She frowned.

He winced.

"Liverpool, Lime Street. Eight minutes."

"Single, please."

Keeping one eye on him, she took the money, printed the ticket and handed it to him. "Platform Two."

He nodded his thanks.

Curiously, she watched him walk away, his two small cases banging against his legs. Something about him didn't quite add up. Should she say something to somebody? She shrugged and went back to her scratchcard.

Barney struggled up a long flight of steps, then down another to get to Platform Two. He put his cases down on the ground by his side. Looked up and down the tracks. Stuck his hands in the pockets of his coat, closed his eyes and took a very deep breath. He would need to get his act together a lot better than this.

11.

The interior of the house in Endell Street was green. Everywhere painted green. An oily green which had been applied over layer upon layer of previous colours so that the mouldings on all door and window frames were smoothed to a shine. And washing drying - always there was washing drying. Towelling nappies, babygrows. Everywhere the smell of baby powder. I hear his crying in the night, waking us from sleep. Me first, most times, being the lighter sleeper. I walk around in the night jiggling him up and down in my arms hoping he'll soon go down again, then sleep, letting me get just a little more. The floral wallpaper in the bedroom, with those strange, orange leaves. The sounds of late-night people outside, going home. That's where he began. So that, I guess, is where I too should begin.

In this age of the computer I should be able to do it all from my armchair. It's all out there. Information on everything imaginable. But I hate computers and the only one I have – in my study in Ludlow – hates me back. I've had it two years and have hardly used it, and then only when I've had no other option. Most of the time at Westminster I got others to do that sort of thing for me - often a little grudgingly, but I made the most of my ignorance, smiled nicely and applied a little charm. It worked. OK - it's all very well. But that way you either forget how to do things for yourself, or never find out in the first place.

I know how to read, write and send an email. I can look up a website. If I had to, I might even figure out how to use one of those memory sticks. Beyond that I flounder. I could learn. I could take a course. But I couldn't sit with other people in night school or an internet café. I'm no celebrity politician but my face is still enough known for me to be recognized. And even if all that were surmountable, there's another thing. Computers aren't that clever. Despite their mind-numbing speed and ingenuity, they can be manipulated - so I'm told - by any devious chancer with the appropriate technical know-how into coughing up all your personal information, down to credit card details and which keys you've pressed on the keyboard. That on its own would be, for me, a deal breaker.

Where does that leave me? Halifax. Endell Street. Number 26. I need to see the house again. To look at it from the other side of the street. The privet hedge that bordered its front garden. The irregular raised lines in the road which marked where once had stood the outside walls of the wartime air-raid shelters. The recreation ground at the end of the road. With the two slides – one for the 'big kids' and one for the toddlers. I used to take Matt on the toddlers'. Put my arms around his warm little body and hold him tight on my lap as we slid down. That slide wasn't much taller than me, but to him it was an Everest and he loved and was terrified by it all at the same time. "Again! Again!" I wearied of it long before he ever did. I never knew in those days what all that meant to me. As I think about it now I'm often overwhelmed with such sadness I feel sometimes my heart will break. God, what have I done?

I have to go to Endell Street.

12.

Stella was working class, her father a bus driver. We met when we were both at Oxford. We had a fling. We spent a lot of time walking hand-in-hand through Christchurch Meadow, punting on the Cherwell, drinking in the town pubs and doing the things undergraduates do. We also spent a lot of time in bed. In those days it was not easy. Colleges were gender-specific, as the toe-curling jargon goes. Trinity was all men, St Hilda's all women. The opposite sex was banned from undergraduates' rooms after about ten o'clock in the evening. It was a brave or desperate couple that ignored it. But then, in those days, most of us were pretty desperate, if not actually brave. If you were caught, the person of the offending gender would be summarily kicked out of the building and the other, as likely as not, booted out of the university. Or at best, rusticated, sent down, summarily sacked.

After our first swift, guilt-ridden and panicky encounter in my cupboard of a bedroom overlooking The Broad, I found us a hotel – a mile or so up the Iffley Road. It was a fleapit. But during our six months together it served its purpose. The end came when Stella suspected I was two-timing her. I was. The lady in question being Licia Harper-Downes.

Licia was a postgraduate student at Somerville College and daughter of Sir Gregory Harper-Downes, a faded member of the landed aristocracy. It had, said Stella, to be all-Stella or no-Stella. I didn't like ultimatums so opted for the latter.

She was a lovely woman, Licia. Strong, proud, sexy and with great integrity. I liked her a lot. But in sheer emotional maturity she was in a league beyond me. We lasted a year. I hardly noticed in those far off days qualities she had which when I look back, cause me even now to regret just a little her passing so soon from my life. But I was lured away by Susie – a curvaceous, flirtatious sexual plum. She hung ripe from a very willing tree. All I had to do was reach out and pick it.

Susie worked in one of the huge vehicle manufacturing plants at the far end of the Cowley Road. They were powerhouses where men earned huge wages. They ran 24 hours a day, weekends included, as they struggled to meet the global hunger for British made. Laughable now. Susie and I met in the Post Office in St Aldates one Saturday morning. One of her heels had broken off. I persuaded a nice lady cashier - it was easier in those days - to lend me some glue and a roll of sellotape with which I stuck the heel back on again, enough at least to get her home.

Susie was cheap, ebullient, provocative, just a little coarse and a pathological flirt. She was irresistible. She'd probably had it off with half the shop floor, and if she hadn't, that was the impression she set out to give. She was good for a thrill. That's what we had, and that's all we had, and it burned itself out in a couple of months. I entered my last term at Trinity – my Finals' term – womanless. A good thing.

After our split, Stella and I had avoided each other for the final eighteen months of our time at Oxford. But something of her was always with me – some trace in the air, some will-o'-the-wisp. I would find myself thinking about her at odd moments – sometimes even when I was in bed with Susie. I'd wonder how she was, what she was doing, who she was with. So it was with utter astonishment, about a year after we'd both gone down, that I bumped into her in a pub one lunchtime - in Halifax of all places. I was nine months into a management trainee course in that town and she was visiting a client on behalf of the textile company she worked for some fifty miles away. She was as delighted as I was. Fate, it seemed, had brought us back together.

Trouble lay ahead. Doesn't it always. Mother had become more British than the British. She seemed to have acquired the belief that if, like us Marshals, you owned your own business, had a big house, a large car and a lot more money than most, then something in the air in this land automatically elevated your social status.

I loved my mother. But her snobbery hurt and embarrassed me. She'd had grandiose plans for me. Her only begotten was to sup at high table. His path into adulthood was to be Rugby School and Christchurch College Oxford. Thence onward into the Civil Service in which he would become a famous diplomat, perhaps an ambassador to some 'important country', as she put it – whatever an 'important country' was.

But already I had punctured many of her illusions. 'Rugby, Christchurch, the Civil Service' was a mantra, burned into her brain which irritated me even in my teens. I asked her where she'd got it from. It was meaningless.

She drew herself up to her full height. "It is well known in all the world," she replied with a splendidly vacuous hauteur, "that Eton, then

Christchurch College, Oxford and the English Civil Service is the best."

"The best what?" I'd asked.

"The best education - what you think? The best there is in the whole world!"

"So where does Eton figure in, 'Rugby, Christchurch, Civil Service'"?

She thrust her still beautiful face into mine and hissed, "You want not to go where your father went?? What is the matter with you?"

I made Rugby. Dad had been educated there - and we had money. They appeared to be the main requirements. I didn't make Christchurch College, Oxford or the Civil Service. I made Trinity College, Oxford which was just as good and more than I'd ever hoped for. As for the Civil Service, I made no attempt. At the end of my three years at university, the thought of working in an office, travelling to it en masse, decked out in bowler hat and striped trousers, looking forward, at the end of it all, to a glass or two of sherry and a carriage clock, filled me with dread. I applied for, and was accepted, as a management trainee with an engineering firm in Halifax.

"For pity's sake!" shrieked Mother. "Not content with doing some working class thing, you go to live in the North!" She spat the word out as though Halifax were only just this side of the Arctic Circle. And with that, Mother's dreams for me were almost in tatters. Though not quite. That was soon to come.

Dad was no more pleased than Mother, though for different reasons. I had long ago made it plain to him that, despite the pressure he put on me, I was not interested in working alongside him in his textile business which he'd hoped I would ultimately take over. Industry had never attracted me – so I'd claimed and so I'd believed. Dad's round of conferences, hotels, big lunches, lobbying dressed up as entertainment, golf, dinner parties with freeloading sycophants, long-haul flights and never-ending office meetings was no more my idea of a life than the Civil Service. So when I announced I was, after all, going into industry – but not his industry – I felt the depths of his disappointment. Even so, he had the grace to mumble, with just a suggestion of a smile on his face, that at least – as he put it - I'd joined the boys.

I'd surprised even myself. But the fact was I'd had no burning ambition to do anything in particular - par for the course with the vast majority of us in Oxford in those days. All my personal associates, with the one exception of dear Licia, acknowledged they wanted a career. They just didn't know which one. There was no pressure. In those days, it wasn't a question of 'if' you got a job – simply of which job you would get. Consequently, the criterion generally became what convivial, well-paid working life could one achieve, doing whatever, wherever. And that is the impression I got of the Halifax job, from the then Careers Office in Oxford. For a traineeship it paid well. Halifax, as I discovered when I went for the interview, was an attractive town, and it was far enough from Northampton for the parents not to be tempted to come a-visiting too often.

Then to cap it all, there, by one of those chances – or is it? - which fate throws in from time to time to confuse you, I meet in a pub one lunchtime, my old flame, Stella. We met up again after work for a drink. We went on to a restaurant and from there to my small bedsit. She returned by cab to her hotel in the early hours. We were on the road to being, once again, an item. A month later, I announced to my parents my intention of marrying her.

That was the final nail in the coffin of Mother's dreams. Her only begotten son really was going to be carried off and cared for by another woman. And a working class woman at that - the final indignity. Right up to that moment I think she had somehow, despite all the evidence, deceived herself into believing that the life she had so long wanted for me – and therefore for herself by proxy – one of prestige and society glamour, independent in most practical senses of Dad - could somehow, in some fantastical, never-never land still happen, thus bypassing the wasteland into which she saw herself otherwise headed. But that closed the door on it. Before her lay a future of making small talk with a bus driver's family.

Stripped of her illusions, she was devastated. She had little to fall back on. Her marriage was one in name only; her wounds from the past were still open and weeping. I feel even now a great sadness. For all her overweening pride and authoritarian arrogance, she was at heart a hurt, confused and seriously wounded little girl. She did only what she could do. None of us can do more.

13.

The rain pounded on the window.

"Draw the curtains, Al!" she whispered hoarsely. "The curtains."

He glanced over his shoulder. "They are closed."

"Not properly, they're not."

He rolled off the bed and scuttled across the room in his underwear. He peered out through the narrow gap between the cheap, floral curtains.

"Hurry up."

"Still pissing down." He drew the curtains together. Then hurried back, dragging his Y-fronts off as he went, and throwing them with a flourish across the room.

"Oooh!" she exclaimed gleefully, "look at that!"

"Full of eastern promise, my dear." He scrambled onto the bed beside her.

"Now there speaks a real advertising man!"

"That's me. Always on the job."

Shrieking with laughter, she threw her arms around his neck.

He nuzzled into her. "You know what they say about real admen, don't you?" He took one of her nipples gently in his mouth.

"No. What do they say? Oi, karamba! Tell me quickly before I lose interest."

"Let me show you." He took one of her hands and placed it gently between his legs.

A little cry escaped her.

He grinned. "Life is short. And lo, the bird is on the wing."

"What?"

"Never mind."

"Come on then, big boy."

He lowered his body down and slowly, gently entered her.

Her head went back, her eyes closed.

"Christ Viki, you feel good." He began to move gently.

She groaned quietly.

His movements speeded up a little.

"Not yet. Not yet."

"I'm not."

"Gently. That's it. Ooh, Al."

He took a deep breath. Paused.

They remained still. The rain beat on the window and the thin roof.

She put her lips to his ear. "You," she whispered, "are the fuck to die for. Did you know that?"

He moved once more.

She responded, and though unsure of each other and a little out of sync they were nevertheless moving towards a more or less joint climax when her eyes shot wide open and her body beneath him went rigid as a plank.

"Christ!" He froze. "What??"

"Listen!"

"'Listen'? What d'you mean?"

"That noise."

"Noise??"

"There's a noise – listen!" She pointed to the wall just behind her head. "There!"

"It's the rain, for Christ's sake. Come on." He moved again.

She tried to extricate herself from under him.

"Fuck's sake Viki, what the - ?" But then he too heard it and stopped. He stared at the faded wallpaper above their heads.

Viki's eyes were wide. "What is it?"

He moved away from her. They both stared at the wall.

"Al?"

"Sounds like an animal." His voice was shaking.

It came again. A short, whimpering cry. Then a long, guttural cough.

The hairs on the back of Viki's neck rose up. "Jesus Christ."

Al bit his lip.

"Do something," she whispered.

"Like what?"

"I don't know."

They looked at each other. The rain battered the roof.

"A man, Al? Is it a man?"

Al put his ear to the wall. Then pulled back, grimacing.

"Let's go!" Viki was off the bed and throwing on her clothes. "Get dressed! Let's get out of here."

"We've got to do something!"

"Like what? You said there's nothing we could - "

"I didn't say there was nothing – I said - "

"Fuck it. Let's go."

Al, protesting, started to dress. The sounds continued. Viki shoved her feet into her shoes. Then grabbed her briefcase, went to the door and flung it open. She looked back at Al struggling into his jacket. "Get a move on!" She ran out through the rain to the car. She didn't have the keys. She stopped and looked back. "Hurry up! I'm soaking."

He came out shoving his briefcase under his arm. He slammed the door behind him, went to run towards her, then turned back and went to the window of the next room.

"No Al! No!"

But already he had his nose to the glass.

"It's nothing to do with us!"

He turned from the window and stood looking at her. His face was ashen. He made no attempt to join her.

She ran back to him. Went to grab him by the arm, but he threw both arms around her body and tried to manhandle her towards the window of the next room. "Look! Look in there!!"

"I've got enough problems!" She tore herself free. "Let's get out of this place."

"Oh, Jesus." Stunned, he allowed himself to be led back to the car.

They got in. He switched the engine on then sat staring ahead.

"Al? Please, let's go."

"This isn't right." He turned to her. "There's a man in there. And what looks like a lot of - "

"Drive, eh? Just drive." She reached across and placed his hand on the gear lever.

He took the wheel. Put the vehicle in gear.

"Al," she said, reassuringly, "it would fuck everything. Your job. Mine. The whole works. They have staff here. It'll be alright."

He put his foot down. The black Jaguar took off, throwing up water and gravel. Splashed and rocked over the rain-filled potholes, narrowly missed a small blue car pulling in by the office, and swung out onto the main road.

14.

Stella peered emptily from the train window. Patches of late winter snow lingered under hedgerows and in the corners of fields. Leafless trees stood out against an overcast sky. She looked down at the small child, asleep under a blanket by her side. He rocked gently back and forth with the train's movement. One little hand lay outside the blanket. She touched the tiny fingers. They flexed just a little. He didn't stir.

She resumed gazing out of the window. Her mother was still on her mind. Scarborough seemed a nice enough town. Just around the corner there was a nice view over the sea. The staff appeared quite caring. And her mother liked them. She didn't like many people these days. It was obvious she was fading. Simply sitting with her in that sweltering room was a form of torture. Her sight was poor, her mind wandered, it was hard to understand what she was trying to say. Then she would stop in mid-sentence as though someone had turned her switch off, and stare into space.

"Mum," Stella would say.

No response.

"Mum?"

Then a sudden, "Eh?"

"Are you alright?"

"Shouldn't I be?"

"You were saying something."

"No. I didn't speak."

Sharon's Dad had to be carried these days by a nurse either side of him. From his invalid chair to the table. From the table back to his invalid chair. To bed, to the toilet. Is that how it was going to be? She prayed not.

The train slowed down as it approached Halifax. Surprisingly, almost on time. The child stirred. Stella picked him up. Then made her way awkwardly with him and the folded pushchair along the corridor.

On the platform she flipped open the pushchair and sat him in it. Tucked his legs up and wrapped his blanket around him. Woken suddenly from sleep, his face began to crumple. She chucked him under the chin. "Not long now, munchkin. Soon be home." She set off towards the barrier.

She was cold. She had no winter coat. One wheel of the pushchair wobbled and squeaked. It embarrassed her. She had been meaning to oil it. The big clock over the booking office said just after six-thirty. If they were lucky and got a taxi fairly quickly, they'd be home by seven.

The child whimpered. She reached forward and tucked the blanket further in around his neck.

They joined the taxi queue.

The newsagent on the corner was open.

"Drop us here, please," she said. "I want a newspaper. We'll walk the rest of the way."

She paid the driver, went into the shop and bought her newspaper. Then set off down Endell Street. There were no lights on at number 26. She was disappointed. He'd said at breakfast he would try to get back before her and put the heating on. On the other hand she was an hour or so earlier than usual. They'd forgotten to let her know her mother had been booked for the physio, which meant that she – Stella - had not needed to stay on till they served dinner. It was a relief. Watching her mother pick at her food with hands she couldn't control was too distressing.

The hinges of the garden gate squeaked. Something else that needed oiling. At the front door of the house she lifted the child out of the pushchair and planted a kiss on his cheek. Balancing him on her hip she put the key in the lock and opened the door. She was surprised to see there was in fact a sliver of rather dim light beneath the closed door of the living room. In her hurry to leave and get the train this morning, she'd probably forgotten to turn the little table light off.

With her free hand she dragged the pushchair in off the step, and leaned back against the door to close it with her weight. Then stopped, stared at the strip of light under the door. Shadows were moving across it. She frowned. Sounds of movement. Silence. Then an unthinkable horror. Struggling to control her breathing, she clutched the child closer.

Approached the door, reached for the knob, hesitated, then in one movement, grasped it, twisted it and flung the door open.

The only illumination was the soft glow from a small table lamp on the TV in the far corner. In this half-light, at either end of the table by the curtained window sat two people - Barney and a young, dark-haired woman. They both had the look about them of people who had been where they were for no more than a second or two. The woman's face was flushed, her long hair in disarray. They both looked at Stella with simulated openness.

"Stell!" said Barney, brightly. "Hi. And Matty. Hi, Matty."

The woman mumbled something inaudible.

Stella looked from one to the other. "What's going on?"

"This is Miriam," said Barney, clearing his throat. "From work."

"Oh yes?" said Stella, cradling the child's head in her hand. "And what's Miriam doing here?"

Miriam herself made no attempt to reply.

"Ooh," Barney gave a dismissive wave of his hand, "there were a few documents needed dealing with. You know – urgent stuff - and we thought it better to bring them here. It's a madhouse at the works with this new contract on the go, and - ."

"Documents?" Stella looked around. "I don't see them."

"No – well we'd largely finished. And - "

"In this light? You were working on documents in this light?" And to make the point she reached to one side and switched on the overhead light.

The pair at the table blinked.

"Or perhaps you have very good eyes, Miriam."

Miriam's face had turned white.

The boy started to cry.

"Poor Matty," said Barney. "He's tired, look." And he stood up and started towards Stella and his son. But she raised a hand and stopped him.

The boy stopped crying and looked at his father. Stella pressed his small face to hers, transferring his tears to her own cheeks. "Well," she said to Barney who stood, thwarted and spare, in the middle of the floor, "at least you did what you said you'd do."

"I'm sorry. What do you – ?"

"You said you'd try and be home before me. You were."

He went to speak, but no words came.

She studied him with a contemptuous, hurt despair. Matt, overwhelmed with the vibes, began to howl.

Miriam scrambled up from her chair, knocking it over. She bundled her coat up in her arms and made for the door. On her way, she snatched up from the carpet a piece of black, lacy material. Shoving it under her coat, she hurried from the room.

Stella pulled Matt closer. Barney reached out to touch the boy but she held him off.

The front door slammed.

"You too," she said to Barney, indicating with a sharp movement of her head the direction of the sound.

Barney's brows knitted.

"Go!" She pointed back towards the front door. "Get out!"

"Wait a minute. It's not what you think. If you'll - "

"Get out!! Get the fuck out!!" And with her free hand she aimed a blow at Barney's head, catching him on the lip and drawing blood. As he spun away, Matt began to scream and kick.

Barney, blood running down his chin, stood looking in wide-eyed disbelief at his wife and distraught son. This could not be happening. This surely was a corner of hell.

15.

'Dear Frank,

Thank you for the kind invitation, but this time I won't if you don't mind. I think I'm starting to come to terms with this, at least as much as I'm ever going to. So it's best I stay here until I'm back on my feet emotionally. Then perhaps I'll come. That's if you and Martha will still have me.

'How could he do this? That's the question I keep asking myself. What had he been keeping from me? In saying that I'm assuming it's of his own volition. I daren't think of the other possibilities. You hear such dreadful things.

'Now the bye-election's well and truly out of the way, interest from the Westminster clan seems finally to have faded away. I've heard nothing from that quarter for a time now. I had become heartily sick of going over the whole thing yet again for some inquisitive nonentity making out he or she was devastated.

'You asked about Barney and me. We've had our ups and downs, but who hasn't? Generally it's been a close and trusting relationship. That's one of the reasons why this whole thing is just so incomprehensible. We've been together over sixteen years.

'HJ came to see me a while back now. Thank you for the introduction. What a strange little man. Have you noticed his shoes, how incredibly highly polished they are? I suppose he knows what he is doing. He seemed mostly concerned with that person B claimed to have seen in the garden. I'm sure in reality he was a figment of B's imagination which could be quite fertile, as you know.

'People are friendly enough here in Ludlow but I don't know any of them well enough to talk to about this and I still get stared at in the street. I would have hoped they had better things to think about after all this time. I had considered going down to London for a while. I love the London flat, but if I were there I'd still feel at risk of odd people dropping round when they had nothing else to do, drinking my gin and going over it all again. Here I feel safe from all that.

'Thank you for your kindness. Love to Martha. I'll write again soon.

'Ellen

'P.S. I may email you - if I can learn how to do it. B hated the computer and I never touched it, but I feel almost drawn to it now. It might be a window on the world. I must sign up for a course. Watch this space!'

16.

I emerged from Lime Street Station. It was my first ever visit to Liverpool. In different circumstances I would have been eager to look around. But the priority was to find somewhere to lay my head that night. I had no intention of stopping someone and asking them. Cabs were out - the drivers talk and peer at you in their rear-view mirrors. I figured the best thing was to walk in a straight line till I came to a hotel. It's a big city, there had to be plenty.

I'd walked for no more than ten minutes when I came upon one of those hotels that has minimal services, but reasonable rooms at reasonable prices. That's the sort of thing. As I approached the double doors I caught sight of my full-length reflection in the glass frontage. I wasn't a pretty sight. I just had to hope they wouldn't hold that against me. I pushed on the door and stepped resolutely inside.

The attractive young lady on Reception greeted me without turning a hair. I presumed the birthplace of so much rock and pop was pretty much at ease with the disreputable and odd-looking. I gave the name of 'Brown', home address – 126 Endell Street, Halifax, West Yorkshire. I was rather pleased with myself – there was no number 126 in Endell Street. Or there hadn't been, back in the old days. She accepted my cash payment for one night plus breakfast box left outside the room at 7.30am. Then smiled, handed me one of those flimsy key card things, and said with a delightful Liverpool lilt, "That's brilliant.".

I went up to my room. Took a few minutes to settle in, then went out again to find the shops. It was time now to get myself a wardrobe as opposed to a disguise.

It was a huge, pedestrianized shopping precinct, packed with people. I had constantly to fight a temptation to look over my shoulder. In this day and age, when you set out to disappear, you soon realize what you're up against. Every step you take is monitored by a closed-circuit camera fixed to the wall of a building or up on its own pole like a stork's nest, swivelling, zooming in. Across the country, uniformed voyeurs must pry, twenty-four-seven. Looking for what? Petty malcontents? Pickpockets? Down women's cleavage? Drunks? Malingerers? Benefit cheats? While the wheels of big business and the City grind us all to fools with impunity.

My heart suddenly hit the walls of my chest. Outside a newsagent's shop - Christ - a hand-scrawled news placard – 'AWOL POLITICIAN – STILL NOTHING'. It was near the end of the day and what few newspapers were left were clipped into a rack on the wall. I daren't look at them, yet I had to. I sidled over to them. The story, though not the main one, was front page on two of them. And those two were folded so that only the first few lines of the story were visible. While trying to give the impression I was looking at something in the shop window, I screwed my head and eyes around to try and read the top one.

"There is still no news of the whereabouts of Barnaby Marechal, Member of Parliament for South Melford, who has not been seen since delivering a talk three nights ago to a local business people's association in Carlisle. Mr Marechal, regarded as something of a maverick within the party, is popular with the public. A close friend of the Marechals, Mr Frank Lippincote who called in the police after being contacted late at night by Marechal's wife to say that he had not returned home, told this paper that there was, as yet, no reason to be alarmed. "Mister Marechal, regarded by many at Westminster as something of a maverick, is given to doing things very much his own way. His often unorthodox behaviour can sometimes be - "

The rest was hidden behind the rack. I walked quickly away. 'Can sometimes be' what, Frank? I'd have given a lot to know the end of that sentence. I headed towards a large Marks and Spencer's. And 'maverick', eh? Seems you don't have to stray far off the beaten track to be 'a maverick' these days.

On the way back from the shops I bought a Chinese takeaway and a bottle of red wine. I took them, along with my shopping, to my room. As it seemed ever more likely I was actually going to go ahead with this brainstorm, I tried to think through, while I ate, the practical problems I was facing. I was looking at a mountain. I tried to bring order to my racing thoughts. My mind however, does not take readily to order. I ended up juggling a plethora of more or less random concerns.

Where was money going to come from? There was plenty in the bank. But I had no way of getting my hands on it. Holes in walls, cheques were out. Anything involving my name was out. Everything today involves your name and/or your address/phone number/email address. I still had most of those few hundred quid in my pocket. But my bank accounts were effectively redundant, I could cash no bonds, sell no shares, sell no property. I was marooned on an island of my own making.

Another thing - what, in the long run, will happen to my property? The flat in London is in Ellen's name. But what about our lovely farmhouse in Herefordshire? If I manage to evade discovery permanently and never, ever reappear as who I was, I will be considered dead after – I think it's seven years. In which case, everything would go to Ellen, being at the moment, the sole beneficiary of my will. A will which, as things now stand, I can't amend. Which means that Matt, assuming I ever find him, will get nothing from me on my death. Had I planned all this in advance, instead of simply jumping off a train one afternoon, it could all have been very carefully thought through. On the other hand, had I planned it in advance I doubt I'd ever have had the courage to do it in the first place. I finished my meal in a state of great agitation, feeling guilty and vulnerable. I found myself almost wishing I had religion. If I believed in a God I presume I'd at least feel less alone.

I picked up my glass of wine, took it with me to the window where I looked out into the Liverpool night. An impressive clutch of neoclassical buildings were bathed in amber floodlighting. Traffic swirled around a busy junction like reflections of lights on water. Beyond that, the brightly lit proscenium-arch-like entrance to Lime Street Station across which passed the silhouettes of pedestrians - walk-on artists in this amateur film of my life.

A strange inner silence was rising up in and around me. The scene before me became just moving images on a screen. My agitation dissolved. I stood very still and held all thought away. The image before me sank deeper and deeper inside me until it was almost as though I experienced it not simply as a sight somewhere out there in front of me but as part of my own self. Or was I part of it? I couldn't tell. Nor did it matter. It felt like a jumping-off point. A moment before birth.

I slept well that night. I took it as a good sign. Perhaps after all, I was doing the right thing, or at least the best thing in the circumstances. Sleep seemed also to have clarified my thoughts. As I sat by the window with my breakfast box, chewing on its depressingly unappetising contents, it came at me out of the blue - there was a source of money - money I had once vowed I would never, ever touch. But in making that vow I could never have envisaged these circumstances. Martin Cosgrove. Do I hear Dad's laughter from the grave? Cosgrove - family lawyer since the year dot. Good man, old school, discreet, utterly trustworthy. And a gentleman.

There was no phone in the room. My mobile was in two separate pieces. There was however a bank of public telephones in Reception.

"Martin?"

"Speaking. Who's that?"

"Bernat. It's Bernat."

"I'm sorry – Bernard - ?"

"No - Bernat. Bernat Horvat-Marshal."

Long silence. Then a muted, "Goodness gracious."

"How are you, Martin?"

"Bernat. Well, well. after all this time! What - ?"

"Martin - listen. Before we go any further, I have not rung you. OK?"

"Sorry. You what, old boy? You have not - ?"

"I have not rung you. This phone call has not happened."

"Right." He thought for a second. "OK. I think perhaps I understand."

"I'm in a public box in a hotel. I'm going to keep my voice down and I have to make this quick. I need to see you ASAP. And I need money. Real money. Think about it - I'm sure you know what I mean."

"Just give me a second to get my head around this. OK. I think maybe I do."

"But I can't meet you in your office. I can't meet anywhere where there are people."

"My house? It's out of town in Woking. A reasonably affluent part of - "

"But you have neighbours, don't you?"

"Is that a - ?"

"Suppose they see me arrive? Or leave? No, it's got to be out in the open. Wimbledon Common. Streatham Common. Primrose Hill."

"In that case, I need a minute to drum my fingers on my desk. Er – think, think, think. OK – how about this then? Two average elderly gents sitting by the river with fishing rods in their hands. Wouldn't excite a lot of interest, would they?"

"Go on. Where?"

"Do you know a place called Laleham?"

"Near Staines?"

"That's the one. I sometimes go fishing there on a Sunday."

"Sounds good. When can we do it?"

"Where are you? And how much money have you with you?"

"Liverpool. And nowhere near enough."

"Do I presume you don't have a mobile phone?"

"You do, yes."

"It would be useful. Dare I say, essential?"

"Nor do I have a place to live."

"Dear, dear, Bernat. This is somewhat off my map. First, I suggest you get a mobile."

"That can be traced."

"I have a couple of old ones. You'd better have one of them. I've got an unused sim card around somewhere. I can put that in one of them and courier it up to you. How long can you keep going with the cash you have?"

"Two or three days. But I really need to get back to London and get myself a cheap room somewhere. Then I can - "

Martin chuckled. "I think you might look a long time for a 'cheap' room."

"I'm not thinking Highgate or Dulwich."

"Kilburn. The Harrow Road even."

"OK. So where - ?"

"Listen. Get down here and book yourself for one night into any really cheap hotel. Can you bear that?"

"I'm getting used to it."

"When you've done that, let me know where you are – use the mobile I'll send you – and I can have cash round to you in a couple of hours. Then you can go and find a room at your leisure."

"Martin - I'm in awe."

"It's the crime fiction I read, Bernat." He laughed, a little self-consciously. "Once that's done we can fix up our fishing trip."

"And Martin - I'm sure I don't need to say this, but I have to stay utterly off the radar. I caught a glimpse of a newspaper yesterday and I seemed to have almost star billing."

"A forty-eight hour Tube strike starts here today. A woman in Surbiton or somewhere has given birth to quads or quins - one or the other. You're cold potatoes. And incidentally, worry not - I won't ask what this is about. If you want to tell me, that's a different matter."

"There's a whole lot of stuff I need to talk to you about."

"I can imagine."

"No Martin, you can't. You really can't"

With Martin's phone in my pocket, I caught an early train to London. I booked a room in a hotel in the Kilburn area - a place calling itself 'Wiltshire House'. By comparison, the 'Welcome' in Wigan bordered on the genteel. The cash from Martin turned up at nine-thirty the following morning. I set off to find myself a bed-sitter. Like he had said, they weren't cheap. In fact, given the state of most of them, they were criminally exorbitant. But I had cash, and by the end of the day, with the help of an agent I would not, in other circumstances, have trusted any further than I could have thrown him, I was the accredited tenant of a bed-sitter. It was on the top floor of a seedy Victorian house in a street just off Kilburn High Road Road. It was mean and it was depressing. But I could hide away in it with more confidence than in any middle-class enclave.

Taking up almost the whole of one side of the room, was a huge double bed. It would have slept a family of four. By the way it sagged in the middle, it looked like it had. I tried hard not to imagine what might have gone on in it. It had ugly wooden posts at each corner, on which I hung articles of clothing and my shopping bag.

The 'kitchen' – as the agent had described it - was simply a partitioned off slice of the same room with a mini electric oven and a cheap fridge which had no freezer. It was cramped, ill-ventilated with just one tiny window. Boil a kettle in it and it steamed up. Cook a whole meal and you'd risk getting trench foot.

A couple of houses along the road, a viaduct carrying the Underground trains crossed the road, vaulting the rooftops. Every thirty seconds or so in the rush hour, the whole building shook as another loaded train juddered by virtually overhead, rattling windows, glasses and crockery.

I shared this top floor with two women. The older one I guessed to be in her mid-forties, the younger around her late twenties. I never saw them apart. Their clothes were so lacking in colour, it seemed that had to be by design. The younger one had very short hair, cut like that of a boy in the 1950's. From their room which was right next to mine, no sound ever emerged – no radio, TV, music, no animated voices. Were it not for the fact that they'd said in unison a rather timid, 'Good morning,' to me the day I moved in, I might have thought they were profoundly deaf. There was never a man around. Although not on that account alone, I sensed they were lesbians. They intrigued me, and via what little contact I had with them, I liked them.

I shared with them the bathroom and the cramped little toilet across the landing. At first, the toilet sort of bothered me. Though I'm not sure why. There was always a can of air freshener in there. And a spare toilet roll. Being the newcomer I was to bed-sitter living, I had to think about what protocol there might be around toilet rolls - especially as the others involved were two women. I could hardly expect them to provide me with toilet paper. And to take my own personal toilet roll in and out with me seemed distinctly mean-minded. The next occasion on which I was the first to start on the standby roll, I left a replacement.

It worked. That's how we carried on – whoever was the first to start on the standby roll, supplied the replacement. The arrangement was never referred to. A discussion with the two women about toilet roll arrangements would likely have embarrassed them hugely. And me, for that matter.

It had been an odd experience. Challenging in its way. And I was pleased with myself. I'd navigated my way successfully past what might have been an awkward social impasse.

The only other resident in that house of whom I was ever aware was a man who lived on the ground floor. I would glimpse him only occasionally when his coming in or going out coincided with mine. He was anything between early thirties and late forties. Though beardless, he looked permanently unshaven with thick, heavy brows. His black hair was long and his clothes never looked really clean. He never spoke. His eyes were black and quite unreadable. He gave me the impression of repressing some terrible anger. His proximity, fleeting though it always was, occasioned in me a troubling uncertainty. Unlike the women next door, he appeared to have no regular hours. There was never any telling if or when he'd be around.

In the time I was there however, he did me no harm. Nor anybody else I was aware of. I decided in the end that he was perhaps just one of the disturbed and disturbing individuals whose presence was par for the course in that stratum of society. How remote from the lives of ordinary people had I, along with so many in the Westminster village, become.

17.

Martin and I arranged to meet by the river the following Monday. Sunday was his usual day for fishing but, as he pointed out, get good weather on a Sunday and the river and its banks would be awash with boats, people, children, ice cream vans, frisbee throwers et al. He would pick me up from the train station at a place called Egham, just a few miles from his fishing spot. Staines would have been closer but Staines was a busy place with a bustling train station. Egham on a Monday morning, he assured me, would be quiet.

I had a week to wait. I decided to use that time in closely observing my own natural behaviour. Then in modifying it where necessary in order to try and create an individual with behavioural traits unlike those of the erstwhile Barnaby Marechal. When the following Monday came, I wanted to feel that in as many ways as possible, I was Mister New Man.

Philosophically it was fascinating. If you want to obliterate the person you have been, and thereafter to be seen and accepted as whoever you now are, you have to go a long way beyond simply changing the way you dress, growing a beard, putting on a flat cap and a pair of shades. You have to give attention to the whole physical and psychological organism that amounts to 'you'. Recognition of another human being takes place at the instantaneous coming together in the mind of the observer of an immensely subtle and complex combination of factors – physical appearance, gestures, facial expressions, mannerisms of all kinds. So if you're going to do the job properly, all those things have to be addressed.

There was a full-length mirror by the head of the bed. I walked up and down in front of it - like Mr. Silvero in the night – studying my walk, how I held myself, how I started off, stopped, turned around. The process began to intrigue me beyond its present purpose. How often does one cast that detailed an eye on one's own self? Not often enough, it seemed. My walk, for a start, almost embarrassed me. It was an odd walk. Slightly snatched and jerky with, even so, a bit of a loping stride. It was not attractive - but it was noticeable. In fact, it was probably one of the main features which, at a distance, would have identified me to those who knew me. It needed modifying.

I set out to study walks. I spent time in shopping malls in and around the capital, Brent Cross, The Whitgift Centre, Bluewater - moronic places, full of people armed with bags they seem determined to fill. We must have developed a great opinion of our own worth, that we lavish so much on ourselves. Or is it the opposite? Is it that deep down, we feel such a lack of worth that we're driven to try and redress the balance by the power of our purses?

In such places I sat down, and from the foxhole of my shades, my burgeoning beard and pulled-low black cap, watched people walking. Walkers come in varieties - the shamblers, the draggers of feet, the slow and weary ones, the totterers, those who take weeny steps and those who stride, the swayers from side to side and the ones who look like they're leaning into the wind. How few walk well. How few are aware of themselves, confident, head up, shoulders out. Once back in my room, I would train myself to be that sort of walker.

I gave time to my interpersonal mannerisms. Before the mirror, I talked to myself as to another person while, at the same time, studying my body language - my hands, my facial expressions, the crossing and uncrossing of my legs. Although happy with this in principle, still I appeared less fluid, less open, free and demonstrative than I'd supposed. I'd work on it. And I tried out a few new gestures. I quite liked the idea of lightly rubbing my chin when appearing to think hard, and of running a hand through my hair when puzzled or when laughing. (Both, I realized with something of a jolt, were common gestures of my Dad's). I practised looking cool and relaxed when sitting. Stretching out a little, lounging, one arm perhaps half over the back of the chair.

By the following weekend I was reasonably happy with my progress. Things seemed to be falling into place.

18.

"I do so adore this view." Ellen stood by the french windows, a hand lightly clutching the heavy curtains. She watched the clouds scurrying before the wind, their shadows sweeping over the fields and leaping the hedgerows. "Those hills in the distance – would they be the Black Mountains?"

Frank Lippincote eased himself out of his armchair and stood by her side. "Where? Show me."

"Those distant grey humps."

He followed her pointing finger. "You know," he said, "I am not as well up on the local geography as I should be. But I suspect they might well be the Black Mountains. Martha will know. We must ask her."

"'Black Mountains'." Ellen savoured the words as she turned from the window. "Fairy tales - spirits and hobgoblins."

He watched her as she returned to her armchair. She was still shapely. Elegant. She moved with an unselfconscious grace. Barney had spoken of her incipient arthritis, but Frank had seen no sign of it. As she sat down again she smoothed her skirt nicely beneath her bottom. She picked up her cup from the little table at her side and took a sip.

He left the window and returned to his own chair opposite her.

Martha came in with another pot of tea. She was a short, overweight woman whose movements seemed often ill-judged and awkward.

Ellen watched her carefully. "How are you today, Martha?"

Martha braced herself, held her breath, then leaned creakily forward to put the teapot down beside the milk and a now almost empty tray of cakes. She stood up, released her breath. "Mustn't grumble, Ellen. Mustn't grumble." She prepared to lower herself into her armchair by first hovering above it. "There are people with worse." She released herself and plumped down into the mass of cushions. "Aren't there, dear?" she said to Frank.

"As you say, Martha."

Each sipped. Teacups chinked in saucers.

Martha pointed to the french windows. "Starting to rain. I had a feeling it would."

Frank set his empty cup and saucer down on a low coffee table. He cleared his throat rather loudly. "So Ellen – the question on all our lips - what about this man of yours?"

"Yes Frank," said Ellen, after a pause. "What about him?"

"Well - is there – I mean – have you or anyone heard anything more?"

Martha, peering into her teacup, said, very quietly, "Ellen might not want to talk about this, Frank."

Ellen waved a dismissive hand. "It's alright, Martha." Then to Frank, "No. That Harry Jardine rang the other day. But only to clarify a detail."

Frank sat back. "You must feel - well – actually, I don't know how you must feel."

"Then I'll tell you – abandoned. Abandoned, dumped, betrayed - " - she paused - " - and quite angry."

Martha shuffled around in her armchair. "I think" she said, "a little top-up on the cake situation." She heaved herself up once again, picked up the plate on which one cake remained. She offered that one around.

The others shook their heads. Martha made her way slowly from the room, biting into the cake as she went.

The first spots of rain were running down the window. Ellen watched them catching sparkles of light.

"Ellen," said Frank.

She turned to him.

The words he'd rehearsed failed him. Others unintended came out. "Er - it's just that – well, you know how it is."

"Do I? How what is?"

"What I mean is – in the circumstances – well, I feel helpless."

Ellen said nothing. She looked again at the rain. The drops had all joined now into a single sheet of water running down the glass, distorting the countryside and the racing clouds beyond.

Frank put the tips of the fingers of both hands together, and pressed them to his lips. He rocked gently back and forth. "I hope you know where I'm coming from when I ask this – but things with you and Barney – were they, well - ?"

"Were they what?"

"As they should be? You know."

She frowned. "I answered that in a letter."

"Yes, you did. But - "

"Then that's your answer."

He retired, nursing the rebuff.

"I certainly had no reason," she said, "to expect him to vanish off the face of the earth. If that's what you mean."

He cleared his throat. "So what view of it all do the police have?"

"They don't suspect foul play. Mr Jardine seems to agree. They're probably right. If it were an accident of some sort – or something a lot worse - you'd expect a clue. But there's nothing. It's like it had all been planned - no loose ends. Some taxi driver - in Wigan, of all places - thinks he might have picked up a man who might have answered Barney's description the day after his talk in Carlisle. But apart from - "

"What would Barney have been doing in Wigan?"

"I'm sure they've got that wrong. The London train from Carlisle stops there, that's all. But it stops at other places as well. And - "

"Was he not on his way to Ludlow though rather than to London?"

"Probably. Does it make a difference?"

"It does. In order to get to Ludlow he'd need to change at Crewe. Now, the thing is, the London train doesn't stop at Crewe. So the police may well have been thinking that he got off at Wigan in order to change for Crewe. But on the other - "

"Oh, Christ, Frank - I don't know. Did he get on the train at Carlisle in the first place? They don't even know that."

"Did no-one drive him to the station?"

"It seems not."

"And if you ring his mobile?"

"It's dead."

There came a sudden crash from the kitchen. Frank shot up, half out his chair. "Martha!"

"It's alright, Frank! Dropped the tray. That's all."

He sat back again.

Ellen said, quietly, "Is it my imagination or does Martha seem not so well again?"

His face darkened. "It's not your imagination."

"Oh, Frank."

"It comes back. It goes, then comes back."

She looked down into her cup. "I do wonder sometimes what it's all about, you know. Not that I'm thinking of doing anything about it, but I can understand people putting an end to themselves."

"I'm afraid I've always avoided thinking too deeply about that sort of thing."

"Have you never wondered?"

He shrugged. "One has a life. One has to get on with it."

She put her cup down on the coffee table. Then sat looking at it.

Frank watched her. "A penny for them."

She turned to him. "Did I do something to deserve this, Frank? If I did, I really don't know what it was."

He had never seen Ellen look vulnerable before. A wave of confusion threatened to embarrass him. "I really do so wish," he said, "that I could help."

"Yes. That would be nice. But you can't."

Martha returned from the kitchen with more cakes. Frank looked at her in a sort of puzzled despair. "We're never going to eat all them, Martha."

Martha hovered once again over her chair. Then dropped herself in among its cushions. "Let's see, eh?" she said, catching her breath. "Let's just see."

Ellen returned to studying the rain on the windows.

Frank picked anxiously at a fingernail. Watched Ellen out of the corner of his eye.

Martha, daintily and with great care, selected a cake from the replenished pile.

The wind rattled the wisteria against the window.

19.

Monday morning. Barney stood before the mirror. In approximately three hours time he would meet with Martin Cosgrove - the first time in over fifteen years. He was reasonably happy with the work he'd done on himself. His hair – although there was not a lot of it– was noticeably longer and just beginning to curl at the sides and back. He had not worn it this long for many years. The touch of it on the skin of his neck, straggling a little as it did in the wind, stirred memories. Its dark brown was now pleasantly streaked with grey. He liked that. It made him look almost distinguished. But be careful – the line between 'distinguished' and 'conspicuous' might be quite fine.

Hair gel was out. However he'd manipulated it, he'd looked

ludicrous. His stubble had grown to where it qualified now as a short beard. He had been concerned it might contain patches of ginger. But the few ginger hairs that had appeared were hardly noticeable. Overall, it was turning out pleasantly darker than he'd expected – almost black around the chin. He would not allow it to grow beyond what he considered 'mid-length' – long enough to be seen as a full beard, but not so long as to attract attention. But it itched. And, to his slight distaste, was subject to dandruff.

He had not entirely come to terms with his new wardrobe. He still had to push past some psychological barrier to avoid putting on a tie. Open-neck shirts still gave him a sense of being half-dressed. And vulnerable. Like the zebras and wildebeest in David Attenborough wildlife programmes being attacked by lions who always went for the throat.

He had splashed out on a pair of Calvin Klein blue jeans. He was pleased with how they looked on him, but he couldn't figure out why they made them so tight that he had difficulty just putting his hands in his pockets. But then maybe if they weren't that tight, they wouldn't look the way they did. You can never have everything.

The footwear question had, for a long time, defeated him. He'd upgraded the grotesque Wigan trainers to a pair of expensive designer ones. But still he had been unhappy. The soles were so thick and rubbery they made him feel slightly unstable. In any case he could not get past the thought that really they were little more than extortionately expensive plimsolls. In the end, he bought himself another pair of Church's brogues. They should not, in theory, go with jeans. But to his eye they did. They looked good.

The pride of place in his new wardrobe was a black leather jacket, made in Italy and bought from a branch of M&S in one of those awful shopping malls. He had not shopped in stores like that since his early days in advertising. But the quality surprised him. The leather was beautifully supple, the cut excellent.

Thus attired, he stood before the mirror that Monday morning. His long aversion to casual modes of dress had all but disappeared. There would no doubt be those who would look on him as an aging rocker – was that the word? - attempting to recapture the unrecapturable. Let them. He looked good. And little like the Barnaby Marechal of old.

He was ready to meet Martin. Ready to start a new life.

He left the train at Egham. The only other person to get off was a young woman dragging along, either side of her, a couple of complaining children. He crossed the tracks via a metal footbridge. He watched the train below him as it pulled out of the station on its way to Weybridge.

'Weybridge' - didn't George Harrison once live there? Paul McCartney? Both?

He had half an hour to kill. He left the station, and looked up and down a street of small shops. A couple of hundred metres or so further on, on the opposite side, was what looked like the gated entrance to a park. He set off towards it. The walk – watch the walk. Head up. No loping. When you imagine all around might be looking at you, it's hard to act natural. A sudden police siren sent a brief shot of panic through him. There'd be flowers in the park. He'd go and look at them. Or watch the ducks. If ducks there were. He liked ducks. They were calming.

He came to a pedestrian crossing and stood with the knot of people waiting for the green signal to cross. He glanced covertly around to see if he could detect any dawning of recognition. They all seemed aware of little outside their own heads. The green light came on. They all crossed. Barney remained buried and unrecognized in their midst. He unwound just a little. He made his way into the park.

There were ducks. On a small lake, they paddled serenely around among reeds and water lilies. He sat down to watch them on a wooden bench dedicated, according to a brass plate in need of polish, to the memory of 'My Dear Sister Florrie'. Their colours were iridescent in the sun. What natural poise. A small black one with a white forehead suddenly attacked – or so it seemed – another of its kind. There was a great deal of splashing, squawking, beating of wings. But only for about ten seconds. Then both of them backed off, shook themselves down and swam calmly away like nothing had happened.

He looked at his watch. Twenty minutes still to go.

"Barney!"

What?? He shot bold upright.

"Barney!" A woman's voice.

His heart pounding, he looked all around. A woman, probably in her forties, overweight and gasping, was half-running towards him waving her hands. Jesus! Who in hell? But wait a minute – he followed the direction of her eyes – to a diminutive white dog, yapping and scuttling furiously along the path towards a dog four times its own size.

"Barney – no!! Come back, Barney! Barney!" But Barney the dog took no notice.

Barney the man sat back and took a deep breath. His pulse rate slowed again. He chuckled to himself. A clock struck some indeterminate point between the hours. He checked his watch. Then glanced in the direction of the sound. Rising up through the jumble of buildings crowding the land on the far side of the park was a square stone tower. Squat, dark, massively built.

Barney was no man for churches. The interior of an empty church with its ancient silence, its gloom and graphic images of pain and torture stirred in him dark shadows. Their silent depths called to that depth within him where childhood demons played. Yet as a man afraid of heights is drawn inexorably to peer over the edge, so such places exerted over him an almost magnetic pull. This dark tower called to him. Like it had risen up through the surrounding buildings in order to be able to see him across their rooftops. And there he was. He got slowly to his feet, and set off towards it.

The heavy wooden door swung ponderously on ancient hinges, opening up a silent chasm. Shafts of sunlight, tiny dust motes floating in them, poured down from the high windows picking out in bright pools irregular sections of the pews and the bright colours of heraldic banners that hung out from the walls. He made his way on near silent footfalls into the centre of the empty space. One other human figure sat, half-lit, across the far side, alone and head bowed. Accusing effigies gazed down at him from walls and windows. He stood for a few seconds, then sat himself slowly down in the nearest pew. Its wood was a rich chestnut colour, polished to a lacquered shine by the rear ends of guilt-ridden generations.

He set his briefcase down by his side and composed himself. Unlike the huddled, bowed figure over there, he sat upright, back straight. Clasped his hands together on his lap and sat very, very still. He was no man for religion any more than for churches. But it seemed the thing to do.

The silence, like some entity reacting to the space he had created for it, moved closer to him. He shut his eyes and took a deep breath. It came closer still, tentatively at first, as though trying him. A sudden urge to start thinking came over him – Martin, money, his son. He pushed it away. Allowed the silence to keep coming towards him, to wrap itself around him.

It was then that he began to experience a most extraordinary sense of space - space that encompassed him, and everything out to and beyond the furthest stars. A limitless and timeless emptiness that took in all things. Asking nothing of him, and incomprehensibly benign. Tears started. But as suddenly as it had arrived, so it began to retreat. He reached out to keep hold of it - but he would as well clutch running water. Then it was gone. He was alone again. He looked up and around. Something had happened. Some thing had reached out and touched him - then slipped back among the shadows.

He stood up. The huddled figure still sat with head bowed. The shafts of sunlight came and went with the movement of clouds across the sun.

"I suppose," said Barney, struggling to work out the geography of a camouflage-green waterproof cape, "this would have to go down as one of the more bizarre moments in my life."

Martin Cosgrove reached out and settled it around Barney's shoulders. "There."

Barney's head projected from the apex of a green tepee. He looked down at himself. "I feel," he said, "like something that's come up out of the river."

Cosgrove smiled. "But you look the part."

Barney held out a hand, palm up towards the sky. "No rain. Won't people wonder why I'm wearing this thing?"

"Fishermen are pessimists."

Barney looked down at their little area of river bank. Two folding chairs. Two rather flashy-looking fishing rods resting in steel supports set in the soft earth, their extremities hanging out over the water. Tins and boxes of fishing paraphernalia. "The last time I did anything like this, Martin, I must have been about ten years old. I had a stick with a piece of string tied on the end, and a hook on the end of that." He pointed to Cosgrove's expensive, many-pocketed fishing jacket. "We didn't wear stuff like that."

"This," said Cosgrove, "is nothing. Some of them leave home on Sunday like they're going into space. Anyway - " - he indicated the chairs - " - shall we make ourselves reasonably comfortable?"

They both sat. "What's happening to people, Martin? Some of them seem to need to wear designer outfits to go for a bike ride or a run round the park."

"One can, I'm afraid, get rather seduced."

Barney looked out over the river. The water lapped gently at the bank by his feet. A breeze stirred the leaves in the trees above his head. "Brilliant idea, this, Martin."

Cosgrove looked him up and down. "It's good to see you. It's been a long time."

"And you. Sad to say though, I can't tell you what all this is about. Not yet. I'm feeling a bit how a fugitive from justice must feel."

"It suits you," said Cosgrove.

"What - being a fugitive?"

"No, no. The beard. The different clothes. The dark glasses. Very 'alternative'. To be honest, I never thought you fitted very well into the suit-and-tie brigade anyway."

"Really? Interesting. I had a bloody good try though, didn't I?"

"And your situation – what I sense of it - sounds somewhat 'alternative' too." Though he smiled a chummily conspiratorial smile, his once sparkling grey eyes had dulled. He was looking old and just a bit tired. His hair, though still thick and wiry, was completely grey now, untidy and not well looked after.

"I hope," said Barney, "that none of this is going to put you in a difficult situation - professionally."

"Worry not. I'm retiring this year." He took from a pocket a pack of cigarettes. Held it out to Barney. "Smoke?"

Barney shook his head.

"Wise man." He lit up. "Not that retirement absolves me of professional responsibilities. But please don't concern yourself with it." He drew on his cigarette. "I'm flattered you're prepared to put the trust in me you already have."

"It seems I've got you just in time. To be honest, I was a tiny bit surprised to find you still in practice."

Cosgrove knocked the ash from his cigarette. "I should have gone long ago. Judy wanted me to. But – well, I didn't. Then it was too late. We'd had no children – sadly. After she died I carried on primarily to keep my mind occupied. I'm not a man for hobbies." He indicated the spread of fishing tackle. "This apart. At which I'm little more than a dilettante, frankly."

The unsolicited intimacy touched Barney. "I'm sorry, Martin. I didn't know about Judy."

Cosgrove shrugged.

"So when do you actually retire?"

"When I've finally accepted that I'm no longer indispensable. Probably later this year." He sighed. "Forty-two years. That's what it will have been then, Bernat. Forty-two years in the same building. Forty-two journeys of the earth round the sun." He looked out across the river. "I sometimes think, you know, that we spend our lives struggling up a winding staircase in the dark, not really knowing where it leads. While outside, the sun's shining, the grass grows. Birds sing."

Barney looked at him in surprise.

Then, with an expression on his face as though his own sudden flight of whimsy had reactivated some dormant impishness, he leaned across to Barney. "Good luck!" He stage-whispered it, as though he feared the trees had ears.

"Pardon?" said Barney, taken aback.

"Bloody good luck to you. Whatever madcap thing you're up to Bernat. I wish I had your courage." The old sparkle was, briefly, back in his eyes.

"Or my foolhardiness."

"Whichever. What the hell."

"So," said Barney, sitting back, "how long is this money going to take?"

"Not long. I'll make sure."

"No-one must know. Not anybody, ever."

"They won't." He smiled.

"I'm sorry. I forget. You're well used to keeping the family secrets."

"I've kept yours a long time."

"I have egg on my face though Martin, don't I? I swore on my life I would never touch his money."

"What you actually said to him in a letter was that if, in spite of your expressed wishes, he still went ahead and left it to you, you'd give it all to Greenpeace or Save The Whale."

Barney chuckled. "You have a good memory."

"I'm a lawyer. I salt away useful snippets."

"So." Barney sat forward, elbows on his knees. "Once it's released, when can I get my hands on it?"

Cosgrove took from a pocket a little battered tin, on its front a faded picture of John Bull. Unhurriedly he removed the lid, took the remainder of the cigarette from his lips, and stubbed it out in the tin. Then replaced the lid and put the tin on the ground at his feet. "You'll have it as soon as I can get it transferred to the new account. Which will be in the name of Bernat Gyorgy Horvat-Marshal. And which will be with an internet bank, such as - "

"Internet? Martin, I know nothing about the damned internet!"

"You don't need to. At least, not very much. That way, everything's done online. It's quite anonymous. You get your money out of holes-in-the-wall as normal."

"What about cheque books, paying-in books, direct debits, that sort of - ?"

"You don't need a cheque book. They're on the way out anyway. Anything else you want, order it online. You do everything online – standing orders, money transfers - everything"

Barney took a deep breath. "I guess I can send an email. Look up a web page."

"You'll manage."

"But where, how do I access the internet in the first place? I can't sit in one of those internet cafés. Somebody's going to see me and - "

"The phone I gave you. The screen's a bit small, but you can get on the internet with it. Once the money's released, obviously it's up to you how you manage it. But I warn you, there's an embarrassing amount of it."

"I might need an embarrassing amount."

Cosgrove waited for the elaboration he felt might be imminent. But Barney turned away, looked across the river, over the meadows that stretched away on the far side towards the village of Laleham. He sat staring into space. Then came round again, and pointed suddenly to the little tin on the ground at Cosgrove's feet. "Why," he asked, "do you put your cigarette butts in there?"

"Er – well, just dropping them on the ground here doesn't really seem the thing to do. And I don't throw them in the river. What would a mouthful of tobacco do to a trout?"

Barney laughed, looked curiously at him. "How long have you been on your own now?"

"Five years. Why?"

"Have you never thought of – well – you know - ?"

"Someone else?"

Barney nodded.

He shrugged. "Look at me. Who'd want me? Anyway - " - he cleared his throat rather loudly - " - talking of women - what's your wife's financial situation likely to be at the moment?"

Barney took a second or two to gather himself. "OK. Ellen has family money of her own. And there's still a fair amount in the joint account. There are bonds in her name. The London flat's in her name. She's at liberty to dispose of any of that if and when she wants."

"And I suppose," said Cosgrove, smiling amiably, "if you're still AWOL in seven years' time you'll be presumed to have departed this life and she can sell the Ludlow house as well." His smiled faded. "You are sure Bernat, are you, that this is what you want to do?"

"'Want' isn't in it. I really have no choice. I'm sorry to be so MI5 about it, but that's all I can say at the moment."

The conversation lapsed. Cosgrove tweaked his fishing lines. Barney looked at the people on a small pleasure boat sliding gently past. Its bow wave rustled the reeds near his feet. A woman passenger in a wide straw hat was looking at him. He returned the look. She turned quickly away. He smiled to himself. "Out of interest," he said, turning to Cosgrove, "suppose, I'd never come to you. What then?"

"I always assumed that one day you would. Despite what you'd said."

"But suppose I hadn't. Suppose I'd died, for example, and the money was still in trust. What then?"

"If, twenty-five years on from the setting up of the trust, you as beneficiary, had still not been located or had been located but had continued to reject the terms of the trust, then it was to be dissolved."

"And the money?"

"The money plus its accrued interest was to be transferred to the account of an orphanage in Hungary."

Silence.

"Excuse me?"

Cosgrove looked expressionlessly back at him.

"Martin? An orphanage?"

"In a town whose name I can't possibly pronounce, but spelled – 'M-a-t-e-s-z-a-l-k-a'. Not all that far from the border with Romania, I believe."

"An orphanage?"

"I know nothing about it Bernat, or about the town, or what connection it had or did not have with your father or his family, or your mother or her family."

Barney ran a hand through his hair. "My mother," he said, very quietly, "was born there."

"In the orphanage?"

"No. Not in the orphanage. In that town somewhere – I don't know where. I've never been there. None of this was ever spoken about. Not in front of me, anyway. I'm stunned."

Cosgrove's eyes narrowed. "Your mother's Jewish parents were her natural parents I suppose?"

"God, Martin – don't."

"It might be worth following up, old boy."

"I haven't the space in my head."

Cosgrove reached into a large bag by his side. He took out a Thermos flask and two plastic cups. He unscrewed the cap and poured. "I do apologize if you prefer your coffee black, but living on my own, I've rather got into the sloppy habit of adding milk before I put it in the flask." He handed the cup to Barney, who sipped tentatively at the rim of the cup. He looked around at the boats, the river, the waving reeds, the trees. "How often," he asked, "do you do this?"

Cosgrove stretched his legs. "Not often enough."

Barney sat back. Listened to the birds, to the ripples as the river murmured quietly to the bank. Some little yellow flowers in the grass by his feet were brilliant in the sun.

Martin ran me back to Egham train station. On the way, we drove past a school. Young children, released for the day, ran across the playground like chaff before the wind. Mothers and one or two fathers waiting for them at the gates in order to shepherd them home. I didn't do that. I could have done.

20.

Al peered through the rain on the windscreen. There was a phone box some way up ahead. He put his foot on the brake.

Viki snapped at him. "What are you doing?"

"There's a phone box."

"So?"

"So I'm stopping."

"What for?"

"I'm going to ring them."

"Who?"

"The motel."

"They'll trace that in five minutes! What's the matter with you?"

He pulled towards the side of the road. "For all we know he might have been bleeding to death!"

She yanked at the wheel to redirect the front wheels away from the verge.

He removed her hand. "Get off!"

"Keep driving!" With which she shoved her right foot between his legs, kicked his foot off the brake and floored the accelerator. The Jaguar leapt forward like a cat, spun and slewed sideways across the wet road right into the path of an oncoming truck. Viki was transfixed. Al, from somewhere, found the presence of mind not to brake or to take evasive action but to continue on that track, shooting straight across the path of the truck which was aquaplaning towards them, its brakes locked, fountains of water spewing from its wheels. The Jaguar mounted the opposite verge, bounced and rocked along the sodden ground as the truck, horn blaring, hurtled past in the opposite direction drowning them in its spray.

The Jaguar came to a standstill in the entrance to a field. Al sat staring out through the windscreen, his heart pounding. The blood had gone from Viki's face. She rocked slowly back and forth, her eyes wide. Then threw open her door and vomited into the wet grass. Slowly, she sat up again and shut the door. Wiped her mouth with a tissue, grimacing.

They sat in silence. Passing vehicles, their lights dazzling through the rain, sprayed the side of the car. Eventually Al sat forward again and started the engine. He waited for a clear road and moved out into the carriageway.

For a long time neither spoke. Then Viki said, "Sorry."

He didn't answer.

She said again, "I'm sorry."

"You said."

"You could be a little more gracious."

"I'm not feeling gracious, Vik. You nearly killed us. And the driver of that truck."

"OK" She shrugged. "Whether you accept my apology or not – I apologize."

They drove on through the rain.

She said quietly, "It's a motel, Al. There's chambermaids. They clean up. He'll be fine."

"That's shit, Viki. I don't like shit."

"Shouldn't be screwing the lady client then, should you?"

"As it turns out - no."

She flicked the vanity mirror down, took a makeup pouch from her bag.

He pointed to her torso. "What have you got in there – a swinging brick?"

"And the rest." And then, with an obscene coquettish lilt. "Remember?" She looked in the mirror, dabbed some rouge on her still white cheeks. Then applied lipstick. She put the pouch back in her bag. "What time back in Bristol?"

"Couple of hours maybe."

She put her face right up to her window and peered out. "Where are we?"

"The last sign said 'Tavistock'."

"It's pissing so much out there I can hardly see. God, I hate the countryside." She turned up the heating, set her seat in the recline position, and lay back. She closed her eyes. "I shall remember this day."

The road curved through tall, dark, water-laden trees. Al turned the radio on. "Money, Money, Money", exclaimed Abba, "In a rich man's world." The car warmed up. Viki's head fell forward onto her chest.

She came to with a start. Looked anxiously around. She was on her own in the car which was stationary. The engine was running and the driver's door open. The rain was blowing in, wetting her maps in the door pocket and her cache of chocolate bars. And there, thirty metres up ahead on the corner of a narrow lane, was Al tugging open the door of a public phone box. "Al!! Oh, Christ - no!!"

But too late. He was inside, and pulling from his pocket a notebook. He flicked through it. She bit her lip. This was going to sink them. Any second now his mouth would be moving - his stupid, silly, fucking mouth giving everything away. She slipped across into the driver's seat. Reached into the rear, grabbed Al's briefcase and flung it out onto the grass. She dragged the door shut, took the wheel and put her foot on the gas. The car rocked and bounced off the wet verge and onto the road then took off, weaved for a few moments from side to side before straightening out and disappearing into the rain.

Al watched through a window of the phone box, his face expressionless.

21.

"Shit!" The heavy box slipped from Ellen's hands and crashed down on the ledge just inside the loft. A cloud of black dust erupted, making her cough. She manoeuvred the box alongside the other three. Then, with a huge effort, heaved herself up from the ladder and sat down with them. She was badly out of breath. Her knees and the joints in her fingers hurt. Her back ached. She was not up to this. Blood was seeping through the finger of one of her gloves. She looked back down through the hatch to the landing. It was an awfully long way down. She wanted to cry.

She turned and peered into the gloom of the loft. It was a land of deep shadow, lit only by a bare bulb dangling from an umbilical cord of flex put up by Barney once, during a very short-lived spell of DIY enthusiasm. It was piled high with stuff shoved away out of sight. It extended the whole length of the house. They'd had plans for it. Double bedroom, bathroom, small study, big windows, big view to the Welsh hills. Plans going nowhere. Still in a drawer downstairs.

She got to her feet. Heaved up the nearest box, and stooping to avoid cracking her head on the low beams, staggered with it through the dusty twilight. Up here, you had to watch where you put your feet. Half the place had no proper floor. One lapse of concentration, and you could have a foot through the main bedroom ceiling. Ending up astride a medieval joist was not something she wanted to think about. With a heavy thump, she let the box down by the water tank. Three more trips like that and her knees were about to give out.

She eased her aching body down onto the floor beside the boxes. Her hair was in her eyes, the blood on her glove had spread. She went to lift the lid of the topmost box, in order to take a look inside. But changed her mind. It would have been like looking into his coffin. She closed her eyes and leaned back against the cladding of the water tank.

She didn't hear the car that pulled up in the lane outside.

"There." Frank Lippincote handed her a gin and tonic. "Try that."
Ellen took a sip, nodded. "Nice. Thank you."

He sat himself in an armchair opposite her. "You look a little discombobulated."

"Not a nice job." She took a substantial swig.

"What were you doing?"

"Something that had to be done."

He pointed to the sticking plaster on her finger. "And you've cut yourself."

"It's nothing."

He sipped his whisky. "I haven't seen you in a while, Ellen. How are you these days – in yourself?"

"How do you think I am? These days or any days?"

He shrugged.

"I'm sorry. That was impolite." She drank again. "I get by – on a day-to-day basis."

"I rather thought from your letter that you were beginning to – so to speak - emerge."

"Some days, that's how it feels. Others - " - she shrugged - " - the road seems long."

He sat forward, elbows on his knees, as though about to say more. But didn't.

"It's nice to see you," she said.

He flushed slightly.

"What brings you to this neck of the woods?"

"I was on my way back from London. I thought I'd call in."

She was touched. "That's kind."

"I think of you."

"It's good," she said quietly, "to know someone somewhere is thinking of one."

He sat further forward. "I often wonder about you, you know."

She smiled.

He smiled back.

She looked down into her glass as she swirled the ice around. "How is Martha?"

For a few moments he was silent. Then sat back. "This thing takes its course."

She picked an imaginary fleck of something out of her drink. Then finished the drink off in one and handed the empty glass to him. "Would you mind pouring me another? Please."

He was pleased to be asked. He was intensely aware, strangely, of the sound made by the chunks of ice as they tumbled into the glass, and then of the tonic water as it splashed, fizzing and cascading over them like sea foam over rocks.

He handed the drink to her. She took it and their fingers brushed. He badly wanted to say something though he didn't know quite what. So he didn't, and whether or not she was aware of his touch as he had been of hers, he didn't know that either. He sat down again, confused and anxious. He looked apprehensively at her. Then frowned. Her eyes seemed moist, as though perhaps on the brink of tears. Please don't cry. He sat quickly forward. "Ellen look - I – er – well - "

"What?"

"I don't know." But then suddenly he reached out and placed a hand over one of hers. Then sat staring at her, stunned by his own action. Gently, she turned her hand up and lightly clasped his. He looked uncomprehendingly down at their two joined hands. Then suddenly took his away. "I'm sorry," he said. "I'm sorry."

"Are you?" she said, without looking at him.

He bit his lip.

"So," she said, withdrawing her hand and arranging herself primly upright in her chair, "what were you up to in London?"

"Meeting with my accountant."

"How intensely boring."

He seemed not to have heard. "I could have helped you, you know."

"Helped me?"

"You had only to ask."

"Help me with what?"

He pointed to the ceiling. "Whatever it was you were doing up there. If you'd rung. What were you doing?"

"Burying Barney."

He started back.

"A one-person, one-woman job. His stuff was still all over the house. Clothes, photographs. Things he would just put down and leave." She sipped her drink. "Barney had this compulsion to expose his inner workings to public view."

Frank shook his head very slowly, as if understanding and commiserating.

"He'd pick things up – all sorts of odd bits and pieces. And bring them home and put them out on display. On that shelf over there, there was a large red stone he picked up off a beach somewhere. Put it in his pocket and brought it home. Like a magpie."

Frank looked down into his glass.

"And a silver dollar. Given to him by a barman in California. I even had to put up with an ancient Oxo tin in the bedroom." She pressed a hand gently to her mouth.

"Mmmm," said Frank, nodding sagely. "Difficult stuff, that. Very."

A cloud crossed the sun. The shadows in the room moved and faded. They sat in silence. Frank looked out of the window.

"It was a good life, Frank. Friends with power and influence. Exotic parts of the world. Did you know - in the early days we lived in Hong Kong? Every morning I took a dip in the South China Sea. Can you imagine that?"

"Sounds idyllic, I have to say."

"A weekend return flight to New York on Concorde - Barney saved the baggage tags. Even they were out on display on a shelf in the upstairs toilet! Why would a man throw all that away? Because either he threw it all away or he didn't. If he didn't, then something awful has happened to him. And if he did – then there has to be a reason. Don't you think?"

He looked away.

"Can you think of one?"

He got up from his chair and went to the window, stood looking out. Ellen frowned. "Frank?"

"Your garden's going to be splendid again this summer."

"Don't be a boor. I asked you a question."

Still he didn't respond.

"Frank!"

He turned from the window. "I'm going to have to be honest Ellen."

"Honest?" She frowned. "What are you talking about?"

He peered down into his drink. "It's like this - "

Her face darkened. "Just - " - she held up a hand to stop him where he was - " - hold it there."

He stopped.

"Is it another woman, Frank?"

He looked wide-eyed at her.

"Jesus fucking Christ! And it never, ever even crossed my - "

"No. No. It's not. I mean – I don't know. How would - "

"Tell me!"

"I'm trying to! How would I know? I haven't seen him for as long as you haven't seen him."

She subsided a little. "Then what on earth are you talking about? What do you mean – you're going to 'be honest'? Have you been lying to me about something?"

"My dropping in here wasn't completely spontaneous."

"Ah. I see."

"I've heard from Jardine."

She froze. "And?" She watched him as he made his way slowly back to his chair and sat down. He clasped his hands round his drink. "There appears," he said, "or – there seems to have been - another side to

Barney."

"Another side? What's that supposed to mean?"

"He's just come back from Cornwall and - "

"Who's just come back from Cornwall?"

"Jardine. And - "

"What's Cornwall got to do with anything?"

"I'm sorry Ellen - I'm trying to put this with some care."

"Well damn the care! Just get on and tell me."

"It seems there is – or perhaps has been - another and – a rather – perhaps troubling aspect of Barney's personality. It may – Jardine feels – and I see what he's saying – it may go some way towards providing us with some sort of clue as to the matter of his disappearance."

She turned on a look of stunned disbelief.

"But he has something to say, Ellen. He has something to tell us. We need to set up a meeting with him."

A breeze stirred the curtains, flicked gently at the pages of a magazine on the table.

Ellen got up and stood looking out the french windows.

"Facts," said Frank. "One has, in the end, to look at the facts."

22.

Till the money comes through everything is on hold. All I can do is sit here and wait. I am not good at waiting. I think too much. There's 'thinking' and there's 'thinking'. The sort I do at times like this is usually of the counterproductive variety. All London's policemen and policewomen - and maybe Interpol as well - carry around with them at all times a photograph of me which they look at many times a day. The country's population have an identikit picture of my face embedded in their brains. Around every corner lurks a know-all looking to grab a moment's fame by outing the fugitive. I take a risk even looking out of this third floor window into the street.

First thing in the morning I go for a walk, usually to the nearby Queen's Park. A half-awake face stuck to a steamed-up window of a passing bus holds its glance just a fraction longer than I deem necessary and my heart's in my mouth. I avoid all newspapers. I have from time to time to go into shops which sell them in order to buy other things. I sidle past them, my eyes averted. And the man or woman in the shop has only to look a little quizzically at me and I'm fumbling my change in my anxiety to get to the door. As I hurry off down the road are they even now dialling 999?

I realize of course that the chances of anyone recognizing me now – or even caring for that matter - are remote. But still I live in a more or less permanent state of anxiety, especially out of doors. Despite the pleasure and the reassurance of my recent meeting with Martin, it is still me over here and the rest of the world over there. I, in my new persona, have yet to be assimilated into the great mass. I am the Alexander Selkirk of Kilburn High Road. The fact that it's all entirely of my own doing doesn't make it any easier. If this whole thing goes tits-up – as I heard the strange man downstairs say to someone on his mobile the other day – the whole weight of failure is on my shoulders, and I'd rather not consider the consequences.

But there is another side to it. When I look in a mirror, when I catch sight of my reflection in a shop window, I like what I see. I'm discovering a new way of being. I'm feeling free of things I didn't know were holding me back before I was free of them. In the train on the way back from Egham, I found myself gazing at the few suited and briefcased men on that afternoon train with what I can only describe as the self-congratulatory pity of the recently converted. That, for most of my working life, had been me. I felt for them. I wanted to take them by the shoulders and shake them.

So until the money is through, I have to kick my heels here in my mean little cell beneath a railway viaduct. It's not an easy place to be. Cooking a dinner which I eat on my own as the trains crash past overhead, borne down with their cargo of humanity on its way home to spouse and family is a telling test of my resolve. Many evenings I go out and eat in some inconspicuous little Indian or Chinese restaurant. I've discovered a number of them around here, all within ten minutes walk. The food is generally good and reasonably priced, the atmosphere pleasantly convivial.

I admire these people from Asia who come to make a living here. What a curious little, half-cast-adrift offshoot of Western Europe this country is. It must seem to them rather like it must have done to the Roman Legionnaires - the end of the inhabited earth, beyond which is only the cold sea and swirling mists. Some of them from little towns and tiny villages whose remoteness I can only guess at – full of wide skies and dirt roads – and here they land with a plate of food in their hands and a smile on their faces too, as often as not. My hat comes off to them – 'Chapeau!' as the French so nicely put it. I can't see many English people – and I include myself in that - having the balls to go to the wilds of China or India to open an English takeaway. 'Roast Beef to Go'? I don't think so.

After my meal I walk home. I call it 'home' for want of any other word. While the rest of the world struts along on someone's arm, I walk alone. Sometimes, from a woman passing close, I catch in the air a trace of her perfume - 'female smells in shuttered rooms'. I am weary of my never-ending maleness.

But I must not let this take hold. Succumbing to the honey trap has been the graveyard of many a high principle. I tell myself it will be alright once I have my hands on the money. Then I can begin.

When Martin did eventually contact me with the details of Dad's money, my first reaction was embarrassment. Then guilt. It was an obscene amount. But then, Dad had always promised as much. He'd amassed it – hoarded it - over sixty years. In the family there was only myself to whom he could leave it. Mother was dead. Dad had two nephews and a niece – my cousins - children of his two brothers. But both brothers had made at least as much money as Dad and he saw no reason to add – financially at least - to what their offspring were already set to inherit. He had no outside interests. Work had been his life. Having given, way back in the past, his lovely Jaguar to Toc H, primarily in a fit of pique, he felt that charities had had sufficient of his largesse. That left me.

After Mother's death however, I had vowed I would never touch a penny of his money. Despite what I knew of their relationship and the roots in both their psyches of its destructiveness, still I blamed him for her alcoholism and her premature demise which, I was convinced, resulted from it. Into my middle age I was hostage to a need to perpetuate, even in her death, my default position by Mother's side. Stockholm Syndrome. It was shamefully unjust, and it had a profound effect on Dad. It led to our alienation from each other which was to continue, on and off, for the rest of his life.

Always I had misread him. Whereas, by some sleight of hand of Mother's I'd felt compelled to try and understand her, it never occurred to me to try understanding him. Dad, after all, was just Dad. It was like he inhabited a separate, second-class world in which little of fundamental importance ever happened.

When his end came, I was not around, and hearing of it devastated me. Only then did it hit home what he had meant to me. He had been no always-there, always-reliable pater familias. But when the road got rough, it was to Dad I turned. He was ever in the background of my mind. When the hills had crumbled and the stars had gone out, Dad - I knew - would still be standing. Probably with a glass in his hand.

I looked down into a long wooden box. His face was white. He seemed at peace. I wondered if, in his last seconds, he'd thought of me.

He hadn't had much cause to.

My new bank card turned up - eureka! I'm across the starting line. As I slid the immaculate, shiny card from its security envelope, I was almost as excited as I had been as a student when I opened my first bank account. And the sight of that name embossed on it – 'Bernat Gyorgy Horvat-Marshal' – gave me a jolt. Last used when I was in my mid-twenties. It was my real name; the one on my birth certificate. It was the name conferred on me by my parents for whom I felt a sudden, profound yearning. Were they still shouting at each other in some ethereal cloud palace or dungeon in hell? Good luck, both. And my love - wherever you are.

I put the precious card carefully away in my wallet. Now I could set things in motion. Buy a few more clothes and some standby shades. Maybe another hat. I'd become quite attached to the idea of me in hats. A trilby perhaps, set at an angle and pulled down low, like in those American gangster films of the '40's. And a new car. A new, secondhand one, that is. Small, modest. Nothing that would attract attention. But I was wary. The prospect of bartering with the trendy spivs running London's secondhand car marts these days was not one I relished.

In fact, I so baulked at the idea that I took a chance on a little garage just a few streets away. I'd walked past it many times. It usually had some sort of vehicle for sale on its tiny forecourt. On that particular day there was a gleaming Harley-Davidson motorbike – for one crazy second it almost tempted me - alongside a little, two-door, blue Ford Sierra. Just the ticket. I descended into an oily cavern, spread with half-dismembered cars. The man who heaved himself out from beneath one of them was as old as I was. I was reassured.

He told me the Sierra was a good runner, low mileage. I trusted him. Its paintwork still shone and it seemed more or less free of dents. I paid him and drove it away feeling proud of myself. It had been accomplished entirely on my own. I found a space to park it in my road. I got out, stood back and looked at it. I liked it. It was a friendly car. One day soon, I would give it a name.

On the way back to my bedsit I discovered, deep in one of the inside pockets of that frightful zip-covered jacket (which I'd worn when I bought the car in order to avoid giving any impression of affluence) my old mobile – the one from which I'd removed the sim card in the taxi that afternoon in Wigan. I would not be needing it. I rubbed it very thoroughly with a tissue to remove any fingerprints – a nice touch, I thought - then dropped it into a skip in the road outside someone's house.

The following morning I planned to be away. To Halifax. It's where he began - so where I too would begin. It was Hobson's choice anyway. Halifax was the last and only place I knew him to have existed. When I thought of it like that, my chances of success seemed ridiculously remote. Maybe I should try reading life's runes. I'd lived long enough by intellect, rule and statute. And perhaps, on my way up north, I'd find some forgotten village well off the motorway, and post that letter.

23.

I've heard from Youssef. He left a telephone message with the man on reception - he'll meet me in the bar, he said, at five o'clock today. 'Five' might not quite mean 'five' as we know it. It's more a statement of broad intent. That's the way it is here. Time seems not to move at the same speed. Or sometimes even in the same direction. I assume he has nothing to add to the meagre bits of information we've put together. In which case, tomorrow we'll be away. I have to return to the UK, regroup, rethink. Then begin again.

I shall not be sorry to leave. I've been to many places in my time, but never anywhere like it. It falls into no known class or category; nobody I've ever known has been to, spoken about, had relatives in, written about or taken photographs of anywhere resembling it. Through no flight of fancy could I have envisaged its reality.

I've lost track of how long I've been here. But however long it is, the town still feels little more than a capricious conjunction of people, animals, mud dwellings, garbage, dust, sand and random objects blown in on the desert wind and which might be gone tomorrow. Except it won't – it's been here thousands of years already. I can't figure out how it hangs together and functions – yet it does. But finding in it and among the people who inhabit it some niche in which a Westerner like myself can feel reasonably at ease has been beyond me. My previous life has been no preparation. I am here, yet not here. If I shout, they will hear. But I am in another dimension.

Sand is everywhere. Some days, the wind off the desert raises into the sweltering air a brown mist of dust particles that drifts around the buildings, irritates your eyes, gets between your teeth, works its way under your arms and into your crotch. The heat presses in on you from above and on all sides. There are no roads – not roads as I've ever known them. Just areas of hard-packed sand, some wide, some no more than alleys lined with low mud houses in whose dark recesses people half-seen sit, cook, move around. Children with no shoes run after you, their hands outstretched for money. For food. For anything. They seem happy enough. Dogs, camels, donkeys, carts. Men with strange conical hats, women with vast bundles of what looks like washing balanced on their heads, leather-skinned men with hard eyes and blue chins. In the air the babble of a language in which I can find no syllable, sound nor intonation on which to hook a hope of comprehension.

The other morning, in a corner of my room, I found a scorpion. It shook the living shit out of me. It was small and almost prawn-coloured, like it lived under stones. That pincered tail curving up and over its back. I think I read somewhere that's how you're supposed to pick them up. I wasn't going there. I found a stick outside and after prodding at it and pushing it along the base of the wall, managed to flick it out through the open door.

I check now. I check every corner, every cranny, every crevice, every shadow. A man who claimed to have been in the French Foreign Legion, told me one evening in the bar that scorpions like to get in between your bedsheets during the day. 'So make sure you check,' he said, 'before you get into bed at night.' How do you check for scorpions in your bed – push a stick in and waggle it around? Pull the bed apart? I pull the one sheet off the mattress. Then I shake it and hope nothing drops out of it. Or that it does – I'm never sure which.

In spite of all that, I wish I'd had the space in my troubled mind to get to know something of the centuries-old culture of this place, to appreciate its life, its colour and vibrancy, its freedom from artifice and affectation. This is the capital of a nomadic people who have been around since way before Christ. If, in Westminster, someone had put a factsheet about it down on my desk, I would have devoured it. Told colleagues about it. Gone home and enthused to Ellen about it.

'Ellen'. 'Westminster'. Words once heard on an outer planet.

I leave my room. The sun hits my balding head like a hammer. I cross the compound moving slowly and carefully. The sores in my groin are raw. I make my way towards the main building of the hotel. 'Hotel' is a word which, in the developed world – whatever that is – conjures up a certain image. It is beyond me at the moment to attempt to define that image. But whatever it would be, it would have nothing to do with the reality of this 'hotel'.

It is a low building constructed entirely of locally made mud bricks, the whole construction then coated all over with a mud rendering. My first view of it had been at a distance through the afternoon dust as we'd first driven into the town. It looked like it had been patted and hand-moulded into shape like a child's sandcastle. "That," said Youssef, pointing to it, "is our hotel."

I had hoped he was joking.

Some of the windows are glazed. Others are just rectangular holes in the walls, often inset with a decorative iron grill. There is a ground floor and one upper floor. One corner of the building supports a diminutive, square tower. The roof is flat. On it is situated an open-air restaurant. I apply to the word 'restaurant' the same reservations I applied to the word 'hotel'. There are perhaps half a dozen tables. Only once have I seen more than two of them occupied. The one waiter, when he is not actually waiting, sits and watches the large TV set in the corner by the tower. The TV service closes down at some point in the late evening, whereupon he switches the set off and turns it to the wall.

I spoke there one evening with an Australian man in his mid-twenties. There was little flesh on his young bones. His black, empty eyes peered out from sockets sunk deep in a face that looked a hundred years old. He had driven alone from Morocco, north to south across the desert, two thousand kilometres. I was aghast - fascinated to know why and how. But he wouldn't talk. There were things he did not want to recall. He put the fear of God up me.

The bar was a small, square room with a few metal tables and chairs. Its walls were painted a deep, dark, gloss green. Endell Street green. There were no other drinkers in that evening. The barman, a stick-thin man of indeterminate age, whose name I didn't know and who spoke a variety of French in which I could understand almost nothing, had open before him on the bar counter a French newspaper. The corners of its pages rustled in the downdraft from a rickety ceiling fan.

I ordered a beer. Ran the ice-cold bottle through the perspiration running down my forehead. I made my way to a table by a small, unglazed window with an iron grille. It looked out over a wide area of compacted sand dotted with mud buildings – a town square of sorts. I peered out. A man's face went by, his dark skin glinting in the low sun; another man, perched high on a camel, lurching past in a curious, swinging motion. A donkey, ears flopping, its poor spindly legs surely about to crack beneath the weight of the panniers strapped either side of its emaciated body. On its back, a huge television set steadied by the hand of a man who walked by its side. People wearing clothes of extraordinary colours. Men somewhere, arguing in loud voices, language indecipherable – Tamajeq? Hausa? The cries of children. The afternoon fast waning.

I shuffled around in my chair to try and ease the discomfort in my groin. I sipped my beer and yawned. Six o'clock came. No Youssef. I ordered another beer. Tomorrow, surely, we'll be out of here.

24.

Al draped his wet clothes over the backs of three chairs which he arranged in a semicircle around the two-bar electric fire. Then took a leisurely, lingering bath. He dried himself on a big red bath towel, wrapped it around himself and sat in the window seat looking down into the narrow, cobbled street. All but the tail-end wisps of the rain clouds had passed and a watery sun was striking highlights from the still wet pavements. He loosened the latch on the little dormer window and pushed it open. Caught the smell of a land after rain. The only sounds were the birds and the quiet music of a stream nearby. No traffic. No noise. Indeed, the absence of noise was so noticeable as to be almost a sound in itself. The scent of flowers drifted in. Beneath the window was a hanging basket.

Al wasn't good on flowers. He didn't know one from another, except really obvious things like tulips and daffodils. These were yellows, blues, reds with big, floppy petals to which still clung a few crystal-clear drops of rainwater in which was reflected – how wonderful!– the sun. He reached down and nipped off a large yellow head. Held it to his nose. He was a child again. Standing in a field with a girl with pigtails who is wearing sandals and no socks and holding a bright yellow buttercup under his chin and it tickles and she says, 'Do you like butter?' He wants to believe it makes sense - that the world really is that simple.

He held the flower as far out from the window as he could and let it fall. He watched as it half-dropped, half-floated down. He regretted having picked it and wanted to call it back. It lay on the pavement, a tiny splash of bright yellow against the damp, grey stone. Summarily executed. Its days measured now in minutes.

He sighed. As the old song says - what a day this has been. He had been soaked to his skin. Rainwater had trickled down his back. Water squelched between his toes. His heavy briefcase banged against his legs. If, in his efforts to keep as far as possible from the passing traffic, he strayed too close to the fence, the brambles that swarmed over it snagged his light jacket. And in the grass through which his waterlogged shoes splashed, and among the grey clouds that raced by over his head there was, inescapable, that tumbled chaos of sheets, the naked man amid the blood. We should have done something, Viki. For Christ's sake, we should have done something.

Every now and then he stuck a half-hearted thumb out into the road in the hope of getting a lift to somewhere where he could get a room for the night. Where he could regroup, take stock. But they all just hosed him down and sped on.

He tripped against a rotted log half-buried in the grass, stumbled and grabbed at the fence. His hand slipped off the wet, moss-covered wood and plunged into the brambles. He cried out. His briefcase fell to the ground.

With great care he withdrew his hand from the brambles. Thorns pulled at his flesh. Blood welled up out of the scratches. Its deep carmine was straightaway diluted by the rain into a light pink and washed off onto the ground. He took a handkerchief from his pocket and wrapped it tightly around his hand. There seemed little point.

He stood looking down at the briefcase sitting among the wet grasses. He picked it up. Examined the name so classily embossed in gold letters on its front – 'AL MARSHAL'. He ran a finger over the letters. Stared at the words, frowning, as though they referred to someone he didn't know. 'Al'? Why, for Christ's sake, had he called himself 'Al'?

He snapped open the catch, plunged a hand inside and tugged out a mass of papers. For a few seconds he looked ruefully down at them. Then took a look along the road in both directions. An articulated truck was bearing down on him. As it roared past, he hurled the papers up into the air. It sucked them into its slipstream, whirled them up and around behind it, before scattering them all across both carriageways and into the trees that edged the woodland. He emitted a manic cackle before grabbing his briefcase out of the wet grass, drawing his arm back, and flinging that over the fence where it disappeared behind the brambles.

He stood, poker-faced, his eyes fixed on the spot where it had disappeared. He heard Viki's voice somewhere among the windswept trees - 'They have chambermaids. Not our problem.' She would be well on her way to Bristol now, racking her ingeniously devious little mind to fashion some monstrous lie out of which she might rescue her reputation before she'd lost it. She'd get by.

As for him, that was the end of his reputation. Gone. Gone with all his sketches and his tortuous rationale for the graphics he'd proposed for their puerile campaign of second class toiletries. Gone like his brand new career in provincial advertising which was to have resurrected his self-respect and set a path for the future. Gone.

He leaned from the window and picked another flower head. A red one. Red for passion, for lust, for life. And you, Viki. Fuck you. Lovely, irresistible, steel-hearted harlot that you are. Looking after your own self - your supreme talent. Where are you now? Telling a tale of innocence, wide-eyed. Mistress of your art, I admire you, hate you and desire you. But all I'm left with is the memory of that room.

What had gone on in there? Then the pair of them had simply buggered off. But this wasn't the end – the law would be onto him. Despite his determination, in the face of Viki's protestations, to at least warn the motel owner, all he'd actually done was pick up the phone and say, 'Hello'. Because at that point he'd seen the Jaguar taking off into the rain. In disbelief, he'd muttered a quiet, "For fuck's sake," to himself before he realized he still had the receiver in his hand. The owner must have heard and was probably, even at that moment, dialling 999. He banged the receiver back on its rest, leapt like a kangaroo out of the phone box and set off at an extremely quick walk along the grass verge. The police might be screaming up this road any second.

What a mess. And the rest – a covert fuck in a run-down motel. There is greater evil. But when the advertising agency got to hear – because they would - of their shenanigans, they'd first try to bury the story. If they failed – and it would not bury easily - they'd turn an affronted face to the world and instruct him never to darken their doorstep again. Screwing the lady client is not an approved activity. Officially, at least. In the pub after work with yet another drink in your hand it resonates differently.

But they'd have no need to ban him. Al had not got the front, the nerve to show his face there again. A three minute, coitus interruptus screw in a rain-swept room, four feet from a man bleeding to death, with a lady client who peddled cheap cosmetics developed on the backs of mutated mice had had enough evil energy locked up in it to blow his resurrected life apart. He was on the move. Again.

He smelled the red flower in his hand. A dog wandered across the road. The thatches of the little houses opposite were still dark with rainwater. In their window boxes blood-red geraniums, recovering from their dowsing, were reaching once again for the sun. The air was intensely clean, fresh and still. He let go of the red flower. It landed by the yellow which had now withered – as it too would, very soon. He was angry with himself.

He closed the window. From the public bar directly beneath his feet came the comforting clink of glasses, the low buzz of voices. The minute his clothes were dry enough to wear, he'd be down there himself. He rearranged his clothes around the electric fire. Then flopped heavily down into one of the two sagging armchairs. He was in great need of a drink.

Life can be crap. Who, given a pencil and a piece of paper would design anything like this? It could all, of course, be some dreadful cosmic slip-up. A chance, one-in-a-zillion nexus in a storm of purely random particles which might and probably would, without any warning, re-randomize once more, annihilating us and our virtual world in a nanosecond.

On the wall by his head, there was a print, its colours faded. A hunting scene. Members of the ruling class. Fat English bastards, men and women in red uniforms, black helmets and overtight white trousers galloping around on horses, leaping hedges and maiming foxes for a weekend laugh. This country stands no chance.

Another clink of glasses from beneath his feet. Christ, he needed that drink. If he slept tonight, he'd be lucky. He felt empty. But then a truly evil idea leapt like a smiling wolf from the shadows. He'd met a girl once - Mavis. He had her number. There would be a phone downstairs. She'd be grateful. How far is Wiveliscombe from here? But where's 'here' anyway?

He checked his drying clothes again and judged they were not damp enough not to wear. He dressed and went downstairs. There was a public phone by the door of the 'Lounge Bar'. A man in a long coat and trilby hat was just putting the receiver down. "Good evening," said the man, and politely tipped his hat.

"Perhaps," said Al, "you can remind me the name of this place, could you?" He pointed to the ground. "This village, town, whatever. I've forgotten."

"Surely," said the man. "Bampton. B-A-M-P-T-O-N. In the county of Devon."

"Much obliged," replied Al.

The man tipped his hat once more, and left.

'What an old-fashioned fellow,' thought Al, as he slotted his coins into the phone. Dialled. No answer. No Mavis. Fuck. He banged the receiver down, retrieved his money and went into the bar where he ordered a triple vodka.

"Triple??" The girl's eyes popped. "You mean - ?"- and she held up three fingers.

"Yep. That's what 'triple' means. Three. Three wise monkeys. Three in a bed."

The girl turned bright red and left to get his drink.

He watched her walk away. Nice bum.

This could be a lonely night.

25.

Halifax.

The word sets up a disturbance in my psyche. I parked the car –

which I'd named Fido - some distance away in a side road. Then walked. I glanced surreptitiously around, half expecting fingers to be pointing from windows. The criminal returning to the scene of the crime.

Little has changed. The main road here looks almost the same. Except of course there's vastly more traffic. High up on the side of a nineteenth century block of small shops there's still that faint – though even fainter now – washed-out, hundred year-old lettering all across the brickwork - 'Anderson's – Haberdashers & Milliners.' I walk past a two-foot tall milestone, half sunk back into a front garden wall. From some bygone, horse-drawn age. 'Leeds 17 miles', it says. I remember it well. I hit it one day with a front wheel of the pushchair.

There is still a shop – a franchise now – on the next corner. On one of its walls there is, as there was then, a huge advertising hoarding. However, it no longer advertises Mazawattee Tea. That has presumably sunk beneath the waves. Taking with it that scary, bespectacled crone and fatface the grandkid whose presences graced their posters in those far-off days and who gave little Matt the willies as I pushed him past them on the way home.

Today, it's all about a toilet cleaner. A bespectacled male child with a rictus of a smile – what peanuts did they throw at you, poor lad, for hijacking a day of your childhood? - says to some bland blonde woman, presumably his mother - that the bathroom smells nice today. Well, well – so nine year olds just back from school are taken these days with the nice odour of the family bathroom. I'm glad you like it, lad, and how thoughtful of you to tell your mother. You'll do well.

Am I just putting myself through the mangle here so I can brag about it to myself afterwards?

I arrive at the top of Endell Street. I stop. I see along its length. There, about a third of the way down, on the left, is the house. What a very, very strange feeling this is. Nostalgia, fear, regret; a need to linger, and a temptation to turn and walk away. I stand still. Is it possible, living in this road and moving around even now unseen within their walls, there are those who remember me? 'Well, well – look who it is. Hello, how's the wife these days? And that little lad of yours? Must have a family of his own by now. Grandchildren?'

I can just make out that at 26 they still have the privet hedge. Though it seems to be just a plain, block of green now. In my day it undulated like the waves of the sea. I hadn't personally sculpted it that way – that's how it was when we moved in. Looked good when it was first cut, and a mess the rest of the time. Privet's an unpleasant beast and trimming it an unpleasant task. When you clip it, it gives off a sour smell, as if in retaliation. Then there's the small, leathery little leaves to gather up off the dusty pavement.

I start down the street. This is unreal. The memories and expectations I brought with me are proving irrelevant. The Vaughans' front garden with its once neatly-trimmed, circular lawn edged with flowers is now a single slab of concrete, home to a motorbike and sidecar, and three wheelie bins. The covered side entrance to old Mrs Rogers' house, once lined with sepia photos from her childhood where she used to sit on warm days is now a car port with automatic up-and-over door which stands gaping, with silver car on guard half-in, half-out, shining in the sunlight like a steel-toothed Cerberus.

I am now within spitting distance of 26. And here is an affront - usurpers have put their own net curtains up at our windows and painted over our green paint with their over-bright blue. Even made a hole in the roof, removed slates and inserted a window. 'Who,' I ask myself, 'do they think they are?' A man is gardening in the front garden where I gardened occasionally in my half-hearted, weekend way. He is bent over, grubbing out some sort of little bush. He has greying hair, is overweight and puffs and groans as he tugs at the roots with garden-gloved hands.

I lean - tentatively - on the gate. Clear my throat. "Excuse me."

He pauses as though not sure he'd heard aright.

"Excuse me."

He looks my way, then stands slowly upright pressing a hand into the small of his back. He too has back problems. They say we are not long down from the trees.

He frowns.

"I'm sorry to bother you," I say, "but - "

"No problem, mate. " This time he presses both hands into his back. "As long as you're not a Jehovah's Witness!" And he guffaws, emptily. "What can I do for you?" He's from the Southeast. Estuary accent. Coarse, careless, but probably well-meaning.

I'm not at ease with his working-class joshery. I apologize again in a self-consciously middle-class way and ask him how long he has lived here. Then before he demands of me what the hell business that is of mine, I hasten to tell him in as casual an over-the-garden-fence way as I can that once upon a time, I and my family owned and lived in this selfsame house.

"Oh yeh?" he says. "When was that then?"

I feel my seniority. "Best part of forty years ago."

"Wow," he says. "Bet you paid peanuts for it in them days!" And guffaws once more.

I'd hoped for at least a smile or an outstretched hand. But getting neither, my momentum falters. I have no idea what to say next. And he just stands looking at me, garden fork in hand. This has not begun well.

Then oddly, he comes to my rescue. "Have a look round inside, mate, if you like." And he tugs off his gardening gloves. "The wife should have got her clothes on by this time of the morning!" And yet again he guffaws. That we should have given way to the vapid.

I follow him through the front door. What am I going to see? What am I going to feel? I blank my mind and drop down into the maw of the past. As I pass for the first time in almost forty years along this once oh-so-familiar hallway, I feel an unaccountable yearning.

The wife was a large woman. She sported a mane of dyed blonde hair and an ample bosom which a pink towelling dressing gown with fluffy lapels struggled to contain. She and her husband together ushered me from room to room. Of us and our lives nothing remained. None of my careful paintwork or our painstakingly chosen wallpaper. None of the shelves I had so struggled to put up. I had thought maybe there'd be – just might be – buried in some dusty corner, a dried-up lipstick of Stella's or iron-hard bread crust thrown one day by baby Matt across the room. But there was nothing. Nothing to say this had been me or us. Subsequent owners had, layer by layer, blanked us out as each played their part in assembling, according to the dictates of DIY mags and TV home improvement pundits, a characterless hotchpotch.

And yet we were there. With other eyes and with other ears I could see and hear us. Ghosts in the mirrors, shadows the far side of half-open doors. Stella pulling on her tights in the morning; Matt in his highchair, his chubby cheeks plastered with poorly aimed food, banging his spoon on his dish; Stella crying one day in the kitchen; Matt calling in the night; people's feet on the stairs; the condensation running down the kitchen windows.

I'd seen enough. It was time to ask them what I'd come to ask them, then go. Yet - what was I going to ask them? If they had any idea where my son, then a baby, was now? If they knew anybody who knew anybody who knew where he and his Mother had moved to more than thirty years ago? What was I doing here? Another bugger's muddle. Shades of the hatter's in Wigan. I burbled something about being grateful and that I must go and thank you both so much.

"Oh, but you haven't met Dad yet," exclaimed the woman. And flung open the door to the kitchen.

"Rather you than me," exclaimed the man, slapping me on the back. Then guffawing, left to return to his garden.

The woman ushered me, with a flourish, into the kitchen. "That's Dad," she said, pointing across the room.

In a corner, warming his hands by an open range, sat an old man in a knitted cardigan that hung on him like sacking.

"Now Dad," she said to me, "has lived in this road since the year dot." She raised her voice to the man. "Haven't you, Dad? Lived in this road a long time?"

He looked our way. I raised a hand to him. "Hello."

He nodded to his daughter but seemed not to see me.

"Him and Mam," she said to me, "lived down the far end. At least till she died." She raised her voice every time she spoke to the old man. "Didn't you Dad? Going on thirty or more year wasn't it, you lived down the far end – you and Mam?"

"When you say the far end," I said to her, "do you mean the end where the recreation ground used to be? Or the main road end?"

She pointed vaguely off to one side. "A couple of houses up from the rec."

She tapped the old man on the shoulder. "This man, Dad," she said, pointing with the other hand to me, "used to live here."

He looked blankly from her to me.

"He used to live in this house." She jabbed a finger towards the floor. "Here."

A light flickered in his eyes.

"Hello," I said again to him, and put out a hand which he didn't take. "When did you move to Endell Street then? What year?"

Called on to recall the past, he started to come to life. He and his wife, then in their thirties, had moved to their house on the opposite side of the road, down by the recreation ground some six months after Stella and I had split up. In those days, everybody in the street knew everybody else, even if only by sight. After some prompting, it turned out he did vaguely remember a young woman. But then he said, there were any number of young women and they all had 'kids'. He had no idea whereabouts in the street any of them lived, but yes, they had husbands. Though pushed a little more, he said well, he just assumed they had husbands because women with children in those days had husbands. But as he said that, a further memory surfaced – of one young woman who, it was rumoured, had no husband even though she had a child in a pushchair.

A flutter went through me.

She lived, he said, somewhere on the opposite side of the road.

The flutter came again. His 'opposite' was the side we were now on. "I wonder," I said, trying not to reveal too much of myself, "does the name 'Stella' ring a bell? Stella Marshal?"

His daughter looked curiously at me.

"Nay, I never knew her name. Nice little thing. Sometimes said 'Hello' or 'Good morning'. If one of us was in the garden, like, when she came by."

I was having difficulty holding onto this. But what he seemed to be saying was that the young woman who was reputed to have a child but no husband walked by his front garden when she took the child in a pushchair to the recreation ground. At least, he thought that was the woman. He had no idea if the child were boy or girl. But then said his wife one day helped bandage a little boy's knee. Or it might have been his ankle. A little boy in a pushchair who had hurt himself in the recreation ground. So perhaps that was the child. But he wasn't sure if the woman with that child was the one who used to say 'Good morning', to them or not.

I was losing it. "So which of those two is the woman who wasn't married?"

He made no attempt to answer the question. Instead, he took it as a starting pistol that set him off at extraordinary speed into a series of random and disjointed reminiscences about a long-gone Endell Street which I guess made sense to him but which just left his daughter and me bemused.

I managed, nevertheless, to extract from the mishmash the bits that might relate to my question. It's best summed up by the following.

It's likely that the woman who pushed her child to the recreation ground and who used to say, 'Good morning' to him and/or his wife was the woman with no husband. News was on the grapevine one day however that a man had actually moved in with that unmarried woman and child. It caused a stir and talk of scandal. No-one knew the man – he was not local. However, a woman from the next street was sure she'd seen him behind the counter at Boots the Chemist's in town. She was also sure she'd heard one of the assistants address him as 'Mr McDonald'. This information was very soon all round Endell Street where people took pleasure in referring to him as 'Mr McDuck' – (here the old man cackled loudly) - though not to his face of course, or to hers. The man and the young woman were eventually married – he was keen to point out that this took place in a registry office. Shortly after the marriage, the three of them moved away from Halifax and were never seen again in Endell Street.

He came to a dead stop, his energy gone.

"Where?" I asked, as casually as I could make it, "did they move to, do you know?"

Yawning, he shook his head.

His daughter looked knowingly at me. "This lady - was she just a neighbour then?"

"Neighbour and friend," I replied. "We lost touch. You know how it is."

"I see." Detecting a promising subplot, she smiled. "Would you like a cup of tea?"

I declined. I needed to go. The old man had given me far more than I could have hoped for or, given my lack of preparation, even deserved. I needed now to digest it, then plan my next step. I said a grateful thank you and goodbye to him as he sat warming his hands again, my existence already forgotten.

His daughter had started to lead me out of the kitchen when she stopped, put a hand on my arm and turned back to her father. "Dad – Dad, you had a postcard though. Didn't you?"

He frowned.

"You and Mam had a postcard from her. That woman."

I looked quickly from one to the other.

He was clearly irritated at having his peace disturbed yet again. "What sort of postcard?" he growled.

"How many sorts are there? A picture postcard – of where they'd moved to. I know you did because Mam kept it. For a long time after." She turned to me. "He forgets, you know. But he showed me this postcard. It was among all the stuff of his we had to chuck away when he moved in here."

"Enderby."

We both turned to him.

"Enderby?" said the woman. "What's that?"

"You asked me where that card came from."

"So where the heck's Enderby then?"

"Nay, I've no idea."

"But 'Enderby' was Mam's maiden name."

"Well, I know that, don't I? That's why she kept the card, wasn't it?"

I was foundering again. "So this lady," I said, "with the child moved to a place called Enderby?"

"Marsh."

"Pardon?"

"Marsh!" he barked it. Then turned back to the range, growling.

I looked at his daughter, "What's 'Marsh?'"

She signalled me out of the room. "Come on." She led me out, closing the door behind her. She put a finger knowingly to her temple. "He forgets. Says funny things."

We walked back along the hallway. I was anxious to get away and search my roadmap for anywhere called 'Enderby'.

The husband was sitting on the front step smoking a cigarette. He looked up at me. "Alright then mate?" He blew smoke out in front of him which the breeze from the garden blew back in his face, making him cough. "Funny, I should think, isn't it? Going back in time like this. Do your head in!" And he guffawed.

I said goodbye to them. Thanked them both for their hospitality. The latch on the front gate sounded much as it had done half a lifetime ago.

Yeh, it's funny alright, mate. And does your head in.

I sat in the car and flicked feverishly through the gazetteer of place names at the back of my road map. And goodness, there was indeed a village – in Leicestershire – called 'Enderby'. But then, wait a minute, another in Lincolnshire – 'West Enderby'. Another in that same county – 'Mavis Enderby' – for God's sake, what a name. And then, just a little to the east - yet another 'Enderby'. But this one had in front of it the word 'Marsh' - 'Marsh Enderby'! Just like the old man had said - or at least, grudgingly implied. I flicked back to the relevant map. And there it was. A village not much bigger than a football pitch.

A swift shot in the dark gave me a journey time of around three hours. With a tingling sense of standing on the brink of life-changing times, I close the map, put Fido in gear, and took off in a generally south-westerly direction.

I drove fast. Perhaps a little carelessly. There was more on my mind than a man at the wheel of a car should have. In fact, my delight at having made what looked like an unexpected early breakthrough overrode any precise sense of what route I was taking. About half an hour out, some instinct whispered to me that the sun, which was on my left, should be on my right. And that I was therefore heading in the wrong direction.

I was the only vehicle on a wide ribbon of road that snaked across high moorland. It was huge in extent. I slowed down. It stretched to the horizon in every direction. Level beyond level of heather-covered moors melting away into the distance. Here and there, splashes of brilliant yellow gorse. Flashes of light where the surface of some hidden stream or pond caught the sun. White clouds hung in a deep blue sky. I was lost.

I pulled off the road. Perhaps I needed to calm down. There was such a weight of stuff in my head. I walked away from Fido and collapsed onto the grass among outcrops of heather. The grass was like the baize on a snooker table, mown to its roots by scraggy, wandering sheep. The wind snatched at my long hair, pulled at my clothes before racing joyfully away into the purple distance. Far away among the hills I could see a large town.

I lay back, closed my eyes. The sun was warm, the grass beneath me soft. Somewhere close by, a bird sang. Its song faded, faded and sank slowly into silence. I drifted in and out of stuff. Stuff from all over the place. Endell Street - snippets with no beginnings nor endings - like old film clippings, off-cuts left on the floor of an editing suite. A face, a moment, here then gone - recalled with an almost aching nostalgia for a time for which, in the years between, I had nursed a gratefulness to have escaped. And children - Frank Lippincote's children. Boy and girl. In their thirties now. The photograph he kept on the desk in his office. Taken when they were about eight or ten maybe. They stood looking straight at the camera. Jamie with an ice cream in his hand, melting and running onto his fingers. Sophie with a wan little smile on her lips. A few strands of hair across her eyes. In the background, people on a wide beach, and a distant fairground. That image always, always stuck in my mind, prodding at me, nagging. I could have done things like that with Matt – taken him to the seaside. Searched rock pools with him. I don't even have a photograph. I wouldn't know my son if I saw him.

"The surgeon's knife." They were Dad's words. "When a thing's over, Barney, it's over. End it." In the mayhem and confusion into which my young life had descended, his words were a beacon of reason and sanity. "The surgeon's knife." But to end it like that, with just one flick of the wrist – the guilt of it would consume me.

Mother poured scorn on my guilt. Stella was as much to blame as I.

"What," I demanded, "has Stella to feel guilty about?"

"Do you not think there is another person in this marriage of yours?"

"You haven't answered my question, Mother. What had - ?"

"It takes two to tango, Bernat. That is my answer!"

There was no reasoning with Mother. As calmly as I could, I told her that I intended making sure Stella and Matt had food to eat and a roof over their heads. If she wanted to stay on in Endell Street, I would continue to pay the mortgage.

"And where will you live – in a tent at the bottom of the garden?"

"I'll manage."

"You," said my mother, thrusting a finger at me like at an accused in the dock, "will be ruined! You think that is what I come to this country for – to have my only son a beggar on the streets?"

I might not have loved; I might not have been much of a husband or father. But I did not want for them this unholy mess. In order to find a path through it that was right and just for the three of us, I needed help. I give Dad his due – he tried. But any suggestion of Mother's was informed almost entirely by her desire – an open secret between the three of us - to see Stella gone.

Dad had nothing against Stella. In fact, hard though it often was to see past his mask, I knew he was fond of her. And he thought more of baby Matt than he would ever let on. The situation was hurting him too. He was right - the kindest end to it would be a short, sharp, quick one. Dad knew more about a lot of things than I ever gave him credit for in his lifetime.

One of the principles on which he ran his business and which was based, he assured me, upon his years' of experience of human nature, was that everyone has their price. He proposed therefore that Stella straightaway file for divorce – on the grounds of my adultery. I would not contest it. He would then pay off the mortgage on Endell Street. The house would be put in her name. He would settle on her a sum of money - sufficient if wisely invested - to enable her to live comfortably at least until Matt were sixteen. This would release me from any untidy financial obligations which could otherwise dog my future. And it would free Stella to live her life in the best interests of herself and the boy.

Good old Dad. Even Mother sat back with a smile on her face. As for me, I was only just about capable of rational thought. All I was clear about by this time was that I wanted an end to the agony. For Stella's sake as much as for my own. Like me, she was up to and beyond her ears. Lined up either side of her, sharpening their weapons as they faced us across the social divide, was her whole family. With battle lines drawn up, threatening an ugly, protracted conflict, Dad's quick, tidy and financially generous solution bought the whole tribe off.

Mother clapped her hands. "That girl will be so much better off on her own. She is young, she is healthy. And my God! - now she is wealthy. I am so happy for her." And if that meant Mother seeing little – if any - of her one grandchild, then so be it. She'd coped with worse.

With the hue and cry finally abating, I said goodbye to the long-suffering friend on whose sofa I'd camped out for the last few months and fled Halifax. I caught a train to Northampton and 'Greenholme'. There, I packed what I could of my possessions into two suitcases and threw them onto the rear seat of a much-dented old Triumph Toledo I bought for a song from the woman who 'did' for my parents. I bade the household adieu and drove south. I had no idea where. Maybe I thought if I drove far enough and fast enough with never a backward glance, a pristine new existence would unroll like a magic carpet before me.

I jolted awake. I was shivering. The sun had gone behind clouds and the blustery wind had turned cold. Peering at me from round a gorse outcrop was a sheep. She looked confused. Struggling to my feet I alarmed her. Tossing her head, she spun around and bounded away. I brushed the grass from my clothes and set off back towards Fido. Butterflies and little flying insects came up out of the heather. I wondered what they were. I knew so little about such things.

I drove carefully and at a very moderate speed. Maybe it was that, along with the rest I'd had that enabled me to look with some clarity on what I was now about to do. Echoes of the hatters in Wigan? And the unexpected success in Endell Street was no thanks to me. How was I going to approach Marsh Enderby? Just roll up there and start asking around? A London smart-arse quizzing the natives about some woman, who might have moved there with husband and young child back in the 'seventies? And if I do, by some extraordinary chance, find her there - or somewhere in the vicinity - and Matt too because she must know where he is and he could even be living just round the corner with his own wife and children - my grandchildren - what a Pandora's box! And Stepfather McDuck - might he straight away be on the phone to The Mirror or The Sun?

Philip Marlowe I am not. This is tinkering.

26.

I pulled into a dismal service area on the A1 somewhere around Doncaster. I was hungry and in need of a pee. I left Fido, locked him, and made my way towards the cafeteria in the main buildings. My new mobile rang. It could only be Martin. I fumbled it out of my pocket and struggled with the unfamiliar buttons. We exchanged the usual pleasantries. Then, "Bernat," he said, "the reason I'm ringing is that something's on my mind. Do you have a couple of minutes?"

I sat down on a wooden bench just outside the main concourse. "OK," I said, "fire away."

"Bit of a tricky one. It concerns your father."

I sat up. "Dad?"

"I should perhaps have mentioned this when we were by the river. But at the time, I felt you had enough to handle."

It sounded like this was going to take some time. I didn't want to sit in public view any longer than necessary. I stood up again and set off back towards Fido.

"In the months before his death, you see, I saw a fair bit of him. Outside of the business we had to do there were things on his mind. He knew he wasn't long for this world. That woman he'd cohabited with for a while after your Mother 's death had - "

"Daisy?"

"He never mentioned her name. Anyway, she'd left him and gone back to somewhere in the West Country. He was on his own and, although he would never admit it, he was lonely. Then one day, out of the blue, he got a letter. From your ex."

I stopped in my tracks. "From - who?"

"That's right. Your ex. Stella."

I plonked down into the driving seat of Fido and slammed the door.

"She was writing on behalf of his grandson, Matthew. The boy wanted to get into advertising."

The apple never falls far from the tree. My head spun.

"But living out there in the country, he had no idea where to start. She wondered if your father, with all his business contacts, might give him some guidance."

I listened, dumbfounded.

"Now – this came at a time when your father had begun to have regrets."

"Regrets? Dad?"

"One that bothered him especially was about the rather unpleasant breakup of your marriage. He had come to believe that its roots lay to some extent in a lack of parental understanding when you were young."

"Dad said that?"

"On both his part and your mother's - yes. He also deeply regretted having effectively cut his only grandchild out of his life."

"Christ, Martin. This is some bolt from the blue."

"I'm sure, old boy. Anyway, your father's time was running out. He wanted to tidy things up. But like the Chinese, he had an almost morbid fear of losing face. Which he would have done had he himself made any overt attempt to try and locate his grandson. So he had been hung on his own petard. At least, until the letter from your ex."

Some sixth sense was beginning to suggest to me that Martin may actually have an idea what lay behind my own current behaviour.

He went on. "He took his time, but eventually he wrote back saying he would think about it. And if, having thought about it, he felt he could help, he'd contact her again."

"And?"

"After leaving it rather a long time he did contact her again and - "

"Martin!"

"What?"

"Where were they living - Stella and Matt? Did he tell you the address?"

"Ah. Sorry old boy, no. I didn't ask. I think he'd been sworn to silence on that.

"Hm. Maybe it figures. And then?"

"He did as he'd said. He gave the boy names of some people he should contact. Your father was respected in the business world. However, it was only a day or two after he'd sent that letter that he was taken ill. And that was the end of it."

"I wish," I said, "he'd revealed half as much of himself to me."

I heard Martin's intake of breath. "On that same line of thinking - " - he became tentative, almost awkward - " - I suspect his reason for telling me all this was - in the expectation that one day I would tell you."

I waited.

"He did not want you to go to your grave believing him to have been simply what he so often - er - perhaps gave the impression of being."

"Which was?"

"In his own words? – 'the philistine businessman'. He didn't want you to believe that's all there was to him."

"Oh, fuck." A lump came to my throat.

"And now, this is me, maybe taking things a little too far, but I don't think so." He paused. "I personally believe it was his earnest hope that the day would come in your life, as it had in his, when you too might want to try and make contact with the boy."

I sat back. Martin knew, didn't he? I closed my eyes. On the road behind me the traffic hurtled relentlessly past.

I had my pee. Bought myself a cake and a cup of coffee – why is it so difficult these days to get a simple cup of coffee without having to go through the names of umpteen specious variations?

I sat at a table in a corner of the cafeteria. Looked out of the window over a children's play area. Swings, a roundabout, some sort of ruddy-faced giant through one of whose eyeholes a boy's grinning face peered. I watched them all running, laughing, shouting. I could hear their cries. One can learn a lot from young children. Them, and ducks.

I finished my coffee. Returned to Fido and headed south for London.

27.

It was arranged I would meet Minxie in a small general-store-cum-café, a couple of bus rides away in Crouch End. I approached a meeting with any woman calling herself 'Minxie' with reservations. The café, owned and run by Greek Cypriots, was busy. Grey-haired men played cards and drank what I presumed was ouzo along with small cups of thick black coffee. There was a lot of cigarette smoke.

It didn't seem Minxie's sort of place. As she came in through the door off the street and registered the interior, her face took on an expression of pained aloofness. She stopped and looked unhurriedly around. I have to say she cut a striking figure. Around thirty, tall, slim, elegant with an incredibly pallid complexion set off by almost black hair and bright red lipstick. Beneath a beautifully cut black coat which she wore open, her clothes seemed to consist of a number of long, multi-coloured layers of some almost diaphanous material draped loosely, even carelessly over her body and reaching to just below her knees. Her shoes had medium-high heels and a delicate little ankle strap. To my un-fashion-conscious eye, I would have said she had a nineteen-fifties look. Few women could have carried it off. Despite her name, she had my respect before we'd exchanged a word. I raised a hand to identify myself, but she had already decided I was her target. I stood to greet her. The action seemed to surprise her. She put out a gloved hand.

"Hello there," she said.

She had strange eyes. They had so little colour I had difficulty settling on the pupils. And for a woman, her voice was extraordinarily deep. Had I heard it over a telephone I would have had difficulty deciding its gender. Either way, it sounded very sexy. Perhaps that was the 'minx' bit. I pulled out a chair for her. Again she seemed not to know quite how to deal with that. She sat down, with a theatrical flourish peeled off her gloves, then lit a cigarette.

I sat upright and carefully composed myself. It had been put to me that this woman might possibly hold the key to the present whereabouts of my son.

Minxie had come to me in a twice-removed way – via a young lady called Marie whose services had in turn been called on by her Mother, that old Oxford girlfriend of mine, the fondly-remembered Licia Harper-Downes. Dear Licia – what times we shared in those far-off days. Summer afternoons punting on the Cherwell; watching the May Morning carol sung at dawn from the tower of Magdalen College; idly wandering, hand-in-hand, through Christchurch Meadows; art-house cinema in Headington; autumn afternoons in bed, talking, watching through the window the dusk settling over nearby rooftops.

I had often wondered what Licia had done with her life after Oxford. She'd set her heart on my old profession, the ambivalent world of advertising. She was going to be a graphic artist, she said, and design ads for glossy fashion accounts in one or other of the big London agencies. What a waste, I had retorted, what an abuse of an Oxford education. She called me in return, a 'dinner-party idealist' and told me my views were 'pompous, turgid and out of tune with the times'. She'd said it with a smile on her face, but a suspicion there might be a grain of truth in it bothered me for a while afterwards.

So if Licia had actually made it, and if I could locate her, and if Matt too – as Martin had indicated – had gone into that same business, a meeting with her could be an altogether more appropriate way of going about things than risking the conflict I could ignite by going through his mother. It was, of course, most unlikely Licia would know of him personally. But she might just know someone who knew someone else who knew someone who had once .....etc., etc.

I tracked her down through her college's Alumni magazine. It was not difficult. But it was some considerable time after my return from Halifax and Endell Street before her name even occurred to me in this context. Prior to that, I'd wasted hours in public libraries. Safe behind my dark glasses and ever-lengthening hair, I'd set myself the task of trawling through the details of all the major and not-so-major advertising agencies in London. I planned to scour their current CEO's, their Creative Directors, all their Account Directors and board members In the hope of finding among them just a few with whom I'd worked in my time in advertising. Those days were long over, and most of those people would have retired. But there surely had to be a few who had stayed the course.

I'd unearthed two - both of them now in senior management positions - before it occurred to me that this was another waste of time. As I looked at their names on a sheet of paper on my table beneath the viaduct, I was forced to confront the question of what I was actually going to do with the information now I had it. Yet again, enthusiasm had trumped pragmatism. What would I do - write to these people – under an assumed name – asking if they knew of the existence in the business of a Matt or Matthew Marshal? Or McDonald? Or anyone with the Christian name 'Matthew'? And if so, who would I – the writer of the letters – claim to be? Some non-existent lawyer? And should I come up with some complex fiction to do with an inheritance due to the elusive 'Matthew'? Would anything convince them I was not just another crank? No – to stand a chance of being taken seriously I'd have to arrange face-to-face meetings on the basis of our having known and worked with each other. And then I'm done for. Because even though I may extract from them cast-iron assurances of secrecy, I would not feel easy putting my trust in either of them. Those who practise advertising - and I include my past self in this - have committed themselves, if only by default, to having no objection to publicly propagating white lies and half-truths. That lack of regard for 'la réalité' which is part of their everyday working lives, can so easily cross a line. And once out on London advertising's gossip circuit, my little game would be over.

I tore the list up. And gave up public libraries.

I was back to square one.

I needed a computer. For Christ's sake! But my reservations still applied. A private investigator? But how could I risk trusting anyone, however luminous their reputation, that I didn't actually know? In desperation, I considered simply ringing round all the agencies and asking quite casually to speak with 'Matt' or 'Matthew'. But Matt or Matthew Who? Marshal? McDonald? I'd spent years calling myself 'Al' - might he too be calling himself these days any old name that came into his head? Or had he never managed to get into advertising? Had he stayed in Lincolnshire to till the land and grow turnips? Or joined the Navy, the Army, the Foreign Legion? The Scouts?

This was another way not to do it.

Then one day, in one of those small franchised shops that sells all sorts of foodstuffs, small household items and newspapers, my eye was caught by a magazine about the Oxbridge Universities. Out of no more than casual interest, I picked it up and thumbed through it. There were photographs of a number of Oxford colleges, mine included. And St. Hilda's – a mixed gender college today, but in my day, women only. That had been Licia's college. Only then did it occur to me that she might be just what I was looking for.

I booked a table for lunch in one of those expensive riverside restaurants to the west of London which I think of as places you go to when you're with someone you shouldn't be with. It was wonderful to see her again. She too was delighted to see me, even though at first – I was gratified to note – she wasn't entirely convinced that I was me. "Bee, you look so different! But my goodness – it suits you. Love the shades, the beard." We were off to a good start. Both of us were larger and wider than in those other days. But the same sparkle danced in her eyes. We'd been OK together, Licia and I. It looked like we still were.

We had a drink in the bar and exchanged airy résumés of our lives in the years between. Then wandered into the large dining room and took our places at a table laid with that self-conscious striving to impress one often comes across in such places. It was a glorious day and the windows were all open to the river, letting in the sounds and smells of summer.

"So," she said, taking her napkin from its ring and spreading it over her lap, "I suspect I'm about to hear something rather interesting."

I told her everything. She was open-mouthed.

"My darling Bee!" She leaned across the table towards me. "What on earth are you thinking of?"

It wasn't what I'd expected or hoped for. I remember shrugging rather meekly. "I have to find him," I said.

"But why?"

"He's my son, Leece."

"And has that only recently occurred to you?"

"It didn't occur to me when it should have done – put it that way."

She picked up her wine glass. "And what about him," she said, "will he want to be found?"

"I'm aware he might not."

"So you're just going to – go looking for him, as it were?" By design or accident, she made it all sound faintly silly. "It isn't the way the Salvation Army would go about it."

"Oh?" I wondered what Licia knew of the Salvation Army.

"I'll tell you what they'd do." She sipped, put down her glass. "They'd first contact your son and ask him if he wanted anything to do with you."

"Fine. But as nobody could tell them where my son is, that approach wouldn't get them very far, would it?"

She shrugged. "OK – touché. But listen Bee - I'm really, really in awe of what you're trying to do. But do you have to give up your whole life to do it? Every single thing you've ever worked for?"

"So should I just do it in my spare time? In the evenings? Weekends?"

"Hire a private investigator. Get them to - "

"And he – or she – leaks my name, accidentally on purpose, to the papers. OK - I'm cold potatoes in one sense, but what a story for the Sundays! Barnaby Trustworthy, MP throws away wife and career to search for the son he abandoned when he was only three years old and never even - "

"OK, OK." She put a hand up to stop me. "It's a pity you didn't think of this twenty years ago, you know. The implications for your life and your career then would have been - "

"I did think of it twenty years ago. And ten years ago. And five. But every time I thought about it, I put it off – in the interests of my life and career. In the end it became too much. I couldn't sleep. I saw him in my dreams. On more than one occasion I really couldn't separate the dream from reality. I tried to keep it from everybody, but secretly I was falling apart." I took a drink of my wine. "It felt like I'd transgressed against some fundamental law."

"Then," she said, thoughtfully, "you have to think of this – if you haven't already. Wherever he is, the boy may be missing you, deep down. Angry with you as well, but longing to know if you still think of him.

But on - ”

"That's exactly what - ”

"But equally he may not. He may be living a happy, secure life. He may have a wife and a family and they may - ”

"My grandchildren."

She looked at me over the top of her glass.

I said again, "My grandchildren."

She went back to her food. "What about your wife?"

It caught me off-guard. I replied, rather snappily, "Ellen is not a children person." Though true, it sounded lame. I expected Licia to challenge it. For some reason she didn't. It hung in the air between us.

Then she surprised me. She leaned towards me across the table, a broad smile on her face. "The point of all I'm trying to say my darling, is that you – Barnaby Marechal - ”

"Sssh!" I looked covertly around with a finger to my lips. In retrospect I probably attracted more attention doing that than if I'd done and said nothing.

"I'm sorry," she said, lowering her voice, " but look – " - she laid aside her knife and fork - " - let's talk real. In only a few years, you built up for yourself a wonderful career. Not one of the party celebs – and thank God, say I - but you'd cornered a sort of niche where you were listened to and respected. You would never have made the front benches because you're too independent-minded and I doubt you'd have wanted to anyway. But people – ordinary people – took notice of you where they turned away, raising their eyes to the ceiling, from the PM and his band of place-men and women. Where might you have risen to, Bee? The phrase 'elder statesman' comes to my mind. And all that you're simply throwing overboard?"

She waited for a response while I turned over in my mind the image of an elder statesman who had turned his back on his only child. "I'm not 'simply throwing it overboard', Leece," I said. "I've thrown it. The deed is done."

"I know!" she snorted. "And after that bye-election, who's in your place now? That poisonous little Eton-educated toad whose daddy is the CEO of - “

"Leece."

"I'm sorry." She sat back. "I just hope you've got this right."

"Anyway - ” - I plonked my wine glass hard back down on the table - “ - politics is shit these days."

"Wasn't it always?"

"Not this shit. All that matters now is getting back in again next time; to look good on the telly and have some con-man PR guru cobble you together a soundbite or two which you can spew out on the box like you thought of it yourself. Principle? – gone are the days." I pushed my wine glass rather agitatedly around on the table. "I couldn't live like it any longer."

"'Thus conscience doth make cowards of us all'. Except with you, it seems to have worked the other way around." She raised her glass to me. "After you, my darling, they threw away the mould."

I looked out beyond the windows to where the sunlight sparkled and danced off the river. A swan preened itself on the far bank.

"Have you got a photograph of him?" she said. "I'd love to see what he looks like."

I turned to her. "So would I."

She frowned. "You serious?"

"I'm afraid so."

"Barnaby! Oh, Barney - I am so, so sorry."

We looked at each other across the table. Something passed between us. I reached out a hand towards her. She gave me hers.

"Barnaby Marechal," she said, " – and I said that quietly enough, didn't I? - dear Barnaby Marechal, after all these years I can still tell you that if you were free, this lunch would not be the last you'd see of me." And she gave me a look that might have come up from the centre of the earth. It stripped me bare and sent a terrible longing through me.

I caught it in time. I took my hand back. "You," I said, breathlessly, "are no more free than I am."

A curious little smile played over her features. "Is that a statement? Or a question?"

I raised both hands in front of me as if to say, 'Don't go there.'

She sat back, wiped her lips with her napkin. "Gerald and I have no relationship whatever. He pretends we do, and I know we don't. I am where I am." She paused. "But only until I'm not." She gave me that same look once again. I felt myself returning it. This was dangerous ground.

We parted in a strangely abrupt fashion. She realized with a shock that she was going to be late for an appointment, and apologized profusely. We hadn't even got round to talking about how she might actually help me find Matt. In a hurried and slightly garbled exchange as she was leaving the table, she said she would ring me the following day and that her daughter Marie who "sort-of, almost works in advertising", was probably the clue to it. That morning I'd bought a second new mobile - for my everyday use as opposed to the one I kept purely for my conversations with Martin. I scribbled that number down on my napkin and handed it to her. We embraced and kissed each other briefly on the cheek. Through the window I watched her drive off in a sleek, silver Mercedes.

I ordered a coffee and took it out into the garden. I watched the river, the boats, the dragonflies skimming over the surface of the water. What appointment was it, I wondered, that had her leave in such a hurry?

28.

I miss Ellen. I miss the skein of perfume that hangs in the air as she passes. I miss her laughter, her voice on the telephone in another room. I miss her touch and the softness of her lips. I miss making love to her. I miss waking up in the morning, touching her still-sleeping hand and knowing she is there. I miss coming home to her.

The attempt to try not to wonder how she's coping or what goes through her head when she thinks of me sometimes takes more strength than I have. At those times I'm all but frozen with guilt and regret.

Even after all this time, I still keep away from newspapers. Not so much because I think they're interested any longer in my whereabouts – I'm not a Lord Lucan. Or even a Reggie Perrin. But what I don't want is to stumble upon some article, included to fill out a newspaper on a news dog-day and designed to jerk tears, about the effect on Ellen of my perfidy.

All the questions come flooding back. Why – why didn't I just level with her? - before I asked her to marry me, before Brockwell Park, before she put her finger on my lips that day and gave me the excuse I was looking for – why did I not simply tell her the truth and take the consequences? Why did I string this albatross around my neck?

Ellen has never been a mother. There are no medical or gynaecological issues. She never wanted children. What she would have done in the earlier years of our relationship had a baby come along - despite our rigorous precautions - I can't imagine. I simply cannot see Ellen coping with that sort of disruption. I remember only too clearly the seismic upheaval the arrival of baby Matt brought to the lives of Stella and myself. A new baby, especially the first, rearranges the domestic dynamics in a brutally disinterested way – and not for just the time it takes you to get them back on track again, because you never do.

I know Ellen well enough to know she would have found the advent into our lives of a child not her own – albeit in the form of a man getting on for middle age - profoundly disturbing and very likely intolerable. She is not, in some respects, the most understanding of women – at least not in matters which fall so far outside her experience.

Something has had to give. Despite Licia's less than overwhelmed attitude towards what I'm doing, I nevertheless believe it is the least dishonourable of the courses open to me.

29.

Licia's contacts within the advertising business were, by this time of her life, few and far between. She had been retired for a number of years and was, as she told me the following day when she rang, rather out of touch. So the fact that she could recall no-one by the name of Matt or Matthew Marshal-cum-McDonald-cum-Whatever wasn't significant. But she was meeting her daughter, Marie, later that week and was hopeful something may emerge from that.

Marie, it seems, had not followed her mother into advertising, regarding it, to her mother's chagrin, as 'a job which society would be better off without'. As if to rub it in, she had taken a post with one of those shadowy organisations whose function it is to keep a critical eye on the content of advertising of all sorts - if necessary insisting on its amendment or even its rejection. The unofficial view of the advertising agencies was that such bodies were there primarily to be obstructionist and to thwart their creativity. The reverse view – that of the bodies themselves, and probably more realistic – was that without them the country's TV sets would be awash with downright lies instead of with just ingeniously worked half-truths.

Although Marie therefore was not working directly in advertising itself, she was involved across the board – sometimes directly, sometimes indirectly - with many of its practitioners. London advertising, although far and away the largest in the UK, is still a relatively small and introverted affair. There seemed therefore, a reasonable chance that if Matt had found his way into it and was still working in it she might have heard of him, or could at least dig around and find somebody who had.

My only concern was that of having to reveal myself to Marie - a third party about whom I was not in a position to make a judgment. In a phone conversation with Licia I was pondering how I should put this to her when she herself saved my embarrassment. "I don't think, by the way," she said, "that you should talk to Marie yourself. Let me do that. I can poke around in Marie's mean little anti-advertising mind without her thinking there's more to it than I'm letting on."

And so it was one morning, wearing my Yves St. Laurent jeans, light blue open-neck shirt, Italian black leather jacket, shades, beard in admirable condition and my hair trailing stylishly to my shoulders that I - posing as 'Mister Peters' - met up with Minxie in the Greek Cypriot café in Crouch End.

Minxie, I'd learned from Marie via Licia, was a copywriter of some repute at one of London's larger agencies. She had apparently worked relatively recently with a man who answered what pathetically few scraps of a description I'd been able to provide. It was flimsy stuff. But Marie had done her best and I had nothing else. Once she'd got a coffee and settled herself down, I asked Minxie simply to tell me, in her own words, all she could about this man.

The very first thing threw me – his Christian name bore no relation to 'Matthew' – it was Gaston.

"Gaston? 'Gaston What'?"

"'Vincent'. And he insisted you pronounced it like in French – Vah-sar. Something like that. I don't know French."

"'Gaston Vincent'." I listened to it as I said it. "Sounds too French to be French. Was this man English?"

"As far as I know. Yes, he must have been – after he'd had a few drinks or got a bit excited he developed a bit of a northern accent. Yorkshire, Lancashire – something like that."

"What about a middle name – did he have - ?"

"If he did, he never said."

"OK. Gaston Vincent. Please go on."

It turned out he worked not in advertising itself, but in one of the many small film companies in Soho that produced TV and cinema commercials for the ad agencies. He was, she said, what they called a Production Manager. It sounded grand enough but even though I'd worked in advertising myself, I'd had too little to do with the production of commercials to have any idea what that involved. When I asked her, she shook her elegantly coiffured head. "There's Production Managers and Production Managers," she observed mysteriously. Then smiled to herself as she stirred her coffee.

I waited for some elaboration. But she just gazed into her cup. "I'm not quite sure," I ventured, "what you mean."

She swept her hair back. "What I mean," she said, "is that there are the names. The guys who do the big ones." She stirred her coffee. "Gaston didn't. Though if he'd liked himself a little more, he could have done."

I was still at sea. "'The big ones'?"

"Pictures. Movies. An elite band – mostly men of course - has it sewn up."

I was sure she wasn't actually trying to confuse me. But she might have been speaking Mandarin. "I'm sorry," I said, "but you're talking of a world about which I know virtually nothing."

"Gaston was an in-house Production Manager. He'd been with them a long time."

"With whom?"

"Leopard Films." She said it as though 'Leopard Films' were words on the lips of half the world. "In that little passageway between Berwick Street and Wardour Street. They were once - " - and here she formed an 'O' between thumb and first finger, held it up before me and gave it a snappy flourish - " - the business!" Then she went back to her coffee. "Times change though. Don't they?"

I struggled on. "You knew him reasonably well, by the sound of it."

"I did." She smiled. "He was wonderfully eccentric. I like that." She threw out a sudden laugh which had little apparent connection with her speaking voice – light, lilting, musical. "Oh," she said, the laugh subsiding into a smile of sweet remembering, "he was delightfully different."

"Was he?" I replied, warily. "What sort of 'different'?"

"He would come into meetings sometimes - " - she put down her cup, leaned across the table and spoke in an urgent, confidential tone - " - dressed entirely in black - black shirt, outrageous black leather trousers, black boots up to here - " - she stuck out one of her own shapely stockinged legs and tapped it just below the knee - " - a black hat with a great wide brim which he called his pet Akubra. On his wrists he'd have these chunky silver bracelets. And round his neck - " - she indicated with both hands - " - the most beautiful silver pendant with a ruby in it. At least it looked like a ruby. I always wanted him to tell me where he got it but he - "

"I understand you worked with him?"

"The Addison's Tea commercials," she replied, proudly. "Bewley's Lager – I wrote all those. Criterion Car Insurance."

"And you knew him over quite a long period?"

"A year - ish"

"D'you know if he'd ever worked in an advertising agency?"

"Probably. Not sure."

"When did you last see him?"

She looked blankly back at me for a fraction of a second. As though something inside had first to be dealt with. That done, she launched into what I can only describe as a piece of personal theatre. She sat back, raised her eyes to the ceiling and placed, with self-conscious elegance, the index finger of her right hand on the little finger of the left. Paused. Then, in a stage whisper, she started to count – slowly and deliberately, "One-two-three - " - and as she did so, with the index finger of the right hand she pressed down on each finger in turn of the left. People have made cabaret acts of less. I watched in a mixture of fascination and profound irritation.

" - four – five – and – er – well - " - she took her eyes from the ceiling and looked at me - " - six. About six months ago."

"And how well did you know him?"

She took a quick sip of her coffee. "Do you mean did we fuck?"

My jaw dropped. "Er - well," I stammered, "in a way, I suppose. But -"

"From time to time. As you do."

I decided to move this up a gear. "Listen Minxie," I said, baulking just a little at that name on my own tongue, "I need to know about him – the man. His background, details of where he came from, colour of his hair etc."

She narrowed her eyes. "You a private dick, Mister Peters?"

I'd hoped not to have to do this. "OK," I said. "I don't know how much Marie told you, but the background to all this is as follows." With which I launched into an elaborate fiction I'd put together in anticipation of some sort of hiatus. I was, I told her, acting on behalf of an elderly female client. This lady had not heard from her only son in five years. He had left the family home in the country one Sunday evening to drive back to London and was never seen or heard of thereafter. He didn't return to his flat in Clapham, his car was never found. He had, at the time, been about to take up a position at an advertising agency. The lady – a recent widow - was now in poor health and desperate to have any news of him, her only child.

I sat back, smiling one of those sad, 'that's life' smiles.

She grimaced. "How awful."

I'd told my story well. Minxie was seriously upset, and quite stripped, for a while, of her affectations. I wasn't proud of myself. But that's the way it had to be. "OK," I continued. "Where did he come from? Had he been married? Any brothers or sisters? You were with him for a year. In that time there must be a lot of things – however insignificant they might seem – that you learned about him and have perhaps forgotten. Can I ask you now to dig deep? For any scrap or fag end that might give this now rather desperate lady something to hang onto." I also needed to ask her about his parents, but as my 'client' was one of them, it wasn't clear yet how I was going to go about that.

She took a few seconds to consider it. Then, with the anguish of the ageing widow in mind, told me anything she could remember and in whatever order.

He was in his late thirties – or at least, that's what she judged. He would never divulge his true age, coming up, whenever she questioned him, with rather silly extremes of one sort or another. From what odd bits about himself he did give away, despite his tendency to play from time to time, the streetwise card, she formed the impression he was a country boy, more au fait with the land and the open air than with the cramped spaces of the city. He came, he had said, from a 'broken home'. But never revealed in what way it was 'broken'. As for his name – Gaston Vincent – nobody, including herself, questioned it. In the film and TV advertising world, it was not uncommon for people to call themselves by 'trendy' or 'fashionable' names in preference to the ones they were born with.

He was about my height, she said, with almost black hair that contained a streak or two of early grey. His eyes were brown. He had never spoken of brothers or sisters. Minxie had assumed he was an only child. He seemed well educated but they had never discussed his schooling.

In private, he seemed often rootless and insecure. Anxious to please and to be accepted. At other times almost to court others' displeasure, to challenge them, to discomfit them. Good-looking, quick-witted, attractive to women. Yet there was a surprisingly vulnerable side to him. The odd innocent remark could sometimes trigger an explosive anger or even reduce him for a few moments to an almost ineffectual ditherer.

All in all, he was very different from other men she had met. He had about him what she termed, 'a permanently edgy buzz, an unpredictability; a feeling that he was slightly dangerous to be with'. He could be very funny, having a wicked sense of humour. "And on top of that," she said, lighting up a cigarette, "with a drink or two inside him, he would talk about things most men shy away from – emotions, feelings, things like that." She had been, she said, 'incredibly attracted' to him. She sat back and drew on her cigarette.

"Did he," I asked, "ever tell you where he came from?"

"I asked him once."

"And?"

"Somewhere south of Inverness and north of Brighton,' he said." She smiled. "He liked playing games."

"Does 'Lincolnshire' ring a bell?"

"Is that where his mother lives?"

'His mother '? My mind went blank. Stella?? How on earth would Minxie - ? No – the fictitious widow. Christ, I was adrift. I dragged things back together. I had to side step the question. I said, in a rather loud, nervy voice, "So do you have any idea where he is now?"

She shook her head. "The last time I saw Gaston was in a restaurant – just off Wandsworth Common – on the day he resigned from Leopard. We ate, he paid the bill, said goodbye and fucked off into the sunset." She was upset.

"I'm sorry," I said. "I didn't mean to pry."

"He wanted out. The film business and the country were off down the toilet, he said."

"Where did he – er – fuck off to?"

"Abroad."

"Where abroad?"

"I don't know." She bit her lip, looked away.

"I'm sorry," I said. "This isn't easy for you."

She shrugged as if to say, 'I can cope.' "All he told me was he was going to 'make serious money'. Bullshit." She stubbed out her cigarette. "He was doing a runner. Don't ask me what from because I don't know. Me - most likely."

Her defences had fallen away. I wanted to put an arm around her shoulder and tell her things would be alright. Maybe that's what having a daughter would have been like.

She looked at her watch. She was becoming agitated and a little distressed. "Just one more question," I said, as a sudden inspiration came to me. "Did Gaston ever say what he felt about his parents? What view he had of them? My client, you see, worries herself sick sometimes that maybe it was something she or her now dead husband had said or done – their relationship with their son had often been troubled."

She thought. Then drank the last of her coffee. She put the cup down slowly. "He never, ever spoke about his parents. I used to tell him I didn't think he had any. But then one day he said he'd had a letter."

"A letter?"

"From his father."

I almost choked on my coffee. My heart pounded. Was I about to be sunk?

"I'd never seen him like that. It had touched some really raw nerve, and he blew sky-high. He wouldn't have told me otherwise, I'm sure. Even then he just blurted out the gist."

"Which was??"

"It was all to do with a woman friend of his father's and a dispute over some property. Putting two and two together, it sounded like the old man had promised it to Gaston, but somehow she'd got her hands on it. He said the old man had betrayed him, that he was a hypocrite and 'a freeloading nonentity'. I told him that was not a very nice thing to say about his father. 'Ah,' he said, 'well that's where you're wrong. He's not my father.'"

An electric shock went through me.

"'He's my stepfather', he said. And he'd never had a lot of time for him anyway.

I had difficulty getting my breath. "So – so – who was his real father then? Did he say?"

She shook her head. "He couldn't remember him. He died when Gaston was very young."

I fell back in my chair.

"Gaston had this weird idea that having a step parent carried some sort of social stigma. He made me promise never to tell anybody. Anyway - " - she started gathering her things together - " - I can't see it matters now."

"Nothing?" I said, my voice faint. "He could remember nothing?" I sat forward again. "A recreation ground, for example? A park? You know the sort of thing? With swings and slide?"

She looked puzzled.

"Or – or anything about a poster – on the wall of a building – an advert that frightened him? No?"

"I'm sorry," she said, standing up, "I'm not sure what you're - "

"And you don't know what part of the country this was in?"

"What was?" Her look was turning to one of concern.

"His father's death. I mean, where did that happen and what - ?"

"I'm sorry, I'm getting a bit - "

"No, no. Right." Confusion and embarrassment were about to demolish me.

She picked up her bag from the table. "That wouldn't have any relevance to where Gaston is now anyway, would it? I mean, he - "

"No. Absolutely not. I just – well, just thought this lady would be interested. In principle."

Her concern was deepening. "But she presumably would have known where he died – his father, that is. Wouldn't she - her husband? I mean - er - "

I too stood up. I was staring at her - struggling to suppress an urge to blurt out the whole truth to this woman. She had known 'Gaston' only a few months back, eaten with him, slept with him. But then - who was this 'Gaston' anyway? He could be absolutely anybody. Yet already I'd pinned my son's name on him. I was breaking up.

Minxie forced a smile. "I hope what I've said helps this poor lady."

"Guaranteed!" Did I really say that? What a stupid response. I didn't know where to look, how to be.

"Look," she glanced at her watch again, "it's time I was heading off now."

We shook hands. "Thank you," I said. "So much."

She turned to go. Then said, "Oh!", stopped and looked back. "One thing. He did tell me once - for what it's worth - that he had a middle name. Which he said he hated. I didn't take it seriously, but whether it's any more believable than 'Gaston' or 'Vincent' I don't know."

"Oh, yes?" I said, flatly. I was out of enthusiasm. I was a fool on a fool's errand. "And what was that?"

"Alec," she said.

"Just – 'Alec'?"

"That's what he said." Then she smiled and went, telling me it had been nice meeting me and that she was going shopping. At least I think that's what she said. I really don't remember.

I got the bus back to Kilburn. 'Alec' - "for what it's worth," she'd said. Well, let's be realistic - plain, unadorned 'Alec' wasn't worth anything. 'Alex' on the other hand, might have been a different matter - Matt's middle name was 'Alexander'. So maybe Minxie's memory had misled her. We all have the right to believe what we want to.

30.

STATUS OF ENQUIRY: I've come into contact by proxy with a man, probably in his late thirties calling himself Gaston Alec Vincent - which has a very odd ring to it. And it might or might not be his real name. He betrays occasionally a hint of what could be a northern accent which may mean he spent part of his childhood (and/or teenage years) in 'the North'. I do not know where in 'the North', but Lincolnshire, though not very 'north' (or at least the southern end of it isn't) is probably not excluded.

He is about my height, with brown eyes – as are a few million other men of his age. Up until around six months ago he worked in the film industry as a Production Manager with a company calling themselves Leopard Films, based in London's Soho. The obvious thing to do now would be to go into Leopard Films and simply ask about G.A. Vincent. But meeting with someone in an office in central London is off-limits. As is writing to them.

At some time within the last six months it is believed (not proven) he went away, possibly abroad – though no-one knows where – to engage in something which would bring him in 'serious money'. That, on the other hand, might be bullshit, that really he was running away, though from whom or from what we do not know. It might have been to extricate himself from a romantic commitment. (Seems a somewhat extreme method) If that were the case, he might have 'run' anywhere, not necessarily abroad. He was probably born somewhere in the UK. Prior to his time at Leopard Films it is at least possible he worked in advertising in London. He was brought up from an early age by his mother and a stepfather. His natural father is said, by him, to have died when he was 'very young'.

That is the sum total of months of my time.

31.

I drive along this big wide road north towards Lincolnshire. I'm on my way once again to Marsh Enderby. Despite my previous confident assertion that trying to find him via Stella could open a Pandora's box, that's precisely what I'm now on my way to attempt. With so many avenues of enquiry denied me due to my fear of being recognized, all my searching has produced nothing that gives me any hope. Carrying on like it could take more years than I've got. Stella, of all people, has to know where he is.

However, I have little idea how I'm going to go about things when I get there. I shall have to trust my instinct – not a thing I've spent much time trusting in my adult life. But as long as I do it sensitively, and don't swoop in like Batman as I was about to do previously, then I probably stand a chance. The whole family could, of course, have moved on years ago from Marsh Enderby and be living anywhere in the UK. Or in the rest of the world for that matter. Or I might crash the car on the way there, or get struck by lightning, or hit a sink-hole and disappear into the bowels of the earth. Negatives abound.

I don't see Stella greeting me with open arms and a big smile. But she was once my wife, and loved me – at least in the earlier days. We had some good times together. If that turns out to mean nothing, then there are obligations of blood I can call on. The very worst thing would be if she sees my reappearance in her life simply as an opportunity to get her own back. Then she could make things difficult - like simply refuse to divulge anything about Matt and his whereabouts. It's possible. Women in her position have done that. And more. If my remorse - which is heartfelt - carries no sway with her, and she chooses to use my openness and obvious vulnerability as tools to wreak vengeance - or to administer justice, depending on one's point of view - then there's nothing I can do about it. Though I can't really imagine the Stella I knew taking that attitude. She may, of course, no longer be the Stella I knew.

Does Matt have my eyes, I wonder? My smile? Does he use gestures and body language which resemble mine? I've heard from people who work in adoption that parents long-separated from their offspring – some since birth - can be overwhelmed on meeting years later to see how their own often trivial gestures are reproduced in those children. How can that be? By no scientific yardstick is life comprehensible. It is a thing of magic. Thank God, and let it remain that way.

Stella could, of course, be dead.

All I know about Lincolnshire is that it's one of the largest counties in the UK, it grows a lot of vegetables and it's flat. Or a large part of it is. I've been there only once before and that was to give a talk in some unnervingly unpleasant town in the northern part. Docks, oil refineries, container trucks. And everywhere an acrid smell, like of chemicals. How do people live in such places? Because they have no choice, I suppose. I guess I've been lucky.

The road is wide. There is not a lot of traffic. The weather is invigorating. Bright sunlight. Puffy white clouds in a blue, wind-cleansed sky. Green fields and hedgerows. And those birds – what are they, what are they? – that hover almost motionless, high over the verges, oblivious to the traffic, with just the tips of their wings and their tails twitching. What are they doing – scanning the ground for prey? Whatever they're doing, that's real flying.

Suddenly I pass a huge sign that shouts, 'Northampton!!' at me. My stomach lurches and I see 'Greenholme' again, that awful Christmas, lights ablaze all over it like a carnival float.

The last journey I made to Northampton along this road was on my own and from London where I worked as an Account Executive on a big, detergent account. It was an important post – if anything in advertising can truly be labelled 'important' – and paid a lot. It demanded a commensurate amount of my time, and I'd seen little of my parents for some months.

Dad had rung me the previous evening to tell me Mother was ill. There had been just a suggestion of panic in his voice. That scared me a little. Big Man - he who coped with all, who had seen it all, had had a slice of it all - was out of his depth. Dad had little time for emotions. You don't build businesses on them. But now his own were breaking loose and he was adrift among them. He was letting me know in his own awkward way that he needed support.

"So what's the matter with her?" I asked.

"Difficult to say, old boy. Sickness. Bit of vomiting. Just – you know

– very tired. Not well."

"Has she seen the doctor?"

"You know your mother and doctors."

I didn't like it. Mother was tough as nails. "How long," I asked, "has she been like this?"

He cleared his throat. "For a while, on and off. You know how it is. She has these – bouts."

"'Bouts'?"

"And you see," he went on quickly, "the worrying thing is, she's on the damn coffin nails again."

"Fuck's sake, Dad!"

"Roll-ups, Barney. Only roll-ups."

"Roll-up smoke is still smoke."

"True, but – "

"And is she eating?"

"Scraps. Not a lot else. Daisy cooks for her but – "

"'Daisy'?" I frowned. "Who's Daisy?"

"Ah. I – er - took on a housekeeper. Just for a short period."

I let that sink in. What – if anything - it presaged escaped me even so. There was a long pause. He coughed again.

I said, "You talked about 'bouts', Dad. Does that mean - drinking bouts?"

Silence.

"Dad?"

"Pay us visit, eh, old boy? Come and see us, if you can."

Leaving London, I'd forgotten my key to the ancestral pile. The door was opened by a woman of around forty or so. A well-built, shapely figure – efficient, motherly, a little bit sexy, with rather more and redder lipstick than I'd think of as normal for a housekeeper. Her shoulder-length hair was dark brown and well-cared-for. This was obviously Daisy. What a very inappropriate name. We introduced ourselves. I followed her inside. Watching her almost strutting along the hallway, head held high, I had a distinct sense that some tectonic plate here was on the move.

"Where's Dad?" I said, surprised he hadn't already put in an appearance.

"Barney – may I call you 'Barney'?"

"Please do."

"I'm afraid he isn't here."

I frowned. "Where is he?"

"He asked me to give you his apologies but he was called away quite suddenly this morning on business. He said you'd understand." And she looked unblinkingly back at me. She had an irritating, almost confrontational, manner – that of one who took it as read you would understand that what she had to say was not open to dispute.

"Business??" I said. "He rang me last night and worried the fuck out of me about – sorry, pardon my French - " -

She shrugged as if to say, 'No matter.'

"I was almost as worried about him as about Mother. Then I turn up here and he's gone to work?" But it was familiar territory. From as far back as I could remember, Dad's involvement in domestic life had been hostage to 'business'. Plus ça change. I pointed up the stairs. "Is she still ill? Or has she taken up her bed and walked too?"

She looked blankly back at me. She was clearly on his side. I didn't want to think what I was starting to think. "So," I said, "did he give you any idea when he might be back?"

"He didn't. But he did ask me to tell you he'd ring later." She threw a glance up the staircase. "Will you - be going up to see your mother now?"

"Yes," I said. "How is she?"

"She's fine. Shall I bring you a cup of tea? Some biscuits?"

I shook my head, and set off up the stairs. Where had he got her from?

I stepped onto the landing. Their bedroom was at the far end. The door was closed. That was unusual – Mother was not one for keeping doors shut. But then, when you're sick you don't necessarily want people wandering in on the off chance. As I walked towards it however, I became aware of a smell. It was an odd smell, one of which I could find no trace in my memory. Not a single aroma, rather a cocktail – part sweet, part acrid, pungent and really quite unpleasant. Whatever it was, it was out of place on a landing and it didn't resemble any of the smells one associates with the sick, such as disinfectants or inhalants. I stood at the bedroom door. The smell seemed to emanate from the other side. My unease deepened. I knocked, very gently in case she was asleep. No answer. I tried again and called to her. "Mother." Still no answer. I turned the doorknob as quietly as I could and pushed open the door. The smell came out to meet me. It bordered on the offensive.

I couldn't see her. But the large hump in the duvet was obviously her, presumably asleep. I tiptoed in. As I did so, I caught sight of something on the carpet at the head end of the bed. It looked like a heap of house dust. But as I drew closer I saw it was actually some sort of fine, grey ash. My stomach sank - in it and all around it were spent matches and the pinched-tight butt ends of roll-ups. Dead matches littered the surface of the bedside unit. The ashtray was overflowing. Ash clung to the bedclothes where they overhung the bed. And amid the ash that lay even on the pillow, were the extremities of a few locks of hair that originated beneath the duvet.

Then a movement. Red fingernails curled out from beneath the duvet and clawed it slowly down. Bit by bit, a face appeared. The skin was like parchment, the eyes black, sunk back in their sockets. Mother. And like a bizarre wig on a shrunken head, her long hair sprouted in barely diminished splendour. Then words all fused into one. "Bernatisthatyou?" She looked up at me with eyes that neither saw nor understood. She was drunk. Hopelessly, incapably, poisonously drunk.

Despite the protestations of Daisy who, I'm sure, resented what she saw as my taking control of a situation truly Dad's, I threw all the windows on the top floor of the house wide open and called the family doctor. He, poor man, was distressed. Said Mother had to be taken in for detox. Had to, and now. He made the appropriate phone calls.

But he hadn't reckoned with Mother. Daisy and I half-coaxed, half-prised her from her bed in order to see if she were capable of standing unaided. Despite her ravaged senses, she caught sight of and recognized the doctor. With a yelp like a stuck pig, she hurled herself back onto the bed in a flurry of wild hair and flapping nightdress, neither aware of nor caring what of her womanhood she revealed in the process. She then burrowed into the folds of the duvet like a hamster into a pile of wood shavings and disappeared from view.

I didn't know whether to laugh or cry. I'd seen nothing like it.

We conferred around the table in the kitchen. "If, as is now pretty clear," said the doctor, looking directly at me, "we're not going to get her into detox without making things worse, there is something you really have to do. I think it extremely likely that somewhere in this house, she has a hidden bottle or bottles.

"'Hidden'?" I said. "I don't think I quite - ?"

"Alcohol - that she herself has hidden."

"I'm sorry. I still don't - "

"Barnaby." He lay a hand gently on my shoulder. "It is likely that somewhere in this house your mother has a secret supply of drink." Then reacting to my puzzlement, "Which she goes to as and when."

The implications were dawning on me but slowly.

"You must find it and get rid of it. It will be well-hidden. Alcoholics are ingenious."

'Alcoholic' – that word, so casually applied to my own mother, was a brick thrown at my head.

And he wasn't finished. "Also, I advise you to take whatever alcohol you know is in the house and lock it away. If you don't, when she regains the use of her legs and can't find that which she's hidden, she'll go to that."

I was reeling. "What will she do if she can't get it?"

"One step at a time, eh?"

"In the end though," I said, "she's going to be alright – isn't she?"

"'In the end'?" His smile was fleeting, cautionary. "Well – she'll be alright as long as she never takes another drink." He looked at me; I looked back at him.

When he'd gone, I went into the sitting room, and poured myself a generous scotch. I sat with it for a long time, looking out at the garden, listening to the birds. That her drinking had come to this should not really have surprised me. But that did nothing to ease the shock-horror I was feeling.

I went back up to the bedroom. With Daisy looking on and Mother still hidden beneath the duvet, I set about going through the cupboards and drawers. Running my hands through her personal and private things – her trinkets, her clothes, her underwear - I feared I might feel like Oedipus. But I was on autopilot. I felt nothing. And I found nothing. I suppose the bedroom was too risky a place. Dad would almost certainly have stumbled across any contraband.

I went back downstairs with Daisy and we ate a very brief late lunch. I had to think this through. Where, in a house where people come and go all day long, can you possibly hide away a bottle – of what, whisky, vodka? - so that only you know where it is? It can't be easy. Daisy had seen nothing untoward, and swore she wasn't getting booze in for Mother on the quiet. I had no reason to doubt her. I asked her to take every single drop of alcohol she could find in the house and lock it away with the wine in the cellar. Then get a man in to change the lock on the cellar door and give me the key.

I went back upstairs to resume my search. I started with Mother's sewing room which was en suite with the main bedroom. I was thorough, scrupulous, fastidious. I turned out every single drawer, cupboard, box, cubbyhole, carrier bag I could find. It was fruitless.

I moved on to the two guest bedrooms. I spread out over the carpets the entire contents of cupboards, wardrobes, underbed boxes. I probed behind radiators, I lifted the corners of rugs and carpets – achieving nothing, I found myself doing pointless things. I similarly and fruitlessly wrecked two bathrooms and three toilets. I have to give Daisy her due in that she insisted I leave the mess for her to clear up. By late afternoon, I was forced to conclude that the upper floor was alcohol-free.

Dad didn't return that evening. He rang to say he'd had to fly to Germany, but would return the following day. I didn't tell him about Mother. He could have done nothing and I didn't want him more disturbed than he already was. I stayed at 'Greenholme' that night. I slept just along the corridor in the room that had been mine as a teenager. It brought on some strange feelings. I found it hard to get to sleep. Not only had the events of that day rocked me to the foundations, but that offensive smell, only slightly less intense now, was once again starting to spread through the upper floor.

The next morning, immediately after breakfast, I set out to crack this riddle. I virtually ransacked the ground floor. The result was the same as the previous day's - nothing.

Then the garages and the outhouses. Likewise. Around lunchtime I came back indoors, thoroughly irritated. I discussed it again with Daisy. Either the doctor had been wrong and there were no hidden bottles; or I had missed a trick. Daisy thought the former more likely. But some instinct told me it was me. I needed to start again from the beginning – this time using my imagination.

I went into Mother's sewing room again, and closed the door behind me. I sat down, then took time to look carefully and attentively all around. Shelves full of little plastic containers. Pins, needles, fasteners of various kinds. Scissors. Some things I had no idea what they were. Dress materials in colourful rolls. Cut lengths of cloth. An electric sewing machine. Her ancient treadle machine with its beautiful Edwardian trade mark. Boxes of threads. Buttons. In a corner, her old dressmaker's dummy - a wooden torso on a pole. My childhood friend and companion. Made from what I imagined in those days to be plates of wooden armour, it had accompanied me to many an exotic land where together we challenged ogres and dragons.

But as I sat there looking around, I felt a chill. Though the small space was crammed and busy with the colourful and ingenious tools of the seamstress's trade, there was about it a sense of decay. It was long-abandoned, it's day done. And indeed, how could anyone in Mother's state have even threaded a fucking needle?

I forced myself to think. I had to try and get inside the head of someone attempting to conceal from others, in a room in a family house, a bottle of alcohol. Well, maybe you disguise the bottle. Maybe you make it look like something else. Like some odd bods do with toilet rolls, for Christ's sake, by slipping a sort of knitted tea cosy over them. So what amongst all this stuff could possibly be a bottle in disguise?

On a little side table there was a doll. An elegant lady, Spanish-looking, about a foot tall, with luxurious black hair piled on her head. Her skirt was bright blue, full length, hooped and belled out by some sort of crinoline. From beneath it protruded a pair of dainty silver shoes. I picked her up, upended her and found myself looking up her skirt. She hid no booze, and I put her down again feeling quite embarrassed.

I sat myself at the treadle machine. Scratched my head. There was nothing in this room that I hadn't already checked and which could possibly be hiding a bottle. Even a bottle as small as a miniature. So what now? I looked absently down at the treadle. I recalled as a child watching fascinated as Mother's feet went up and down, to and fro on this same treadle. I put a foot on it and pressed it down. With a soft clickety-clacking sound, shiny metal parts of the machine started to move, sliding smoothly back and forth. What an exquisitely precise mechanism. I remembered watching her once skilful hands as they guided and coaxed the material she was working on past that fast-jabbing needle. One day she let me have a go. I was only about ten. I made a mess of it and jammed the machine.

On a shelf above my head I caught sight of a box containing different coloured reels of cotton. A childlike eagerness took hold of me – although I'd jammed the machine all those years ago, now surely I could figure it out. I could just about remember how to load it with cotton. You slotted the reel onto the top spindle, threaded the cotton around a sort of tensioning spring, then on down to the eye of the needle.

I stood, reached up to the shelf for the box. As I did so, I banged my hip against the corner of the machine. I staggered slightly, and instead of getting a hold on the box, edged it a little to one side. It was enough to topple one of those slim, delicate vases often used for single roses which stood beside it. I shot out a hand to catch it, but too late. It rolled off the shelf and fell to the floor, shattering as it hit a wooden footstool and spattering water on the carpet.

I got down on my haunches, and with a tissue from my pocket, dabbed rather pointlessly at the damp area of carpet. As I started gathering up the broken pieces I saw, in one large fragment whose curvature remained intact, a tiny reservoir of water. I was about to soak it up with my tissue when a light flickered on in my brain. I dipped the tip of a finger into the water, then put that to the tip of my tongue. It wasn't water. I tried another drop. Let the aroma drift up into my nose. It was gin.

And so it was virtually throughout the house. The only rooms not harbouring at least one small vase, scent bottle or decorative container of some sort which held a few centimetres of either gin or vodka were the sitting room, Dad's study and the main bedroom. In the kitchen, the bottle in question was an old white wine vinegar bottle, its label still intact. Quarter full of vodka, it had been pushed right to the back of a shelf unit amongst the cooking oils and sauces.

Whatever gloss any of us might be tempted to put on it, the plain fact was Mother was in the process of killing herself; committing suicide in front of our eyes. The black despair which that brought on turned to an equally black anger. Was I - was Dad - not worth remaining alive for?

I took the stairs two at a time. I threw open her bedroom door and winced as that same foul smell came out to meet me. Her head and shoulders were now clear of the duvet. But her eyes were closed. Asleep? I stopped. Then stood very still, and looked at her.

My anger evaporated. Beneath the bed, I could see the pretty bedroom slippers she herself had hand-embroidered years ago. I heard her slow, deep, seemingly peaceful breathing; watched the unhurried rhythm of her shoulders. I had once been a part of that body. And there she lay, a lonely, wounded little girl. For so long the final authority on so many things in my life. Now so much at the mercy of some destructive aspect of her own self that all authority and self-respect had left her.

I flopped down in a rattan chair by the window.

But then that smell again. Christ, what is it? I'd scoured the whole room the previous day and found nothing that could account for it. I stood up and walked around sniffing like a bloodhound. It was strongest near the bed. I got down on my knees, pushed her slippers to one side, and peered under the bed.

Another pair of shoes – Dad's. Dust. One or two used and screwed-up tissues. And over at Mother's side - I frowned - two strange, pale, sphere-like objects the size of large marbles. I lay flat down, stuck my head and shoulders beneath the bed, stretched out an arm and scooped them towards me. I looked at them. Then stood up, took them to the window and examined them in my hand. Garlic. Cloves of fresh garlic. With teeth marks in them.

I flopped down once again in the chair. Let me get my head around this. For this is the icing on the cake. My mother, the haughty Hungarian beauty, turner of heads and the cause of such envy in female eyes, had resorted to chewing raw garlic in the hope of masking the smell of alcohol on her breath.

Dad returned later that day. I brought him up to date. He showed little surprise. He went up to the bedroom. There, he stayed for over an hour with the door closed. He emerged at dinner. Mother, he announced to Daisy and myself, had asked that everyone stay out of her room until the following day. She was recovering and needed time.

I had no problem staying out of her room. I intended leaving early the following morning and returning to London. I would go in and say goodbye to her before I left.

At nine o'clock the following morning, she was sitting up in bed looking like Cleopatra. The evil cocktail of alcohol and well-chewed garlic had been replaced by the subtle and rather lovely aroma of a perfume I remember buying once for Licia in days gone by - 'Je Reviens'. She was wearing a pristine white nightdress with a delicate lace collar. Her hair, brushed and shimmering, hung in gorgeous, springy tresses across her shoulders. Around her swan-like neck a little emerald pendant Dad had given her in happier times. She looked wonderful. All my childhood adoration of her flooded back.

Then just as quickly evaporated. For the reality was she reminded me just a little of Gloria Swanson in 'Sunset Boulevard', a sad - and dare I say slightly grotesque - caricature of the beauty she had once been. I wanted to hold her and let her cry the tears she surely needed to cry. But Mother would never have allowed that.

I drove away, disturbed and unhappy. Even so, I persuaded myself things at 'Greenholme' would soon be on the mend. I was convinced that Mother, after such a deeply humiliating experience, would surely do whatever it took to cure her addiction. Daisy was going to be around all the time, and the doctor had promised to keep a watchful eye on her for as long as it took. The conditions were in place. Beyond that, all it required was Mother's cooperation. But - you can lead a horse to water..... When I kissed her goodbye that morning it was the last time I was to see her alive.

Some months after her death I learned from Dad that a bemused workman, fitting a new cistern in one of the downstairs toilets, had discovered, lodged inside the old one, a half-full bottle of vodka. Dad checked the rest of the toilets in the house – there was a bottle in the cistern of the main bathroom and in one guest room toilet. Neither had labels. He had at first assumed the paper had simply come off in the water. But why then, he wondered, had it not obstructed the flow nor left any trace? He'd had to conclude that Mother had anticipated that and removed the labels before hiding the bottles. Alcoholics, as the doctor had said, are ingenious.

32.

I am in a room in a house in Lincolnshire. Over to the west, the dying sun is visible between torn layers of black cloud. From the east I can hear the sea and the shifting of a shingle beach.

The land round here is flat, wide-open. Like a tabletop. The wind sweeps across it like a tribe of mad dogs, bending before it the branches of the few trees that can stick this sort of thing out and still carry on. And the sky is as wide as the universe, drowning you out. There are farms, isolated houses dotted about, looking like they fell from a passing plane. And these narrow rivers - streams. 'Dykes', as they're known. Thin lines of water, silver as the sky reflects off them, running straight as a die to the sea, legacy of the Dutch engineers who first drained this once-waterlogged land four hundred years ago. I'm told that even now, only constant pumping keeps the sea at bay. It is a strange place.

I look around this room in the gathering dusk. It is a guest bedroom in 'The Willows' - a nice enough Bed and Breakfast I happened upon in the late afternoon. It's clean and smells of polish. Autumn is almost with us, sharpening the air, shortening the days, lengthening our nights. The leaves are turning brown, auburn. It was autumn when I stepped off that train. Time accelerates as you get older.

I look at myself in the mirror. I've got myself a pair of rimless glasses now. I bought them in W.H.Smith's for just a few pounds. I reserve the shades now for days of bright sunshine. My refurbished appearance seems to have bedded itself down. Like the engines in new cars of years gone by that had to be 'run in', the new me is, I feel, pretty well run in now.

This is not a homely room. They've tried - there are plates fixed to the walls as ornaments. One is pallid, intertwined flowers, poorly executed and signifying nothing. Another says it's, 'A Present from Prestatyn'. A woman with a face straight out of the fifties, grins at me across the Prestatyn rooftops. The sash window is draughty and rattles with the strongest gusts. I have had my dinner. They had no wine and I had brought none with me. Dinner is not dinner with just a glass of tap water.

In my briefcase is the ageing letter to Ellen. It is always with me - in case the moment takes me and I drop it into a postbox. But is it any longer relevant? So much time has passed. I feel very strange.

Marsh Enderby is just a few miles up the road from here. The fact sends a pulse of nervousness through me. I had intended arriving there this evening. Finding a room at a local pub, being outgoing, friendly and chatting in the bar with the locals – just to get a feel for the place. But I changed my mind. What if – despite the years between – she really is still there? There are people who stay in one place most of their lives. And I bump into her? In the street, or rounding a corner? I need to see her coming; I need to have prepared myself.

33.

"Harry's just reporting what he's heard, Ellen. That's all."

"Thank you, Frank. I think I got that."

Frank Lippincote stood upright and awkward, the tips of his fingers drumming on the table. Harry Jardine sat at the other end of the table, his notebook closed in front of him. Ellen, her face darkly anxious, sat opposite him. Martha sat in one of the large armchairs. She was not comfortable in other people's houses. She had come along only to provide refreshments.

Frank looked from Ellen to Jardine and back again.

Ellen looked at Jardine. She raised her eyebrows. "So?"

Jardine opened the notebook. Martha began prising herself heavily out of her chair. "I think perhaps a cup of tea to get us going. And I brought some cakes. Will you have a cake, Mr. Jardine?"

Jardine shook his head. "Thank you, no."

She turned to Ellen. "Do you mind awfully if I use your kettle?"

"Do whatever you want, Martha."

Ellen watched with mounting impatience as Jardine flicked through the pages of his notebook. Frank eased himself down onto a chair. Then arranged himself precisely, carefully and slightly nervously - upright, hands placed symmetrically on his knees, his head slightly forward in the direction of Jardine.

"Before you start, Mister Jardine," said Ellen, "do you mind telling me the source of whatever it is you're about to reveal?"

Jardine smoothed an open page in his notebook. "A number of people. All of whom are either living in Cornwall now or were at that time. This was in the general area of Newquay, Padstow."

"And these people knew Mister Marechal personally, I presume?"

"One or two."

"Just one or two?"

"It is long time ago now and - "

"Quite." She sat back.

"Which is not to reflect on their veracity."

"I'm sure they meant well." Her smile was empty.

His was tolerant. "I can usually tell."

Her sting somewhat drawn, Ellen looked away,.

Jardine referred to his notebook. "He rented a room in a village called Saint Mawgan."

"Used to be an RAF base there I believe," chirped Frank, anxious to keep things pleasant.

"The period we're talking about is roughly from 1975 to 1980. Mister Marechal had actually left Halifax two years prior to that but I've little useful information yet about that period. It seems to have been spent in a fairly peripatetic progress to Cornwall. I suspect he had no planned destination – just that Cornwall was where he ended up. But by March of 1977 I do know that he – and a friend who accompanied him on at least part of the journey there – were renting two upstairs rooms in Saint Mawgan. The landlady was a woman by the name of Davina Cassells. She was not local. She'd recently moved there from London."

Ellen shifted awkwardly in her chair.

"Mister Marechal had taken work as a barman in a pub in another village nearby. Village's name is - rather nice name - St Columb Major. The 'Seven Stars'. A family owned and run pub. It still is. The father of the present landlord, a Mister Malcolm Trevithick remembers him. As for the friend – man of about the same age as Mister Marechal – he got a job working at a local farm. I doubt a pub would have employed him in those days - he wasn't white. According to Trevithick, he was 'of a mid-brown colour'. So probably Southeast Asian or North African. He was known only as Raffie. He and Mister Marechal were seldom seen apart. In a place like that, they were an item of some interest."

Ellen frowned. "Meaning?"

"Rural Cornwall in the mid-seventies. Two young men, one of whom was black, always together and both far from their usual haunts." Eyebrows raised, he looked at Ellen. "If nothing else, it was uncommon."

"Tea up!" Martha appeared in the doorway with a loaded tray.

Ellen's irritation got the better of her. "Alright Mister Jardine - interesting though this biography of my husband as a young man may be, I would be grateful if we could just deal with the veiled allegations Mister Lippincote here has indicated."

Frank bridled.

"Could we not – as they say – cut to the chase?"

Jardine pushed his notebook to one side. He picked up his briefcase and drew from it a document in a transparent sleeve which he held out to

Ellen. She took it, frowning.

She glanced cursorily over it - an old newspaper cutting. A grainy black and white photograph beneath which was a paragraph of text. "What," she said, looking up, "am I supposed to make of this?"

"There is a man. Do you recognize him?"

"It's so faded I can hardly see him, let alone recognize him." She went to hand it back across the table. Jardine held up a hand to stop her. "Would you mind please taking another look? Perhaps tell me what you see?"

Frank looked nervously out of the window.

With an irritated flick of her wrist, she all but snatched the document back. "I see a man. A young man in a dark suit. And a young woman leaning out of a car window – seems to be smiling at him. And it seems to have been taken through somebody's window." She looked at Jardine. "I say again – what am I supposed to make of it?"

"Have you read the headline to the text beneath it?"

She read it out loud. "'Have you seen these two?' I'm supposed, I imagine, to know who he is."

Jardine waited.

"Alright,"she said reluctantly. "Then I imagine it's a very young Mister Marechal."

"And would you now mind reading the first paragraph of that article, please?"

Her eyes flicked back and forth. Jardine watched. Frank examined a cufflink.

Ellen's face slowly darkened. "How come," she asked, "there's a photograph of them? Where is it? Who took it?" She handed it back across the table.

"It was at a motel." Jardine slipped the cutting back into his briefcase. "At the request of the local police, the manager made a practise of covertly photographing his customers with one of the then new Polaroid cameras. There'd been some drug trouble. It was widely known locally that you could rent rooms there by the hour, and dealing had been - "

"Why," said Ellen, "would anyone want to take a hotel room for an hour?" But even as she said it the penny dropped. She struggled with the flush that came to her cheeks.

Jardine continued. "The couple in the photograph were thought at first to be implicated in what turned out to be a drugs-related crime. Mister Marechal and his lady friend were in their room – which they booked for two hours – for only about half an hour. When they left, they did so in a great hurry and without returning the room key. Their car – the Jaguar in the photograph - drove off at high speed almost hitting another car parked by the Manager's office."

Ellen's eyes were now riveted on Jardine.

"The manager thought nothing particularly of that. People forget room keys, and people drive recklessly. But when his wife, who was a sort of acting, unpaid chambermaid, went to make up the room an hour or so later, she came running back saying that sheets and pillows were all over the floor, the curtains were still closed, the lights on. Couple of chairs had been knocked over – all the signs of a panicky exit. And there were some very strange noises coming from 409 next door. The manager went himself to take a look. He got into 409 and saw what he saw. He rang the police and the ambulance service."

"And what," said Ellen, guardedly, "did he see?"

"The occupant, a man in his late fifties, had been attacked. Rather badly. I'll spare you the details."

Ellen took a second to marshal her thoughts. "Alright - however intriguing this may be as a detective story, I have yet to see where it - "

"Bear with me. Please."

She sat back, tight-faced.

"When the ambulance arrived, the man in 409 was still alive. But he died soon after arriving at hospital twenty miles away in Exeter. One of the doctors who had attended him told the local newspaper that had the ambulance been called even half an hour earlier – i.e up to an hour and a half after Mister Marechal and his woman friend had left the motel – it is almost certain he would have lived." He looked up from his notebook.

Nobody moved or spoke.

"There is," said Jardine, "one further thing. While the manager was waiting for the police and ambulance, he had taken a phone call. It was from a public box - he could hear traffic in the background. The caller sounded like a young man. He was clearly nervous and flustered – he said just, 'Hello'. Then what the manager described as, 'A muttered, 'For fuck's sake' - excuse my bluntness - but then no more. After that, all he could hear was traffic before the receiver was put down with something of a crash." He closed his notebook, pushed it from him and looked up. "I guess you know who that young man was."

Frank looked at Ellen.

"At least," she said, very quietly, "he tried."

Martha topped up the teacups.

"And I suppose," she went on, "one could also say the man might have lived had the Manager been up to his job. If he'd checked the room when the other two drove off in such a hurry."

Nobody commented.

"The man and the woman," said Jardine, "were eventually traced. The man's name was Bernard Marshal, age 26, born in Peterborough, Northamptonshire. He was commonly known as 'Al'. He worked for a Bristol advertising agency. But only briefly. At the time of this incident he'd been there only six months. On the strength of it, he resigned."

"'Al'?" said Ellen, perplexed. "Why 'Al'?"

"I've no idea."

Martha tapped Ellen's arm. "Don't let your tea get cold."

Ellen took no notice. She said, rather meekly, "I don't know about you Mr Jardine, but I would not want to be judged today by how I occasionally behaved in my twenties."

"Quite so, Mrs Marechal. But your brief to me was not only to try and trace your husband, but also to try and dig up any information which might possibly throw light on his recent seemingly out-of-character behaviour."

Ellen looked down at her fingernails.

Jardine went to say more, then stopped. Looked at Frank who was looking steadfastly the other way.

They all sat in silence.

Ellen very slowly put her cup down in its saucer. "Thank you, Mr Jardine. I think that's enough for today."

"Ellen." Frank raised a hand. "I think if you would just - "

"This is not what I wanted, Frank! I don't want to sit here and listen to Barney's memory being trashed on the basis of a single sin of omission best part of forty years ago."

Frank looked back at her, blinking.

"Mrs Marechal." Jardine's tone was oddly compulsive.

She turned to him.

"I'm not trashing your husband's memory. I'm not apportioning blame. The scene he walked into at that motel was seriously distressing, and frightening for anyone, let alone a young man with a young woman on his arm."

Ellen's irritation softened. "Thank you."

"On top of that, I'm aware how much the still recent events in Mister Marechal's own life at that time must have affected how he conducted himself. Divorce and breakup of a young family are profoundly disturbing events which reverberate for many - " He stopped. Ellen's face had gone rigid. He frowned. "I'm sorry – is there something that - ?"

"What did you just say?"

Frank was leaning forward, his elbows on his knees, peering intently at the carpet.

"What," Ellen repeated, "did you just say, Mr Jardine? 'Divorce'?"

"And the breakup of - "

"What divorce? What are you talking about?" She stared at Frank. "Frank? What's he talking about?"

Frank indicated Jardine. "I – er – I think that he'd better – you know – continue."

"What do you two know that I don't? What divorce? What young family? Who are we talking about here??"

Jardine just looked at Ellen.

She frowned, incredulous. "Barney?"

Jardine said nothing..

"My Barney?" She laughed. "That's ridiculous. Who on earth are these people you've been talking to?"

"He was married in 1965."

"He could not possibly have been."

"I'm afraid he was. On the 14th of May that year to a lady by the name of Stella Jordan."

Ellen sagged.

Martha's jaw dropped.

"But how," said Ellen, "can you possibly know this?"

Jardine reached once again into his briefcase. He drew out a folder from which he extracted and held up a large brown envelope. "In here is a copy of the marriage certificate." He offered her the envelope.

She went to take it. But changed her mind.

Frank, for no apparent reason, stood up.

"Children?" said Ellen, very quietly.

Jardine slipped the envelope back into his briefcase. "One. A boy."

She nodded as if to say, 'I see.' Then stood up. "Like I said - I think that's enough for today."

She turned from the table and walked away. She stopped at the door and looked back. "So I'm a stepmother. To a middle-aged man. Whose father has vanished. Well, well. Has he kept in touch with this boy? Like - has he been living some parallel existence about which I know nothing? Is that what this whole sordid business is about?"

"Not," said Jardine, "as far as we know."

Separating the words out and emphasising each one, she mimicked him. "'As-far-as-we-know.'" Then turned and went from the room, leaving the door open behind her.

Frank sat down again. He and Jardine looked at each other.

Ellen's footsteps mounted the stairs.

Martha gathered up the plates, cups and saucers and left the room.

Frank smiled wryly. Said to Jardine, "I admire your technique."

Jardine shrugged. "I've been here before."

34.

As Barnaby Marechal drove his ageing Ford Sierra through the Lincolnshire countryside, he was in a strangely excitable frame of mind. Autumn leaves in their browns, reds and yellows swirled across the road in front of him – 'like ghosts from an enchanter fleeing' - driven by a wind off the sea (he assumed it was off the sea, coming as it appeared to do from the east). He felt a sort of contained nervousness mixed with a tingling anticipation. He wound the window down, let the wind play in his hair and worry at his beard. He raced, like Mister Toad, past fields of black-dark earth ploughed to a devastating precision. He turned on the dashboard radio. The volume knob came off in his hand. He forced it back on its spindle. Wound the tuning knob through a chattering cacophony till he hit on some pleasant pop which, though it thumped and dinned his ears in the small space seemed, even so, all of a piece with the speeding car and the swirling leaves. Then high above him, a huge flock of small birds, moving and manoeuvring like programmed dust across the wide sky, one mind among their hundreds. How wonderful. And quite beyond comprehension.

But then a large road sign was sweeping up on his left – 'Marsh Enderby'. Near panic removed all else from his head. 'Marsh Enderby '. And splashed on beneath it in red paint - 'Twinned with Hell'.

He pulled himself together. 'PLEASE DRIVE CAREFULLY THROUGH OUR VILLAGE.' He slowed down. Turned off the radio. Round a bend in the road appeared the first few houses. He sat up, grasped the wheel in a solid, respectable manner.

His imagination, fired mostly by wishful thinking and Oliver Goldsmith, had made of Marsh Enderby a place of contemplative rusticity, where flowers would bloom in the window boxes of thatched cottages and on a bridge over a crystal stream, small children might even play Poohsticks.

It wasn't like that. He drove past a nondescript terrace of small, run-down old houses. The front garden of one was filled with a grotesque family of huge gnomes. Then a tiny, franchised general store overshadowed by an anonymous modern warehouse with no windows. Across its flat roof he could just see the spire of a church. He pulled up alongside a communal green. There was an undersize football pitch with a single set of goal posts. On the other side, swings and a roundabout. Beyond them, on the corner of a narrow side street a pub with the unlikely name of 'The Amsterdam Freighter'. A woman hung washing out in a rear garden. Somewhere the intermittent whine of an electric drill.

He drove around the green and pulled up outside the pub. Its paintwork was peeling. A mud-splattered Morris Minor was the only vehicle in its small car park. A board announcing food and coffee had collapsed and lay on the ground. There were one or two lights on inside. He shook his head. Put the car in gear again and returned to the main road. There had to be another pub in the village.

There wasn't. He was already driving past a sign saying 'THANK YOU FOR DRIVING CAREFULLY THROUGH OUR VILLAGE'. Then he was back among the ploughed fields. It was either return and chance the 'Amsterdam Freighter' or follow this road wherever it led. He drove on. There had to be another village and another pub.

He settled to the drive. Turned the radio on. Some people calling themselves the 'Pussycat Dolls' threatened to sing to him. He switched it off again. The sun was high in the sky. A few white clouds.

What, oh what, Stella, brought you here, of all places?

Celeste Johanssen yawned. Picked up the phone and dialled. It rang and rang. She yawned again, and was about to replace the receiver when a woman's clipped tone at the other end snapped, "Freighter. Yes?"

"Lilly?"

"Who's that - Celeste?"

"Yes. Checking if you want me in the morning. I was on my way to bed."

"Sorry - coach party appeared out of the blue. I wish they'd take the trouble to book. We're run off our feet." She tutted. "Mick took pity on them - as usual. Anyway - yes please, if you would. There's three in for breakfast."

"Any specials?"

"Nobody's said anything."

"OK. See you at the usual time."

"Thanks Celeste."

Celeste put the phone down. She switched off the downstairs lights and went upstairs to the bedroom. She took off all her clothes and hung them neatly back in the wardrobe. Then padded into the bathroom. Splashed cold water on her face and dabbed it dry. Opened her eyes wide, thrust her head towards the mirror and examined the skin of her face, particularly around her eyes. She grimaced. Then undid her hair and watched it fall down around her shoulders. 'Genuine auburn,' an admirer had once told her. That was a long time ago. There was almost as much grey now as auburn.

Back in her bedroom, she climbed into bed. Even in the coldest weather, Celeste slept naked. She was ever conscious of the intimate relationship between sleep and gestation. It was as primal, and merited being experienced in as primitive a physical state.

She had thought she might read for a while, but in the event was too tired. She switched out the bedside light. Pulled the covers up to her chin and lay looking out of the window. She always slept with the curtains just a little apart. That way she felt that even in sleep, she remained in touch with nature and the earth. Tonight there was no moon. But the air was clear and there were lots of stars. It had been a windy day. The sky always seemed particularly clear after windy days. Perhaps tomorrow would be the same. Then maybe after work she would drive to her special place by the sea.

I ended up in a village with the bizarre name of Old Leake. Leaving Marsh Enderby I'd followed the road wherever it took me, doing little more than an 'eenie-meenie-minie-mo' when I came to a junction. Now, that's a thing I never would have contemplated in my former existence. I had to have a map, for Christ's sake. "Someone go and get a map. How the hell are we going to know where we are without a map?" It's satnavs now. So those 'in charge' are no doubt saying these days, "Someone go and get a satnav. How the hell are we going to know where we are without a satnav?" So things change while at the same time remaining exactly the same.

Arriving in Old Leake I drove around its few narrow streets and discovered an attractive-looking pub called 'The White Hart'. Its large car park was almost full. I bought a cheese sandwich along with a half pint of locally brewed ale and retired with them to a corner of the low-beamed bar.

The place had a good feeling. The staff were friendly and efficient. And they had a free room. I booked it, initially for a week. I had more or less formulated a modus operandi. I would base myself there, then, starting with Marsh Enderby, work my way around the local villages in say, a twenty mile radius. Twenty miles was pretty arbitrary, but I had to set some limit beyond which I would stray only on the strength of a worthwhile lead. Based on what the old man in Endell Street had told me, I had to make the assumption that Stella and family had moved either to Marsh Enderby itself or its fairly immediate surroundings. With a young child nearing school age, they would have stayed for some years. There seemed therefore a reasonable chance there would be those around today who could recall the family McDonald. Families put down roots. Through their children's schools, through social activities, through work they establish networks. The youngsters grow up, marry, have children themselves and the networks widen. My basic premise, I was convinced, was sound.

One thing concerned me, however. Something of which I had taken no account back in London. Now I was here, it was obvious - this is a wide and empty part of the country. A stranger is an object of curiosity. Especially one who goes around asking questions. I will have to be discreet. I don't want people questioning me – Who are you? What's your business? As for my attitude - I think casual and friendly is the thing - 'Up here on business for a few days and thought, while I was here, I'd look up an old friend I lost contact with some years ago – you know how it is - and who moved into this general area. Name of 'McDonald'. Don't happen to have heard of him, do you?'

I don't have to say more than that. And if they ask what business I'm in – then maybe I say something like 'Environmental Research'. It's vague yet plausible. Do I, in my leather jacket, jeans and beard look like a man who might be so nebulously employed? I think I do. But I have to be careful. I am not, nor will I ever be, fireproof.

In order to get up to speed on the local background, I bought both local newspapers and read each of them from front to back. I thought there was a chance that somewhere in them, I might even come across mention of a 'McDonald'.

Life in this rural backwater was a bizarre read. At a cattle market in a place called Louth, an argument between three farmers had escalated into fisticuffs. The police had been called. Two officers had turned up in a car, but had then been penned in by heifers panicking in the confusion and had had to be rescued by the three farmers who put aside their differences when they saw the plight of the police. A middle-aged woman in Spilsby had won a thousand pounds on the Premium Bonds. She planned to spend it all on roller coaster rides in theme parks. I read a report on the deliberations of a Parish council about the noise caused by scramble bikes on Sundays. I read about the latest goings-on in Boston Magistrates' court which – oddly – was situated 25 miles away from Boston in Skegness. A man had poisoned his neighbour's dog by putting food out for it laced with rat poison. He claimed that the holes the dog persistently dug under the fence that separated the two properties encouraged 'all the vermin in the county' into his garden to wreak havoc with his vegetables. A recently divorced woman in her forties had been charged with a public order offence. She had taken to hanging articles of her obese ex-husband's oversized underwear over the heads of the two-metres high Scotch thistles he had once cultivated in their front garden. London seemed tame by comparison. I read through the list of entries in a ladies' bowls tournament. I checked the Births, Deaths and Marriages. I checked for anybody who for any reason had their name in the paper. But I found no 'McDonald'.

Questioning the locals was a tricky business. You have to work to a stratagem. You can't just approach anyone in the street, or just tap the person in front of you in a queue on the shoulder and ask them if they happen to know or have heard of a family McDonald. I was quite pleased with my solution. First, you ask a dummy question - one that breaks the ice. Then you can get to the meat of the matter. I noted down a few ideas. Like – 'I'm sorry to bother you, but do you happen to know where Such-and-Such Street is? (And here you have to be quite sure that Such-and-Such street does not exist anywhere around – often not as easy as it might sound). Their answer - at least, as long as you've done your homework - is going to be 'No, sorry, can't help, etc'. Which then lets you lead quite naturally into - "Ok, thank you. I'm just trying to locate a very old friend who – etc., etc. - name of 'McDonald'." And if, by any remote chance, they do know of a 'McDonald', they'll hopefully give you whatever information they have.

But not only wasn't it easy - it was often quite uncomfortable. My first few attempts – people in shops, and one or two whom I approached almost at random in the street - caused me much embarrassment and general awkwardness. I fear, in retrospect, I may have covered that up by being pushy, perhaps even slightly aggressive. Just the sort of thing to make them remember you. Shades once again of the hatter's.

I'd thought of cafés as having potential. People there are captive, seated, hopefully relaxed. But during the day I found such places patronized more by women than by men. Going up to a woman sitting on her own drinking her coffee and asking her if she knows Such-and-Such Street is likely to be interpreted as a cheap come-on. On one occasion I approached, without really thinking, a woman with a small, demanding child in tow. She was civil enough, but hadn't really the time or the patience. And I felt in any case she wasn't entirely sure of my motives. I avoided similar situations. However, on the one occasion when I went up to three female pensioners drinking tea and eating cakes I was perfectly at ease. Two of them were openly flirtatious, to which I responded likewise. Though it produced nothing about McDonald, it made for a pleasant few minutes.

I thought maybe I should find workmen's cafés, truckstops. I found a couple of the latter on the A16 road that runs between Grimsby in the north of the county, and Peterborough in the next county to the south. They were never very full. It clearly wasn't a major trucking route. But in any case, almost every one of the drivers I spoke to - most of whom seemed to take me for some sort of upper-class screwball - came from hundreds of miles away, often right the other end of Europe.

Pubs should have been easy. In theory. The theory being that people – especially men – with a glass in their hand were likely to be more genial and helpful than if they were accosted in the street. But time and again, as I set foot in a new pub, conversation would stop and suspicious male faces turn in my direction. It was very off-putting; a sort of silent aggression.

If my initial overtures were snubbed – as was often the case - I couldn't persist. And what I did manage to elicit amounted to little. There was – or had been – a McDonald just outside Skegness. A man who kept a hardware store. But he'd gone out of business. I nevertheless drove there. It was a 'Nail Parlour' now. And questioning those living close by, it seemed he'd left the area some years ago and had been unmarried anyway. In a remote area right on the edge of my twenty-mile limit, a woman in her eighties with an off-putting amount of hair on her upper lip – a Marian McDonald - ran a farm with her two sons, both unmarried and in their fifties. They knew of no local McDonald. The three of them were strange to the point of creepy. They appeared to live together, and I found myself seriously wondering just what was the relationship between Marion McDonald and her sons. An old man in the bar of the White Hart itself had a recollection of a Peter – or was it 'Michael'? - McDonald who many years ago ran a smallholding on the outskirts of Boston. I went there. A block of flats was built on the land in the 1970's.

It was depressing. Though not enough to suggest the principle was at fault. Indeed, I booked my room for a further week. What did however persuade me I was not entirely on the right track was an incident which occurred the following Monday in a village some miles to the north. It was in a pub called 'The Jolly Farmer' – which, from what I'd seen of the local agricultural community, was a bit of a misnomer. I walked into the saloon bar mid-morning, ordered a half pint of shandy and, there being no other drinker, soon got into conversation with the landlord. It was easy enough to slip in, along the way, a more or less airy, "Do you happen to know of anyone – any family – in the area by the name of McDonald? Just out of interest?"

"McDonald?" His eyes narrowed. "You must be the bloke from Old Leake they say's been asking about."

Time to go. Time to drop the principle. The sparseness of inhabitants around here was clearly no bar on the rapid transmission of gossip. I looked at my watch and brought the exchange to an end. I drank up, thanked him, bade him a good morning and left. He knew no McDonald anyway. Every driver in every vehicle I passed on the road was surely looking at me, thinking, 'Ah, there he is - the bloke from Old Leake.'

I needed to go to ground. Have a rethink.

It was warm for October. A few flowers were still in bloom in the pub garden. I sat at a solid, reassuring wooden table. Twirled my half-pint glass thoughtfully around. How I needed the damned internet! Never mind asking questions of graceless bumpkins. I needed access to all the things I knew were there for the taking by those who can use computers. I needed a researcher. Like in the old days. And outside of Westminster, the only person I knew with the mind of a researcher was Ellen.

Then all the doubts once again came flooding back. Licia, by the river that day - "For God's sake Bee, are you sure you've got this right?" No, not any longer. Should I just chuck it all? Shave off the beard. Cut the hair. Go back to being 'me'. Get measured for another Savile Row suit. Wear a tie. Call it a day, and go home.

'Home'? Where's that? You, Friend, have no home. An outcast by your own hand. And that old 'me' you might return to – is that the real 'me'? Or is this latter one you've so carefully crafted the real one? Or is there a real real 'me' which might yet emerge from this one? Fact is, old boy, you've no longer any idea who you are.

And then there came a voice in my ear – familiar even after all this time - tender, compassionate, understanding as it had always seemed. 'Have a drink. Be kind to yourself. For a while, let it all go hang. What is this life, so full of care – and all that?'

Ah - but I can't. Not again. Never again.

I took my empty glass back into the bar, then went upstairs to my room to lie down. I felt really despondent. Had I simply left it all too late? All things have their moment; miss it and you play catch-up forever, but never do. That day in the park, I should have removed her finger from my lips and spoken up. That is the sin at the heart of all this.

As I ate my dinner that evening I was in an agitated state. If I'm to continue with this, I have to learn how to use a computer. Then I can do all my research sitting on my backside instead of this never-ending running around, annoying others and embarrassing myself. Why I had accepted so readily that IT was beyond me, I've no idea. It may be I've no inborn talent for it, but I can surely learn enough.

On the other hand, I had to admit to finding something appealing in this running around – never knowing quite what was going to happen next, the fresh air, new faces, new and unfamiliar places. The idea of exchanging it for sitting in front of a screen, day after day, in Kilburn with the Underground rattling the teacups hardly stirred my blood.

But then, as I thought a little more about it, the obvious occurred to me – internet research was not confined to Kilburn. Or to anywhere. I could rent a cottage - sun-drenched and bougainvillea-encircled - in the Dordogne; work with the scent of herbs drifting in through my window. Get fresh baked bread from the village boulangerie. Nobody there would point me out as 'the bloke from Old Leake.'

Lay the ghost of the computer – I had my answer! My agitation eased off. I finished my dinner feeling almost elated. So much so in fact that I treated myself to a double measure of my favourite malt whisky - Laphroaig. I took it and sat in a quiet corner away from the bright lights around the bar. There were a lot of people in and I didn't want to get drawn into conversation with any of them.

Some way through my Laphroaig, musing idly on whether it should be the Dordogne or a pleasant corner of one of the smaller Canary Islands, I sensed I had company. I looked up. A man stood looking down at me. He seemed utterly out of place in a pub. He was wearing a black trilby hat, black leather jacket and waistcoat. At his neck a large, floppy blue cravat hung loosely down over a deep red shirt. His trousers matched his shirt, while over his shoulders he wore a flowing grey cape. I was nonplussed. Then panic hit me. Some strange, covert arm of government had tracked me down.

He inclined his body forward in a clipped and practised movement. "Please excuse me," he said, and smiled.

I uttered what I hoped was a passably calm, "Good evening."

He removed the trilby. "I'm sorry to disturb you." He was soft-spoken with what I took to be an Eastern European accent.

I took a hold of myself. He was more likely having a drink after an am-dram rehearsal than on an errand for MI6. "Can I help you?" I asked.

"I believe," he said, holding the trilby rather nervously in both hands in front of him, "you look for Mister McDonald?"

I sat up. "Yes!" I said. "I do. How did you know?"

He pointed back towards the bar. "Mister Mick."

Mick was the landlord. I knew him by no other name. When I'd asked him about McDonald he'd frowned and shaken his head.

"Yes," I said. "I am looking for Mister McDonald. He's a very old friend of mine. Do you know him?"

He shook his head. "But there is a lady knows about him."

I frowned. "Knows 'about' him? What lady?"

"His name is not McDonald round here."

"His name is not McDonald 'round here'?"

He shook his head. "It is 'Jordan'."

I pulled a chair from under the table. "Look, please sit down."

"Thank you. But I am with a friend."

"Do you mean Mister McDonald changed his name to 'Jordan'?"

"You have to talk with the lady, sir. She is in Marsh Enderby. It is not far from here."

"I know it. Who is she, this lady?"

"Celeste."

"Just – 'Celeste'? Where do I find her?"

"'Amsterdam Freighter' pub. She works with the tables there – you know – food. Brings food for breakfast and - "

"She's a waitress?"

"Yes. That is it. Breakfast waitress."

"But does Mister Jordan still live around here?"

"I don't know," he said. "But Celeste knows about him." He looked back towards the bar where a woman with dark hair was looking in his direction. "I have to go. I hope that is a help." He turned to leave but I stopped him. "When I meet this lady," I said, "who shall I say told me about her?"

"Ah." He thought. Then said, with a twinkle in his eye, "Tell her 'Mister Mackeson'."

I frowned. "Mister Mackeson?"

"She will know."

I watched him weave his way back through the other drinkers. 'Mackeson'? Like the drink? He joined the woman with dark hair at the bar. She kissed him on the cheek.

I sat back, sipped my whisky. This had a strange feel to it. Was I being set up? A lady with the slightly pretentious name of 'Celeste'? A man who is known 'round here' as – and then I almost spilled my Laphroaig– 'Jordan'. 'Jordan' was Stella's maiden name.

35.

Dusk moves in off the desert. Lights come on in the bar. I finish off the remains of a second beer. Seven o'clock. Still no Youssef. With the dusk, come the flying insects. They flitter about the two bare electric bulbs that hang from the ceiling. I have spun two beers out beyond their natural life. I resist a third. A third would send me to sleep. Even without it, my eyelids are drooping.

Someone to talk to would help me stay awake. But I can make no sense of the barman's French, and he in any case has retired to a windowless cubbyhole at the back where he watches a black and white television with the volume turned up. Two other drinkers sit across the far side of the room. They are not local. Their faces are too black, too round. They talk to each other in guttural, staccato voices as though angry with each other. The next minute they're laughing and slapping each other on the back. I have them down as Nigerian. I shake my head and look away. The world needs more understanding than I can bring to it.

I wipe my brow with a tissue. I fold my arms on the table, lean forward and rest my head on them. My eyes close and I drift into a semiconscious confusion of sounds and images.

He is European. English. And white. 'Gaston'. Maybe 'Matthew' or 'Matt'. Or anything else he might have made up – 'His intimate friends call him Candle-ends', said Lewis Carroll. Late thirties. Came here to earn money. Doing what we don't know, but within the last few months. Look, a photograph. Taken twenty years ago, I'm afraid. No, you're right, I don't suppose he does. Apologies for troubling you. But then – then there was the kossai woman. She looked too old and fragile to be outdoors on her own – the woman who sold kossai by the side of the road. 'They fry black-eyed peas,' Youssef says to him, in his half-dream. 'With garlic. Very nutritious. You should try.' And Youssef speaks with the old woman in Hausa and she says, "Things are not good. The world comes here now."

"We're looking for a white man. An Englishman."

"What," she asks, "is 'Englishman'? An American?"

"A white man."

"There are white men from some country."

"Which country?"

She shrugs. She is uncomfortable.

"You've seen them?"

"They are here now. There is an American with them."

"An American? How do you know? Have you seen him?"

She glances around. Shakes her head.

"Then how do you know that - ?"

"They stopped and bought kossai."

"Who did?"

"I don't know." She shakes her head again. "I have to work now."

Youssef persists. "Please – tell me. Who stopped and bought - ?"

"Two white men in a truck. One man came and bought. The other shouted for him to get one for the American. But I did not see the American."

"What sort of truck?"

"Red."

"Was it big? Small?"

But she is agitated now, and fearful. "Go. I am busy." She grunts and emits a sibilant noise from between what teeth she has left. They walk away with their kossai. Youssef is strangely excited. "She says, there is an American." He said it like he'd turned up a stone and found a diamond. "What help," says a lost Barney, "is an American?" "It is the same thing to these people – white man speaking English is American. This 'American' could be an Englishman – that is what I am saying."

I am floating across the rose garden. The roses are fading now but the philadelphus is still in full leaf. It bushes out wide, wider than I've ever seen it. I know that I will see only what I always see. I drift closer. And there - there is the red scarf trailing to the gravel path in this yellowing October light. The long, black coat and then the man - seated, head turned the other way, never this way. Closer still, till I am so close I could almost reach out and touch a lock of the hair which overhangs, just a little, the red scarf at the back of the neck and which is still as fine and of the same light brown colour as when it used to hang over his crumpled collar as he rocked from side to side in the pushchair. Please turn my way. But leaves, blown hither and thither by the wind block my view and when they've settled again the man is not there. But on the seat where he sat, I see a bright metallic object. It is silver, and like a pendant, inset with a stone, red like a ruby. I bend down and am about to take it in my fingers when, in the last of the dying sun, the stone catches fire, flooding my world and blinding me with a deep, blood-redness.

Something is touching my shoulder. Crying out, I spin round.

The Nigerians are staring at me. The flies buzz about the lights. Youssef, in his Western T-shirt and trademark wraparound, rimless shades has a hand on my shoulder. He is looking down at me, smiling.

Youssef delved into his briefcase. I watched. I never got used to the fact that in such a remote and primitive place – as it was to me - there were people, like Youssef, wearing Ray-Ban shades, Breitling watches and sporting leather briefcases that would make those of many of my erstwhile colleagues look cheap by comparison.

He pulled out a large, spiral-bound notebook and lay it before him on the table.

"What time," I asked, "do we leave tomorrow?"

He looked at me.

"What time tomorrow?"

He flicked through the pages of the notebook.

"We are leaving tomorrow, Youssef. Aren't we?"

He tapped the book. "They found a vehicle."

My heart went haywire. "Who," I said, struggling with my breathing, "found a vehicle?"

"The police."

"What police?"

"In Iferouane."

Iferouane. I winced. "What sort of vehicle?"

"Suzuki pickup."

"Red?"

He nodded.

"Fuck." I took a deep breath. "Where," I said, "is Iferouane?"

"In the Air Mountains. But the vehicle is in the Tenere."

The Nigerians called for more beer. Glancing back over his shoulder at the television, the barman emerged from his cubbyhole.

"What," I asked, "is the Tenere?"

He shrugged. "Part of the desert."

"When you say it's been found, what do you - ?

"They saw it from a helicopter."

"Just – 'saw' it? Didn't they go down and - ?"

"It is like that." He imitated, with an outstretched hand, the steep, up-and-down wave-configuration of the dunes. "Helicopter cannot land there."

"Are there footsteps around it, or leading away from it? Anything that might indicate - ?"

"No footsteps. But the sand drifts all the time, so – we have to go there."

"We have to go?"

He nodded. "It has not been there many days."

"How do they know that?"

"By the way the sand is. How much is drifted against it."

I turned away, looked out through the grill into the night. The few street lamps flickered. Some youths kicked a football around. Am I, in this African darkness, about to journey to the centre of the maze? My heart has not yet stopped its pounding.

The Nigerians resumed their noisy chatter over recharged glasses.

I breathed deeply, calmed myself, then turned back to Youssef. "How far?"

"Four days. But first we go to Iferouane."

"Why?"

"We have to go to the police. That part of the Tenere is a protected area. We have to tell them."

"Why is it protected? What's special about it?"

He shrugged. "Famous. Very big desert."

"How big?"

"Four hundred thousand square kilometres."

My jaw dropped. "Four hundred thousand square kilometres of sand?"

He nodded. "One town."

"Just one?"

"Bilma. Where they get salt."

I wiped my brow with my tissue. "Why," I asked, "would anybody be driving on the dunes in the middle of the desert?"

"People do these things. Some for some crazy reason."

"And if you broke down?"

He shrugged. "You stay with your vehicle."

"Mobile phone?"

He shook his head. "No signal."

"But what if you don't stay with your vehicle? Some get out and walk, don't they? Then what?"

Again he shrugged. "Where you walk to?"

"That place - Bilma?"

He chuckled. "You know which way - East? West? South?"

I persisted. "But suppose you do know. How far?"

"Two hundred kilometres."

I blanched.

"Temperature - 50C. Maybe more."

I gave up.

"You walk?" He shook his head. "No chance."

Laughing loudly, the Nigerians stood up and made their way from the room. The barman, his elbows on the bar, was gazing idly at the pair of us.

36.

Open on Ellen's desk beside her new laptop was a small desk diary. Its well-thumbed pages were covered in neat, handwritten notes. Off to one side was a low table, one half of which was taken up by two photo albums, one of them open. The other half of the table was covered in photographic prints of varying sizes. Each of them showed herself or Barney singly, or the pair of them together, often with other people. Each print had stuck to it a Post-it note bearing a handwritten code number.

She transcribed from the open diary. 'Jan 11. Friday. B was approached today with a view to standing for Parliament – of all things! One of the clients on this political account – which he really doesn't enjoy working on, poor man – is an old Oxford acquaintance who apparently told him quite seriously that he'd make a good - '

The telephone rang. She stopped, stared at it, hoping the caller would hang up. They didn't. She took off her spectacles, placed them carefully on the desk in front of her and picked up the receiver. Her, "Yes?" was intentionally off-putting. But then she smiled. "Oh, hello. Right. Mmm - that would be nice. Yes - I'm working on it right now. Stay afterwards for a spot of lunch if you've time – there's some cold lamb in the fridge. See you soon then." She replaced the receiver very slowly. Placed her hands gently against her cheeks to ease the slight flush she sensed rising there. She sat quietly for a few seconds. Then stood up and left the room.

In her bedroom she took off her jeans. Selected a loose, casual skirt which she lay carefully on the bed. Then stood before the mirror. Her legs were horribly white. Between finger and thumb of both hands she took her slip, and hoisted it an inch or two. They would need tights. She sorted out a pair of black ones and tugged them on. She settled them around her waist with fingers that hurt just a little in the joints. She stood once again before the mirror.

After a moment's thought, she glanced at her watch, pulled the tights off as quickly as she could and threw them on the bed. She took from her underwear drawer a pair of black stockings and matching suspender belt.

She continued typing where she'd left off.

'One of the clients on this political account – which he really doesn't enjoy working on, poor man – is an old Oxford acquaintance who apparently told him quite seriously that he'd make a good politician. B wasn't sure he felt it was the compliment the man had intended. Apparently he laughed out loud! Then apologized. However, we decided it might be worth at least following up. B is not proud to be working in advertising. But I reminded him that it's through advertising that he's met all these influential people. We agreed we'd think more about the proposal.'

Ellen pushed the diary aside. Looked through the photographs, selected one, placed it by the keyboard and continued typing.

'Photo No. H/LP90/32. 'B's father dies. Quite unexpected. B hadn't seen him for a long time. He is seriously distressed. It surprised me. He always claimed to have little time for him, blaming him for his mother's alcoholism and her general degeneration. I don't see that. Alcoholism is a personal choice. I never knew her. B and I met at her funeral. I said to him what a strange place for a first date. He wasn't sure how to - '

She heard a car outside. Stopped and looked up. She left her desk and went to the window. The familiar blue Volvo was turning into the gravel drive. She straightened her skirt, fluffed up her hair, and went from the room.

"Thank you, Ellen." Frank Lippincote took the glass of wine and sat himself down in an armchair. "I hope this isn't inconveniencing you – my just dropping in like this."

"You haven't just dropped in. You rang."

"Even so, I didn't want to - "

"How could you possibly inconvenience me Frank, when you'd rung to ask and I'd said, Yes?" She sat herself in the chair opposite.

He laughed rather nervously. "One says these things."

"Anyway." She raised her glass. "Bottoms up."

"Indeed. Yes." He too raised his glass and they drank. "Mmm." He savoured the wine. "Very nice. One of Barney's, I guess?"

"Where else?"

"Knew his grapes, didn't he?" He settled back in his chair. "So," he said, summoning up his avuncular tone, "how's Ellen now?"

She smiled a wan smile. "Ellen's life goes on."

"Good. Good." He twirled his glass around in his fingers. "I'm sorry I felt it necessary the other day to leave it to Jardine to do the deed. If you know what I mean."

She looked down into her drink. "It depressed the hell out of me, Frank. However – It was better I heard it that way than find out accidentally at some future time." She sipped her wine. "And in a way, it did me a favour – it got me up off my backside."

"Excellent." He rubbed his hands together. "And how is the book coming on? Or perhaps it's still too early?"

"I'm still making notes. Creating a shape. You have to remember I've never done this sort of thing before. Progress is hardly rapid. But – well, it's ok."

"Listen." He put his glass on a small side table and sat forward. "I've heard from Osborne. He says he'll be delighted. I knew he would be."

She smiled. But said nothing.

"Doesn't that – well – excite you just a little? Osborne's one of the best, and - "

"Frank - if I'm honest, I'm not one hundred percent at ease with the whole thing. It still feels a little bit like cashing in on a tragedy."

"Whose tragedy?"

She looked out of the window past the beech tree, towards the distant hills. "Mine as much as his – yes I know."

"And as you yourself have said - life goes on."

She turned back to him. "I'm just not sure it has to go on in quite this way. It's not as though I need the money." She shrugged. "Even so – let's keep going as we are."

"Bravo. I'm sure that's right. The book will do well." He nodded, sagely. "People really can't get enough of the domestic lives of those in the public eye."

"I would hardly have classed Barney as having been 'in the public eye'.

"Sufficiently so though, I sense. Especially as the man disappeared overnight, without trace. That gives his profile an enormous fillip."

"That aside, I can't think where the fascination lies."

"Their lives, Ellen. Their lives."

"Whose lives?"

"I've sat in on Gillian Mountfoot's surgeries. There's a sense of pointlessness out there. An undertow even of anger."

"Pointlessness and anger about what? They've got more now than they've ever had. Far more than you and I had, Frank, thirty or forty years ago."

"Then maybe they've got too much."

"There's all that binge drinking. There's thousands on benefit. Yet they can still go out and buy big televisions, drive cars. I really don't have a lot of sympathy."

"Well, whatever the reason, those same people are in awe of the lives of those they see as glamorous – the 'celebs' as the current jargon has it."

"Life with Barney was never 'glamorous'."

"No? Flying around the world? Gala dinners and balls, dressed up to the nines? Hobnobbing with the famous?" He raised his eyebrows questioningly. "Not to you, perhaps."

"Alright. But then I'd have to ask – isn't this sort of book - " - she pointed to the laptop - " - just catching a rather dubious ride? Wouldn't we do better to try and kill those illusions?"

He chuckled. "Having said all I've said, the world works the way the world works. Who are we to tell others what to like and what not to like?" He smiled his knowing smile.

Ellen looked hard at him.

He found it a touch unsettling. "What? " he asked.

"We've never talked much before have we, you and I? Not really talk. I see another side to you. I quite warm to it." And she raised her glass to him.

Frank, enormously encouraged, though not entirely sure by what, went on enthusiastically. "I'll set up a meeting with Neville Osborne. Consummate professional. He asked me, by the way, if you had a working title. I said I wasn't aware of it if you did. Have you thought about it?" He picked up his glass. "It'd be a nice gesture if we could give him one."

She thought for a second. "'Life and death with Barnaby Marechal'. How about that?"

He was horrified.

"Oh God!" She buried her face in her hands "I'm sorry. I don't know where that came from." She shook her head slowly from side to side. "It was horrible."

Frank watched, his brows knitted.

She removed her hands from her face. Looked straight at him. Her eyes were moist. "Where's he gone, Frank?"

He went to say something, but didn't. Shook his head, muttered something inaudible.

"D'you know," she said, quietly, looking at the sun slanting across the hills beyond the window, "I have to think now to remember the sound of his voice." She turned to him. "I would never have thought that possible." She paused. "And after that meeting with Harry Jardine I do sometimes wonder if he's run off with another woman."

Frank reached for the wine bottle and topped up their glasses.

"And that son of his – has he been living some double life with the man that I know nothing about?"

"Jardine said not."

"Jardine said not as far as he knew. Not quite the same thing."

"This has all been terribly hard on you, hasn't it?"

She pulled a tissue from a box and dabbed her nose.

They sat in silence. Outside a breeze rustled the last few leaves on the beech tree.

He looked into her eyes. He was reminded of the eyes of a hurt child. Before he knew it, he had left his armchair and was kneeling before her, his arms resting on her knees. He looked up into her face. Though she kept her eyes from his, she made no attempt to move him.

"Ellen. Ellen, I can't bear seeing you like this."

Her eyes were still on some point beyond the horizon. "I have to get past it, Frank. I have a life to lead." She looked down at him for the first time. "Don't I?" Her eyes remained on his, as though awaiting his affirmation.

Time for him had stopped. The world was those wide, wide eyes. A tear appeared and started slowly down her cheek. He reached up and with the tip of a finger stroked it tenderly away. Her eyes remained on his. Her face was coming gently down towards him, her mouth just a little open, her lips soft, swelling. A sort of horror hit him – that this might be a dream. Did she mean this? Did she know what she was doing? Was he thinking things he had no right to think? But her face was now so close he could feel her bodily warmth. Her perfume filled his head, flinging his judgement to the winds. His heart pounded, he caught at his breath. Her cheek was then laid against his, so soft, and her lips were suddenly, urgently seeking his out – they touched and the years, all the years, fell away.

Outside in the garden he heard a bird singing, singing to them, a song to them. This was no dream. They were no longer used, either of them, to tearing off their clothes in the heat and swirl of passion. They fumbled, trying not to look at each other. Limbs that once moved like the wings of birds, though having no less urgency, creak now, stretch and take their time. But there are things that will be. They shuffled and juddered in a frenzied confusion towards the sofa where, in the fullness of their own time, they lay among the cushions and moved, cried and held each other in the shifting sun.

"Probably best not to make a habit of it." Ellen's voice eventually broke the silence. Despite her stockings crumpled around her knees, she managed somehow to pull them off then wriggle into her knickers, all while still sitting.

Frank looked the other way as he tugged on his underwear.

Ellen stood up.

Frank kept his eyes averted.

She picked up her skirt.

Frank cleared his throat.

They dressed, avoiding each other's eyes.

Frank tied his tie, put on his suit jacket and sat upright in his armchair like a man about to be interviewed for a job. Ellen's bra and stockings were on the floor right at his feet. There was now the problem of how to move forward in this fundamentally changed landscape. He and Martha had not made love – had sex, whatever - in years. Martha had been only his second ever. He felt jangled, disturbed. Not knowing where to look, he kept his eyes fixed in front, letting them encounter whatever passed before them.

The clock ticked. The bird in the garden still sang. Ellen finished off the last dregs of her wine. Placed the empty glass on the table. "Well," she said, "as we observed earlier– life goes on. Time for lunch." She went to the door, then turned back. "Didn't talk an awful lot about the book, did we?"

Frank sat staring straight ahead.

37.

In pursuit of the enigmatic Celeste, Barnaby Marechal cancelled the rest of his week's booking at 'The White Hart' in Old Leake and moved to 'The Amsterdam Freighter' in Marsh Enderby.

His first impressions of that place, all acquired on that first day from the window of Fido, had been quite misleading. The staff turned out to be friendly and courteous. The woman who booked him in even asked a young man in a white apron to take his case up to his room for him. The room itself was comfortable and warm. The bed had a nice firm mattress. That evening he enjoyed a nicely-cooked dinner of local roast chicken and vegetables which he washed down with a couple of glasses of a more than passable house rosé. After which, he went back up to his room to sit down and mull on this developing situation.

He was hopeful. Even a little excited. If the things the odd 'Mister Mackeson' had told him in the White Hart were true, then it seemed he really could be onto something. But then he'd been 'onto something' before, and got nowhere. He needed to be calm. And just hope the 'Celeste' woman was indeed on breakfast duty the following morning.

In anticipation of that encounter, he needed to prepare himself. The overriding requirement was that he - a perfect stranger in her eyes - should come across as personable, open and trustworthy. But then an accidental glimpse of himself caught in the wardrobe mirror gave him a shock. His hair straggled in lank wisps to his shoulders. The beard had bushed out, almost to eccentricity. His Calvin Klein jeans had gone slightly baggy at the knees. And having lost some weight, his lovely black leather jacket rather hung on him. He looked like the sort of oddball who might accost you in the street and thrust into your hand a leaflet warning you the world would end next week.

The hair was the most pressing. In the early days of this mission he'd bought a pair of special, hair-cutting scissors. With them he'd been able, every now and then, to hack at his lengthening locks without having to be too concerned about the end result. Tomorrow was different - her first impression of him would be crucial. Another of his amateur choppings would likely make matters worse rather than better. The answer came to him in the shape of that dreadful hair gel he'd bought in Wigan. He still carried with with him. A judicious blob of that would tame the more straggly ends, at least for the duration of breakfast.

Trimming the beard was no problem. Nor were the baggy jeans. Just along the corridor he'd noticed an iron and ironing board for the use of guests. As for the black leather jacket - wear it open maybe. A touch of nonchalance, casualness seemed a good idea. He mustn't appear staid or too conventional.

He lay in bed, composing his mind. Assuming a woman is on breakfast duty in the morning, how is he going to know if she is Celeste? I guess, he told himself, I'll just have to find a reason to ask her name. It can't be that difficult.

Barney stood in the doorway of the lounge bar, looked around, and smiled. The morning sun through mullioned windows set ablaze a deep red carpet. It lit up cut flowers in polished copper bowls, glinted off horse brasses and reflected off highly-shone tabletops. In a huge open fireplace, a fire was laid ready for lighting, logs stacked either side of it.

A corner of the room had been set aside for breakfasts. The tables were nicely laid - a red flower in a little vase on each. He was relieved to note however there was only one actual place setting. With what he had to do he would feel a lot more at ease with no audience. He sat down and looked around. So where was she? On the far side of the bar counter was a door with a small porthole-type window. Presumably the door to the kitchen. If she were on duty she was perhaps in there. He sat back. He looked around. Find something to occupy his mind.

He could see his head and shoulders reflected in a mirror behind the bar. His hair looked just about OK. He smoothed it nervously with both hands. He turned to look out of the window. On the far side of a narrow lane, half hidden by shadowy yew trees, was a church, its yellowed stones warming in the sun. A black bird with a bright yellow beak stood on a wall, flicking its tail up and down. Late autumn leaves drifted past the window. He closed his eyes, listened to the birds and sensed his own breathing of this clean, fresh country air.

"Good morning!"

His eyes shot open.

"Apologies for the delay. Problems with the toaster."

He sat forward and took her in in an instant. Tallish and shapely. Fiftyish? Silver rings on the fingers of both hands. Brown eyes and auburn-if-slightly-greying hair tied loosely back. A 'womanly woman' with nothing coy or flamboyant about her, natural, refreshing. Beneath a short apron, decorated with pictures of the Lake District, she wore nicely-fitting blue jeans.

She put a hand over her mouth to mask a yawn. "They keep saying they'll get a new one. Sorry."

He smiled. "I'm not in a hurry."

From a pocket in her apron she produced a little notepad and a pencil. With the pencil she indicated the view beyond the window. "You've brought the nice weather back." She hovered the pencil over the pad. "Ready to order?" She looked expectantly at him. Her eyes were sharp, intelligent. Was this her? He rather hoped it was.

"Continental or full English?" Her voice was attractively modulated. She was well-spoken with a touch of an accent that might have been almost Scottish. The ordinariness of her waitress's outfit didn't conceal her style. Her vibes seemed hardly those of a country girl.

"Full English please," he said. "I'll indulge myself."

"Why not? A bit of what you fancy. And would you like your eggs fried, poached or scrambled, and how many?"

"Poached, please. And two."

"Toast, marmalade, coffee?"

"Please. All three."

"The full works. That's nice." She pointed towards a large antique dresser against the far wall. "Cereals, milk, sugar, fruit juices etc. over there. Help yourself." And with a breezy, "Back soon!" she left and headed towards the kitchen. He watched. She almost swept out, as from a country house ballroom, leaving in her wake, a faint but unmistakable hint of – of all things - Chanel No.5. The intrigue deepened.

He sat back. He'd pass on the cereals. He'd wait. And think. What a very nice shape the lady was. He hoped this was indeed Celeste.

"Nice to see an empty plate!"

Barney brushed the napkin across his lips. "That's what my mother used to say."

"Ah - Mother knows best!" She picked up the empty plate, and as she was doing so, said casually, "Here on business, are you?"

Excellent! She had handed him the opening. "No," he said. "I'm here on what you might call a personal mission. I'm looking for a lady."

"Oh dear," she said, balancing the empty plate on her arm. "You might look a long time."

He frowned, puzzled.

She smiled, and he caught up. He felt rather foolish and grinned. "Sorry," he said. "A bit early in the morning." He gathered himself together. "I'm looking for a lady who I've been told works here - in this pub. I don't know her surname – just 'Celeste'. Do you happen to have - ?"

She dropped a snappy and skilfully executed curtsy.

"You?" He pointed to her. "You are Celeste?"

"Sir, I am Celeste. Well - at least I'm a Celeste. Do you mind telling me where you got my name?"

He said, with some slight misgivings, "Does 'Mister Mackeson' ring a bell?"

"Oh." She looked pleasantly surprised. "Do you know him?"

"I met him. In a bar a couple of nights ago."

"Andy – at least we call him 'Andy' – Andrzej Kowalski. Polish. He wants to be an actor. Hence the cloak. I presume he was wearing a cloak?"

"He was indeed."

"He wants to act but never really does anything about it. So he acts the actor. Anyway – you didn't want his life story." She rested the empty plate on the table. "So - now you've found me, I'm intrigued."

"OK. Your Andy told me that you might know something about some old friends of mine who used to live in this area. I'm hoping they still do, but I lost contact with them some years back. You know how it is."

"Well, I don't come from round here myself, but I'll do my best." But then suddenly she was looking curiously at him. "I'm sorry," she said, "I hope you don't mind my saying this, but haven't I seen you somewhere before?"

His heart leapt into his throat. There was always going to be a first time, but it was unexpected after as long as this. Speak slowly, calmly as though nothing could be less likely. "I really don't think so," he said. "This is my very first time in this part of the country."

"Mmm. Yes, I'm sorry. I must be mistaken."

He cleared his throat. "The name of the family I'm looking for is 'McDonald'."

Did he detect just the slightest widening of the eyes? "Or," he went on, "it might possibly be Jordan."

She looked rather blankly back at him for a second or two. Then uttered a strangely flat, "I see."

"Does the name, 'Stella Jordan' mean anything to you?"

"I – er - it depends what you want to know, I suppose."

Her sudden discomfort spurred him on. "So you do know them? Or you know of them?"

She picked up the empty plate. "I may have heard the name. I'm really not sure." She turned to go. "As I told you, I don't come from - "

"Can I just ask you then – did you ever know if - ?"

"Celeste!"

She looked towards the kitchen.

"Laundry!" An older woman's face was peering round the kitchen door. "It's only you and me today, remember."

"I'm sorry," she said to Barney. "I have to go." As she turned to leave he shot out a hand and grabbed her by the wrist. She cried out.

"Sorry!" He released her instantly. "I'm so sorry. But please – please stay for a second."

She rubbed her wrist.

"Please forgive me. But there's something I really need to ask you."

She remained, looking warily down at him.

"It's possible you may be able to help me with something that's very, very important to me. Please, may I just give you my mobile number, and ask you to ring me when you're free?"

She said nothing.

While he'd still got her, he grabbed the pen from his pocket and scribbled his mobile number on his napkin.

"Celeste!!"

"Coming!"

He handed it to her. Without a glance at it, she tucked it into the back pocket of her jeans and hurried away to the kitchen.

The door closed behind her. Her shadow crossed the circular window then was gone. He sat back, ran a hand through his hair. He'd been on the point of bungling that. Indeed, there was nothing so far to say he hadn't. But at least she'd put it in her pocket. What was certain, was that here at the Amsterdam Freighter he'd stumbled across something.

He heard nothing from Celeste that day. He'd hardly expected to. But nor was she on duty at breakfast the following morning. Her place had been taken by the young man who had carried his case for him the previous day when he'd arrived. Then, he had been affable; now he was surly and seemed to be working under protest. When asked where Celeste was he said he didn't know but she probably had the collywobbles again. Which, being asked, he translated as, "Gut ache." He said she wasn't permanent staff anyway, and worked only when she felt like it. He didn't conceal his irritation. Barney ordered his breakfast. He too felt irritable.

After breakfasting he went out, bought the latest edition of one of the local newspapers and sat on a bench by the green to read it. There was no 'McDonald' in it. Or 'Jordan'. He wandered aimlessly around the village, most of his attention tuned to the mobile in his pocket. What few people were about looked curiously at him, making him feel distinctly uncomfortable. He made for the church. The thought of sitting for a while, alone in silence appealed to him. But the church was locked. If you wanted the key you were asked, via a handwritten notice sellotaped to the door and faded almost to illegibility, to contact one or other of the churchwardens. The sun had gone and it had turned cold. Winter was coming.

He returned to his room in 'The Amsterdam Freighter'. He took his scarf from his suitcase, went back down to the car park, sat himself at the wheel of Fido and headed for Skegness. The only thing he knew about Skegness was that ancient poster of the ageing old salt prancing along the sands – 'Skegness is SO bracing'. It wasn't today. The skies were leaden. A car park the size of a prairie had three cars in it. The windows of one were steamed up. It rocked gently from side to side. He ventured onto the pier, sat looking out over the sea. A wind straight off the Baltic whipped up white crests on the grey water and threatened to cut him in half. He left the pier and walked around the town.

It was surely a shadow of its former self. What few people were on the streets seemed in a hurry to be off them. The pinball machine arcades were full of noise and flashing lights and almost empty of punters. 'Vacancies' notices hung in boarding house and hotel windows. Lingering along every parade of small shops, was the odour of over-used cooking fat. Barney returned to the car and escaped back out into the countryside.

He headed south for Boston – a town he knew less about even than Skegness. But at least it seemed alive, like it had a future. He sat on a public bench by a quite magnificent church. He gazed in admiration at the height of the tower. An old man came and sat beside him. "Boston stump," he said. "That's what they call it." And his rheumy eyes glowed with what Barney took to be civic pride. "Tallest parish church tower in England. D'you know that in years gone by you could see it from twenty miles out to sea." Barney wanted to ask him why you couldn't see it from twenty miles out to sea now. But it was too cold to sit around and chat. And besides, he'd had a sudden brainwave. He'd find a bookshop and buy a book on computers.

Back in his room at 'The Amsterdam Freighter' again, he closed the book and put it to one side. Had it been written in Sanskrit he would have understood only a little less. He looked at his watch. Thirty-six hours now and still no phone call. He lay down on the bed and gazed at the ceiling. Was this trail too going cold? And if it did, where could he possibly turn next?

He got up again, went into the bathroom to shower before dinner. As he was drying himself, he heard his mobile ringing in the bedroom.

A gusty onshore wind rattled the marram grass and struck tiny spurts of sand from the dunes. The sea birds, their heads into the wind, hung almost stationary in the air. Two small cars pulled up side by side facing the sea. As Barney got out of one, the door of the other was opened from the inside. He got in and closed it again.

Neither spoke. Celeste played nervously with one of her rings, twisting it back and forth on its finger. Barney surveyed her from the corner of his eye. She was no country girl. What was she doing on her own in this empty neck of the woods? She wore a loose-fitting and wonderfully hairy jacket, an affair of many colours and shades. South American? And blue jeans – good ones, and perfectly fitting. They hugged her long thighs and sent through him an unexpected and rather unsettling surge of desire.

He edged his body a little more round towards her. Still she tweaked at the rings on her fingers - silver rings on the fingers of both hands. She was a handsome woman. The grey in her rather lovely, long auburn hair aided that impression. One of her earrings glinted where a lick of sunlight caught it. Small, simple, gold. Old gold. The real stuff. And wafting softly across to him, just a suggestion of Chanel No. 5. Bought so many times in Duty Free for Ellen – that now distant figure in an ever-widening landscape.

Who would be the first to speak? He wanted to get on with this.

But then she turned to him. "You're a Scorpio," she said, "aren't you?"

He was nonplussed.

"Aren't you?"

He cleared his throat. "Are you interested in all that?"

"All what?"

"The stars. The zodiac."

"Are you?"

"Not really, no." He shook his head. "I'm afraid I've always rather regarded it as mumbo jumbo."

Looking disconcertingly straight at him, she said, "How do you know?"

"I don't know. But then again, all I've ever had to do with it is read my horoscope in the newspaper every now and then. Mostly for a laugh. But I've never - "

"There are patterns."

"'Patterns'?"

"Psychic patterns that accord with star signs. Are you a Scorpio?" And she smiled.

"As it happens - yes."

"How did I know?" She was pleased with herself.

"You took a guess."

"Twelve to one against?"

"You're obviously something of an expert."

"Not really." She sat back. "It was just a hunch."

He frowned. "Based on what?"

"Look." She pointed to a large, yellow-beaked gull strutting across the ridge of a nearby dune, its feathers ruffled up in the wind. "As you're not into the zodiac, are you into birds?"

"No," he said, thrown again. "I've sometimes wished I were. And flowers. But - "

"That there's a herring gull. I've no idea if it eats herrings."

He frowned. He couldn't somehow catch hold of this.

She resumed looking out of the window. Then, without turning to him, she said quietly, as though she were just passing the time of day, "I have something to tell you."

"Ah." He sat quickly forward. "The McDonalds? Jordan?"

"I know who you are."

His mind emptied.

She turned to him, smiling.

He stared back at her.

"You don't look anything like you used to in the papers. I wouldn't have recognized you at all - under normal circumstances. You know – with the beard and all that."

"So what," he asked, speaking very slowly, "is different about these circumstances that make them abnormal?"

"I know you," she said, her voice and whole demeanour softening, "from an old photograph."

"Uh-huh. Photograph in a newspaper?"

"And I once knew a man who looked like you."

He caught his breath. "Oh?"

"Whose gestures were like yours. Who spoke like you speak."

He ran a hand nervously through his hair.

"A man who ran his hands through his hair like that." She pointed to his hands. "And had the same, slightly flat, wide fingernails."

He looked down at his own hands. Then slowly back up at her. "Are you saying," he said, "what I think you're saying?"

She smiled. "Probably."

His heart thumped, his breath caught in his throat.

The sun was low, and the marram grass rustled in the wind. They walked a narrow path between shoulder-high dunes, Celeste in front with the beach bag, a faraway and bemused Barney wandering along behind, carrying a rolled up beach towel. His head was in a desert space, empty of sign or signal.

He hadn't dressed for a walk in the sand. It was edging in over the top of his brogues, working its way like marbles beneath the soles of his feet. Three or four metres up ahead of him a strange woman - fifteen, perhaps twenty years his junior - who carried with her his son, unborn to him in all these years. This was not how he'd imagined things. How could he have done? He stared at her back. How beautifully she walked. Was any of this real?

They emerged from the seaward edge of the dunes. The beach opened up before them, a plateau of hard, yellow sand stretching on either side to the far distance. The sea was so far out it seemed hardly in this country. A little knot of small birds scuttled comically along the shoreline dodging the breakers.

"Now." Celeste put the beach bag down. "Close your eyes. Let the Spirits of the wind and the sea rejuvenate your soul. Like this." And she turned into the wind, eyes closed, arms spread wide, fingers extended, her long auburn-grey hair rippling out behind her.

Under normal circumstances, Barney would never have dreamed of doing what she'd asked. But as things were - what the hell. He put the towel down on the sand at his feet, and even though he felt rather silly and self-conscious, closed his eyes. Then immediately opened them again. Seeing hers still closed, he closed his again. Then stood still, settled down, and let himself go - just a little. Allowed the wind to play with his hair, worry at his beard. He let it sweep the skin of his face, felt its careful, blustery pressure on his eyelids. Then he held both hands out before him, felt it coursing between his fingers then up an inch or two into his sleeves to nibble at his arms. He filled his lungs with air that could be making its first landfall since Denmark or even Russia. And held it as long as he could. Then slowly, slowly he breathed out. He let his arms hang loose by his side, stood as still as he could. He was a post in the sand and would never move from this spot.

His self-consciousness returned and he opened his eyes.

She was looking at him. "OK?"

He nodded.

"There." She pointed off to one side. "That's my hidey-hole."

Sculpted in the sand by the wind was a wide depression sheltered on all but the seaward side by dunes. "Where I come and sit. Look at the sea. Watch the birds. And think." She spread the towel out on the floor of the depression.

"What," he asked, "do you think about?"

"Things."

"Cabbages and kings?"

"Yes. And whether pigs have wings." Smiling, she sat down on the towel.

He arranged himself, with some effort, beside her. He yanked off his brogues and poured the sand from them. He waggled his freed toes around in his socks. She too took off her shoes and burrowed her bare toes into the sand. Then drew her knees up again, wrapped her arms around them and rested her chin on them. She closed her eyes.

He looked at her. On the skin of her neck was the softest of peach down, bright in the shifting sun. Drifting to him, every now and then a waft of that perfume. He was on very, very strange ground.

"How are you feeling?" she asked, without turning to him.

"Bemused. Excited. Befuddled."

"Scorpio's survive." She looked round at him. "D'you want me to talk about him?"

"Perhaps I should have a drink first."

"There's probably a bottle of wine in my car."

"I wasn't serious. But I wouldn't say no."

She started to get up.

"Let me. Got your keys?" He held out a hand.

She took them from her bag and handed them to him. "If there is one, it's probably just rolling around on the floor. Or it might be in a plastic bag."

"Anything to drink out of?"

"Should be a few plastic cups under the dashboard."

He pulled his shoes back on and left.

She kept her eyes on him till he was out of sight among the dunes. For a few moments longer she stayed like that, her eyes fixed on the spot where he had disappeared. Then went back to resting her chin on her knees. She remained like that until he reappeared at her side.

He unscrewed the top and poured wine into the first plastic cup. He handed it to Celeste then poured one for himself.

Cups in hand, they looked at each other.

"So," she said, "what are we drinking to?"

"To Matt?"

"To Matt then," she replied, brightly.

They raised their cups and drank.

"So," he said, taking a deep breath, "describe to me then, if you will, my own son."

"This," she said, "might not be easy." She put her cup down, screwing a little depression for it in the sand. "It was a strange period of my life - the months with Matt McDonald."

"Is that what he called himself – McDonald?"

"It was his name. Why wouldn't he?"

"It wasn't the name he was born with."

She shrugged. "Everyone around here knew the McDonald's had two sons. He was one of them."

"OK. I guess I'll get used to it."

She pulled her jacket up around her shoulders. "When I met him he was coming up twenty-one. The family had a florist business. I used to drive the delivery van for them sometimes when they were very busy. Matt usually came with me. I did the driving and he took the orders into the houses, the shops, wherever. That's how we got to know each other."

"What was he like? Describe him to me."

"Very bright." She took a swig of her wine. "Great company. He made you laugh. At least, he made me laugh. He had a pretty dark sense of humour but he could be very funny with it." She paused. "He was attractive. Good-looking."

Barney smiled.

"Unfortunately he knew it." She looked down into her drink. "Women liked him. How many he'd slept with or screwed behind the bike sheds before I met him, I've no idea. But I don't think you'd count them on the fingers of one hand."

Barney's smile persisted. So his son was something of a Lothario. Well, well.

"It was almost a reflex with him - meet a woman, turn on the charm. The easy smiles. Eye contact. It seldom failed."

Barney looked at her; wondered if he should ask the next question.

Celeste wondered if he might be about to. "And no," she said, smiling, "it didn't fail with me either. But I wasn't going there. I'd seen a bit of the world. I wasn't going to end up on a twenty year-old's trash pile." She shifted slightly to get the sun out of her eyes. "We became just friends. I think with me he felt free."

"Free of what?"

"His innate compulsion to try it on. I'd made my feelings clear. He had the opportunity to walk away. But we got on well. We liked the same things. The odd couple – him twenty and me – well, the wrong side of thirty. We went bowling. To the cinema. He loved films. He said he'd like to work in the 'movies' as he called them. I sometimes wonder if he ever did."

Barney drank some wine. "So - where is he now? Do you know?"

She shook her head.

"When did you last see him?"

"A little over ten years ago. The day he left Skegness."

"Where did he go?"

"London. So he said."

"What was there for him in London?"

"He had a call from somebody he knew – he wouldn't say who. So I guess it was a woman. Whoever it was, they worked in advertising there. They told him that was the game to be in. Where the money was. And –

as he said to me - 'full of chicks with short skirts and long legs, anxious to make friends and a name for themselves'." She looked down and fell silent.

Barney watched her.

She was a long time peering into her glass.

"I was a few years in advertising," he said.

She looked up. "The photograph of you I'd seen - was that to do with advertising? You were with some men and women on a beach in the sun."

"Tell me more."

"You were all eating and drinking at a long table under a large awning. You were laughing and looked very young. The other side of some palm trees was a hotel - 'The Carlton'."

"Cannes. The advertising film festival."

"He always had that photograph with him. He'd cut it out of some trade magazine. He said one day you'd come looking for him. If you didn't, then he'd go looking for you." She looked questioningly at him. "But I guess he never did."

He smiled. "How would I know?" A gust of wind off the sea brought a chill with it. He cleared his throat. "Did he leave you no address when he went? No contact number?"

"Nope. That was Matt. When a thing was over, it was over."

"What, in this case, was 'over'?"

"His time here. His mother and stepfather had divorced. The family business had collapsed. His brother – or rather his half-brother - had not long ago died of meningitis. His stepfather had moved away and he hardly ever saw him. Everything he'd trusted had fallen apart - for the second time in his life. He got out to pastures new."

"And what happened to his mother – to Stella - after all that?"

"The last I knew she was living in Skegness. But I've lost track of her now."

"It sounds like he's vanished off the face of the earth."

"And that," she said, with a sigh of resignation, "is just how Matt wanted it. I'm sure of it."

"Wherever she is though, she has to know where her son is."

"I wouldn't put money on it."

Barney looked away out to sea. The similarity between his own and his son's apparent determination to sever all links with the past did not escape him. He watched the flickering ripples where the dying sun's reflection lit a wide red swathe across the surface of the dark water. "Looks like I've got quite a job on," he said. "Doesn't it?"

A gust of cold wind sent some grains of sand into Barney's eyes. He rubbed them.

Celeste shivered.

He finished off his wine. "Let's go. It's getting cold." He stood up and reached a hand out to her.

The sun had quite gone from their hollow. They picked up their belongings and set off back to the cars through the now darkening dunes.

They sat side by side in Celeste's car with the engine running and the heater on. The little dashboard lights – a toytown set piece in red, blue, green, orange - gave off a comforting glow. The only light left in the seaward sky was a thin skein of almost transparent cloud, pink-tinted, reflecting the sun's light as it slipped beneath the landmass behind them. In the distance, to the south, the slow-moving sweep of a lighthouse beam traced a silver-white arc across the waves before disappearing over a black horizon.

Celeste looked across at the dark shape that was Barney. "I used to smoke in years gone by," she said.

He turned to her.

"This was the sort of moment I'd light up. Did you ever smoke?"

He shook his head. "I did most of the things I shouldn't have done. Smoking wasn't one of them."

"Been something of a roué in your time, have you?"

"'Think of all the good times I've been missing having good times.' Remember that line?"

"'Wasting'" she corrected him. "Not 'missing'. 'The good times I've been wasting.' Eric Burdon and the Animals.."

"Goodness," he said. "I'm impressed."

"There must be something about politics – so many politicians seem to have had colourful pasts."

"I'm not a politician."

"You were."

"Not really. It was a part I played. I did it so well I convinced most people. Myself included."

She watched the lighthouse beam as it swung across the dark water.

But the elation Barney had begun to feel out there in Celeste's hidey-hole was fading now. Leaving aside any gossip surrounding the breakup of the McDonald marriage, Celeste seemed to have come to the end of what she could usefully tell him. She had no idea where Matt was now or what had happened to him in the years between. So tempting though this tête-à-tête in the gathering darkness was, there seemed little point just sitting here.

"Celeste," he said, quietly.

She turned to him.

"Thank you."

"Really? What for?"

It seemed an odd question. "For most of my life my son has been a bundle of fading memories. Now he's looking like a real person again. Thanks mainly to you."

"Oh, I'm so pleased!" she almost gushed. "Barney, I'm so pleased. Can I call you 'Barney'?"

It took him by surprise. "Please do." He felt flattered.

He sensed her eyes searching his. It seemed a long time before she said, "But - what happened? Can you tell me?"

"'Happened'? I'm not sure I know what - "

"You seem to be throwing away your whole life - everything you've ever worked for. He must mean the absolute world to you. And yet it's - "

"More than I ever knew."

"And yet, you've let it go on all this time."

He said, after a long silence, "It's a long story."

She looked at his head and shoulders, ill-defined against the background darkness. The dazzling headlights of a passing car momentarily threw the hairs of his beard around the side of his face into a bizarre silhouette. Matt had once tried to grow a beard.

She had touched a nerve, and Barney was about to tell her how he could still remember Matt's voice as a child; to tell her about the lock of his hair that used to bounce up and down as he wheeled him along in the pushchair. Then something stopped him. Something about her breathing of which he had become suddenly aware. It seemed oddly disturbed, breathless – as though she were a little scared. Or even slightly aroused. This was going to some strange places. He cleared his throat, asked her if she was alright.

He took the movement of her head as a nod.

"So," he said, brightly, gathering himself together, "before I go back, I'd like to buy you a meal if I may. To say, Thank you?"

"That would be lovely," she said. "Where are you going back to?"

"London."

"Oh dear. Everyone goes to London."

"Will you be on breakfast in the morning?"

"I will."

"OK. See you then." He opened the car door and was about to swing his legs out when she put a hand on his arm.

"Don't."

At the touch of her hand, he stopped, sat very still.

"Don't go. There's something else I need to tell you. I'm not sure why, but – I do."

He didn't move.

"Please. I don't really know who the hell you are - but I sort of do. If that makes any sense. And I've told you almost everything already."

Very gently, Barney closed the door again. Then waited.

"I did, in the end," she said, "break my promise to myself."

"I'm sorry. Which promise was that?"

"Or I would have broken it."

"Which promise? I don't know - "

"Let me just go on." She collected herself. "OK - it was a Saturday and I was going out of my mind. I was sick of looking out of the windows of the cottage and seeing nothing but green. The fields, the trees, the leaves, the hedgerows. Everlasting bloody green. I thought I'd turn green myself. I'm not a big city girl but even so I'm a townie. And despite Matt – who I only saw from time to time anyway - I was alone. Weekends were the worst. They'd all go by in the lane in their cars, on their bikes, scooters. Kids, dogs, mums and dads. Couples. The whole world had somebody. Except me. And that Saturday I suddenly thought, 'Fuck it. Just – fuck it.'"

She stopped. Coughed into her hand. "I made a plan. I'd wash my hair. Put on a nice dress - I've still got a few. I'd show a little flesh. Put on some perfume. I'd really make myself look good. I can. Then I'd drop in on Matt. Just turn up. He'd be pleased to see me. Then I'd play up to him and – well, you know what I'm saying. Sod the promise. Life's short. I'd end up on the pile with the rest but it'd have been my choice and I'd have had a good time getting there." She tried to gauge Barney's reaction, but it was too dark to see his eyes. "So – I drove over to Skegness, primped myself up in the vanity mirror, went up to his flat, and made an entrance. And there he was - packing. Shoving everything into bloody great cardboard boxes he'd got from Sainsbury's. He told me he was leaving for London in the morning. My world fell apart. It went through my mind in a feeble sort of way to give him some line about wouldn't it be nice to say goodbye in a really memorable way? But even I hadn't the stomach for that."

She stopped, sat looking down into her lap.

Barney had no idea what he should say or how he should say it. He ran a hand through his hair.

"There. I've told you. You probably find it strange. Maybe even distasteful. I'm sorry. But you're his father and I needed to tell you. I don't really know why."

Along the coast to the north a ship had appeared. A ferry out of Hull probably - porthole lights ablaze in lines along its side. Where, Barney wondered, was it going? Where are any of us going?

"There is," she said, "just one more thing."

Barney steeled himself.

"Although I never heard from Matt ever again – I do have a photograph."

He sat bolt upright. "Of Matt?"

She nodded. Held up an index finger. "One photograph. That's all."

"Can I see it?"

"I think you should have it. It's old. It's black and white and all crumpled. It was taken in the garden of the house in Skegness where he rented the room."

"How old was he then?"

"Twenty. Something like that."

"Have you got it with you?"

"It's back at the cottage. It was the only photograph of himself that he had and I don't know why he'd kept that. He was weird about photographs of any sort. He gave it to me that afternoon. I don't know why he did that either. He was just tipping all the stuff from a drawer out into one of the cardboard boxes when he caught sight of this little photograph. He picked it out and handed it to me. He said hang onto it. It seemed important to him. I tried not to see it as any sort of compliment to myself because I'm sure it wasn't. But giving it to me and then insisting I hang onto it seemed odd and out of character."

"Can you bring it with you tomorrow – at breakfast?"

"When we have dinner."

"OK - dinner." He shrugged. "Whichever."

"You see," she said, thoughtfully, "I wonder now, looking at you, here with me, that if – and this may sound really strange and New Age to you – I wonder if, by some movement of things within things of which we know little – that he knew."

Barney frowned. "'Knew' what?"

"Not 'know' – in the normal sense – but felt that afternoon, sensed, had no words for, but just reached out and grasped at something passing."

Barney tried, without success, to get into it.

"Do you have any idea at all of what I'm trying to say?"

But then he was in the church in Egham once again. And felt just a wingbeat of that presence which there, in the silence, had come to him. Bringing with it that mysterious, all-encompassing emptiness. Had Matt, with Celeste that afternoon in Skegness, snagged all unknowing on the edge of a star which lit up for him, however dimly, the tiny corner of space-time in which he and Celeste now sat? There are things we are not equipped to know. Who was he to say that what she was intimating could not possibly – in any possible world - have been?

38.

It was some time after our meeting by the sea that Celeste took me to see the house. That part of Lincolnshire has a strange feel. Like somewhere left behind and only half-remembered. It's flat like a pancake. In order to avoid flooding, the roads that run across it are built up a couple of metres or so above the surrounding fields which are, in many places, below sea level. These roads are narrow and dead straight, crossing each other at right angles forming an extended rural grid system. Running alongside many of them, but below them at field level, is a narrow, man-made drainage dyke. With that wide Lincolnshire sky reflected in them, they look like rods of steel as they run away into the flat, unfathomable distance.

Stella and Giles McDonald – as the old man in Endell Street had said – moved to this part of the country shortly after their marriage. Why anybody would choose to live there I found at first hard to imagine. The closest settlement was Marsh Enderby, five miles away and with a population not much bigger than the average bus queue.

The house the McDonald's had lived in was, in itself, quite ordinary. Built probably in the 1920's, three, perhaps four bedrooms, and extensive rear garden. Its situation however was as crazy as a Magritte painting. Apart from one or two distant farm sheds there was no other building in sight. Its very existence looked accidental, like a child's toy left on the carpet at bedtime. It stood in the corner of a huge sunken field, five or six metres from the road and two or three metres below it. The bedroom windows were therefore virtually on a level with the average car occupant. The only access from the road to the house was via a bridge across the dyke which ran alongside the road at field level. The outlook from their front sitting room could have taken in little more than the dyke itself and the grassy slope leading up from it to the road above their heads. It seemed the weirdest place in which to choose to live. And how dared they have taken my child-son and dumped him down in such a place? Where were the other children, the neighbours' children he would play with? Where was the equivalent of the recreation ground where I used to put my arms around him as we whooshed together down the slide?

It turned out that the intention had been to set up a smallholding growing flowers, so I suppose their choice of location was not as odd as it had at first seemed. They called themselves 'Jordan Florist'. "Why 'Jordan' rather than 'McDonald'?" I asked Celeste. She didn't know. Maybe it just came a little more trippingly off the tongue. Or perhaps some obstinate spark of individuality in Stella had prevented her from completely abandoning her maiden name. Whatever the reason, 'Jordan Florist' was the name of the company.

Their first few years had been relatively happy and successful. Stella gave birth to a child of their own, another son whom they named Philip. And the business did well. Most of their trade was with private houses, hotels, pubs. They bought a small transit van in which they did deliveries. Both Giles and Stella became well-known in the local business community.

Emboldened by the rapid progress of the early years, they started up a mail-order business. It dealt exclusively in a few rare and exotic species of house-plants. But they were in over their heads. Neither of them had sufficient specialized knowledge, nor did they have the infrastructure or the basic business nous. Things went slowly downhill. Their customer base dwindled until, after a few years of limping along - exacerbated by serious domestic problems - the business was wound up.

Times thereafter for the McDonalds were hard. Work had never been plentiful in that part of the country and Giles was on the dole for a long period. Their debts mounted. He moonlighted for cash in hand with odd gardening jobs and labouring on farms. A year or so later however he succeeded in getting a permanent job as an assistant in a pet food shop in Boston. That enabled the family to live within their means and it gave back to Giles some measure of self-respect.

But there was more to come. Philip, now fourteen, contracted bacterial meningitis and very soon after, died. Stella, once a familiar figure around and about, disappeared from the scene. In the immediate aftermath of such a shattering event, it gave rise to little speculation, though it was regarded as odd that she called on none of her friends for help and support in that time.

As the weeks and months passed and still there was no sign of Mrs McDonald, she became the subject of more or less enthusiastic conjecture. She had been seen shopping on one occasion in a small supermarket in Horncastle, fifteen miles away. To be shopping that far from home for what looked like everyday provisions was, in itself, unusual. Also, she had seemed jumpy, reluctant to engage in conversation with the woman who had bumped into her, a woman she had known reasonably well. This encounter was taken as confirmation of whichever of two widely promoted theories you preferred – either she was nursing some secret she didn't want to get out, or she was suffering from depression and was fearful of social contact. The latter was the more generous and the more likely. It was however, the less interesting. Hence the majority opted for the former.

The majority were eventually proved right. News got out on the gossip circuit that she'd had an affair with a local farmer. He and his wife were close friends of the McDonalds. If there are to be degrees of outrage surrounding adultery, there can be few greater. What was left of the family McDonald fell apart. Matt was already, by that time, living in his rented room in Skegness. But now Giles too moved out. He went to Boston where his work was, and little was ever heard of him again in the area.

As for Stella, she had, to all intents and purposes, vanished. The house lay empty. Rumour had it that she had gone back to Halifax; or she had been so devastated by Philip's death and the breakup of the family subsequent to her own adultery that she was now in a mental home. Or – for those with a taste for the macabre – she had walked out into the treacherous salt marshes that stretched all along that length of coast and had been cut off by the tide, then swept out to sea.

To the best of Celeste's knowledge, only she herself, McDonald, Matt, and presumably Stella's family in the north of England, had known of her living at that time in Skegness. But even she, Celeste, had now lost track of her. The last time she had rung her number, she had encountered the answerphone of 'Rowan, Gwyneth and Baby Jane', all of whom were sorry to have missed her call.

I was becoming ever more impressed by the facility with which members of the McDonald family seemed able simply to vanish. But then, as I myself had done exactly the same thing, and - so far at least - with great success, it appeared I was similarly talented. Perhaps it runs in families.

After leaving Celeste, I drove back to The Amsterdam Freighter in the gathering darkness feeling a little sorry for myself. I had learned far more about Matt from Celeste than from any other source. Yet the day, which had seemed to promise so much, had ended in a similar sort of cold trail as my time with Minxie. I still had no idea where he was or where to look next.

I made my way wearily up to my room after dinner. I went to the window, drew back the curtains and looked out into the night. There were a few stars. I opened the window just an inch or two and breathed in the smell of early winter and of the cooling earth. Could I hear the sea, murmuring in the distance to the shore? Then voices and the clink of glasses came gently up from the bar beneath. Like on another night in another pub so many years ago. I closed the window. Then closed the curtains. I felt a strange sadness. I couldn't pinpoint its source. It seemed to be oozing from so many points of my life. I prepared myself for bed.

And Celeste. Well, I guess I liked her. But there hung around her some indefinable strangeness. Like a jigsaw in which just one or two pieces don't quite fit - just enough to discomfit you without your knowing quite why. I closed my eyes, and she was there in front of me. I could not easily put together the image of her and my son, fifteen years between them, driving across this flat land together and wandering into a local Odeon. She was attractive. Though when all was said and done, not really my type.

I dreamed that night of an old photograph. I was holding it in my hand. It was black and white, crumpled. There was a man in it. And a woman. They were both old. They stood, rather formally, side by side. Behind them was a sort of ugly floral wallpaper that reminded me a little of Endell Street. I didn't know the woman. But the man was me, fifteen or twenty years down the line. Each had just the suggestion of a smile on their faces as they gazed out past the camera. There was pride in her eyes. 'Look, here we are now, old and grey. But it's been a good life. We've had our ups and downs. But I wouldn't have wished it any other way. I'm happy.'

His smile however was with reservations. Like there was something he could not open up to. Something that made him inconsolably sad. She seemed unaware of it. And he would never, ever be able to tell her what it was.

39.

So we were to go into the desert. It had always been on the cards. No part of this country is for the faint of heart - but the desert's a step beyond. Even the capital, a city of some three-quarters of a million people, is tough going - hot (45C), noisy, chaotic, alien, edgily unsafe. The drive from there to here is one thousand kilometres, fifteen hours down a plumb line of a road across a baking, rock-strewn tableland. I had peered, bemused and shocked, from the window of the Land Cruiser on this moonscape. The occasional mud-walled village flashed past, some with an associated area of scrub on which tethered camels grazed a few trees. Men with only the upper half of their faces visible beneath swathes of cloth stared at our passing; children shoeless, laughing, running after us till they were out of breath.

We stopped at some point in the day to relieve ourselves by the side of the road. Three or four hundred metres away across the barren plain, a tiny group of people, the only moving objects in an empty landscape, were doing something with what looked like a huge, wooden cage.

"Nomads," said Youssef.

Some middle-class myth about the enviable simplicity of a life close to nature took hold of me. "Are they likely to be offended," I asked, "if we go and take a closer look?"

It was a family of seven - man and wife, with five children between the ages of about three and fourteen, along with a few scrawny goats who wandered freely all around. The 'wooden cage' which the two adults were engaged in settling onto the rough ground, was the frame of their new home. It was a surprisingly delicate affair of thin branches stripped of their bark, bent and lashed into a dome-shaped formation around two and a half metres high in the centre.

Without pausing what they were doing, the man and his wife greeted us in a friendly, though slightly formal fashion. But their faces, when they looked our way, shocked me. Their eyes were milky white, both pupil and iris almost invisible. They must surely have been all but blind. Where, for pity's sake, are the doctors, the medicines, the care for these people? I felt helpless and uncomfortable. "Who are they?" I asked Youssef. "Where have they come from?"

He said he could not speak their language and wasn't sure. "But they may be Peul."

"What," I replied, "is Peul?"

"Nomad tribe. Many Peul in Africa. They have cattle herds."

"These people seem to have nothing but a few goats."

"This family, I think, is very poor. Today is not good time for nomads."

The children looked healthy and happy. The two smallest, a boy and a girl, both ran around naked. The brightly coloured clothes on the three older ones were immaculately clean. The man and his wife worked away with an impressive, quiet dignity.

This wooden cage had been set down around the frame of a large double bed which had been put in place earlier. This bed was constructed of stout, straight branches, also stripped of bark. At each corner was an ornate 'foot' – a disc, set upright like a wheel, of a dark metal that looked a little like pewter, each carved with some sort of quite intricate design. I wanted to take a closer look, but felt it would be intrusive even to ask.

Close by was a large wooden rack loaded with animal skins. These, said Youssef, would be draped over the domed frame to form the roof.

Hanging among the branches of a nearby thorn tree - the only tree in sight - were the family's water gourds, along with a collection of metal pots and pans which gleamed in the sun.

The man and his wife smiled at us as we left; two of the children waved. I felt an uncomfortable sort of gratitude towards them, and the shock of their situation stayed with me. As we made our way in silence back to the vehicle I felt humbled and slightly guilty.

We resumed our progress along the relentless ribbon of road. In a mud village, barefoot children ran after us, waving, shouting. Three men chased a whiplashing, panicking snake across the road, shouting and hitting at it with sticks. A youth pushed a ghetto blaster almost into our open windows as we passed. A thumping beat and a wailing, alien voice set my teeth on edge. A camel's antediluvian face sneered at us. The sun beat down.

This was Africa. Sub-Saharan Africa. Black Africa. It was not the Africa of diplomatic or trade missions; not the Africa seen from the window of the Ambassador's residence. This, I assumed, was real Africa. The Africa with which I would have to form some interface acceptable to both myself and it. It would not be easy.

We set off for Iferouane. We took two Toyota Land Cruisers, more jerry cans of fuel than I'd ever seen in one place at one time, and a great deal of food and water. Mattresses and tents were secured on the roof-rack of one of the vehicles. 'We' was Youssef and myself, Sam - a member of the Hausa tribe - who had driven us from the capital, a Tuareg cook whose name I was never to discover, and a strangely taciturn man, probably somewhere in his forties, who looked Southern European - Greek or Sicilian maybe. He had appeared at the last minute, apparently out of nowhere. What his function was I had no idea and it was never made clear. I decided not to question it, at least for the time being. I did not have a good feeling about him.

We travelled in convoy. I sat in the rear of the lead vehicle. Youssef, navigating, sat in front beside Sam, the driver. The cook drove the following vehicle, with the European man in his rear seat. As we left the town behind, what little vegetation there was soon petered out and we processed into an infinite sand-coloured emptiness onto which the sun blasted down. No trees, no shade. And there was no road. Just a few tyre tracks in the sand which, for a while at least, we seemed to be following. But they too petered out as the ground beneath us came to resemble a sort of dark brown rubble over which we moved with a juddering, vibrating motion.

I settled down and made myself as comfortable as I could. I

determined to look on this foray into the desert as a great adventure and to try not to think too much about what may lay at the end of it.

That first night we made camp in a dried-up watercourse. There was a short run of mature trees along one of its banks. The cook collected some dead branches and stowed them on the roof of his Land Cruiser. I wondered why, in a rather disinterested way. Mattresses were laid down on the ground by the side of the vehicles. I was offered a tent to sleep in but refused, saying I wanted to experience the reality of the desert. I did not sleep well. In fact, I slept very little. The stars were so bright in that unpolluted atmosphere that I could see by their light alone. And however hard I tried, it was impossible not to think and wonder about the red Suzuki pickup somewhere up ahead of us, abandoned in the sands of the Tenere.

In the first light of dawn, I sat up and looked warily around. I started violently. Motionless, among the trees, seated high up on a camel, was a man. All I could see of his face were his eyes, bright as steel bolt heads in that cold, early light. The lower part of his face was obscured by the indigo Tuareg veil. He too saw me. With no change of expression and in no hurry, he pulled the head of the complaining camel around and set off into the desert the far side of the trees. I told the others when they awoke. They expressed little interest, and got on with their day. I was left to assume that people wandered around the desert on camels as in Europe one might ride around the lanes on a bicycle.

The two Land Cruisers bucked and rocked across blackened, rubble-like rocks that strewed the floors of empty plains that stretched on all sides to infinity. And I had thought the desert all sand. After some hours of this, my head ached, and I felt just a little nauseous. But what a story I would have to tell. While my former colleagues, even now, were stifling their yawns in meetings in airless rooms, here was I, looking like what we used to call a hippy, with long hair, beard, shades and jeans, being driven, not in an air-conditioned government limo by a uniformed chauffeur, but in a rolling, swaying Land Cruiser by a Nigerian Hausa driver named Sam across the Sahara desert in temperatures high enough to fry an egg.

On the second day both vehicles' air conditioning gave up. The others expressed no surprise. In these temperatures, I was told, it was more or less par for the course. We drove with all the windows down, and sat in the resulting furnace blast of air. We moved across a flat emptiness so devoid of features that our forward movement was hardly detectable. In the distance was a range of mountains, black against the backdrop of a dusty, cloudless sky. But they were so far away that they too seemed hardly ever to change shape or angle. Black mountains. I felt an ache for the life I'd left behind.

The sun was merciless, its heat beyond anything I had thought possible or tolerable. You dehydrate at dreadful speed. They don't tell you that in school geography lessons. I doubt they know. Until you experience it, you've no idea the human body – your body - can so readily lose its substance. Like an alcoholic, you live from one drink to the next. But this drink is water. Go just a little too long without enough and you need no telling that without more you will soon be on the edge of survival. Staying alive in these conditions is a damage limitation exercise.

On the second day we stopped to change a wheel on the cook's vehicle. A short distance away was a low outcrop of reddish-brown rocks. There had been so little to look at for so many hours that this series of irregular shapes jutting up out of the sand was an interesting oddity. I had to go and investigate. I wandered over to them, selected one with a more or less flat surface, and sat down on it. I yelped and jumped straight up again. I might as well have sat on a hot iron. I felt rather stupid, and avoided looking towards the others grouped around the ailing Land Cruiser. They were not people to laugh at another's discomfort. But it must have raised a smile or two.

I had just started to walk back towards them when I felt something cold land on the back of one of my hands. Startled, I looked down. A drop of water? Then another on my forearm. It took me a second to connect. I looked skyward. A small area of thin, grey cloud was sitting right above us. And from it – rain! Then more. The cool drops landed as a balm on my face, my lips, ran down my cheeks. Quite instinctively I spread my arms wide, closed my eyes and opened my mouth. Water! It caressed my eyelids, ran onto my hot, dry skin, into my mouth and around my tongue. I stood quite still, letting it soak into what few clothes I wore.

It lasted perhaps a minute. Then petered out and stopped. Steam rose from the hot rocks by my side. In seconds they were once again bone-dry. I walked back to the others, offering silent thanks to whoever or whatever had provided me with my own personal shower of rain. There might be no more in this place this year.

Two days later. We are still pitching and rolling in this terrible heat and still I am peering out at the same never-ending desert. A sun-blasted tree or distant range of sand dunes provide occasional moments of excitement. I need to talk to someone. I am developing Saharan cabin fever. Aside from the European man, from whose lips so far I've heard not one word and therefore have no idea what language or languages he speaks, the only one with whom I can hold any sort of conversation is Youssef. But he is busy driving, navigating. I fear the onset of panic. My previous lives in engineering, advertising and politics have been no preparation for this. They are parlour games. I take out my wallet, draw from it the battered little black and white photograph. Its ragged corners flap in the hot blast through the open windows. The English Victorian house and its little rear garden are unreal. There are flowers round the lawn. Tulips. I know tulips. They come in the Spring. He smiles at me and at the desert. I have to be prepared for the worst. Have I had a part in this madness?

I was developing a wary fascination for the European man. He travelled in either vehicle, sometimes in ours which always led, sometimes with the Tuareg cook in the one following. If he came in with us, Sam would drop back to drive the rear vehicle and Youssef would drive ours. I would then sit in the front by Youssef while the European man sat behind us. He never spoke. What informed the man's choice of vehicle I had no way of knowing, but the decision seemed entirely his.

I made a point of keeping a surreptitious eye on him. The others would, from time to time, exchange the occasional polite greeting with him. But there was a wariness in their manner. And as they spoke always in a language which meant nothing to me, I had only his looks by which to guess at his origins. His swarthy, olive complexion and black hair said 'Mediterranean' to me. But I was nowhere near as confident these days of my knowledge of the world as I had once considered myself. Central American? Colombian? Who knows?

At meals, whether taken in the vehicles or sitting outside under whatever scant shade we might find, he would sit slightly apart. He carried about him an aura of mid-level officialdom. Like he might be representing some covert arm of government – an arm that had no truck with boundaries, social or national. Terrorism and hostage-taking were on the rise in this country and we were already far from civilization. I was more than ever convinced his joining us had not been optional. He disturbed me.

The further we progressed into the desert, the more I became concerned about our isolation. As Youssef had pointed out to me in the bar, no mobile phone signal penetrated this wilderness. On top of that, he had switched off the satellite navigation system in both vehicles. "Why?" I asked him. He said he was convinced the one in the cook's vehicle was giving faulty readings. He had come to that conclusion because its readings seldom agreed with those of the GPS in our own vehicle. And the readings in our own vehicle were, most of the time, more or less accurate. How, I asked, could he judge their accuracy? He told me simply that he knew the desert. Therefore he saw little point in keeping even our own switched on. What if, he said, that too, developed a fault? With GPS coverage as patchy and unreliable as it was out here, how would you know a fault with the device from simple lack of coverage?

Put like that, it, seemed unarguable. And although it didn't ease my concerns, I couldn't see what difference it was going to make. He had seemed in any case to use GPS only as an occasional 'second opinion'. The rest of the time he appeared to navigate by a combination of huge maps which he would spread out and study on the bonnet of our vehicle (maps which to my eye were little more than high-altitude pictures of sand), by the stars and by some sixth sense which seemed to tell him pretty well exactly where we were at any time of day or night. I was in awe of him.

The days were interminable. We were for ever on the move yet seemed never to get anywhere. The journey started to take on in my mind, the character of an asymptotic curve - however close we came to the end of it, even when the distance left to travel had shrunk so little as to be immeasurable, we would never actually arrive. The more I thought about it, the more this piece of mathematical chicanery- which had so intrigued me in Rugby Upper School - started to take on the aura of prophecy. Were the five of us on a quest that would simply go on and on and on till food and fuel were gone, and we were bleached bones on the sand, with Iferouane still at infinity from us?

I am not coping. Toilet protocol in a shared bathroom gave me problems enough. But things here are right off my map. And speaking of toilets – Saharan ones are simple matters consisting of a hole in the sand – custom-made by shovel – into which one shits.

The procedure: clutching toilet roll and a bottle of water, one walks a discreet distance from one's fellows, then digs one's self a modest hole in the sand. One then crouches over it, and concentrates. I amuse myself imagining the PM in the same situation. Or his insufferable Home Secretary. The task completed, one then wipes one's self and puts the used toilet paper on top of one's waste in the hole. One then scrapes enough sand back into the hole to cover up that which one has left there. Then, holding in one's hand the bottle of water – with top off – one reaches across one's shoulder and pours water from the bottle down one's back allowing it to run through the cleft in one's buttocks so that one might clean one's self.

I was drifting down, like in a parachute, into a Hieronymus Bosch landscape. A picture of his - 'The Garden of Earthly Delights' - electrified me when I first came across it as a young man. Perhaps his mind when he painted it was as far out of true as I sensed mine becoming. In it, grotesque insects devour naked people. Men and women fuck and fornicate their short lives away and devils excrete the damned. These images, embedded in my head, started to take on a semblance of reality. Hobgoblins ran along beside us in the sand; I knew – bizarrely, I was aware – that I was hallucinating. I told myself therefore that the part of me that 'knew' - that did the knowing - wasn't therefore itself doing any hallucinating. So I wasn't completely hallucinating. And I saw ostriches – they were real. A long way off. A dozen or so of them, a herd, a flock, a bevy – strange, weird, Bosch-like creatures themselves – I wanted to laugh out loud but thought that would show lack of respect - neither fish nor fowl, travelling at great speed, all their lanky, cranky legs in unison like the external valve gear of old steam locomotives, across the floor of the plain. And I remember moments when, as I stared from the window of our vehicle on the endless parade of baking rock and distant sand dunes drifting aimlessly past, I so wanted to believe that what I was really looking out on was a huge painted canvas being dragged past my eyes by Tuaregs on camels, and that eventually, like a curtain being drawn back, it would reveal on the other side a village in the Cotswolds on a sunny day with a sparkling, cool stream burbling along beside the road. And are there muffins still for tea?

I was becoming sick. A sickness with which I was unfamiliar and had not much idea how to treat. What I did know was that a couple of paracetamol weren't going to do the trick.

I had never been one for searching for one's so-called 'real self'. Too many opportunist amateurs, in paperbacks and Sunday supplements, have demeaned and degraded the whole subject for my liking. In any case, my view had always been that life is just what you see - it's short, sometimes good, sometimes nasty, and when it's over it's probably all over. Why waste the little time we have agonizing about things to which there are no answers. But again, those few moments in that church return to me. Was that silence and the peace I felt part of the fabric of the place, available to all who come through its doors? Or, by some means with which my rational self is not capable of engaging, is it something that resides somewhere deep within my own self and which the circumstances of that moment drew up, like from a well, to the surface? If so - if that same peace is somewhere within me even now, please, please may I find it?

Controlling as best I could my trembling fingers, I took from my bag the mobile reserved for calls to Martin Cosgrove. He knows I'm here. I'd even given his number to Youssef in case anything should happen to me. And now I needed to hear his voice. That reassuring, measured tone. To hear in the background as he spoke, the gentle rumble of traffic in Lincolns Inn Fields. Perhaps even hear the slow ticking of that ancient clock on the wall by his desk. I dialled his number.

Youssef saw. Shook his head.

"What?" I demanded.

"No signal here."

Hadn't he already told me? Even so, just in case everybody else had got it wrong I put the thing to my ear. I got a continuous, high-pitched whistle. I put it back in my bag. Stared sightlessly out of the window.

At night I sleep in my tent and dream. I dream of that empty vehicle abandoned in the desert with the wind blowing through its open windows, rattling the pages of old newspapers, and at the wheel, turned as always away from me, a young man in a black coat and red scarf. I reach out and take him gently by the shoulder and turn him to me. But as his face is coming round to mine I can't take what I might see and I wake up shouting to the stars.

40.

"I don't like jokes about sex." Ellen pulled the duvet up to her chin. "They're always more smutty than funny."

"OK. How about this then. 'Do you - ?'"

"Frank - no. Stop it."

"This isn't smutty. 'Do you smoke after intercourse?' 'I don't know, I've never looked.'"

Silence.

She burst out laughing.

"See what I mean?" He waited. "Well, do you?"

She stopped laughing, frowned. "Sorry. Do I what?"

"Let's have a look." He went to pull the duvet off her. "Let's see if you do smoke after - "

"Frank!" She yanked the duvet back up over her breasts. "No! That's crass." She looked at him in puzzled surprise. "Frank, that's really, really crass."

He sat up, his face blank. "I'm sorry. I'm so sorry."

"So you should be. Christ." She turned her back on him.

He went to say something. Held a finger poised to tap her naked shoulder. But decided against it.

She said, without turning to him, "There's a bottle of some sort of red open on the unit in the kitchen. Get me a glass please, would you?"

He climbed out of bed. Then stood there, embarrassed by his own nakedness.

She could see him reflected in the cheval mirror. "If you're looking for something to put on, there's a dressing gown - " - she withdrew an arm from beneath the duvet and pointed across the room - " - in that wardrobe."

He opened the wardrobe, looked around inside, and drew from it a heavy, multi-coloured dressing gown. He looked at it with curious distaste.

"Yes," she said, watching in the mirror, "it was Barney's."

He looked at it again. Put it on and went from the room.

"I watched you for years, you know. Gazed at you from afar." Frank leaned back against his pillow. "I never, ever thought I'd be here with you like this."

Ellen sipped her wine and looked out of the window. It was very dark outside. There was no moon, no stars. She could just about make out the nearest branches of the maple Barney had been threatening for years to have removed. Its roots, he had claimed, were going to disturb the foundations of the house before very long. Then what sort of a mess would they be in? What indeed?

"I used to watch you - the things you did. At meals - how you held your knife and fork. When you were thinking hard, how you would frown and touch your upper lip with the very tip of your tongue. Silly things."

She looked at him.

"Were you ever aware of that?"

"No," she said, apologetically. "Not really."

"And I used to wonder what would it be like to hold your hand." He looked down into his glass. "Feel my face against yours."

"Listen," she said, finishing off her wine, "about MS. I guess it might make that aspect of life a little difficult. Or not? I hope you don't mind my asking."

He gave a noncommittal grunt.

"I'm sorry. Perhaps that was a little gauche of me."

"No, it wasn't. And yes, it does." He held the wine bottle up, questioningly.

She nodded. He refilled her glass.

The chimes of a church echoed distantly across the fields. He looked at his watch.

"Where does she think you are?" She tried hard to keep from her tone any suggestion of guilt.

"Having a drink with a couple of local party members. I didn't say which members. Or where."

"So how long is it then since you and she – well – tasted the joys, as it were?"

He shrugged. "Four years. Five? I've lost count."

"But surely," she said, "having MS doesn't actually mean you can't. Does it? Or does it?"

"No."

"So – ?"

"Some people do."

"Right. And some don't?"

"It's not for everybody."

She frowned. "What's not? I'm sorry, I don't think I - "

"It affects things. Not everybody copes too well with the ways around it. Put it that way." He looked away.

"I think I understand," she said. "I'm sorry."

The telephone by the bed suddenly erupted. They both started. Frank sat forward anxiously, peering at it.

It rang on.

Ellen said, quietly, "Does she have this number?"

He nodded.

"Let it ring."

He shook his head vigorously. "She wouldn't ring here."

Ellen said nothing. Studied her reflection on the surface of her wine.

Frank kept his eyes on the telephone. It seemed to be going on for a very long time. It stopped and he sat back.

"We're entering difficult waters Frank, you and I."

A train threaded its way through the night, slowing down towards Ludlow. The nine-forty-six from Paddington. In those other days it was so often her signal to half fill a glass with ice cubes, and pour a scotch over them. By the time he arrived from the station it would be just as he'd liked it.

Frank sat forward again.

"What?"

"Listen," he said, "I'd better go." He drained his glass.

"Oh." She frowned. "That's very sudden."

"I need to be back by half-ten."

"You didn't say."

"I didn't think. I'm sorry." He slid awkwardly out of the bed.

"OK. Well – er - do you want anything before you go? Coffee?"

"No. Thank you." He picked up his clothes from the chair over which he'd earlier draped them and started to dress.

Ellen watched, slightly bemused.

He turned away to pull on a brightly coloured pair of boxer shorts.

"Are you alright?" she said.

"Yes."

"You're not acting alright."

He turned to face her. Threw his shirt on and started doing up the buttons. "I'm a little concerned."

"About what?"

"What do you think?"

"I don't know, Frank. That's why I asked."

"As you said – 'difficult waters."

"That surely was obvious from the start."

He stepped into one leg of his trousers.

"And Frank."

He stopped. Looked at her.

"Don't you think you'd better have a shower?"

He stepped into the other leg and started to pull them up. "I'll be alright."

"It's not you I'm thinking of. We have been – rather close."

He stopped again.

"Please."

He stood quite still. His shirt was half out over his trousers which he held up with his hands, unzipped and crumpled like a clown's. The penny dropped. "OK." The word was a staccato jab which seemed only just to escape his mouth. He yanked himself back out of his trousers, one leg of which got caught round his foot. With some difficulty he kicked it away. Then pulled off his shirt and boxers and threw them down on the floor. "Shower," he said, and naked, stalked from the room.

Ellen watched him leave. Listened to his bare feet padding along the polished oak boards of the landing. The few moments then of near silence as he traversed the Axminster rug. The padding continuing. Then stopping. The opening and the rather noisy closing of the bathroom door. The shower starting up, grumbling a little before getting into its stride. So banal, so familiar. Twisted painfully out of true in these now and forever changed times. She lay slowly back down.

Martha's bedroom door was a tiny bit ajar. Frank put his face to the gap. The room was in darkness, but the light from the landing was sufficient to give him sight of a slight movement of the bedclothes.

"Hello dear." She sounded sleepy. "I'm not asleep. Was it a successful meeting?"

"The usual sort. Are you alright?"

"I watched a bit of telly. It wasn't very interesting."

"Did you have your warm milk?"

"I did. Why do you ask?"

"It's just that I didn't notice a used milk saucepan in the kitchen, and I wondered."

"I think I remember washing it up." He heard her yawn. "And Frank, by the way I locked the back door. And the conservatory. To save you having to check."

"Thank you. So - goodnight then." He turned to leave.

"Frank."

A fleck of apprehension shot through him. He looked in again. "Yes?" he said.

"A kiss? To say goodnight."

He went to her bedside. The light behind him threw his shadow across the bed so he could hardly see her face. He bent and kissed her cheek. The skin was loose, the flesh slightly puffy. He had lived a life with this face. Seen joy, pain, heartache, laughter in its company. He felt a sudden, almost overpowering need to tell her where he'd really been, what he'd really done. "Goodnight," he said, quietly.

"Thank you, Frank." She turned away on her side. "I'm glad you had a successful meeting."

He went slowly to his own room. Closed the door quietly and sat down on the single divan bed. He took off his shoes, lay them neatly side by side on the floor. He stood up again to close the curtains. Through the trees that bordered their land he could just make out the public tennis courts lit dimly by the lights from the street on the far side. A fox emerged from the shadows and wandered across them. He closed the curtains. He found himself cursing Barnaby Marechal. But what's done is done, and done for all time.

41.

Barney Marshal brought the car to a skidding stop just past the 'You are now leaving Glastonbury' sign. He turned to look back. The man was running towards him along the verge, his holdall banging against his legs. He looked OK. Mid-twenties. Indian or something – brown anyway. He turned the radio off, then leaned across to the passenger side to wind the window down. The handle jammed. "Fuck." He banged it with his fist. It hurt. "Shit!" The man had his face to the glass, mouthing something. Barney shouted, "Window's stuck! Hang on." He picked up a shoe from the floor and banged the handle with it. It gave. He wound the window down. "Where are you going?"

The man pointed up ahead. "That way."

"Yeh, I got that. But where – what place?"

The man shrugged. "I'm not sure. Where are you going?"

"No idea. Get in." Barney threw open the door.

The man frowned, hesitated, then climbed in. He settled the holdall on his lap and closed the door.

Barney put the car in gear and pulled away. He pointed to the holdall. "Sling that in the back."

The man turned round. The rear seat was a piled-high jumble of clothes, newspapers, books, towels, toilet bag, plastic cups, food, a camera, a portable television.

"Shove it on top," said Barney. "It's all fucking rubbish anyway."

The man shrugged and did so.

"You been to that music thing?" said Barney.

"I'm sorry – 'music thing'?"

"Glastonbury. Some sort of music festival again this year."

"No, no. My last lift dropped me there yesterday. Where did you say you were going?"

"I didn't. I'm just going. You know – driving? Following the sun. The wind. My nose."

"Ah." The man turned to the front. "Then you are a true wanderer."

Barney was intrigued by the man's accent. Subcontinent-cum-sort-of-north-of-England. "Where are you from? Do you mind my asking?"

"I don't mind. Leeds."

"Leeds? You must have been there a while – you've got the accent."

The man looked at him, confused. "I was born there."

"Ah. Yes." Barney felt the colour rise to his cheeks. What an old-fashioned, English fool. He went on quickly, "My own neck of the woods. Near enough, anyway. Halifax – me."

"Ah." The man's face lit up. "Your football team is no good. Ours is much better." And he grinned broadly. "FA Cup winners last year!"

Barney shrugged. "Don't know much about football, I'm afraid."

The final few houses of Glastonbury slipped away as they headed west.

The man looked again at the clutter behind him. "I think you have been on the road a long time."

"A while, my friend," said Barney. "A while."

The man settled into his seat. "Nice car. Comfortable."

"Triumph Toledo. Classic motor. Nought to sixty in five minutes."

Again the man looked confused.

Barney turned the radio back on. 'When,' asked the Three Degrees, 'will I see you again? Will I have to wait forever?'

A little brass bell above their heads emitted a twee tinkle. The tea shop was small, warm, crammed with brown furniture. Steam hissed out of some device by the counter. There were four other customers. Two white-haired, elderly women with their coats still on, were deep in an earnest, whispered conversation. A middle-aged woman with china clay skin and blue-rinse hair sat beside a choleric man in cavalry twill trousers, check shirt with cravat, and a black blazer with military-style crest. They all looked up. Disapprovingly, Barney felt. Somewhere a clock ticked.

Barney led the way to a table by a window. It looked out over a small, drab square. The man from Leeds took in his surroundings. He was bemused. Shelves filled with ceramic tankards in the shape of heads, some with cloth caps, one with a tricorn hat; a plaster figure of Charlie Chaplin, of Winston Churchill with cigar; behind the counter, Annigoni's portrait of the Queen. And on the wall right by his head, a large, gilt-framed painting of a World War II Lancaster bomber breaking dramatically through the clouds; under it a printed notice - 'Say NO to the European Community'.

"I've never been in a place like this before," said the man, half whispering. "It seems a little – well – old fashioned."

"A little 'English'." Barney corrected him. "'English' equals 'old-fashioned'. Here we venerate the past and live in it as far as possible. Or hadn't you noticed?"

The man looked round at the other customers. He smiled behind his hand. "I do not think they like us very much," he said.

"That," said Barney in a loud voice, "is because I have long hair and wear jeans. And you are the wrong colour."

Four heads turned their way.

The man looked down, avoiding their eyes. Slotted in between a pepper pot and salt pot was a menu. He picked it up and made as if to read it.

"What's on offer then?" asked Barney.

The man handed the menu to him. "I do not know these things."

"OK." Barney scrutinized it. "Well - you can have tea, coffee. Cakes and buns, various and sticky. Then there's - " - but he stopped as his nose encountered some sweetly pungent and slightly objectionable perfume. He looked up. By his side stood a large, middle-aged woman with permed blonde hair, dressed in expensive country casuals. In one hand she held a notepad, in the other a pencil.

He stared questioningly up at her.

She returned the look. "Yes?" she said, without enthusiasm.

His looked turned to one of great puzzlement.

She pointed to the menu in his hand. "Have you decided?" Her accent was self-consciously upper-class.

"Ah!" His face lit up. "You're our waitress."

She bit her lip.

"Well, we've hardly sat down. However - " - he ran a finger slowly over the menu - " - let's see."

"All homemade." She said it as though, on that account, there really was no need to pick one item rather than another.

"This – " - he jabbed a finger on the word 'teacake' - " - what sort is it?"

"'Sort'? It's teacake."

"Well," said Barney, smiling, "we're from the north, my friend and I. And in the north there's teacake and there's teacake."

"I see. Well, I'm afraid this isn't the north and the only teacake we have is that one." She aimed a finger again at the menu.

Barney looked across at the man. "Teacake?"

The man dithered, not sure if this performance merited a serious answer.

"Did you make it yourself?" said Barney to the woman.

She gave him a look like he might be a little demented.

"You said it was all homemade so I naturally - "

"Shall I come back when you've - ?"

"Teacake for two, and - "

"Is that one teacake between two, or two separate - ?"

"The former, if you wouldn't mind. Coffee twice, please. Mocha, if you have it. Thank you."

"Coffee here is Nescafe. Blend 37. Assuming that suits." With which she turned on her heel and walked away.

Barney turned to the man. Shrugged. "There. Rural hospitality in the birthplace of freedom and democracy - leaving aside the Greeks, that is. What do you make of it?"

The man was about to answer when Barney winced. "Sorry – I keep treating you like you arrived yesterday."

The man looked at him with dawning admiration. "I like the way you stood up to her."

"If you're running a country tea shop you're running a country tea shop, aren't you? Not fucking Harrods."

The man nodded enthusiastically. "I get on with you nicely. My name is Raffie. Would you mind telling me yours?"

For a second Barney's face was blank. Then he reached a hand out across the table. "Likewise. Mine's Al. Call me Al."

Raffie gripped the proffered hand and shook it. "Nice to meet you, Al."

Barney sat back. "OK Raffie – so where are we going?"

Raffie peered out the window at the little square beyond. "Where is this? Where are we?"

"Dunno. Haven't got a map." Barney too looked out into the square. Ornamental trees in discoloured concrete tubs. A dry cleaners and a Co-op. A woman with a huge pram like a sailing ship. A billboard outside a newsagents flapped in the breeze – 'UFO sighted over Taunton'.

Raffie pointed to the front cover of the menu. "Look – is that where we are?"

Barney picked it up. "You got it. 'Ye Olde Tea Shoppe, North Street, Wiv - '" He stopped, stared at the menu and grimaced. "'Then some place I dunno how the hell you're supposed to pronounce it – but it's in 'Somerset.'" He stared down at the word. "'Wivel'. Then 'is'. Then 'combe'" He looked up at Raffie. "'Wivel – is – combe.'"

Raffie, grinning, shook his head. "I will not be trying to say that."

But Barney's attention had shifted. Looking fixedly across the room, he mouthed quietly to himself, "My goodness. She walks in beauty, like the night."

Threading her way between the neighbouring tables was a slight, fresh-faced young woman. She wore a white lace pinafore over a short, frilly black dress with black tights. She carried a wooden tray containing teacake and coffees, and she was heading their way. Barney kept his eyes on her till she came to a stop by his side. Then fixed her with an adoring gaze. She looked blankly back at him.

"Hello," he said, grinning seductively.

She went rigid. Then turned bright red, set the tray down with a crash on the table and hurried away.

Barney sat back, pointed to her fast-retreating figure. "Innocence fleeing the rapist. Oils, by Blake."

"I think," said Raffie, chuckling behind his hand, "that this place does not want us."

"Well, that's OK, Raffie – we don't want this place." Barney picked up a knife. "I'll be mum." He cut the teacake and put the two halves on separate plates.

"Where is Newquay?" said Raffie.

"Newquay?" Barney pushed Raffie's helping across the table to him. "Cornwall. Why?"

"I have a friend there. Abdul."
"That's a good old Cornish name."
"Is Cornwall this way?"
"Sort of. Eat your teacake. It's homemade."

Barney opened as much of one eye as he dared. Then snapped it shut again. He'd seen a misted-up sheet of glass. And cold – God, I'm cold – chilled to the marrow, though apparently fully clothed. His legs were half-buckled under him. When he tried to stretch them out, his feet came up against some hard, irregular objects. He opened his eyes again. His feet and ankles were somehow twisted and tangled up with the clutch, brake and accelerator pedals of the car. He struggled to extricate them. His head was pounding, his mouth tasted foul.

Condensation obscured all the windows. He drew the backs of his fingers across the nearest. Cold water dribbled across his hand and up his sleeve. He put an eye to the cleared area. A small car park, empty. Beyond it, a few houses and a pub - 'The Bear'. The sun was orangey and threw long shadows. A crow scavenged in a waste bin. He looked down at his watch. Coming up to eight. Then - Christ! - with a jolt he remembered Raffie.

He spun round and peered into the rear. No-one. But the accumulation of clothes and junk had been arranged into a bed of sorts. It had clearly been slept in, using his towelling dressing gown as a cover. It had to be a lot more comfortable than where he was right now. He kicked off his shoes, heaved himself in amongst the jumble, pulled the dressing gown up to his chin, and lay there, shivering.

A clock somewhere struck the hour. Were they still in – wherever the hell place it was? And was there still a 'they'? Or had Raffie done a runner? Bloody hell! He shoved a hand into the pocket of his trousers. His fingers encountered his loose change. He pulled his wallet from the inside pocket of his jacket. The paper money was there. He lay back again. Shit. Keys - where are the car keys? Should he get out of his cocoon and look for them? Then he could turn the engine on and get some heat in here. But he was warming up now. He decided against it.

Where was Raffie anyway? And God, now he needed a pee. Plus - he was becoming aware of an ominously sticky feeling around his privates. What had he been up to?

The front passenger door burst open, letting in a blast of ice-cold air. "Good morning, Al!" Raffie stood there, beaming. In his hands, a tray bearing two large steaming mugs of coffee and a large plate of bread rolls.

"Fuck's sake, Raff – shut the door!"

"Breakfast! Rolls and coffee." Raffie clambered in and slammed the door. "You will think you're in the Ritz!"

Barney manoeuvred himself upright and eyed the plate of goodies. "Where the hell did you get all this?"

"Mind, it's hot." Raffie handed him a steaming mug. "There is a greasy spoon caff down by the main road."

"Christ, you're some sort of genius." Barney saw the car keys sitting on top of the dashboard. He pointed to them. "Hand me those, will you?"

Raffie did so. Barney selected the ignition key and handed it back to Raffie. "Turn the engine on, warm us up, eh?"

Raffie eyed the key and frowned. "I do not drive. I don't know how – er - "

"Put it in that slot there - " - he pointed to the ignition - " - then just turn it to the right."

Raffie did as he was told. With a crash and a whine the car leapt like a kangaroo, shooting coffee out of the cups. The tray hit the floor, bread rolls disappeared under seats. "Oh God! God!" cried Raffie. "What have I done??"

"You bloody idiot!! The thing's in gear!"

"I do not know about cars! You said to - "

"OK, OK. Forget it. Not your fault." Barney stretched across the front seats, took the car out of gear and turned on the engine.

Raffie retrieved rolls and wiped up spilled coffee.

They ate and drank. The car warmed up. The condensation dried from the windows. The sun came in. Other vehicles began trickling into the car park. Wiveliscombe's day was beginning.

"Raffie."

Raffie looked at him over his coffee cup.

"How come you look like you do?"

Raffie was puzzled.

"I'm feeling about ninety. And you're sitting there looking like a newborn babe."

"I do not drink alcohol."

"Not at all? Ever?"

Raffie shook his head.

"That some sort of religious thing?"

"With my family it is. I personally don't have anything against it. But it was never part of my life. So I just don't."

"You should give it a try some time." Barney sipped his coffee. "Give yourself a zip and a zing."

Raffie smiled. "Is that what you have now - 'a zip and a zing'?"

"OK. Touché." Barney shrugged. "So – tell me - " - he took a bite out of his roll - " - did we have a good evening?"

"I don't know. I left you there."

"You left me?" Barney frowned. "Where?"

Raffie pointed across the car park. "In the pub. I came back to the car. You gave me the keys."

"And you left me in the pub? Oh dear. Where I doubtless quaffed my fill and more." He chuckled indulgently at his own excess. "Well, as I always say - 'Better a glimpse within the tavern caught than in the temple lost outright.'" He chewed on his roll.

"With the girl."

Barney stopped chewing. "Girl?"

Raffie nodded.

"You left me in the pub with a girl?" He shifted around to get a corner of the portable TV out of his back. "What girl?"

"Innocence fleeing the rapist."

The wheels of Barney's brain started to turn. "Tell me you don't mean that, Raff."

"Nice girl. She liked you."

"Mavis," muttered Barney, looking blankly out of the window. "Mavis from Bridport." He turned back to Raffie. "I don't know what you know about women, Gunga Din, but beware the ones that scream and run away. It's part of the agenda." He cupped his hands around his coffee.

Raffie was struggling with 'Gunga Din.'

"I said I'd take her to the bloody seaside, and all." Barney shook his head in despair.

"When," asked a bemused Raffie, "will you do that?"

"And you know what, Raff? I didn't use anything. Nothing." He ran a hand through his hair. "Just have to hope she's on the pill. Or she's infertile. Or they all missed. Jesus."

They finished off the food and drink. Raffie gathered up the empty mugs and plate.

"By the way - did you see a bog in your travels?" Barney grimaced. "I'm about to explode and dowse Wiveliscombe."

"There is one the other side of the car park. But may I warn you? - it is not nice."

They climbed out of the car.

"Listen," said Barney, "fancy a trip to Newquay? See your mate, Abdul?"

"What about Innocence fleeing the rapist - and the seaside? You told her you'd - "

"Raff." Barney lay both hands on Raffie's shoulders. "A bit of cautionary advice. English girls - right? - another day, another punter, another roll in the hay. The sixties blew the lid right off." He raised his eyebrows. "Know what I mean?" He turned away and headed across the car park towards the public toilets.

Raffie stood looking after him, frowning.

Barney called back over his shoulder. "And we get a move on, eh? Chop-chop!"

Raffie walked over to the rubbish bin and scared off the crow which flew away with a large piece of something in its beak. He dropped a half-eaten roll into the bin, then set off, still puzzling, for the greasy spoon.

The brake lights on the car in front came on yet again. Barney brought the Triumph to a stop. He hung his head out of the window and peered up and down the street. Large, once proud Victorian houses were splattered with notices in their windows and on wooden boards in their front gardens – 'No Vacancies', 'Home-from-Home Guest House', 'Sunnyside Holiday Apartments', 'Dining Room Open to Non-Residents', 'Atlantic View Hotel'.

"Welcome to Crapsville-on-Sea," he muttered, putting his head back in. He drummed his fingers on the wheel. Both ahead and in the rear, the traffic jam extended further than he could see. Cars, over-stuffed with people, pumped out petrol fumes alongside pavements thick with families, pushchairs, children sucking lollies, long-legged young women in tight shorts and kiss-me-quick hats, transistor radios, balloons, buckets, spades, crying babies.

Barney looked across at Raffie. "What's Indian Abdul doing in this madhouse then?"

"He works in a restaurant. In the kitchens."

"So where's his place then? The sooner we're out of - "

"I don't actually know where his house is, but - ."

"You don't know?" Barney ran a hand through his hair. "How are we supposed to find him if you don't know where he lives?"

The car behind hooted.

Barney looked in his rear-view mirror. "Fuck off!" He put the car in gear again and edged it forward. "I thought we just had to turn up at his pad to get a bed for the night."

"Oh dear. I'm sorry. I should have made things clearer."

"Having said that though - " - Barney grinned as he braked again and scanned the scene outside once more - " - this has to be one hell of a town in which to spend the summer."

"I certainly think we could make some money here, Al."

"We can make more than money, Gunga Din! You seen the totty out there?"

Raffie frowned. Thought about, but then discarded the idea of commenting upon 'Gunga Din'.

They sat staring at the stationary traffic ahead of them. In the rear window of the car in front, a small boy stuck his tongue out at them. Barney responded with a grotesque mimed kiss. The boy turned away in disgust. Barney turned to Raffie. "What is this Abdul to you, then? A friend?"

"More like an uncle – but not a real uncle. He used to go with me and my Dad to football. But he moved away. Some people from home were not kind to him."

"'Home' being - ?"

"India. My parents still think of India as 'home'." He looked away, clearly not wanting to pursue that.

Barney checked the dashboard clock. "Listen – it's nearly one, and I'm in dire need of a drink. There's got to be an Indian restaurant somewhere here. What was the name of the one he was working in – d'you know that?"

"Yes! I do."

"Good."

"The Taj Mahal."

"Taj Mahal. OK, Taj Mahal - here we come."

But they couldn't find a 'Taj Mahal'. So they had lunch in 'The Star of India' and asked where the 'Taj Mahal' was. There wasn't one in Newquay, and none of the staff had heard of an Abdul who worked in a local restaurant kitchen. Their lunch was bland and indifferent - what Barney called, 'Cotswold Indian'. But he drank half a bottle of their red wine and said he felt a lot better. "Not very authentic," was Raffie's over-generous verdict on the food.

They left the restaurant and wandered off. Barney was disgruntled. "I can't believe none of them knows a bloody Abdul. Aren't half the men on the subcontinent called 'Abdul'?"

"I don't know," said Raffie. "I've never been to the subcontinent."

"Shit. Sorry. I'll catch up one day."

They mooched around, looking in shops, sniggering at saucy picture postcards. Barney ate a chocolate lolly, Raffie an ice cream. They went into three other Indian restaurants to ask about Abdul but were met with blank looks and shaking heads. Barney said Raffie must have got his friend's name wrong. Raffie said that was ridiculous. Barney agreed.

By mid-afternoon, hot and tired, they had achieved nothing. Barney announced he needed to revive himself with a paddle in what he called 'the briny'. Raffie said he wondered where the sea was. Barney said there were bound to be signs pointing to it. But in any case, he added, as Newquay was sited more or less on a peninsular, whichever way they went they had a three-to-one chance of finding it. Raffie struggled with that but was, even so, impressed with the reasoning behind it.

They elbowed their way through the crowds, down one narrow street after another until they stumbled quite by chance upon a road, one side of which overlooked a wide beach hemmed in by black cliffs.

"There!" exclaimed Barney, pointing triumphantly towards the sea.

A steep stairway led down from the road to the sand. The tide was out. The beach was swarming with people. Barney looked around in despair. "Ants. Look at them. Who'd part with money to do this?"

Picking their way between exposed bodies, sandcastles and deckchairs, past a plodding, lop-eared donkey loaded with a brace of more or less jolly children, they made their way towards a low, rocky outcrop.

It was hot and there was no shade. Barney, wearied by the tortuous drive from Wiveliscombe, and the listlessness that follows a bad hangover, flopped down on his back, closed his eyes, and was soon asleep. Raffie sat by his side, propped up against the rocks. He lobbed little white shells and whatever tiny pebbles he could find at his own feet. Then he too lay down and slept.

He was rudely awoken by being dragged by his shoulders along the sand. The lower half of both legs were wet. "My God! What is happening?? My God!"

"Get up, Raff! Bloody tide's in on top of us. Get up!"

It was late afternoon. The sun had gone behind heavy clouds and a wind had sprung up off the sea. The last few holidaymakers were packing up and leaving. At the water's edge a tiny dog barked and jumped ridiculously up at a seagull hovering high in the air above it.

They made their way back up to the road. They stood among a red-skinned tide of adults and children wending their end-of-day way back to their hotels and boarding houses for the evening meal.

"Lemmings," snarled Barney. "Lemmings."

"Where," said Raffie, looking anxiously around , "are we going to sleep tonight?"

Newquay was full. The toiling classes of the Midlands and the North had booked the town. Barney drove the length of one street after another. Every guest house and third-rate hotel had a smug, 'No Vacancies' sign in the window. He threw the car around the last corner of the last street. Beyond that, the town petered out. The open road snaked away, up the hill towards the cliffs. He pulled in to the side of the road.

Raffie took that as a signal Barney was about to come up with a practical suggestion.

He wasn't. He sat back and ran a hand through his hair. "Newquay too," he observed, "appears not to want us, Raff. And by the look of those clouds up there, it's going to piss with rain before long."

"Where will we sleep tonight?" asked a plaintive Raffie.

"Dunno. Have to press on. There's got to be a pub or something." He put the car in gear once again, and pulled away. "A large whisky. That's what I need. Smelling of peat and the misty Highlands."

"My Dad drank whisky once. It made him ill."

The road coursed in a twisting, roller-coaster ribbon up and down along the tops of the cliffs. Raffie looked out at the black clouds now piling up to the west. Then down to the darkening waters of the Atlantic far below. As they crested a sharp rise, there came a sudden explosion of orange-red light as the heavy clouds, blown by a strengthening wind, cleared the lowering sun. The whole wide sky, the earth and the interior of the car were instantly suffused with an intense, orange light.

"Oh, my God!" exclaimed Raffie.

"What's up?"

"Nothing! It is wonderful. This light – it is a lantern of God!"

A blast of wind, slicing up off the sea, slammed into the car, sending it into the middle of the road. "Fuck's sake," muttered Barney, yanking it back on course.

Raffie continued peering out, mesmerized. An orange shaft of sunlight, miles wide and of biblical proportions, was sweeping, with the movement of the clouds, majestically forward across the sea. As it moved over the dark waters it turned them orange too, and the white horses pink where the wind plucked at the surface.

Barney slammed the brakes on.

Raffie spun round. "What??"

"Look." Barney slowed the car to a crawl and pointed through the rain which was now starting to fall, to a road sign up ahead. "'Tregurrian', 'Mawgan Porth', 'St Mawgan'" He stopped the car and turned to Raffie. "Which d'you fancy?"

"'Fancy'?" Raffie frowned. "What are they?"

A car passed them, hooting in protest at their stopping on a yellow line.

"Why did he do that?" asked Raffie.

"Because he's ignorant. They're place names - what d'you think they are?"

"Not like English, are they?"

"Cornish. Gaelic. Something like that."

"Is that not English?"

"Listen - d'you want to drive around in the rain all night, or - ?"

"But I have no idea, Al."

"OK. Nor me, Gunga Din. However - the closet hagiologist in me inclines me towards Saint Mawgan." He put his foot down and pulled away again into the now pouring rain.

Raffie frowned. He really would have to say something before very long about 'Gunga Din'.

That explosion of orange light was the prelude to some majestic - and intimidating - weather. We set off again, but had gone on only a short distance when the rain started to come down in sheets blown by raging winds now battering in from the Atlantic. They hit the cliff face, shot vertically upwards before levelling out again and throwing the rain diagonally at the land. It was so dark I drove with dipped headlights. Gusts hit us with such sidelong force I had to keep pulling on the wheel just to keep the car on our side of the road. Looking back on it now, part of me was savouring this joust with the elements. I was aware only of the present moment and my own mortality. Even our need of a bed for the night and the whereabouts of St Mawgan had become more or less hypothetical. It flashed through my mind that war was probably a bit like that.

Raffie, poor lad, was terrified. He sat with face drawn, staring wide-eyed ahead – probably praying to some Hindu god. I didn't blame him. I don't think he had a very good opinion of my driving anyway. After one especially violent squall which came close to propelling us onto a collision course with an oncoming motorcycle, I threw the wheel over in a near-panic and shot us off down what looked like a narrow lane.

I was preparing to breathe a sigh of relief when we were plunged into deep darkness. Vegetation slapped at the roof and windows. It was precipitously steep. I flicked the headlights on full beam. We were racketing down a narrow, rutted track strewn with loose rock. Floodwater bubbled down the middle in a frothing stream. The car bounced and rocked, throwing the pair of us around like pebbles in a can. The lower branches of overhanging trees thumped on the roof. Our speed was increasing. I put my foot on the brake. The wheels locked. We simply carried on down the hill, riding on the loose rocks. I had the sense – though from where, I know not – to release the brakes and then keep tapping on them to avoid their locking again, slowing us down little by little until we finally came to rest. The rainwater river gurgled out from under us and swept on down the hill.

I turned to Raffie and he turned to me. His face was white – or as white as his face was ever going to be.

"My God, Al," he croaked. "Where in the Lord's name are we?"

I waited for my own heart to slow down. Then said, rather breathlessly, "Christ knows, my friend. But at least down here we're not going to be blown off into the sea or sucked under a truck."

He mopped his brow with a tissue. "It really would help, I think, if we had a map."

"I doubt this badger track's on any map."

We sat with the engine running while we gathered ourselves together. I fancied I detected some lightening of the sky and with it, a slight easing of the rain and wind. "OK, Raff," I said, "let's have another go."

I released the handbrake, and very carefully let gravity take us. The gradient eventually levelled out. We crossed a line of trees and found ourselves joining a narrow, metalled road. A watery light was returning to the sky. A hundred metres ahead of us, a road-sign appeared. We both leaned forward and peered past the windscreen wipers.

"My God," said Raffie, prodding the windscreen, "it says -

"Saint Mawgan!"

"We have triumphed! We should plant our flag here, Al – like they did on Everest."

Saint Mawgan turned out to consist of a church, a shop, one pub, a few houses and little else. Not surprisingly, there was no-one about. But there were lights in the pub, 'The Magpie'. Thatched, half-timbered with attractive dormer windows. After our recent dice with death, it looked wonderful. We parked in its small car park. The rain had all but stopped. As we walked towards the door of the 'Lounge Bar', a delicate pink glow was slowly spreading from one side of the building to the other as the dark clouds moved away.

They had rooms at 'The Magpie'. We took one each. There was no-one else in and they seemed glad of the business. We were hungry. We hadn't eaten since lunch. But this was in the days before pubs did meals as they do today, and all they could rustle up for us was tinned salmon sandwiches. That was OK. We were warm now, we had a roof over our heads, a bed for the night and we could go on eating sandwiches till we were full.

We took ourselves and the food, along with a bottle of red wine for me and a glass of orange squash for Raffie to a table in a corner by an open fire. We had the place almost to ourselves. Until the food had hit our stomachs we ate and drank in silence. Then I sat back, yawned and stuck my feet luxuriously out under the table. The fire was warm, the effects of the wine lulling, comforting. I wiped my lips with a paper napkin. "So Raff," I said, "you going to tell me what you're up to?"

"'Up to'?" He looked at me over his glass of orange.

"Yes. Come on. The normal life of normal respectable people doesn't bring them to places like this on nights like this. What were you doing wandering along a country road with your holdall three hundred miles from home?"

He looked down into his glass.

"Show me yours," I said. "I'll show you mine."

He looked up, an embarrassed grin on his face.

"Tell me what you're running from, Raff. I'll do the same for you."

"Why do you say I am running?"

"'Where are you going?' I said. You answered by asking me where I was going. 'No idea,' I said. So you jumped in and shut the door. That's a man who's going for the sake of putting distance between himself and somewhere else."

Raffie took a mouthful of his squash. Telling the story wasn't easy. But he said afterwards he was relieved to have done so.

His parents, he said, were Hindus. They had arrived in the UK from India in the early 1950's – two of that hopeful band who, tempted by the British government's promises of a warm welcome and plentiful work for immigrant labour 'of good stock', came here to help rebuild a shattered economy. They were from a remote part of the state of Gujarat in the north west of the subcontinent. They had not thought, nor had they been encouraged to think, about the upheaval their simple lives were about to undergo.

Within a year of their arrival in the UK, Raffie was born. Two years later, a girl, Naseem. As Naseem approached her ninth birthday, tentative arrangements were made with another Indian couple in Leeds, for her and their son, then a boy of ten, to marry when Naseem reached the age of eighteen. Naseem herself was told nothing of this until her eighteenth birthday. The announcement, when it came, shocked and horrified her. She refused point-blank to even meet him. Born and brought up in England, she considered herself at least as British as Indian. And the British didn't make marriages that way.

To her parents that was shocking enough. But when she went on to reveal that she was already seeing a man just a little older than herself – white, English, with no particular religion - and that if she were to marry anyone it would be him, they got out the big stick. They forbade her to see him ever again. She refused, and over the following weeks a cocktail of distrust, anger, and resentment insinuated itself into what had been a relatively peaceful household. Raffie tried to intercede with the parents. To get them to see how, in the same way that they themselves had been conditioned by the society in which they'd been born and raised, so Naseem had been conditioned by this very different one.

They could not – or would not – get their heads around it. They were adamant - as was Naseem. Rows were a daily occurrence. The family struggled on in a state of permanent tension. It was, said Raffie, the most unhappy period of his life.

One evening, after a particularly long and bitter exchange involving all four of them, Naseem ran from the house in tears saying she would go where she was wanted and respected. She did not return that evening. Raffie knew where her English boyfriend lived. He went to his flat the following morning, a Saturday, to try and persuade her to return home and attempt to come to some agreement with her parents. But the boyfriend had not seen her. The police were called. Three days later, a man walking his dog on the moors near Hebden Bridge twenty miles away, came across her body in the waters of a disused quarry. There were no signs of foul play.

Raffie had been beside himself. He blamed his parents for caring more for their culture and traditions than they had done for their own daughter. Immediately after his sister's funeral, he packed a bag and walked out the front door. He walked until he found himself on the main road out of Leeds going south, the road to London. There he hitched a lift and thereafter just kept going. And going. Like me. Just going.

He stopped. Finished off his orange drink. Put the glass slowly down on the table in front of him and sat gazing into it.

I sat in a shocked silence. He was such a gentle, unassuming soul I found it hard to imagine such a tragedy occurring in his life. I didn't know what to say. I mumbled that I was sorry. Tears came to his eyes. I remember trying to persuade him that this really was the time when a double scotch would do wonders. But even in such straits, he refused, and I grudgingly admired him. And at the same time, felt oafish for even having suggested it.

"Anyway," he said, pulling himself back together, "that is my part of the deal. Now – show me yours!" And he went into a fit of embarrassed giggles.

"Me? Ah well." I poured the last of the red wine into my glass. "Not a lot to tell, really." On two accounts, I felt upstaged and humbled. His bearing and self-possession throughout the telling of his dreadful tale had been impressive; my own story, by comparison, was going to sound like the autobiography of a heel.

"Not much to tell," I said again, airily. "Nothing like that. Standard stuff really. I was born into a well-off family. My Dad was – still is - a successful industrialist. Mother a one-time beauty from Eastern Europe. I have a cousin who I never, ever see. I went to a posh school and somehow – God knows how – got into Oxford. Got a pretty crummy degree, then an equally crummy job in engineering, up in Halifax. 'Management', it was laughingly called. I stuck that for four years. By which time I was cracking up with boredom. There had to be more to life. I got out. Hit the road. And here I am." I took a sip of my wine. "And that's it."

Raffie looked puzzled. "And that is it?"

"That's what I said. What more do you want?"

"It is a very – how shall I say – sparse life."

"You got it, Raff - sparse and simple."

"You did not have a girlfriend?"

"Er - yeh – girlfriends, of course. Quite a few in fact. But – well, only ships in the night."

"Oh." His puzzlement continued. "I had assumed – I don't know why really - that you were married. Or that you had been married."

"Why," I said, trying to laugh it off, "would you have thought that?"

He shrugged. "One gets feelings about people."

That irritated me.

"And you really have not been?"

My irritation grew. But I had not got what it took, once challenged, to follow the lie right through. I had to fabricate a half-truth. Then perhaps I'd be only half-culpable. I apologized for breaking my side of the bargain. Then set about digging myself an even deeper hole.

"OK," I said. "Yes. You're right - I was. But only for a few months and it was a disaster. We were like chalk and cheese - you say 'tomayto' and I say 'tomarto'. It was sex – that's all. We couldn't keep our hands off each other. OK - that's great. For a time. We shagged each other senseless. Then there was nothing. We shouldn't have married. We agreed to part, got a divorce and that was that." I shrugged. "It's not something I like talking about."

Raffie sat in a thoughtful silence so long I felt my irritation returning. Eventually, all he said, quite quietly and without looking at me, was, "It is lucky then that you did not have any children."

A hole in the ground opened up in front of me. My own voice came back at me from afar. "That would have put the mockers on things, alright," it said. But I saw his face. Felt my arms around his little body as we whooshed down the slide. I stood up quickly, went and ordered for myself a double whisky.

In the mirror behind the bar I saw Raffie looking at me across the room.

42.

'Dear Mr Jardine,
Re- Mr. Barnaby Marechal
I am writing to inform you that after due consideration of the facts as I now know them, along with the protracted length of time this matter has remained unresolved, I am calling off any further enquiries regarding the fate and whereabouts of my husband. I would be grateful therefore if you would regard your work for me as being at an end. I would ask that you now send me your final invoice which should include all expenses you have incurred up to receipt of this letter.
I thank you for all you have done on my behalf.
Sincerely,
Ellen J. Marechal'
Harry Jardine frowned. How very sudden. One minute she's crying for him in the night; the next, she's called the whole thing off. There has to be more to it. One thing wrapped up and bundled away in order to leave the field clear for something else? This isn't a good business to be in if you want to retain a faith in human nature.

So what's going on? Frank? Easy-going Frank Lippincote? It was, after all, Frank who, as a favour to Ellen, brought him into this in the first place. Jardine had originally dismissed an early suspicion he'd had of a frisson between them. But at that last, rather uncomfortable meeting, there had been a look or two exchanged across the room. And considered dispassionately of course, life with Martha must involve some rather delicate limitations. It made sense. Goodness knows however what it would do to Martha were she ever to find out.

He read the letter again. Lay it slowly down.

He wasn't sorry that was the end of it. It had not been a comfortable assignment. He was not keen on Ellen Marechal – something about her didn't ring true. As for Marechal himself, he quite admired him. He was his own man. Whatever his reasons for doing what he'd done – for surely his disappearance was self-engineered – he wished him well. Perhaps he had never been as happy with his domestic situation as he'd made out. Though you'd hardly go as far as wiping yourself from the face of the earth simply in order to get out of a marriage. Something else had to be afoot. That abandoned son of his – was that a clue? Though Harry Jardine had no children of his own, he could imagine that turning your back on your own child like that might eventually tear you in half.

He got up and poured himself a beer. Took it to the window of his apartment and stood with it in his hand as he looked out over the river towards Docklands. Wheels turn within wheels.

"Best of luck to you, Marechal," he murmured.

43.

Despite the slight sense of disillusionment which had settled over me at the end of my day with Celeste, I walked into the Lounge Bar of 'The Amsterdam Freighter' the following morning for breakfast with a spring in my step. I still had no solid clue as to Matt's whereabouts, but he was, nevertheless, no longer just a dimly recalled memory of a very young child; I had now a sense of his adult reality. And there was the photograph to come. I was about to see what my own son looked like as a young adult. From that it must surely be possible to make a reasonable guess as to what he looks like now.

I said a breezy, 'Good morning' to a couple who came in rather furtively, and sat on the far side of the room. They clasped hands beneath the table, and whispered, each into the other's ear. They were, I guessed, in their forties, and should not have been together. I felt protective. They looked just a little lost – babes in the wood. I wished them well. Who knows from what emptiness they were running?

It was then that I discovered, with a sense of pained disbelief, that Celeste, once again, was not, after all, waiting at breakfast. The same surly young man presented himself. "Where," I asked him, edgily, "is she this morning?"

He shrugged, said he had no idea. He told me he should really be at college and was doing this only because his mum had press-ganged him into it at the last minute because Celeste had had to cancel. Why, I asked him, had she done that – i.e. cancelled. He said he had no idea, but he'd ask his mum to come out and tell me if I liked, except she was on her own in the kitchen as a result, and with all these breakfasts in she was 'up to her gills' so wasn't going to be very pleased.

I told him not to bother. I gave him my order and he ambled off.

I was angry. She'd said quite clearly she would be on duty. I looked at my watch. Ring her? Dare I? She hadn't given me a phone number. But the previous day, when I'd gone to her car to get the wine, I'd noticed a landline number on the keyfob she'd given me. It had to be hers. I'd copied it down on a scrap of paper I had in my pocket, and despite feeling some guilt, had nevertheless been rather pleased with myself. But still I dithered. My wanting to see her seemed not entirely due to practical matters. I wasn't sure how I felt about that. I decided not to think about it.

But what else was there to think about? Should I ring? Perhaps she was unwell. Maybe she'd been taken ill and had had to call an ambulance. I discounted that. Drummed my fingers on the table. Should I wait till the breakfast rush had eased and ask young Steerpike to get his mum to come out and talk to me? But then I had a sudden urge to bite the bullet. I pulled out my mobile and rang her land line. It rang and rang. Then went to her voicemail. Bugger. I left a rather irritated message saying I'd rung, then put my mobile down on the table in front of me and sat looking at it.

That felt stupid - sitting at the table looking down at a lump of black plastic. On a shelf nearby was a stack of glossy, country magazines. I slid one from the pile and flicked through its pages. Stuffed with adverts for the clothing of jolly sporting gents armed with shotguns. I had once been invited to a weekend pheasant shoot in West Sussex. I don't know what I'd expected, but being in the company of grown men armed with shotguns who, for entertainment, were blasting at birds bred for the purpose and so all but tame and virtually unmissable, sickened me. I left and drove back to Ludlow.

I tossed the magazine back onto its shelf. My mobile rang. I snatched at it, knocking it to the floor. I reached down and grabbed it.

It was her. She sounded harassed.

"Are you alright?" I asked. "Where are you?"

"I'm sorry I didn't answer just a minute ago – the phone's in the sitting room and the floors are all wet and I didn't want to walk on the bits I'd done."

"I thought you were going to be doing breakfast this - "

"I should have been. But I came down this morning to get ready for work and there was water everywhere. I'd put the washing machine on last night when I went to bed and the hose had split and water had obviously been pouring out of it for hours."

Though I felt for her, I was hugely relieved. "So," I said, "you've got a whole house to dry out."

"Well, most of the ground floor. I've opened all the doors and windows, but it's going to take me most of the day."

"Sounds a big job for one. Would you like me to come over and help?"

Silence.

"Celeste?"

"Er – I don't know. I'm not sure. No - really, it's no big deal. Just a nuisance."

"It's no problem. I'm doing nothing else now."

"You're going back to London."

"I hadn't planned which day. And in any case, I'm not going without that photograph." And then I said something I hadn't intended to say. "And indeed, one or two other things have occurred to me I'd like to ask you about anyway."

Silence again.

"Have a think about it," I said. "Then let me know. You've got my number. Or if not today then - "

"Well, I suppose we could, couldn't we? As long as you're sure."

"Would I offer otherwise?"

"I don't know. You might."

"Give me your address then." I took out my pen and prepared to write on a corner of the napkin.

I drove out into another brilliantly clear late autumn morning. It was cold. The sun was still low and in sheltered places, the roadside grass was brushed white with frost. There were still a few leaves on the trees. Birds were in the sky. The die-straight lines of the still-water dykes glinted like steel as they ran away to nowhere. I felt full. How life had changed.

The journey to Old Bolingbroke – Lincolnshire has some weird and wonderful place names - took me only twenty minutes or so. 'Christmas Cottage' stood alone some way out of the village itself. It was a small, low, huddled-together building, half-timbered and thatched, with diamond-pane windows. One or two faded roses lingered still around the door. It didn't somehow seem Celeste's style. It was set in a large plot of land most of which appeared to be given over to grass on which was tethered a goat. All the doors and windows had been flung wide open. Assorted rugs and a few smaller items of furniture had been set down on the grass.

I stood at the open front door. There she was in the hallway, on her hands and knees, in a bright yellow apron and red rubber gloves, sweeping a cloth back and forth over the wet floor. She was not aware of me. There was music from a radio, and she had heard neither the car pulling up nor the click of the front gate. I watched her. She sat back on her haunches and wrung the cloth out into a large green plastic bucket by her side. Then back onto her knees again. She reached forward and swept the cloth in an arc all around her in one direction, then back again in the other. All her movements, even those of washing a floor on her hands and knees, had an extraordinary, unforced grace. Where had she acquired that?

"Good job it's not raining," I said, raising my voice over the radio.

She looked up, startled. "Oh! Oh hi." She smiled, and pulling the loose strands of hair from her face, got to her feet.

I pointed to the floor around the door which seemed almost dry. "Can I come in?"

"Uh-huh."

I stepped inside. "Shouldn't your stars have foretold this?"

"What stars?"

"Your astrological ones."

"They're not 'my' stars." She dropped the floor cloth into the bucket at her side. "And in any case, they don't predict the future." She pulled off one rubber glove. But the other clung, half inside-out, to her fingers, its floppy wrist-end hanging limply off her hand. She held that out towards me and stood just looking at me. It took me a second to catch on. "Oh – right," I said. I took its slippery wetness in my fingers and pulled. She too pulled. As we did so it stretched, but the tension around her fingers kept it firmly in place until with a sudden rubbery snap, it came off and hung, dangling from my hand. A weird awkwardness hit me. I handed it back to her feeling deeply embarrassed.

She smiled. "Thank you."

"So," I said, clearing my throat, "what can I do to help?"

"Let's have a cup of tea first. And I'll get the photograph."

Her house was the sort of place which, had it been described to me, I would have put down as the home of a weirdo. Some of the walls were virtually papered with what I can only describe as astrological bric-a-brac. Bizarre creatures from some alien mythology peered out through intricate designs part-borrowed, it seemed, from ancient navigational charts - along with sundials, and cards depicting a fool, death, a hanged man. As we picked our way around the still wet patches on the hall floor, we passed the half-open door of a toilet through which I caught a glimpse of what looked like a silver moon suspended from the ceiling. For someone who claimed, as she did, only a passing interest in this sort of thing, I found it rather puzzling.

She showed me into a small sitting room, the floor of which had largely dried out. I sat on a sofa at a low wooden table while she left to make the tea. I heard what I assumed was water splashing into a kettle. Then her footsteps going up the stairs.

I waited, tense and nervous. The incident with the rubber glove wouldn't go away. I was unsure what to make of myself. I tried to think of the photograph I was about to see. I listened to her moving around on the floor just above my head. I looked around. On one wall was a picture of a pair of scales. Some loose scrap of information floated to the surface – the star sign of Libra. I presumed that was Celeste's own sign. She seemed to be taking a long time. Perhaps she'd forgotten where she'd put it. And maybe she wasn't taking a long time at all – maybe my own agitation was getting to me.

A piercing whistle from a boiling kettle brought her clattering back down the stairs. She hurried into the room and slapped something down on the table in front of me. "There," she said, then went out again to attend to the kettle.

I was looking down at a small brown envelope. The sort you would buy in any corner shop. It was not sealed. I wanted to take it up and open it, but my muscles wouldn't respond. When I looked at the photograph, would he be able to see me looking at him? What would he think of me?

"This is hard for you, isn't it?" said Celeste, standing at the door with a cup of tea in each hand.

It was a small, black and white print, faded and a bit dog-eared. A young man in a dark suit stood on a tiny lawn in the rear garden of a small Victorian house. In the background an older woman leaned against a wall. Whoever had taken it had not held the camera straight, setting everything slightly off-kilter.

The young man looked a bit like me. He truly did. But I really cannot describe my feelings. They burst explosively up at me out of that blurred image like something released from beneath the earth, overwhelming my judgement and my ability to handle them. But as they did so, some in-built defence mechanism kicked in and I found myself sitting back, looking at him with a calm and curiously objective eye.

He stood a little awkwardly. He was about my height. Black hair, quite long and a little curly. The jacket of his suit was open and his tie loosened at the neck. He was indeed a good-looking young man. He was mouthing something at the camera and there was amusement, laughter in his eyes. I ransacked myself for a sense of that being my son and of my fatherhood of him. I so wanted, and would have been overjoyed to feel what I had imagined would be an electric vibe of recognition. But some inner part of me - some part which I've come recently to realize can deal only with what is - was forced to acknowledge that the figure before me was a stranger where once he had shared my flesh and my soul. On the lawn there, in that far-off rear garden, standing in his suit by a flower bed just this side of a low hedge beyond which was the God-forsaken emptiness of south Lincolnshire, my son – for that's who they say he is - was a stranger. There were others to whom he was not. Others who had grown up with him, tended his childhood, been with him through illness and trauma, laughed and cried with him, cared and looked after him. Others. Between my Matt and this Matt before me was half a world and half a lifetime. And even this Matt wasn't today's Matt. What a desert I had to cross.

My hand shook as I indicated the second person, the woman. She was leaning against a wall of the house. Between the fingers of one hand she held a half-smoked cigarette. She was overweight and a bit blowzy, with untidy hair. I asked Celeste, by my side on the sofa, if she knew who that was.

"His mother."

"His - what?"

She nodded.

"You sure of that?"

"Yes."

I peered again at the photograph. Ran a hand through my hair.

We drank our tea in silence. There was only the one subject of conversation and neither of us was going there. Once again - yet again - I found myself asking if I should call the whole adventure off.

Well - my life doesn't end with that photograph. Words by an American writer - H. L. Mencken - are going through my head - 'We are here and it is now; further than that all human knowledge is moonshine'. Look around me - I am here - here now, in the morning sun. Hearing the sounds of the countryside. Here, beside this woman. The slight breeze through the open window toys with the wisps of loose hair along her cheeks. This - not my search, nor the abandonment of it - is my true reality. The rest is memory of the past, or future hope. Moonshine.

She sits very close to me and I feel her warmth. I delight in the delicacy of her hands, how elegantly her index finger and thumb entwine about the curved handle of her cup. From the corner of my eye, I glimpse the slight upthrust of her breasts as she inhales, sharing with me the same breath of morning air.

The note of a tractor wafts in from the fields. I clear my throat and wave a hand around in the air. "You – er - obviously take all this astrology stuff more seriously than I thought." It's crass, I know. But I feel a need to say something. "And is that you - Libra?" I ask, pointing to the picture of the scales.

"Yes," she says, "it is."

I stir my tea.

She stirs hers. The only sound in the room is that of both teaspoons as they hit the sides of both cups. I clear my throat once again. "Astrology,"

I say, "is not a thing I've - "

And she, at precisely the same moment, starts up, "It's not what people - "

And we both stop. Look at each other. Then burst out laughing.

We calm down, the laughter fades. "It saves papering the walls," she says, and looks oddly at me - as though the remark, being redundant, had nevertheless ridden out on its own momentum. She looks quickly away.

Silence again.

I watch her as she sips, then puts the cup down again. She pauses, her fingers still on its handle. Her rings glint in the slanting sun. "Should we, do you think," she says, without looking at me, "finish the floors now?"

We stood together in the hallway. The breeze through the open doors and windows had dried the floorboards enough to walk on.

"Looks as though that's it then, doesn't it?" I said. "Job done."

She shook her head. "There's still the kitchen. I left the floor in there till last so I wouldn't mess it up walking in and out filling and emptying buckets." She led the way.

I looked around. Muddy footprints weaved back and forth across its wet, tiled floor. "OK," I said, taking off my leather jacket and hanging it behind the door. "Tell me what I do."

She filled a red plastic bucket with warm water. Dropped a cloth into it and placed it on the floor next to her own green bucket.

I pointed first to my bucket, then to hers. "Port and starboard," I said.

She handed me a small kneeling mat. "Well," she said, "if Mister Port would like to start over there - " - and she pointed to the corner by the door that led out into the garden - " - Ms Starboard will begin in the opposite corner."

And so it was. Both of us, on our hands and knees, wiped up the water and the mud from the floor, and wrung our cloths out into our plastic buckets. As we did so we moved away from our respective starting points towards the centre of the floor and each other. It was when we'd arrived at a point where we were both kneeling and working almost side by side that it occurred to me that the pair of us were now occupying an island of still wet and muddy floor, surrounded on all sides by that which we had cleaned and was now drying.

I tapped Celeste on the back. In the middle of executing a long, sweeping arc with her cloth, she stopped and looked questioningly back at me over her shoulder. With a gesture of my hand I indicated first our little island then how the two of us were cut off. It took her a second or two to catch on. Then she burst out laughing. I expected her then to sit back on her haunches to take stock of the situation. But she remained as she was, on her hands and knees, a little ahead and just a few inches to one side of me. And there, like that, she continued laughing. Then stopped laughing. And still remained in that position, not looking round at me, her head hung down and the ends of her hair almost touching the floor. Her hips and bottom were turned half towards me. They were no more than a foot away. She was wearing a skirt that morning. Being on her hands and knees its hem was halfway up her thighs. I had a moment of intense embarrassment. Surely she knew. I really could not help looking and seeing. Nor – as I was suddenly and devastatingly aware – did she wish me to. The air around us grew thick with static. I started to tremble.

I have not the words for the next few moments. I don't want it to sound crude – it was not. Nor do I want anyone to think I'm exaggerating for dramatic effect – I'm not. I shall try to tell it as it happened. That of it at least that I can remember clearly – a lot of it has gone – burned out even as it was happening. I placed a tentative palm lightly on the delicious rise and fall of her buttocks. I heard her gasp. With the very tips of my fingers I pressed gently down. A tiny cry escaped her and her head dropped a little lower. I reached out and taking her hips in both my hands, turned her rear end gently but firmly directly to me. She offered no resistance. I was shaking so I could hardly control the finger and thumb of each hand as I took the hem of her skirt and gently, slowly lifted it. I was in an agony of anticipation – but also possessed of an enormous sense of privacy and privilege. I caught my breath, my heart leaped and the blood pounded in my temples - her buttocks, clad only in a pair of brief, lace-edged pink knickers, were presented to me. I recall then, as I slid them down towards her knees, only the warm smoothness of her flesh, her heaving back and her breath that came in gasps. My head was swimming and though I can see again now her thighs as she parted them to reveal – just – that beautiful soft warm centre into which both she and I were bound - the rest is gone. What remains is like a memory of summer lightning.

When it was over and with me still inside her, we toppled sideways like a pair of rag dolls to the floor. Very slowly I withdrew from her, turned her to me and put my arms around her. She buried her face in my neck and whispered my name. There, clinging to each other we lay, our clothes around us on the wet floor, a red plastic bucket on one side of us and a green one on the other.

We remained like that for a long time, just being, together with the sounds of the birds, the wind in the trees, a vehicle passing every now and then. Things like that are not supposed to happen to people of my age. Was I not old enough to know better? No - it was wonderful. A miracle out of its time.

But then the idyll was shattered. With a strangled little yelp, she jerked herself out of my arms and sat up.

"Christ - what??" I shot bolt-upright beside her. As I did so she turned away from me, putting both hands to her mouth.

"Celeste? What's the matter?"

She shook her head slowly from side to side. "Nothing. Nothing."

"What d'you mean - 'nothing'? Tell me. And look at me - please."

But still she kept her back to me. "I'm sorry," she said. "So sorry."

"'Sorry?' What for? It was wonderful." I took her shoulders intending to turn her face very gently to me. But as I touched her she struggled to get to her feet on the slippery floor.

"Please just tell me what - "

But she was up and starting to walk away.

I too struggled to my feet. "For Christ's sake, Celeste!"

"It's OK," she muttered. "I'll be alright. It doesn't matter." She headed into the hallway. I started after her. But she held up a hand to stop me. I watched her walk away. Naked, apart from the yellow apron which somehow remained flapping loosely around her body, and with her pink knickers dangling from the crook of one finger, she continued to the bottom of the stairs, where she stopped, paused a second or two. Then turned. And gave me the strangest of looks. Never had I encountered such a complex of emotions in one glance - guilt, sadness, elation, affection, embarrassment, even fear. Then she turned away and started off up the stairs. Her footsteps padded across the floor above. Then the gentle closing of a door.

Silence.

I looked down at myself. I was wearing my shirt. Nothing else. I could see my bare knees and my feet. I was standing amid the muddy scuffles left by our love-making on the still wet patch of floor. And cast off all about me - my socks, my jeans, my underwear. Barnaby Marechal, sometime Member of Parliament. Then from outside, there came a loud bleating from the goat. A fitting comment. The farcical absurdity of our lives.

I guessed I would go back to the 'Amsterdam Freighter'. Then later in the day, ring her. What the hell had that been about? Should I be feeling a bit of a fool? I gathered up my clothes. They were too damp to wear. As was the shirt I still had on my back, but I kept that on because it kept my privates covered – just. Why, in the circumstances, that mattered, I had no idea. I needed to dry the other stuff out. I went in search of a heater of some sort.

The radiators on the ground floor were all cold. I made my way very quietly up the stairs. Three doors, two of them closed, led off a small, square landing. One of the closed ones was presumably Celeste's bedroom. The second, adorned with a small metal fish with a speech bubble coming from its mouth saying, 'Pisces' had to be the bathroom. The third was ajar. I went into a small box room lit by a prettily-curtained window. It contained only a single divan bed and another cold radiator. I looked in a large fitted cupboard. Might there be a fan heater? No. There was no heater anywhere. I was going to have to put my damp clothes back on and drive as quickly as I could back to Marsh Enderby.

My clothes still draped over my arm, I made my way back out onto the landing. I had just started back down the stairs when there came a voice, tentative, uncertain.

"Barney?"

I stopped, one foot hovering above the step below.

"Barney – are you there?"

I turned towards the closed bedroom door.

"Come and see me."

And what else might I be letting myself in for?

"Please."

If I'd wanted to avoid the turn my life was about to take, that was the moment. But I dropped my damp clothes on the stairs and went to her.

Beneath a low ceiling crossed with dark oak beams, we stayed in bed for three days. We got out only to eat or to go to the toilet. We drank a lot of red wine and champagne. Celeste - to my surprise or not, I wasn't sure – had ample supplies of both. When we did finally emerge it was primarily because we were out of fresh food.

It had been a time of glorious excess. For too long I had been captive inside my own head and skin. Our true home is the wind and the sun, the shadows of clouds that race over the fields, the falling rain, the stars, the running seas. I astonished myself. I had given in, held and been held. There had been moments when I had an almost blissful sense of oneness - that 'me' and 'she' were all but momentary irrelevancies. And all this so late in my life. One thing was certain, Ellen – my dear and long-beloved Ellen - was gone from it.

We'd been happy, Ellen and I. That at least is how I'd spoken about us to others and how others, I think, had seen us. But perhaps things had not been all I'd made them out to be, even to myself. I'd compromised. We both had. But how else will you get through life? I suppose it depends on the extent of the compromise. In the forcing frame of day-to-day living with another human being, any ill-judged one is going to bring trouble. As for me, I'd compromised in about as fundamental a way as possible, all in the interest – as I'd seen it - of holding onto Ellen. And if Ellen too were making her own ill-judged compromises vis-à-vis me, then we'd both been living in some place to one side of reality. Advertising and politics may have made a cynic out of me, but I reckon it's what most couples do.

One thing Ellen and I congratulated ourselves on was our sex life. 'If the sex is good,' Ellen used to say, 'then the rest is good. And if the sex is good it's because the rest is good'. There was a playful shrewdness in those words – oddly untypical of Ellen - which appealed to me. I also knew from oblique references in conversation with many of my colleagues that she and I were still enjoying something often grown threadbare in their own relationships.

The sex was good – on occasions, even slightly wonderful. But we always did it in bed. At night. Among sheets, pillows. In the missionary position – albeit with the light on. Ellen had been brought up with, and maintained too respectful an eye on convention to dig down into the fecund subsoil of living where Celeste and I played - wherever, whenever and however - as natural as the wind through trees, the sun over water. With her, I was reminded of that very old joke about the couple who also felt like that about it and got banned from the Café de Paris.

I'm not maligning Ellen – it was my marriage as well as hers. I didn't spend it burning to swing from chandeliers. It was simply not in the manual. We had our way of life. What I brought to that way of life was the result of careful planning a long time before she and I met. Around my mid-thirties, as the green shoots of adult decency had started to show through, I'd taken a textbook to the compulsive and disordered young man I'd been. I re-formed him on a template of stylish convention. The result dressed well, talked the talk, walked the walk and made no waves. Hence my success, my popularity with all and sundry. Hence my marriage to Ellen. Hence my rapid rise up the ladder. Hence my welcome into the establishment. Hence my prison. Celeste sprung me from that prison.

I love her for it even now.

I returned to the 'Amsterdam Freighter' to collect the rest of my clothes. I'd paid them well in advance so I was still in credit. Celeste came with me. But only for the ride. She wouldn't come into the pub. People would talk, she said. I'm sure she was right – people do. But why that should be a problem I didn't know and didn't ask. So I dropped her off to wait for me by the little recreation ground on the corner of the green. It was quite early in the day and there were few people about. I left her sitting on a swing, pushing herself to and fro with her feet.

As I approached the pub, I noticed that lights were on in the bar-cum-breakfast room and that a number of people were eating breakfast. I wondered, in passing - and thought no more of it at the time - why she had not been asked to work that morning. Or on any of the mornings when I'd been with her in Christmas Cottage.

When I returned with my briefcase and suitcase, Celeste was still on the swing, but standing by her side was a small boy. He seemed to be showing her something in his hand. As I approached he ran off back to the woman I assumed was his mother, sitting on a nearby bench. "Bye!" Celeste called after him.

I went and stood by her side. "Who was that?" I asked, feeling unaccountably irritated.

"He said his name's Kevin. He was showing me his pet dinosaur." She chuckled. "He told me it lives with him in the big wood."

"Where's that then?" I demanded. "'The big wood?"

"I wouldn't take it too literally. He's only little."

"I see," I said, tight-lipped and feeling rather foolish. "I'm afraid I don't know much about children."

She reached out from her swing and put her arms around my waist. Buried her head in my chest. My irritation eased. I pushed my fingers into her hair, ran them gently down to her neck and felt its warmth. I suggested we went to the sea.

"And then will you stay with me?" she said.

"Stay with you? For how long?"

"For ever."

"For ever," I said, "is a very long time."

I am not in love with Celeste. In fact, I'm not at all sure what being 'in love' means. But as I understand it, I'm not. We've done a lot of the things those in love are reputed to do. We've walked hand in hand by the sea. We've laughed together, cried together once or twice, and talked. We've talked indoors, out-of-doors, in bed, and with our hands around wine glasses warmed by an open fire. We've sat on the grass and watched the sun set. And we've made love. Many, many times we've made love, had sex, been intimate, screwed, fucked – all of those. We've done all that. But I have no sense of being 'in love'.

And I have to leave. This time is over. We're burning out. As the flames flicker and die, there, standing alone among the ashes, is my son.

And there's something else - Celeste's bizarre behaviour that first morning at Christmas Cottage. Behaviour she has never explained. My questions have been met with smiles and evasions. It has left me with the uncomfortable feeling that whatever secret she's keeping, she's getting some sort of buzz from keeping it.

Last night I dreamed again of the man in the garden. The black coat, the long red scarf trailing on the gravel path in the wind, and his face, as always, turned away from me. The wind picked up the scarf this time and swirled it around in the air, up, right up into the trees that mark the boundary of the meadow that leads down to the river. And faint, fading on the wind, there is Ellen's voice as she calls to me from the open door of the kitchen.

"It's been good Barney, hasn't it?"

"Yes. It has."

She hesitated. "There's been an elephant in the room though, hasn't there?"

"We knew it would come."

"So - " - she took a deep breath - " - when will you go?"

"Tomorrow."

She didn't argue or try to dissuade me. She said she understood. But didn't want us to sleep together that final night. On one level that didn't seem to make much sense; but on another, I knew where she was coming from. I slept on the small divan bed in the spare bedroom. I say 'slept', but I did little sleeping. I doubt she did either.

I got up to a cold, grey dawn. I left my room on tiptoe and was about to make my way along the landing to the bathroom when I hesitated. The bathroom door was open a fraction – just enough to give me a view of two bare, flexed knees protruding from under the hem of a blue nightdress as she was seated on the toilet. Her calves were whiter, thinner, more fragile than I would have remembered. She seemed so vulnerable. And I was about to walk out on her.

I turned away and went back to my room. I stood just inside the door, waiting for her to go back to hers. But after the flushing of the toilet, I heard her soft footsteps padding up to my door. They stopped outside. I took a step back as the door was very slowly opened. She stood, looking up at me. Her hair was dishevelled, her eyes dark and unslept. I asked her – it sounded vacuous - if she was alright. Her response was to reach out and take my hand in hers. She went to lead me from the room. I held back. This was over.

"Once more," she said, quietly. "Just once. So I don't forget."

We lay side by side, on our backs, in a silence that grew more painful by the second. Our hands were just touching, fingers careful though not to entwine. The clock in the hallway downstairs ticked. The sun cast shadows of the net curtains on the wall opposite. A breeze brushed the wasted tendrils of the clematis against the window. A car passed in the lane outside. Who would be the first to make the move?

The car outside stopped. Reversed, then stopped again. Its engine was left running as footsteps – heavy, irregular – started up the gravel path.

I turned to Celeste who was very slowly sitting upright, frowning.

"Postman?" I said.

She shook her head.

The footsteps arrived at the front door. Then a sharp metallic crash.

I got up on my elbows. "What's that?"

"The letter box."

More crashing. Then a heavy thump against the door, and what sounded like the tearing of paper.

Celeste clutched my hand.

I slid out of bed, grabbed my shirt and struggling into it, ran down the stairs to the front door. One corner of a huge brown envelope, its contents bulging, was jammed in the letterbox and whoever was on the other side was attempting, against the odds, to ram the whole thing through.

"Wait!!" I banged the flat of my hand on the door. "Wait! I'll open the door!" But as I was drawing the bolts I heard the footsteps starting away again down the path. "Hey! Just a minute!" Tugging my shirt down over my privates with one hand, I threw the door open with the other.

An old man in a shabby suit was hobbling away down the garden path as fast as his uncertain legs would take him. His long grey hair trailed over his collar, his trousers were way too short and he wore socks with sandals.

"Oi! Come back!!"

He stopped, paused, and seemed about to turn to me, when Celeste appeared by my side. Coincidentally or not, he changed his mind and loped on out of the garden. He fell into the open door of his car, slammed it, rammed the car in gear and shot away down the lane.

I turned to Celeste by my side. "Who," I said, "was that?"

Her eyes were wide. She shrugged and slowly shook her head.

"You don't know? He seems to know you."

She looked at me, saying nothing.

I peered down at the bulging brown envelope. He had managed to shove only one corner of it through the letter box, so the vast majority of it was hanging precariously off on the outside of the door. "And what the hell," I said, pointing to it, "is this?"

Celeste fiddled with the belt of her dressing gown. She watched agitatedly as I lay the unwieldy envelope down on the kitchen table. I read out the spidery handwritten words on the label. "'Mister Bernard Marshal, c/o Christmas Cotage, Old Bolingbroke.' 'Cottage' with only one 't'." I looked up at her. "'Bernard Marshal' is a name I haven't used since my twenties."

Her agitation increased.

"Who was that, Celeste?" I said, very quietly.

She looked at me, but said nothing.

The corner of the package was torn. Inside I could see papers of some sort. I thrust my hand in through the tear and with one yank, ripped the whole package apart. Celeste gasped as an avalanche of paper fell out across the table and the floor - letters, folders, scribbled notes, exercise books, drawings.

I gazed at it in a stunned silence. Fallen at my feet, was a sheet of dark grey art paper. I bent down to pick it up. As I did so a dreadful foreboding swept over me. It was a child's crayon drawing.

44.

"What do you all get up to on Saturday nights in Wiveliscombe then?" Barney pushed the dirty pint glass down into the automatic washer.

Mavis sipped her Cherry B and shrugged. "Get pissed." With a precise, double tap of her index finger, she knocked the ash from her cigarette. She hoped she seemed worldly and sophisticated.

"I'd heard Wiveliscombe was a with-it place. You know - far-out, and trendy." Barney pulled the glass out of the washer. "No?"

She drew on her cigarette and coughed. "Dunno where you get your information."

"Listen - " - Barney started drying the glass - " - how did you find me?"

"You told me."

"Told you what?"

"Where you were going."

"I told you?"

She nodded. "That night."

Barney frowned. 'That night', for him, remained a virtual blank.

"You said you were taking your friend to the seaside and did I want to come. And if I did, to bring my bucket and spade, you said."

He reached up and put the glass in the rack above his head.

"And I said yes. But you didn't wait for me."

"It was a bit of a joke, really."

"You didn't say it like it was a joke."

"Anyway, the 'seaside's' not 'Newquay'. How did you figure Newquay out?"

"There's a coach that - "

The street door burst open, flooding the bar with sunlight and a chattering gaggle of middle-age holiday couples in jumpsuits, Bermuda shorts, T-shirts, baseball caps, wedge heels, white socks with sandals.

"Grockles!" exclaimed Barney. "The crock of gold."

"What on earth," said Mavis, eyeing them with crushing distaste, "have they got on?"

Barney moved towards them as they came up to the bar.

She raised her voice above their chatter. "What time do you finish?"

He looked back over his shoulder. "No idea. Late."

She wrinkled her nose. Stubbed out her cigarette, then took her Cherry B and sat down at an empty table in the corner.

Barney, pouring the first Babycham, frowned as he looked at her across the room.

From the cliff top they watched the sun setting across the western sea. Mavis's cigarette glowed red in the dying light. She drew on it. "You said 'late'. Nine isn't late. Not – 'late'."

"Ah. But you see, I had you down as a nice, well-brought-up young lady who kept respectable hours." With a loud fizz, Barney pulled the tab out of a can of beer. "Early to bed – early to rise, and all that. Cheers." He drank.

She looked askance at him. "After that night in Wivi, you thought that? Cripes. You must have been with some corkers in your time."

He drank again and handed the can to her. She took a long swig. Grimaced and wiped her lips with the back of her hand. "Don't like that much."

He took the can from her. "Don't drink it then."

"I don't not like it that much."

Far out on the black sea the lights of a small boat rose, dipped, disappeared and reappeared in the swell. Behind them, down the hill, the lights of Mawgan Porth flickered. Music drifted up to them, rising and fading on the air. Mavis closed her eyes. "Lovely this." she said. "Really lovely."

"I still don't know," said Barney, "how you come to be here."

"That'll be my secret then won't it?" she said, without opening her eyes.

He put an arm around her shoulders and drew her to him.

"A woman needs her secrets."

"You got any others?"

"That'd be telling, wouldn't it?"

He placed a hand very gently on one of her breasts.

"Cheeky," she said, dreamily.

He drew one finger down towards the nipple.

"Oooh," she cooed.

He took her in his arms and kissed her. Ran a hand slowly down her back and around her buttocks. "Nice bum, Mavis," he said. "Cute."

"I didn't come all the way here just to do this, you know."

"We'll do other things as well."

"It's nice to see you again, Al."

"And you."

"I'll bet you never gave me another thought after that night."

"You were never out of my mind."

"Shameless." She put a hand between his thighs. "But I like it." She slid her hand slowly upwards.

"Oh, Christ," he said.

She started to undo his belt. "Do it like you did it that night – nicely. Ever so nicely."

He had no recollection whatever of how he'd 'done it' that night.

She wriggled out of her knickers. "Don't think we're going to get an audience up here, do you?" she said. "On a bloody clifftop?"

"Nobody comes up here in the dark."

"I hope I do."

"Do what?"

"Come – up here in the dark!" She cackled.

"Jeez, you're something else."

She giggled. "Come on then."

He eased her thighs a little further apart. "Let's make it snappy."

"Not too snappy. Ooh – that's nice."

They lay on their backs looking up at the stars. Mavis puffed on a cigarette. "Do you know about stars?" she said.

"Do I know what about them?"

"Which is which. That sort of thing."

"Like the Plough and the Bear, you mean?"

"Stars, I said. Not pubs." She wriggled her body around on the grass. "Oooh - ooer!"

"What's up?"

"I'm all sticky."

"What d'you expect?"

"I'm not complaining."

"Stars," said Barney, sipping his beer, "are the ones that twinkle."

"They all twinkle, don't they?"

"Planets don't."

"What's a planet?"

"Like where you are now. The earth's a planet."

She peered up into the sky. "So which is a planet up there now then?"

"Can't tell. You'd need binoculars."

"So what's the difference?"

"Between a planet and a star? For a start, you couldn't lie on the grass on a star."

"Why not?"

"Stars are all just gas and flames."

She looked disbelieving. "Who says?"

"Astronomers."

"They been up there then, have they?"

"Shut up."

She giggled. Drew on her cigarette. Watched the stars' light dulled through the smoke she released into the still air above her. The sea churned gently and unseen against the rocks at the foot of the cliffs. The music came to them again through the darkness.

Barney felt in all his pockets for another can of beer. "Disaster." He pulled a face. "We're out of beer."

"Is that a fair – that music?"

"Dunno. Might be. Let's find out. And get some more beer." He stood up, reached out and pulled Mavis to her feet. She brushed grass from her skirt.

"How old are you, by the way?" he said.

"Old enough."

"I know that. But how old? Twenty?"

"Take away one, baby snatcher."

They set off down the hillside towards the lights of Mawgan Porth.

Mavis took his arm. "Did that friend of yours come here with you, like you said? The one that was in The Bear that night?"

He didn't answer.

"Al? That friend you had in Wivi. Did you - ?"

"Raffie. Yeh. But well – he's around – but we don't go about together a lot now."

"He was nice. Where did he come from?"

"Leeds. I think."

"No – he was Indian or something. Where did - ? "

"Leeds. I told you. England's multi-cultural now. Or hadn't you noticed?"

"Didn't fall out, did you?"

"No. He just likes living in the village. I got pissed off with it. Me - I thirst for the noise, the temptation, the glitzy buzz of the town."

"I like the way you talk."

"So I moved. I've got a bedsit. Or 'bedshit' as I prefer to call it. Full of character - if you like squalor. Come and see it if you like."

She squeezed his arm.

They carried on down the hillside. "So," she said, "what does Raffie do with himself now then?"

"Dunno. He had a lot of personal stuff going on. His sister topped herself not long ago."

"Fuck. Poor guy. Let's go and take him out for a drink, eh? Cheer him up."

"No chance. He doesn't drink."

"Gosh. Why not?"

"Some religious thing."

"Well," she said, cosily wrapping both arms tightly around one of his, "I know a drink that'll cure any old religion."

"Mavis - Raffie doesn't - "

"It's magic. Me and a friend made it up one pissy-arse weekend when - "

"Eh - listen!" Barney stopped. Turned to her. "Raffie does not drink. OK? Does not want alcohol. Does not want to associate with those who do. Does not. Ever. OK?"

She looked straight back at him. Blinked. "OK. Keep your shirt on. Raffie doesn't drink."

He went on ahead.

She hurried after him. "Are you alright?" She tugged his arm. "Al - what's up?"

He stopped, turned to her.

She searched what little she could see of his eyes in the near-darkness. "You got some problem with Raffie?"

He looked at her, saying nothing. Then placed a hand gently on her forearm. "Leave it, eh?" he said. "Please."

She smiled, nodded. "OK."

He pointed down the hill. "Beer. I'm in dire need."

With a sudden, "Whoopee!" she took off down the grassy slope. She stumbled across the uneven ground, then stopped, yanked off her shoes and waving them above her head, continued on ahead of him, laughing, down towards Mawgan Porth.

Barney followed at half her speed. Her frail figure, her shoes bobbing around in her hand, her skirt flapping about her thin legs and her hair trailing out behind her as she ran was silhouetted just for a moment against the silver reflection on the sea way below of the light from an almost full moon. The image lodged in his head. He had a sudden sense of life about to get out of hand.

45.

Frank switched off the engine. Reached into the rear seat for his briefcase. He glanced at Ellen who sat looking blankly out of the front windscreen. He frowned. "Are you alright?"

"Shouldn't I be?"

"You don't look it."

"I'm sorry. I'll try and look it."

"Listen." He lay a hand on her knee. "It'll be alright." Then leaned across to kiss her. With a hoarsely whispered, "Frank!" she pushed him away and pointed towards the house.

He smiled. "No problem. Not today."

"What do you mean – 'not today'?"

"Today is Martha's awayday. A minibus from a local charity picks her up every Wednesday. Her and three others. They go all over the place - the Black Mountains. Tintern Abbey. They went all the way to Barmouth last week."

They got out of the car and made their way towards the front door.

"What do they do when they get there?" Ellen asked. "Sit and look at the scenery?"

"Probably. Have tea. Talk." He put the key in the door. "When you're stuck in the house twenty-four hours a day six days a week, drinking tea and looking at scenery's like a night at the opera for you and me."

He opened the door and ushered her into the hallway.

She took off her coat and handed it to him. "I have to be honest and say I can't stand opera."

"You serious? I'd always thought of you and Barney as opera-lovers."

"Goodness knows why."

"But you went, didn't you?"

"When we had to. As like as not dragging along with us some half-cut 'captain of industry' – plus floozie."

He looked shocked.

"Oh, come on, Frank. You know how it is." She watched as he hung their coats up side by side. "Anyway," she said, "now you can kiss me."

He caught her arm and drew her to him. As they kissed she pushed her fingers through his hair. "So," she murmured, "are you actually telling me you and I have the house to ourselves?"

"Till six this evening. At the earliest."

They kissed again. He ran a hand down her back, eased her groin in towards his.

"But work first, eh?" She placed the flat of both hands on his lapels.

He sighed. "Work first, work first - the story of our lives." He took her arm and propelled her along the hallway towards the study. She swept a hand all around - ahead towards the tall window which gave onto the rear garden, up the curving sweep of the staircase and along the balustraded landing that ran around two sides of the upper floor. "This house," she declared expansively, "feels a lot bigger today."

Frank placed the box containing the manuscript down before him on the desk. Ellen pulled up a chair beside him. He removed the lid from the box and sat looking down at the contents.

She looked expectantly at him.

He turned to her. Smiled.

"So?" she said smiling in return. "How are we doing?"

He lifted the manuscript out and lay it gently down on the desk. "Well," he said, in a self-congratulatory tone, "we are almost, almost there."

Her smile faded.

He patted the topmost sheet, gently as he might a baby's head. "May I read a little of it to you?"

She frowned. "'Read' it? Why?"

"If I may. To make the point."

"What 'point'? What are you talking about?"

"The opening para for example. If I may - "

"Just a minute, just a minute! 'Almost, almost there', did you say?"

"Indeed. So just let me - "

"Frank - this was going to be the final check. This, you said, would see us home."

"Words from Osborne who I saw yesterday afternoon - 'Tone,' he said. That's all it is now – a matter of tone."

"And what - may I ask - is that supposed to mean?"

"Let me read and clarify." He picked up the top sheet. "The opening para - *'A girl does not go to a funeral expecting to meet there the man she is to marry. But that is what happened to me. For that is how I came to meet my Barney - better known to most as 'Barnaby Marechal, MP.'"*

Ellen struggled to contain her confusion and irritation.

" '*The funeral was that of Barney's own mother. At the moment he lost her, so he found me. As father used to tell us girls, 'Life is a wheel of perpetual motion. The ending of one thing marks the beginning of another'.*" He looked up, smiling. "Do you not sense here a touch of stylistic, contextual conflict?"

"No."

"OK - well, Osborne has pointed out that on the one hand there is a tone of quite charming naiveté. But that naiveté delivers the sort of punch many might find just a tad - might I say - distasteful as an opener - funerals and all that, you know."

She looked askance at him. "I have not the least idea what he's talking about - and nor, do I think, do you."

He coughed loudly into his hand, then continued reading. "'*I was living in Edinburgh at that time and I was already engaged to be married. My fiancé was one -* '"

"No Frank - spare me! What the fuck is 'tone'? Pardon my French."

"His word, Ellen. Not mine."

"Meaning?"

"Well – the - er - spirit of the work, the timbre of it, if you like, needs just a little - "

"'Timbre'? What's that - apart from half the French for a stamp?" She lay a hand gently on his. "Frank - have you actually asked yourself what this man is trying to say? Mmm?"

"Well – and these are his words again – the overall resonance of the piece could do with a little - "

"Ah," she said, sitting back, an ironic smile on her face, "the 'overall resonance'. Well, now I see."

"And he assured me there is absolutely no - "

"Frank! What he's trying to tell you – and what you're not hearing - is that you and I are wasting our time. We're wasting his time. He doesn't like what it reads like, what it sounds like and what it is. That's the 'overall resonance'. Right?"

He rubbed a finger nervously around his chin.

"I need a drink." She stood up. "Will anyone mind if I go and pour myself one?"

He transferred his finger to his brow and rubbed that. "I guess not."

"Do you want one?"

He shook his head.

She left the study.

He listened to her footsteps retreating along the hallway. He smoothed out the pages in front of him. Then sat staring down at them.

She came back with a gin and tonic in one hand, a large whisky in the other. She handed the latter to him. He frowned. "But I said I didn't - "

"I know what you said. But you're going to need it."

He watched her as she sat down beside him. She raised her glass. "Bottoms up."

They drank. He waited.

She took another sip. Then put her glass down on the desk. "I'm through."

He leaned towards her as though more surely to hear and understand. "You're – through? How d'you mean, you're through? Through with what?"

She picked up the top page of the manuscript and waved it in his face. "That."

"The book?"

"Just so."

"Ellen, just a minute. You can't. I mean that you're - "

"I can." She tossed the sheaf of paper back towards the pile. It missed and slithered away across the floor. "My book is written. Done. Finished. Your man of books can take it or do the other thing."

"But -"

"I told you at the start that if I were going to open my wounds to the scrutiny of the great unwashed, I would not have some whippersnapper of an agent telling me what to say or how to say it."

"I think," he said, turning his glass slowly around in his fingers, "one should respect professional opinion."

"I do. The man does not like the way I write, and that's his professional opinion. I respect it."

Frank bit his lip, his brows deeply knitted.

"I'm sorry Frank - I am not a writer. You convinced me I could be. You persuaded yourself I was. But I'm not. He knows that and so do I."

"Oh, dear." He turned and looked out of the window. "This, you know, is an awful shame."

She shrugged. "Worse things happen at sea."

"The most awful shame however, is that Barney - " - he spun round to face her - " - big, moral Barnaby Marechal whom everybody loves and looks up to, ups and leaves his wife - abandons her – then cruises off into the blue and is not ever, by anybody – even by you who is the most sorely hurt by his actions – called to account, criticized, or exposed. This - " - and he banged the flat of his hand down on the manuscript - " - is the only conceivable instrument of restitution. And you're abandoning that as he has abandoned you." He stopped, wide-eyed and a little breathless. "Mister Nice-Guy turns Traitor!" - that's your title."

She gazed at him in amazement. "My, my. How very muscular of you, Frank. Not to say, how insanely jealous." She chuckled and looked at him over her glass. "Now there's a thing I'd never suspected."

"We can't just throw it to the winds, Ellen."

"I think I agree." She put her glass down very slowly. "And with you in such a furnace of passion, I think we should seize the very moment."

He frowned. "Which moment? I'm not sure what - "

"Carpe diem? In an empty house?" And she turned on him a sidelong, coquettish look.

The penny dropped. For a few seconds he just stared at her. Then quite suddenly, with a hoarse, "Oh, God!" and his eyes locked on hers, he leaned forward, put a hand under her skirt and ran it gently up the inside of her thigh. She jerked violently away. But her reaction was entirely involuntary and as the ends of his fingers approached her pudenda she flung her head back, grasped his wrist in both hands and guided his hand the rest of the way. He half-heard some animal-like noise escape his own throat and as his fingers encountered, through the thin material of her underwear, the pliant ridge of soft, warm flesh, he lost himself. He lurched up out of his chair and fell on her. She rescued some fragment of her own self-possession and pushed him away, "Not here!"

"It's alright. It's alright" He fumbled frantically with the belt and zip of his trousers. "They won't be back!"

"I mean not on the floor!" She kicked off her shoes. "Let's find a bed. And hell, I need a wee!"

"Christ!" Holding his trousers with one hand as best he could, half-up around his knees, he pulled Ellen after him with the other as she staggered along trying to unzip her skirt and unbutton her blouse all at the same time. The pair of them coalesced into an eight-limbed organism as it made its way, octopus-like, up the staircase and along one side of the landing to Frank's single bedroom. He kicked open the door. Ellen held back – "I need a wee, Frank. I'm sorry but I really have to have a wee." She looked around the landing. "Where is it? Where's the - ?"

"Door at the far end." Frank pointed to the limb of the landing that ran at right-angles. "And don't be long!"

Throwing away her blouse and kicking off her skirt as she went, Ellen half-ran along the landing.

He went into his bedroom and tore off all his clothes. Stood stark naked in the middle of the floor. He caught sight of himself in the mirror. Goodness. Look at him. Not quite what it was twenty years ago, but nevertheless worthy of respect. Standing and admiring his own arousal however, in his own middle-class bedroom designed by Martha with coordinated floral furnishings, genteel paintings of rural scenes, along with photographs of the grandchildren crossed a line. He looked quickly away, climbed into the single bed, pulled the duvet up around his neck and waited, waited in ever-mounting tension. God. He had not thought there could be, at his age, such need. For months now they had, in Ellen's phrase, 'been at it like rabbits'. And hell, he wished she'd hurry.

There came the distant flushing of the toilet. His hands tightened on the duvet. He waited for the sound of her padding footsteps hurrying back to him along the landing. He stretched right out, felt gloriously tensed. The sound of the toilet cistern refilling, faded. Then silence. She seemed to be taking a long time. He frowned. There came an odd little cry, like a whimper. He sat slowly upright, listening. A second or two more of silence - before a piercing scream suddenly ripped through the whole upper floor. He shot from the bed and hurled himself out onto the landing.

Ellen, naked and trembling, her arms limp at her sides, was making her way towards him. Seeing him, she stopped. Her eyes were big, black, looking straight at him out of an ashen face.

His mouth went dry. "Christ. What?"

"That room – the one next to the bathroom."

"What about it?"

She shook her head very slowly from one side to the other.

Pushing past her, he strode through her discarded clothes along the landing, round the corner onto the other limb, slowing down just a fraction before taking the last step that would bring him level with Martha's bedroom.

The door was half-open. Things inside looked pretty much as they always did in Martha's bedroom. Sunlight was flooding in from the window in the opposite wall. On the table, in a pool of light, the book she was currently reading. To one side of that, her tray with biscuit tin, plate, sugar bowl, teapot, cup and saucer ready for her elevenses. And Martha herself was sitting where she always sat – in the high-backed chair Frank had bought for her last birthday. With her head resting on her chest, it looked like she had fallen asleep. One hand lay in her lap, the other hung limp over the arm of the chair. On the low table in front of her was a handwritten sheet of notepaper.

46.

Mavis threw a pebble at a nearby rock. "All I'm saying is why don't I move in with you? Just for the summer. I'm not asking you to marry me, for Christ's sake. After that we go our separate ways." She shrugged. "If that's what we want."

Barney gazed out to sea.

"You're on your own in a crummy bedsit and I'm on my own in a crummy old hostel. Sharing a bedroom with a load of women. Doesn't have to be like that."

"How did you find me? You've never told me."

"It wasn't difficult."

"All I told you was that I was going to take Raffie to the seaside. So how come you fetch up at 'The Fountain' in Newquay?"

"What's it worth?"

"What's what worth?"

"The answer."

"It's not worth you taking up residence, if that's what you're getting at."

She picked up another pebble. "Not quite sure what your problem is, Al."

"And what's that supposed to mean?"

"Nothing." She lobbed the pebble. It plopped into a small rock pool. She turned to him. "Your friend Raffie went into the caff down by the traffic lights in Wivi and got some breakfast for you. Didn't he?"

"Go on."

"Then you turned up a bit later and bought a can of beer. Right?"

"For the journey. I wasn't in good shape."

"I'm not surprised. Anyway, you got talking to the old alkie who hangs around in there. Everybody calls him Pisspot. He drinks Worthington 'E' till he gets offensive, then they chuck him out."

"I didn't 'get talking' to him – he hijacked me. And how do you know all this anyway?"

"Me and some friends hang around in there. Coffee's crap but it's better than nothing and there's nowhere else. Anyway, you upset Pisspot because - "

"He asked me was I a tourist and where was I going? I said I wasn't a tourist and I was going to Newquay. He said if I wasn't a tourist what was I doing going to Newquay? I thought 'What's it to you, anyway?' and told him that I - "

"You said you were going to work in a bar there because you were a student at Oxford and you needed work for the summer."

"And that lit his fire. 'Oooh,' he went, waving his hands around, 'Mister La-de-dah here is at Oxford University'. Mummy and Daddy must be loaded and did I play football for Faggots United?"

Mavis giggled. "Wind a saddo like him up, what d'you expect?"

"I didn't wind him up."

"You told him you were at Oxford."

"So I was. Once."

Her mouth fell open. "You serious?"

"Yes. Trinity College - where I got a Bachelor of Arts degree in PPE."

"Mmm," she said, grudgingly. "Clever, aren't you? What's 'PPE'?"

"Philosophy, Politics and Economics."

"So what are you doing working in some old pub?"

"That's my business. You talked to Pisspot. Then what?"

"Easy-peasy. I get a coach. There's one comes to Newquay from London twice a week that calls at Wivi. I get a room at the YWCA down the road. Start looking in the pubs in the centre of town. The fifth one I look in – there you are, pulling pints. Took me a couple of hours."

"Clever, aren't you?"

She pulled her knees up and rested her chin on them. "You also told Pisspot you were going to screw as many women as you could fit in while you were here. How many have you managed so far? Not including me, that is."

"No idea. I lost count."

They sat for a while in silence. Then, "Fuck you, Al," said Mavis, quietly. She got up and wandered down the beach to the shoreline. She stood alone, looking out over the sea.

Barney watched her. Watched as the wind caught her hair and trailed it out to the side. Then dropped it back around her shoulders. Her legs were really nice, shapely. She let the waves come in over her feet. They swirled and bubbled around her ankles. She never seemed to wear many clothes. Perhaps it was just that what she did wear always seemed to be light-coloured and of thin, delicate material that hung loose on her small, angular frame. Where did she come from? The house they'd made out in that night – what little of it he could recall - was big with expensive furniture. Whose was it? She'd told him she came from Bridport. Not far from Wivi. Did her parents have money? She was a feisty little person. Not educated, but knew what was what. He liked her. But he didn't want a relationship. Not a real one. He was only here for the beer.

47.

Youssef switched off the engine. He turned to me. "Please, they will need your passport." It was the middle of the day. The heat was intolerable.

"Where are we?" I asked.

He looked puzzled. "Iferouane."

I tried to claw back the reasons for all this. "What," I asked, "do they want my passport for?"

"It is police post. They check passports."

"I'm not leaving the country. What do they need my passport for?"

He shook his head as he held out his hand. "Please. I am sorry."

I gave in. You do. I drew from my shoulder bag the leather wallet containing my passport. I slipped it out.

I am no nationalist and no little Englander. And when all's said and done, I'm probably not even much of a patriot either. But out there in no-man's land, the sight of that imperial coat of arms and the words 'British Passport' embossed on the front threatened to bring a lump to my throat. I handed it to Youssef. He got down out of the vehicle and walked away with it towards the low mud building visible through the trees. I put the now empty wallet back in my shoulder bag. I felt exposed and vulnerable.

I sat back to wait. Then started violently. Eyes were on me in the rear view mirror. The European man. I'd forgotten him. He was easily forgotten. He sat forever silent, impassive in the back, saying nothing, hearing everything. His breathing was laboured. Like he had some sort of chest problem. The eyes looked unhurriedly away.

We were parked in the shade under trees. I was running with perspiration. The rash in my groin made sitting comfortably impossible. In the other Land Cruiser, Sam the driver and the Tuareg cook had their eyes closed. They dozed peacefully like middle-aged men in the sun on the promenade at Bexhill. I envied them. Then felt irritated by them. Three days being shaken around in a four-wheeled oven across these interminable rock-strewn plains had stripped me of all but a veneer of tolerance.

I recall those few hours in Iferouane as one recalls a film seen once a long time ago – snippets, odd images, bits and scraps of dialogue. There was a meeting. Half a dozen of us – more or less - around a table. All men. You don't see the women. Except around remote water holes where they haul up goatskins full to bursting with beautifully clear, cold water and you find yourself wondering why the hell don't we all just grow up, stop fighting each other and pump this stuff up from under the desert and feed the world's malnourished, but I guess that's too simplistic by half. The meeting was in the open air under an awning with some sort of red design on it. It flapped gently in the wind off the desert and cast a constantly shifting red pattern over us and the table. I sat by Youssef. The European man was there. At the end of the table. Why? He said nothing.

Just listened – all he ever does. I recall in detail the surface of the table right in front of me – women wearing yashmaks, Moorish arches, camels, sand dunes, mud houses, palm trees - all in beautifully wrought brass – 'Brave Lover, never canst thou kiss, though winning near thy goal. But ever wilt thou love and she be fair'. The men around the table are wrapped in voluminous swathes of white linen like sheets blowing in the wind on suburban washing lines, only their strong brown hands and the upper parts of their dark faces visible. Their eyes glint, twinkle in the sun. Youssef tells me they are the police. I have to believe him. "They want to know," he says, "why you think your son might have been driving." I'm trying to gather up the wind-blown pages of my mind. "Flight AF 732 from Paris," I say. "Paris Charles de Gaulle. He was on that." Who was? "Gaston Vincent who Minxie spoke of, Gaston Vincent – my son." So you say that's your son, Gaston Vincent? 'Say it is,' I say to myself, 'say it is', else we'll be here for ever – "Yes, that's my son." Then why is his name not your name? "He likes his new name better. In the United Kingdom – the 'Royaume Uni' - you can use whatever name you like. He took a room at that big hotel in the capital." Which hotel is that? "Began with a 'G' but I can't recall more than that. He got a second-hand Suzuki pickup there – what colour? - red." From a garage there. Did he hire it, buy it? "I don't know. It might have been arranged from London that he would pick it up and No, I have no idea who arranged it or for what purpose nor do I know its registration number. It had a faulty battery so he bought a new one. Here's a copy of the receipt." Where did you get this? "I got the garage to do it for me." What did he need a pickup truck for? "I don't know, I don't know." I hear Youssef's words in the bar – 'Some people drive on the dunes for crazy reasons.' This is scaring the shit out of me. Another leans at me across the table. There were tourists here once monsieur. People with good money. Times have changed. And he looks at me with a steely twinkle like he knows that I know that he knows what I know, so it's all between men of the world, I've nothing to lose and he understands. But it's not, I have and he doesn't. Men with no names come here now, he says. This is drug country now – you understand? What in Jesus' name brought you here, Matt? I'm losing track. I don't know what he was doing here! Maybe, I say – maybe – and like in the hat shop somewhere, I resurrect a talent for rapid fabrication. I claw 'Nigeria' from the air – probably because it's nearby on the map - maybe he was taking stuff for a friend to Nigeria. Perhaps. Derisive laughter greets it, but one of them says – one who doesn't join in the laughter says, why would your son be in the Tenere if he was going to Nigeria? They lie in opposite directions. "I don't know," I say, "I don't know where he was going – I'm guessing. Just guessing."

The laughter dies away. The wind rustles the few papers on the table. The men look silently at me, then at each other. Then at Youssef. I don't like this.

An argument breaks out. First among the men themselves. Then Youssef is drawn into it. It's all in Hausa or Tamasheq or whatever else language. It got to feel ugly. The European man stood up and walked away through the trees. I am not here. Peering down, I run my fingers lovingly around the brass figures on the table – 'Oh little town, thy streets for evermore will silent be; and not a soul to tell why thou art desolate, can e'er return.' Youssef grabs me, pulls me up out of my chair and leads me away. A man shouts as we hurry through the trees. Youssef is jabbering angrily to me half in French, half in English about things I can't grasp. A vehicle revs up wildly and roars off. I don't know what is going on.

It is late afternoon when we get away from Iferouane. And then only after both vehicles have been systematically stripped and their contents strewn around on the ground. The implications of this dawn but slowly on me. What they are looking for – or perhaps what they are pretending to look for – is obvious. Youssef, with whom I usually communicate with ease, keeps his lips tight buttoned. Even he is on tenterhooks. All of us are aware of the potential for serious unpleasantness. I struggle to ward off some of the more wayward excesses of my imagination. There is profound relief all round as finally we escape back out into the desert.

Youssef drives furiously across a baking rubble prairie. We are thrown from one side to the other. From his still angry bilingual outbursts, only half-heard over the straining of the engine as it struggles across the uneven ground, I manage to piece most of it together. They had accused him of working in some unspecified way for the South Americans. But their primary problem had been me. Me? - I stared at him in fearful disbelief. They'd implied they weren't being told the real truth behind a hugely expensive, five-man expedition to an empty vehicle abandoned in the desert, funded by a rich white Westerner who gave them a fanciful tale about searching for a son he hadn't seen for years, of whom the only photograph he had was twenty years old, of the nature of whose business in this country he had no idea and of whose name he wasn't even sure. It was clear, said Youssef, that the only way it made sense in their minds was if I knew something about that vehicle - and what it may contain - that they didn't and which I wasn't revealing. Getting no good answers to their questions, they'd ended up threatening us. Claiming to believe us incapable of finding the abandoned pickup unaided, they'd insisted on our being escorted – by whom and under what circumstances they wouldn't say - to the abandoned pickup.

Youssef pointed a finger at his own chest. "I find it. No problem."

I didn't doubt it. I'd trust him to find an abandoned golf ball in the Tenere. But I had to rein in my imagination as to what we might have escaped from. In the hope of calming myself, I took a few deep breaths.

And then Youssef told me something that wiped everything else from my mind. It was only the presence amongst us, he said, of the European man that had prevented them from forcing their threat on us and so virtually taking us hostage. They could have held us - they had pretext enough. We would have been at their mercy.

The European man! He is behind us in the rear seat. I spin round to look at him. The merest nod of the head acknowledges me before he looks away. Stunned, I turn back to Youssef.

"Police in Iferouane," he said, "are more corrupt than the criminals. they are paid to arrest."

I am so far out of my depth. It's like the wild west out here. And the European man sitting behind us - I still had no idea who he was or why he was with us. But the power his very presence appears to have wielded over members of a corrupt desert police force has utterly thrown me. I owe him – we all do - a profound debt of gratitude. I will look upon him henceforth with respect.

An hour or so later, I ask Youssef why he's still driving so fast. Does he think they might be following us?

He shakes his head. Points out the front windscreen. "Sandstorm."

I sit bolt-upright and follow his pointing finger. But what's he pointing to? It all looks mind-numbingly similar to how it's always looked. I'm squinting though - why? The atmosphere outside has developed a bright misty glare. The distant black mountains which have been in the background almost since the day we started out have all but disappeared. I look up to the sky. The sun has collapsed to an innocuous, cream-coloured disc. A flash of white light hits the corner of my eye. I glance in the wing mirror. The headlights of the cook's vehicle behind us have come on. Sand is streaking horizontally across them.

Sand is now pouring out of the sky and hitting our windscreen. The air is darkening. The vehicle receives a sideswipe from the wind. I look in alarm at Youssef. But he can deal with sandstorms - I'm sure of that. He's hunched over the wheel and doesn't look my way. The European man in the rear is impassive. Things deteriorate. Our windscreen is being sand-blasted. Everything around us is brown. The sky has gone. Youssef strains to see through an ochre gloom. We're under a sea of sand. How long before we bog down? Or it gets in the carburettor and we grind to a halt with a fucked engine?

We continue like this for a very long time. Where are we going? Anywhere? None of us speaks. I try to get the eye of Youssef but he drives us blindly onward. Then quite suddenly, for no reason I can see, we do a sharp ninety-degree turn which almost capsizes us and I gasp, as out of nowhere, a wall of black rock is rushing up at us. Youssef slams on the brakes and we come to a halt right in front of it. The other Land Cruiser pulls in beside us. My heart is pounding. I glare at Youssef. I need him to acknowledge me and my anxiety. He sits back in his seat and turns to me, smiling. Only then do I recognize that all around us is now calm. No wind. No sand hitting the vehicle. He points upwards through the windscreen. I lean forward and follow his pointing finger. I can just make out the very top of the rock face. Sand, blown by a howling wind, is still streaming horizontally across it. But where we are, down here in the lee, there is calm and near silence.

I am, yet again, in awe of this man and these people. I know my way around London by the characters of streets – a left turn here, a crossroads there, by advertisement hoardings, pub signs, prominent buildings, road signs. These people navigate this empty desert, even in a sandstorm, by instinct and by signs I can't even see.

And I sense a pulse of elation. Far away, men and women I once knew, stifle their yawns in centrally-heated rooms, eye the clock and nod sagely in unison with their leader. If I have to be in one or the other of these places, I'll stay where I am.

We spent that night in the lee of the same rock face. The two small tents were put up as usual for the European man and for myself. (By this time I had, rather shamefacedly abandoned my early attempts at sleeping in the open). Youssef, Sam and the cook slept inside the vehicles. The sandstorm continued into the night. I lay awake on my back, strap-hanging from the ridge pole to prevent the wind getting in under my fragile shelter and whisking it off across the desert. It was some time in the early hours when the storm eased enough for me to feel it safe to try and get some sleep.

I crawled out at first light. I was shocked to see, on the lee side of the tent, a cavity in the sand the length of it and almost a metre deep where the wind, swirling over the tent in the night, had scooped away the sand. Had the storm not eased when it had, I might have toppled into that in my sleep. If there were anyone up there among the stars - like whoever it was who had sent me my own rain shower - I thanked them I had not had to cope with that.

But I had not really slept. I was weary to my bone marrow and the encounter with the red Suzuki was still at some unknown point in the future. I'd lost track. The days had all run together like spilled water-colours. As we breakfasted, I asked Youssef how much longer. "Soon now," he said, quietly. "Morning of third day."

48.

I rummage among the papers and come upon a bundle of letters. I remove the rubber band holding them together and select one at random. 'Dear Mr and Mrs McDonald, Matthew's teacher, Miss Crossfield, tells me she is a little concerned about him. She feels he is getting rather withdrawn and anxious. The other children seem to be a problem to him, and on one or two occasions, he has been a little aggressive towards them. Miss Crossfield has asked him if something is troubling him, but he will not say anything. I wonder, is there any situation at home that you think might have a bearing on it? I would be grateful if you could get back to me on this.'

Shuffling some loose papers I find an essay.

"My Day off School". By Matthew McDonald (14). 'My Mum will pack an apple with my brown bread sandwiches and I will ride my bike to the sea. I will get the ferry to the Isle of Innisfree where the girls like being kissed and Mars Bars grow on trees. I shall build myself a house from stones I'll find on the beach. I'll lock the door and only let the fishes in. I'll leave when the music stops and come back home. But my parents will be very old by then and I shall still be fourteen. Amen.' 'Far too short, Matthew. Also flippant and rather silly. See me.'

Then a child's crayon drawing. Rectangular block of a house with a central front door, and a window in each of the four corners. A chimney with smoke curling up from it. In the sky one puffy cloud and a spherical yellow sun. A path from the door coming towards us. The front door stands open revealing a stick silhouette of a man. In the top left corner of the coarse, thick paper, in red crayon, the one word – 'Matthew'. I run the tip of my finger slowly, gently along the word as his fingers once did, struggling as young children do to make the lettering legible. This is the closest I've been to him in most of my adult life.

I pushed all the papers to one side, looked out of the diamond-paned kitchen window. The sun was shining but grey clouds were coming up from the east. Autumn was almost winter. Celeste had gone out. She had remembered – quite suddenly it seemed - that she had promised to go into the 'Freighter' to help them with a coffee-morning coach party. Who is the ragged old man who tried to push this through the door? She has to know. I must gather it all together. Index it Put things in folders. Then I shall take it with me and go from here.

As she walked in the door, she announced airily and with a big smile, that it was time for a cup of tea. As she went about it she chattered, passing on aimless tittle-tattle from the 'Freighter'.

I let it go like that. Waited for her to put the full cups down on the table between us. Then "Thank you," I said.

"Ooof!" she exclaimed, "mad house. Coach party from London, going to Durham. Had to be in and out in thirty minutes." She picked up her cup and sipped. "Crazy."

It crossed my mind that going from London to Durham via Marsh Enderby seemed a strange route. But I let it go. I said, quietly, calmly, "Who is he, Celeste?"

She looked innocently back at me.

"Who? You must know. How otherwise would he know I'm here?"

She looked down into her cup.

"And what's he doing with all this stuff – these letters, pictures, Matthew's old school reports?"

Still she said nothing. I was getting angry. "Christ, Celeste!! If you don't tell me who that old tramp is I swear I'll - "

"McDonald!"

I stopped dead.

She took a deep breath. "You asked who he is. He is Giles McDonald."

Stunned, I let the name reverberate around my head. "That?" I said, eventually, "that dishevelled tramp is Giles McDonald?"

She nodded. "Matt's father."

My blood froze.

She blanched, closed her eyes tight, and pressed her clenched fist against her lips.

If I were ever tempted to hit a woman, that might have been the time. "Jesus fucking Christ!" I was trembling. "How many times do I have to tell you Celeste that - "

"I know! Yes. I'm sorry. Barney I'm so sorry."

I sat down. I was shaking.

So was she.

A flurry of leaves skittered against the window pane. A breeze disturbed the curtains.

I forced some calm on myself. "So please just tell me how he knows I'm here. And is he going to spread my name all over the place?"

"He doesn't know your name. Not that name. He doesn't know who you are. Just that you're Matt's father."

"How can he not know?"

"Because Stella never told him who Matt's real father was. She never even told Matt. Some women don't."

I was forced to suppose there was some justice in that. If you walk away as I had, you can hardly expect to be included thereafter in the family album. "So how then," I asked, "did Matt know the photograph he kept on him – the one taken at Cannes - was of me?"

"Because his mother told him it was."

"But you just said - "

"She told him the man in the photograph was his father. That's all. But the photograph was twenty years old when he found it - in a box in the attic."

"What was it even doing in the house then if - "

"How would I know? Maybe she just saw it in a magazine in the dentist's and cut it out. She was probably hoping you'd show up again some day."

I turned away.

Her tone softened. "The caption underneath named you as, 'Georgie' Marshal. Why 'Georgie'?"

"My middle name is 'Gyorgy'. My mother was Hungarian. The people I worked with thought it was cute. Or something."

"How old were you then – late-thirties?"

"About."

"As far as Matt was concerned," she went on, "there was nothing to connect the man in that photograph with Barnaby Marechal, M.P."

"So how," I said, "does McDonald come to know I'm Matt's father then?"

"Because I told him."

"Jesus." I couldn't keep up.

We sat in silence for a while. Then pointing to her empty teacup, she said, "I could do with a real drink. What about you?"

I nodded.

She stood up, and went from the room. She returned with two glasses of brandy. Sat down, slid one across the table to me. "Cheers." We raised our glasses and drank.

"So now," she said, "you know it all."

That seemed unlikely. We sat in an awkward silence. I broke it. "Can you let me have his address? I'd like to meet him, talk to him."

"McDonald?" She shifted uncomfortably in her chair. "Why?"

"He may know things."

"What things? I'll guarantee he's no idea where Matt is."

"You don't know that."

"And I'd put money on Stella not knowing either."

"What the hell has gone on round here Celeste?"

"Nothing very complicated - what was left for Matt? 'Jordan Florist' was moribund. His half-brother had died. His parents were at each other's throats. He was running out of money for that horrid little room in Skegness. His mother goes and screws a local farmer - whatever was left of the family McDonald, that put paid to it - bingo. The second family in his life is up the spout. Why would he hang around here?"

I felt raw. I said, "I'd still like McDonald's address. Please."

"He can be difficult, I warn you. He lives with a foul woman who spends his money and drinks like a fish. He's not short of money - owns three or four shops. But his life's a fuck-up."

"I'll take my chance."

"I told him about you a day or two after you and I'd met. He went ape-shit. He thinks you're the root of all his problems."

"Me?"

"You were always the spectre at the feast." She toyed absently with her glass. "Stella never really got over you. He knew that." She paused. "OK. I'll give you his address." She took a little note pad and a pencil from a kitchen unit. She leaned forward to write. Her loose top fell down just enough to reveal the soft upper curves of her breasts. She knew. She raised her eyes slowly to mine.

I was tempted. I finished off my drink.

She watched the movement of the empty glass as I set it very slowly back down on the table. "Goodbye dear, and amen?" she said, with a little smile.

I nodded.

She finished writing. "Here's hoping we meet now and then." She tore out the page and handed it to me. "It's a shame," she said. "And I wonder."

"What's a shame? And what do you wonder?"

"You and me here. Like this, now. And so much gone astray."

'So much gone astray'? I was on the point of asking what she'd meant. But something in her look, some quirk of her body language warned me off. I said nothing. My time here was over.

As I drove away from Christmas Cottage I did not look back. In one of the wing mirrors I caught a glimpse of Celeste by the garden gate, still waving. I raised a hand in response. Whether she registered that or not I've no way of knowing. I turned down the lane towards West Keal and she was gone. I wound my window down and breathed in the rush of cold, fresh air.

I headed south towards Boston. Instinct told me if I were going to risk a joust with the bizarre Giles McDonald I should do it as soon as possible. And without an appointment - just turn up on his doorstep and surprise him. I was intensely curious to meet the man who was my son's stepfather and my first wife's second husband. I was also nervous. Not so much on account of the possibility of his going ape-shit – as Celeste had warned - as out of embarrassment. For best part of twenty years he had looked after and provided for my son. Fed him, clothed him. Seen him through the spats and traumas of childhood, school days, and teenage years. And while all that was happening, I was out there at what I'd thought of as the sharp end, being what I'd thought of as important. Whatever sort of fruitcake McDonald turned out to be, I owed him. I hoped, when the moment came, I would find the generosity to say so. And maybe he in turn would be able to accept my thanks. Though 'Thanks' seemed a paltry thing to offer in return for his years of dedication. But then, I don't suppose he did any of it for me.

49.

Mavis was beginning to irritate Barney. All women irritated him in the end. They were never satisfied with just cruising along and having a good time together. They started out like that. But before long they wanted to live with you, have your children. Own you. It was a design fault.

He looked at her through the partying crowd as he waited at the bar for the drinks. She was but a slip of a girl. When he had his arms around Mavis there was not much to get hold of. Especially compared with the woman who, at that moment, appeared by her side and struck up a conversation. A large lady who shimmered like a cascade in a full-length gold lamé dress. Her blonde hair was piled high on her head and she had a large, mobile mouth full of bright red lipstick. Her voluminous boobs whose upper arcs bulged above her low bust-line, vibrated alarmingly with her laughter. Mavis, by her side, was an Oxfam case.

"Anything else, mate?" The barman plonked two drinks down on the bar counter.

Barney handed him the money. "No. That's it. Thanks."

"Listen, you on staff here?"

Barney leaned forward in order to hear over the music. "You what?"

The barman raised his voice. "I'm just casual – like - for this shindig.

But somebody said you work in this boozer."

"That's right. It's my night off. Why?"

"Who's this lot you've got in then?" And he pointed into the jostling crowd. "Brought some talent with them, haven't they?"

"Advertising Agency from Bristol. Staff summer outing."

"Advertising, eh?" He was impressed. "Can you tell Stork from butter?" And he guffawed. Then leaned forward, suddenly confidential. "Any chance of a – you know - intro to any of it? When they close the shutters, like? I wouldn't mind getting in amongst that."

"Not a monkey's." Barney picked up the drinks. "Crumpet's all spoken for. It's a day by the sea and a night on the nest. And anyway, if there was a chance of a nibble, I wouldn't be telling you about it, would I? Nudge, nudge, know what I mean?"

"British bulldog!" The barman banged the flat of his hand down on the bar and guffawed again.

'Idiot,' thought Barney as he pushed his way back through the throng towards Mavis and her new companion.

It was as he was handing Mavis her Cherry B and saying the most cursory of 'Hello's' to Gloria – a name which, it struck him, sat ill on her – that he spied, on the far side of the room, a vision. It was but a glimpse through the crowd. But the image burned itself into his brain. She wore a simple, low-cut black dress. Her slim, lithe body was draped across a sofa, eyes closed, an arm hung languidly over the side. Her long black hair trailed in glorious abandon over her bare shoulders and both long legs were stretched out before her, each exposed to just above the knee. And she was alone. But then the crowd heaved, bodies filled his vision and once more, she was gone.

"Gloria's in advertising" said Mavis.

Barney didn't hear.

She prodded him. "She works on the Lawley's Bacon account."

He came round, winked at Gloria. "Bacon, eh?"

She lit up with the sudden attention.

"Keep the home fires burning," he said mysteriously.

She had no idea what he meant, but assured him she would.

"Good Lord!" he said, suddenly pointing across the room. "I'm sure I just caught sight of old Robbie."

"Old Robbie?" Mavis followed his eyes. "Who's old Robbie?"

"Robbie from the Isle of Dogs. We go back a long, long way, him and me. It looked like he was on his way through into the other bar. I'll just go and say a quick Hello."

"Now?"

"Fear not - back in seconds."

She called after him, "I'd like a dance soon."

He raised his glass in the air, stuck his rear out, did a comedian shimmy and disappeared into the throng.

Mavis, crestfallen, turned back to Gloria.

Gloria shrugged. "Men." She pointed to Mavis's Cherry B. "Drown your sorrows, girl. They're all the same."

Mavis downed half of it in one.

Gloria smiled a surprisingly sweet, naïve little smile. "He's nice though, isn't he?"

"That," said Mavis grudgingly, "is the trouble."

Barney made his way into the other bar. In case he was being watched, he buried himself for a few seconds in the throng, then edged surreptitiously out again back into the main bar. He sidled up to the girl in the black dress, still draped across the sofa. Her eyes were closed. "Excuse me," he said.

The girl in the black dress paused before opening her eyes.

"Mind if I join you? Just for a second."

She eyed him up and down. Then shrugged.

He took that as an affirmative. Sat by her side. Cradled his whisky in both hands. "Not a bad old do, this – don't you think? As do's go."

She closed her eyes again. "As do's go."

He took a swig of his whisky. Twiddled the glass around in his hands. She was extraordinarily attractive. Though slim, she was subtly curvaceous. She wore little makeup - that was nice. Smooth, pale skin. Lustrous, black hair. And a tantalisingly discreet cleavage. What beauty there was in that soft, subtle upthrust. He cleared his throat. "So," he said, rather loudly, "how's the advertising business, these days?"

She paused. Then opened her eyes again, this time very slowly. "I haven't the least idea. How's your business these days - whatever it is - brain surgeon?"

"Close," he said. He was impressed.

Then lazily, she crossed her legs. As she did so, a slit in her dress fell open revealing a long length of thigh. She left it like that.

He was clearly in with a chance. "You don't seem to have a drink," he observed.

She reached under the sofa and drew out a glass containing what looked like whisky. She held it up.

"Ah good. I see you're not a member of the Cherry B girlies' brigade."

"What are you talking about? And who are you anyway?"

"But you seem to be on your own." He indicated the milling, chattering crowd. Couples were dancing. "While the rest of your lot seem highly convivial."

"They are not 'my lot'."

"You said you were in advertising."

"No. You did."

"So –what are you in then?"

"It's actually none of your business. But as it happens, I'm one of their clients. For my sins, I happened to be working in this one horse town today. They asked me to join them." She downed what remained of her drink. "Wasn't that noble of them?"

"And then they go and abandon you – tut!" He pointed to her empty glass. "Refill?"

"Scotch." And as she handed him the glass, she turned on him such an unfalteringly straight look he had to fight to keep the blood from his cheeks.

To avoid the eyes of Mavis and the gold-encrusted Gloria, he bought the refills in the second bar. When he came back with two full glasses of whisky and a broad smile on his face, the girl in the black dress had gone. In her place on the sofa were two overweight young women, one black the other white, sitting either side and very close up to an older, suited man who seemed oddly unmoved by their self-conscious sparkle.

"Fuck," said Barney. "Page one." He looked at the drinks in his hands. Shrugged. Then downed one of them in one.

"I hope that wasn't mine."

He spun round. She was back.

"Actually," he said, instantly revived, "it was. I thought you'd done a runner." He offered her the full glass.

She took it and held it up. "I went to make some room for this." She took a generous swig and handed it back. "And I don't do runners."

The music was turned up a notch. 'I don't wanna talk about it,' sang Rod Stewart.

"Do you dance?" she asked.

"Do I dance??" He turned on an expression of pained disbelief. "Like Gene Kelly."

"Really? Got some front, haven't you?"

"I grew up on a council estate. Without front you didn't exist." He put both glasses down on the floor by a large pot plant. "Or perhaps it's Gene Autry I dance like. I can never remember."

"Who the hell," she said, "is Gene Autry?"

"The Singing Cowboy."

She let out a shriek of laughter. "Who are you?"

"Shall we dance?"

"Seriously," she said. "What's your name?"

"Al. What's yours?"

"Viki."

"Viki. OK, Viki, come on then. Let's limber up."

They moved towards the dancers in the centre of the floor. As they did so, the slight figure of Mavis, buttoning her coat, slipped through the door and silently away into the night.

50.

The coach finally slowed to a stop. Barney peered from the rain-spattered window. Other passengers were already on their feet, struggling past him, shoving and pushing like there was an award for first off. Barney waited until the tide had eased. Then prised himself awkwardly up out of his seat.

His knees were stiff. His back ached. He was unfit. He should do more exercise. He reached up and pulled his travel bag down from the overhead rack, slung it across his shoulder and made for the exit. He stood on the top step and surveyed Bristol bus station. A 'fifties concrete concoction with puddles like lakes reflecting leaden skies.

The wind whipped rain into his face. It trickled down inside his collar. He was hungry and thirsty. He'd got up too late to have breakfast and had brought no food or drink with him. He was dying for a pee. This had been his first experience of long distance coach travel – if you can call a hundred and fifty miles 'long distance'. It could be his last.

But – and the thought brought instant comfort – it was Friday afternoon. In his travel bag, two bottles of Veuve Cliquot nestled among his clean shirts and his underwear. In the inside pocket of his jacket, a jumbo pack of condoms bought from the new machine in the gents' toilet of 'The Fountain' in Newquay. He smiled, took the few steps down to the ground.

"'Scuse me."

He stopped and turned. Peering uncertainly down at him from the top step of the coach was a young woman. On her hip she balanced a young child, and from her arm hung a full shopping bag. Clutched precariously in her one free hand was a pushchair which had slipped its lock and was hanging half-open. The child was struggling and close to tears.

"I'm really, really sorry to bother you," she said, "but would you mind - " - and she held forward as far as she was able, the pushchair - " - just taking that for me while I get down the steps?"

He reached up and took it from her. "Do you want me to open it?"

"Oh, would you mind? Thank you." The child started to cry. She 'shushed' him and jigged him up and down as she made her way with some difficulty down the steps.

Barney took a handle of the pushchair in each hand, and in one movement, flicked the device open. Then leaned forward and patted the seat down flat.

The woman's face broke into a smile. "You've done that before," she said.

He was startled. "Pardon?"

"I said you've opened a pushchair before."

He looked emptily down at her as she settled the child into the pushchair. The heavy bag slipped off her arm, spilling vegetables and fruit out onto the concrete. "Oh no!! Now look."

Barney went down on his haunches.

"No, no. I'll do that. Just let me get his waterproof on him."

Barney was rescuing apples from a puddle. "It won't take a second."

She manipulated the protesting child into an uncomfortably stiff yellow waterproof. His cries grew louder. Then quite suddenly faded and stopped. Barney, still on his haunches, turned curiously to the child. Their heads were level and only a metre or so apart. The boy's eyes, wet with tears, were wide, deep and fixed silently on his. Barney looked into them. The child looked unblinkingly back. Something passed between them. Very slowly, Barney reached out with his free hand and was about to lay the backs of his fingers gently against the child's cheek when he stopped. Drew the hand back. Then got quickly to his feet and held out the bag of apples to the woman.

She went to thank him. But something in his face stopped her. A sound came from him - clipped, like the sudden closing of a door. Then turning on his heel, he slung his travel bag over his shoulder and strode away through the rain. She went to call out a 'Thank you', but there seemed little point. She shrugged and looked down at the child who was looking up at her from his pushchair. She mimed a kiss to him, bent down and pulled the peak of his yellow rain hat further forward. She stood up and glanced once more in Barney's direction. He was nowhere to be seen.

By the time he arrived at 'The Sacrarium', Barney's mood was black. He had walked through pouring rain, taken a number of wrong turnings, and exchanged insults with a man who had bumped into him. He looked up at the building. It was modern gauche, flashy and bloody tasteless. And the name - 'The Sacrarium'. Typical of the inflated view those in advertising have of themselves!

He approached the faux-baroque entrance and pressed the bell of

Number 12. No answer. He pressed again. No answer. "Fuck." Pressed a third time. Waited. He wasn't in the mood. But then he noticed another, smaller bell – 'Concierge'. How very middle-class and continental. He pressed that and almost before his finger was off the button a disembodied voice, which he assumed to be male though it was too distorted for him to be certain, came out of a tiny metal grill right in front of his face. "Yes?" it said. "Can I help you?"

"Allardyce-Hopkirk & Partners." Then as an afterthought, "Please."

"This is the concierge."

"Yes. I pressed a bell saying 'Concierge'."

"Can I help you, sir?"

"I have a meeting with one of their directors." He consulted his watch. "Half an hour ago, actually."

"Just a minute please."

He waited.

The voice came back. "Their suite, I'm afraid, is unattended at the moment."

"I know that. That's why I'm talking to you."

"May I have your name, sir?"

"Marshal. Mister Al Marshal. I have a meeting with Miss Morgan."

"Thank you."

Silence. Barney kicked at the brickwork. Then at the face of an ugly little animal he presumed was a dog, moulded into the side of a metal footscraper.

"Hello – sir?"

"Yes?"

"I have no note of your name, sir, I'm afraid."

"Look, I am meeting Miss Viki Morgan. She is Head of PR at Bijou Cosmetics. They are clients of Allardyce-Hopkirk."

"Even so sir, not having a note of your name, I'm afraid I have no authority to let you in."

"I see. So what do you propose doing about it then?"

"In the circumstances sir, I fear there's not a lot I can do. What I might suggest - "

"Really? Well, I fear the Head of PR at Bijou might have you sacked for an unresourceful nincompoop!"

Silence.

"I assume," Barney continued, "that you have a record of the fact that the Allardyce-Hopkirk suite is booked for the weekend?"

"I can't divulge clients' arrangements, sir. All I can suggest is - "

"'Arrangements', eh?" Barney reached down to a small flower bed, took up a handful of black, wet earth and held it poised before the grill.

"Well, how's this for an arrangement?" With which he slapped the sod of earth onto the grill where it stuck, blocking the holes and silencing the concierge.

He walked away, angry and frustrated. He felt like crying. The rain was easing off. A low wall edged the lawn which fronted the building. He sat on it, his travel bag by his side. He was cold. Where was she? He had been half an hour late himself. Had she stood him up? He kicked his heels against the wall. He was behaving like an arsehole. So what? This is not how this sort of weekend should begin. He was considering walking back to the bus station and getting the first long-distance bus to wherever the hell it went and splurging the Veuve Cliquot on the first sad, lonely woman who was sad enough and lonely enough to want a warm body by her in a bed. But a long blast from a car horn spun him around.

"Sorry, I'm late! Bloody, bloody meetings!" Leaning out the of window of a shiny black Jaguar was the woman of his dreams with her black hair, red lips – not to mention the rest of her too. Oh joy!

"I'll park the motor then let you in." She turned into a service road that led round to the rear of the building. "I'd kill for a drink!"

"Fear not!" He tapped his overnight bag. "We have ample supplies of the Widow!"

"The what??" But she and the car disappeared from view round the side of the building.

Smiling, he wandered up to the main door again. He waited. Looked down at the footscraper. Gave the dog another kick.

"Bit of a bummer isn't it?"

Barney shrugged. "Temporary. It's just temporary."

Viki eased herself upright in the bed. "Hardly a compliment though."

"That attitude's not going to help."

"It's not an 'attitude'. It's a fact."

"It happens."

"To you? Has it happened to you before?"

Barney looked away.

"So - there's a reason. Right?"

"Everything has a reason."

"Everything has a 'cause'," she said. "'Reason' implies intent and I doubt you intended it."

"How very existential. It was your word - 'reason'."

"So what's the reason then?"

"Just one of those things."

She swung her legs out of bed. "Cup of tea? Coffee?"

"I'll stick with the widow." He reached for the bottle of Veuve Cliquot on the bedside unit.

Viki pointed to it. "Maybe it's too much of that."

"Or not enough."

She disappeared to the kitchen.

He topped up his glass and drank half of it. Then surreptitiously pulled the duvet off himself and considered the miscreant between his legs. It lay sullen and uncooperative. Like a dog that didn't want to go for a walk. He covered himself again. This happens to other men - not me.

Viki came back with her tea and sat beside him on the bed. Even naked, she was gorgeous. Though she was slim, her curves were almost Rubenesque; her smooth, slightly tanned-looking skin, and that black hair cascading down her back which led his hungry eye on to the tantalising outward curve of her hip. He watched as she sipped her tea. Her brownish nipples were proud, hard. God, what was his problem? He lay down once again and gazed at the ceiling.

"Listen," she said, "I'm sorry. It's obviously just as difficult for you. Perhaps more so."

"Thank you." It hadn't been said with feeling, but at least she'd tried.

She got up from the bed, took her tea and stood looking out of the window. It was early evening. The skies were clear. The sun was dipping down behind the tall buildings of the city. The warehouses by the docks were square, black silhouettes with orange windows. A swirling curtain of small birds, wheeled and spiralled across the rooftops on their way to roost.

Barney wanted to fade away to nothing. Other things were so normal. Streetlights were coming on, their reflection turning the ceiling above his head a strange silvery-green. The murmur of traffic. A distant police siren.

"Got an idea!" She spun round from the window, her eyes alight.

He gazed listlessly back at her.

She put her cup down on the windowsill. "Are you game?"

He frowned. "For what?"

"I saw a film once. Don't ask me what it was called – it was at the end of the day at a conference and we'd all had a few drinks. It was one of those films – you know. Not porn exactly but – well, anyway. And there was this amazing scene in it. It had us all gasping."

"What's that got to do with anything?"

She hurried from the bedroom. "Batwoman to the rescue!"

"Game for what?" he called out. But the only response was the sound of her busying herself in the kitchen. A couple of minutes later she reappeared in the doorway, one hand behind her back and a broad grin on her face.

He didn't like it. He sat slowly upright. "What?"

"Lay down again."

"What's behind your back?"

"Please."

Warily, slowly, his eyes on her, he lay down again.

For a couple of seconds she stood quite still by the bed. Then reached out and got hold of the duvet. Sensing she was about to pull it off him, he grabbed it with both hands, yanked it right up to his neck and peered wide-eyed at her over it. She shot out her free hand, snatched up the foot end of it and whipped the whole thing right up over his head, exposing the full length of his naked body. He was just as quick. He rolled away from her, taking the duvet with him, and fell off the bed on the other side.

"Fuck you!"

He scrambled to his feet, wrapped the duvet around his body. "What's behind your back?"

"Spoilsport - you're ruining it!"

"Ruining what?"

"Not telling you!"

"I'm not moving from here till you do."

Slowly, cursing him under her breath, she brought the hand out from behind her back and held up a red plastic jug. Water dripped from it.

His eyes popped wide open. "What the - ?"

"It's what they did in the film."

"What – did they do in the film?"

She put a finger and thumb into the jug and held up a single ice cube.

His jaw dropped.

"This guy in the film couldn't get it up so she goes to the freezer and gets this handful of ice cubes and holds them right up round his balls and then - " - but the look of incredulity on his face silenced her.

They stared at each other across the bed.

"It worked," she said, lamely.

Silence.

He looked her up and down. One of her breasts was hidden behind the red plastic jug which dripped water onto the bed. The nipple on the other was tantalisingly erect. Just below that, her neat triangle of black hair hovered a few centimetres above the bed sheet. He smiled. "But I've got a better idea."

"Uh-huh?" It was her turn to be wary.

He narrowed his eyes. Then in one movement, peeled the duvet off, jumped onto the bed and leapt at her. She screamed and ran. Ice cubes spilled and bounced across the floor as she fled into the kitchen. Looked frantically around for somewhere where she could defend herself. She threw open the door of a floor-to-ceiling cupboard. He tried to grab her from the rear, but she wriggled herself in amongst a polish-scented accumulation of brooms, dusters and cleaning materials, then turned to face him. In her hand she had the jug still half full of ice cubes and water. He reached out to take it from her. But she batted his hand away, lunged at him, and with a yelp of triumph, emptied the contents over his head.

He gasped as the freezing slurry ran down the length of his naked body. She went to dodge past him. But he put out an arm and pulled her body right up against his own icy skin. She screamed, and wriggled as though to get away - but wriggling, he sensed, was all she was doing. He loosened his hold. She stayed. Raised her face to his. He paused. Then leaned forward and cupping her head in his hands, gently kissed her lips. Locks of his wet hair lay on her closed eyelids. And like that they remained, holding each other, their bodies' warmth intermingling.

She let out a sudden squeal of delight.

He smiled. "Like I said – only temporary."

Barney and Viki were good together. Sexually, that is. For there was little else. Beyond that, her head was filled with ambition; his with a need to bury recent events and move on; to forge for himself another new identity and set of standards. Armed with these he would start again. Again.

Cornwall was going to cast a long shadow. It was a failure of a different kind from that of Halifax, yet the wellsprings, he was aware, were the same. 'Raffie' and 'Mavis' were names, the embarrassment of which on being recalled would, he hoped, be neutered by time. It seemed unlikely however to do the same for 'Abdul'. Abdul was a different matter.

The Abdul incident haunted Barney. To that point in his life, he had found himself able without too much effort to put from his head those things from the past which disturbed his peace of mind, and proved an obstruction to clear thinking in the present. Even the breakup of his marriage and the whereabouts of Stella and young Matt ruffled the surface only from time to time. But Abdul kept floating back into his ambit like flotsam on a pond the running stream can jostle but not dislodge.

Meantime he and Viki made love to each other – 'making love' being simply the phrase commonly applied to their almost everyday activity. There was little actual 'love' in it. Not that that was to take from what they had. There was understanding and a certain affection. All of which was eased along by the freedom they had to meet and 'make love' whenever and wherever they fancied.

The one potential complication was that Viki was herself married. But, as she explained to a momentarily stricken Barney, she was married – happily she added – to a man who worked in international water conservation. He spent long periods abroad, often months at a time and in strange corners of the world. These absences, she assured Barney, had forced them to an understanding. One's intimate needs take no account of schedules. Accordingly, of those periods spent apart, they asked no questions of each other. None.

"So you see," said Viki, taking Barney's hand, "we can roger away till the cows come home."

"Or till Desmond comes home."

"Listen," she said, "Des won't be back from wherever he is now for another six weeks. And then he's sure to be off again soon after."

"Where is he now?"

She shrugged. "China, somewhere. But even when he's back - " - and she smiled a knowing smile - " - I'm sure things can be arranged. If you get my meaning."

He did. It was clear enough. Perhaps a bit too clear. He didn't want her getting ideas. Like Mavis. And a married woman would be more difficult to dislodge. On the other hand, this was a fast-burning fire. He just needed to be wary. And when it had finally sputtered out he would move on without ties or encumbrances. Though where he would move on to, or what he would do when he got there he had little idea. That was at least until Viki told him what she thought should be his future 'metier'.

"Advertising?? Me?" He pulled a face.

"You say it like it was on a par with child molestation."

"So it is – in a way. All those innocent kiddiwinks watching TV while some lying tripehound of a commercial pushes food down their throats that'll make them fat and their teeth fall out. Where's the difference?"

She shrugged. "It's an integral part of today's society."

"You don't have to make a living from it though."

"Lots of money." She turned on her coquette's smile. "Trips abroad."

"Where abroad?"

"Depends. Last year we had a commercial shot in Martinique."

"'Martinique'? Where's that?"

"Caribbean somewhere. I went. Ten days of sun and sand and sea. Stayed in the Martinique Hilton. The dining room there was open on one side to the Caribbean. Went scuba diving. Saw flying fish. Hummingbirds. All on expenses."

"What were you doing there?"

"I was the client. The money. A client representative always goes along to a commercial shoot."

"What do you know about shooting a commercial?"

"Not much. You don't have to. Just keep an eye on things - make sure they don't get all creative and carried away."

Barney seemed unimpressed.

"And I got my leg over the focus puller. A gorgeous guy who looked like Robert Redford."

"What the hell's a focus puller?"

"Someone who works on the camera."

"Shouldn't you have got your leg over the director?"

"Maybe I will next time."

Barney thought about all that. "Lots of money, you said."

"Sky-high compared with what you'd get in an office."

"You're in an office. You're not actually in advertising, are you?"

"As good as. I'm PR Manager. I work with the agency all the time." She leaned forward, a confidential gleam in her eye. "And I'll tell you this - the agency is always on the lookout."

"What for?"

"Writers. Artists. Young people. Creative people. Advertising is the game." She lay a hand on his arm. "I could put in a word."

"I'm not creative. And I'm hardly what they'd call 'young'."

"You're as creative and as young as you'd need to be. They'd see you."

He tried hard not to sound as interested as he was becoming. "What's Bristol like as a place to work?"

She did a thumbs-down. "London's the crock of gold. Within a year – you watch - I'm out of West Country Wurzel management and into London hot-shot advertising." She sat up, preened herself, stuck her pert breasts forward. "I shall be account director on the Elizabeth Arden account. Or Chanel. Watch this space."

Barney didn't doubt it. She was ruthless enough.

"That," she declared, "is where I'm headed. Fancy the ride?"

He sat back, smiled. "OK," he said. "Like you say – put in a word, eh?"

51.

After their arrival in St. Mawgan on the night of the storm, it took Barney and Raffie only a couple of days to find themselves permanent accommodation. A would-be exotic and rather self-promoting divorcee by the name of Davina Cassells, recently arrived from London, had bought a big nineteenth century house at the end of the village. She was looking to rent out rooms to 'paying guests of good class.' Barney and Raffie intrigued her. She saw them as oddballs, outsiders – especially Raffie. Their presence in her house would be a challenge to the parochial and often bigoted views of the locals.

As soon as they'd settled in, both men set about looking for summer employment. Barney had little problem - he was soon working as an assistant barman in a popular tourist pub, 'The Ring O'Bells' in the neighbouring village of St Columb Major. Raffie had to struggle. People of his skin colour were few and far between in rural Cornwall. And what few there were were viewed with suspicion, resentment, even apprehension. Eventually however, he was taken on as a general labourer by a local farmer - a job which, to his and to Barney's surprise, he came to love. The hours were long, the money poor. But it was enough – just – to live on. The real bonus was that he was in the open air most of the day. The animals, fields, trees, birds, streams and open skies fed Raffie's soul.

Barney bought a secondhand bicycle on which, in the interests of getting fitter than he was, he planned to ride to work every day. But the long, steep hill out of St Mawgan defeated him more often than not. He would get off some way up and push. On wet days he drove. Raffie on the other hand, walked the three miles to and from the farm every day, whatever the weather.

Their very different jobs meant they saw little of each other. Barney worked evenings and left the house to go to work at just about the time Raffie was leaving the farm to walk home. It was midnight or later when he returned, by which time Raffie was usually asleep. By the time he got up the following morning, Raffie had already been at work two or three hours. Only on Barney's evenings off did they have the opportunity to get together. It was on one of those evenings that the Abdul incident occurred.

They were sitting in the bar of The Magpie. It was around six o'clock. Barney was thumbing idly through a local newspaper when he sat up and turned to Raffie.

"Raff - look." With a noisy rustle he folded the newspaper back, handed it to Raffie, and pointed to a small advert near the bottom of a page. "'New Bengal Curry House, Market Hill, St. Austell'".

"St. Austell?" said Raffie. "Where is that? We have not been there."

"No. And look what is says afterwards." Barney read out the few words in brackets that followed. "'Formerly the 'Taj Mahal'" He looked at Raffie. "Taj Mahal? Your mate, Abdul?"

In the time they had been in Cornwall, they had eaten in every Indian and Pakistani restaurant within thirty miles along the coast in both directions. In none of them however did anyone know anything of the elusive Abdul from Leeds. Raffie had been forced to assume his old friend was no longer in this part of the world. But for no reason other than a lack of thoroughness on their part, the restaurants they had visited had all been in towns on the north coast of the Cornish peninsula – Camelford, Padstow, Perranporth, St Agnes. St. Austell however was on the southern coast, about fifteen miles away.

"What's the betting," said Barney, "that's the place?"

"I think," said a cautious Raffie, "we will need to be very, very lucky."

"Well tonight, Gunga Din," said Barney, slapping him on the back, "could be our lucky night!"

They downed their drinks, jumped in the car and headed for St. Austell and the New Bengal Curry House. Raffie still had said nothing to Barney about 'Gunga Din'. But these days, he hardly noticed it. In fact he'd come to see it almost as a term of affection.

It was indeed the place - Abdul, Raffie's old, old friend from Leeds, still worked there in the kitchens. Raffie's face was aglow. Barney, seriously pleased for his unassuming companion, slapped him once again on the back.

Tonight however, said the Manager, was Abdul's night off.

"So where does he live?" demanded Barney, buoyed up by their success. "Far from here?"

The Manager shook his head vigorously. "No, no," he said, "just a few minutes if you have a car."

"Have you got his phone number?"

The Manager hesitated. Then said, "His phone is – er - out of order at the moment. But I can give you his address." And clearly pleased to be able to help an old friend of Abdul's, he wrote down on an order pad, 'Flat 3a, Second Floor, Pendragon Court'. "It is by the sea," he said. "Very desirable location."

Barney and Raffie decided that first, they would eat. The Manager himself showed them to a table by the window.

It was an evening cursed from the outset. Despite having at last located his old friend, Raffie over dinner, became morose and uncommunicative. It puzzled Barney; it was very unlike Raffie. But it wasn't until halfway through the meal that he succeeded in getting him to talk about it.

"It is my parents," said Raffie, sadly. "I am concerned for them."

"What's concerning you, Raff?"

"It's a long time ago now that I walked out of the house. I have not contacted them. I was so angry and disappointed with them, Al. Naseem would not have done what she did if they had shown her more understanding. But I cannot stay away for ever. They are still my parents. They must think they have lost both their children."

"Send them a card. A letter." Barney waved an airy hand. "Just to let them know you're OK. You're alive and well. You and your funny white friend - " - and here he spread his arms wide - " - are having a ball!"

Raffie smiled. "You have indeed been a friend to me, Al. But I cannot just think of myself. My parents are on their own, and almost strangers in this country."

"Strangers? How long have they been here?"

"More than twenty years, but my mother still speaks hardly any English."

"Fuck me."

"One day they will get old. My place will be by them. I am their only child now. But – oh dear - the thought of going back to Leeds is – well, very depressing. I do so love it here."

"What," said Barney taking a generous gulp of his beer, "has brought this on?"

Raffie pushed his food aimlessly around his plate. "Finding Abdul. I cannot stop thinking of home." He sat, hangdog and disconsolate.

Barney was not having it. The evening had begun with great promise and he wasn't going to let that go without a fight. He'd downed a few beers by this time, and was in a jollying, expansive and not too understanding a mood. He pressed Raffie to have a drink – a glass of wine – just to take the edge off things. Raffie, as expected and as always, refused. But something had got into Barney. He pressed him and pressed him, worrying him like a dog with a slipper – assuring him he would feel a whole lot better for it – until finally Raffie, more in hope of shutting Barney up than out of any desire to numb his own anxieties, agreed. Like many nondrinkers taking a drink for the first time, he drank the wine down almost like a glass of water. Then grimaced.

"British bulldog!!" exclaimed Barney, clapping his hands. "Done like a trooper!" And he called for another glass.

Raffie despatched that almost as quickly. Then went back to his food. But his hand and eye co-ordination wasn't what it had been and his clumsy attempts to pick up food with his cutlery sent him into fits of giggles.

Barney's spirits lifted. He paid the bill. Then ignoring Raffie's protests that Abdul was a non-drinker, bought half a dozen bottles of Ben Truman pale ale from the off-licence next door - "Just to keep the mood nice and light." He took a holdall from the rear seat of the car, tipped the contents onto the floor, and stuffed the bottles into it.

And so, in the gathering dusk, they drove towards the sea. Barney, on the way, half-sang, half-hummed drinking songs half-remembered from his Oxford days. Raffie sank into silence as the euphoria from the wine wore off.

Pendragon Court was an ugly, red-brick building, built probably in the early years of the 20th century. Four stories tall, strangely narrow and standing entirely on its own on a high bluff overlooking the sea, it looked like something that had risen up overnight out of the ground. Its isolated silhouette stood out stark and black against a sky lit by the recently departed sun. Gulls wheeled around its topmost chimneys.

"Christ." Barney brought the car to a stop by a pair of ornate and rusted iron gates. "Welcome to the Bates Motel." The gates were wide open. From the grasses which had grown up and swallowed their lower levels it was clear that was their permanent state.

Barney wound his window down. The land around the building was part long-neglected garden, part rubbish dump. Half a motorcycle sidecar sat among a low spinney of cabbage plants gone wildly to seed and which struggled up through a mat of brambles and coarse grass. Wire frames strung with some previous year's runner beans had collapsed sideways over an upturned refrigerator. At the side of the house, a pre-war Morris saloon sat wheelless on the ground. Old motor tyres lay about.

Raffie was aghast. "Abdul," he croaked, "is living here??"

"Looks like he might need a bit of cheering up, Gunga Din. Come on." Barney left the car parked by the side of the road. Bottles clinking in the holdall, they picked their way along a crazed concrete path towards the house. Then up a short flight of steps to a heavy wooden door, most of whose paint had long ago peeled off. It was slightly ajar. Barney scanned a bank of doorbells. 3a was in the name of 'Gilani, Floor 2'.

"That his surname?" said Barney, "Gilani?"

Raffie, tight-lipped, nodded.

But where the pushbutton for 3a's bell had once been was now just a corroded brass contact. Barney shrugged. Leaned against the heavy door and pushed it open. "Can't ring a man who has no phone and no doorbell."

They stepped into a cavernous, unlit hallway. A dank, stale odour drifted out past them. Very faint, coming from somewhere above them, was music. A wide staircase, lost in deep shadow apart from a small patch of late evening light from a window on a half-landing, led to the upper floors.

Barney started up, followed by an increasingly apprehensive Raffie. The higher they went, so the music grew in volume. They stepped out eventually onto the second floor landing. A single light bulb swung gently to and fro in a current of air from somewhere.

Raffie was devastated. "This," he said, "cannot be Abdul. Abdul would not live here. I do not understand this."

"Maybe this Abdul is not your Abdul after all."

They stood before the door of number 3a. The music was coming from the other side.

"So what if this is not him?" said Raffie.

"So knock and find out."

Raffie raised his hand, hesitated, then rapped on the door with his knuckles. Then again. The music was turned down. He knocked a third time.

"Yes?" A gruff male voice came from just on the other side.

"Abdul?"

Silence. Then a wary, "Who is that? What do you want?"

"Is that you, Abdul?"

No answer.

"It's Raffie, Abdul."

Still no answer.

"From Leeds. Remember? Jimmy Patel's son."

"Raffie??"

"Yes! I'm here to see you with a friend."

With a sudden crash, a bolt was drawn, and a tiny slit opened up between door and door frame. Peering from it, a watery, red-rimmed eye. A second later, the door was flung open. A big Indian man with wide eyes and dishevelled hair was filling the doorway and peering out at the pair of them in utter astonishment. "Raffie! My dear, dear boy!" And opening his arms, he pulled Raffie to him and enveloped him.

"My God, oh, my God!" muttered Abdul to himself, over and over again. He was awash with a tearful, effusive delight. He was also drunk. The room was airless and thick with cigarette smoke. The music came from a radio in a corner. On the mantelshelf a flame flickered in a small silver shrine to the elephant god, Ganesh. Among the dirty plates and dishes on the table, was a mammoth can of Watney's Party 7 beer, already open. Abdul insisted they share it with him, then crowed with delight when Barney opened the holdall revealing the six bottles of Ben Truman. "We shall have," declared Abdul, "a wonderful, wonderful time together!"

Barney was overjoyed. This had the makings of a memorable evening. Raffie, on the other hand, was adrift. He refused the glass of beer thrust at him by a grinning Abdul. The effects of the wine had worn off and he was feeling unwell.

"But this is a celebration, Raffie my very old friend! Tonight we must have good fellowship. Drink each others' health after all this time."

Raffie stared uncomprehendingly back at him. Something was being pulled out from under his feet.

Again, Abdul pressed the beer on him.

With a trembling hand he took it.

"Good! Very good!" Abdul, a cigarette in one hand, his own glass raised high in the other, looked from Raffie to Barney and back again. "So let us drink to each other! Let us call on the Lord to grant us his blessing."

"Hear! Hear!" chimed in Barney. "See you in hell!"

The three of them banged their full glasses together, sloshing beer onto the carpet, and drank. Barney emptied his in one and slammed the glass breathlessly back down on the table. Abdul took one large swig, then a long pull on his cigarette. Raffie, in the absence of any idea of how to conduct himself in the circus which had broken out around him, gave in and abandoned himself to the disorder. He drank slowly but consistently like with a large glass of water, on and on, with a few sharp intakes of breath, until he saw the bottom of the glass. Then he put it down empty on the table and looked at it. Despite an uncomfortable sense of having succumbed to some sort of darkness, he nevertheless felt a twinge of triumph. He wiped his lips with his hand, and looked around at the others.

Barney pointed in admiration to the empty glass. "Will you look at that! Abdullah, my friend, this upstanding protégé of yours makes out he doesn't drink. But just - "

"His name," said Raffie, struggling to enunciate clearly, "is not 'Abdullah'. It's 'Abdul'."

"'Abdul'; 'Abdullah' – what's in a name? A rose by any other - "

"One is right, the other is wrong."

"Then I'll call him 'Gunga Din-Two'. You don't mind, Abdullah, if I call you 'Gunga Din-Two', do you?"

"My friend," said Abdul, waving the smoking cigarette aimlessly around in the air, "you can call me whatever you bloody like – just so long as it's not late for dinner!" With which he exploded into raucous laughter. "Oh dear, dear!" He took out a tissue, and as his laughter subsided, wiped the tears from his eyes. "It is an English thing my first dear landlady used to say. But you are probably confused. So I will explain."

He had opened his mouth to do so when Raffie, without any apparent warning, folded at the knees and collapsed into a sagging armchair. And there he remained, motionless, his eyes closed.

"Raffie?" Barney's antennae shot up. "You OK?"

Raffie nodded, his eyes still firmly closed.

"You drank your beer too fast."

Abdul, oblivious to Raffie's condition, lay a confidential hand on Barney's arm. "The Patel family, you know, never touched drink. Not one of them, ever. Staunch people."

"Well then," said Barney, side-stepping the pang of conscience which loomed up before him, "it's just the die-hard and intransigent left now - you and me." He refilled both glasses. They clinked and drank. Abdul turned the music up, lit another cigarette, and the pair of them launched into a serious assault on what remained of the evening. Lost amid the joy of being teamed up with another free-wheeling drinker and wandering soul, Barney forgot about Raffie.

They talked, laughed, shouted. About what, Barney in retrospect, had little idea. But it was good. One of those great times - nothing but the present laughter, the present noise, the present amnesia. What a night it was with Indian Abdul. Cigarette smoke, the sweet reek of joss sticks, the flame flickering across the silver elephant, the lurid colours on the posters of Indian gods, loud music, enough booze to float a ship, and the wind and the rain which, at some point in the evening, started to spatter the windows and blow the tattered net curtains around.

It was well into this session that Barney, returning on uncertain legs from the one lavatory at the end of the corridor outside, looked again at Raffie still slumped in the chair, eyes closed, arms hanging limp over the sides. How long he had been like that Barney had lost all idea. And for an Indian, he was strangely pale. He put the backs of his fingers to Raffie's forehead. It was disturbingly clammy. "Abdul," he called across the room. "Come and look at Raffie."

But Abdul, at the table with a beer in his hand, tears coursing down his florid face, had turned the radio off and was singing what he declared was a religious song - a 'bhajan' - loudly, emotionally, from his heart.

Barney nudged Raffie. "Raff! Wake up." He bent down and peered into his face. "Are you alright?"

Nothing.

He stood back, looking down at the other man.

Abdul sang at the top of his voice.

"Shut up, Abdul!!"

Abdul continued unabated.

Barney was reaching out to put a hand on Raffie's shoulder in order to give him a shake, when his eyes popped wide open and he shot bolt upright .

Barney stumbled backwards.

Raffie remained like that for a moment or two - quite still, his eyes fixed straight ahead. Then slumped forward and vomited across the threadbare carpet before falling off the chair, face-downwards into it.

"Aaah, shit, Raffie!"

Abdul stopped singing. He gazed uncomprehendingly at the scene in front of him.

Barney grabbed Raffie by the shoulders and started to drag him across the floor. "Open the door!" he bellowed at Abdul. "He needs air."

"Ah - air – yes!" exclaimed Abdul who stood up, rocked back and forth before making his way uncertainly across the room. After one failed attempt to get hold of the knob, he yanked it round and threw the door open. "Air. Get it in his lungs!" he said, pointing in the general direction of the stairs. But then stood in the doorway, completely filling it.

Barney was on the edge of panic. "Get out of the way!"

Abdul's face was a blank.

"Fuck off!!" He reached out and dragged the bemused Abdul back into the room, and in the same movement gave him an almighty shove to one side. It sent the big man reeling and crashing into the table, his arms windmilling in an attempt to stay on his feet.

Barney dragged the now moaning Raffie along the corridor and half-carried, half-slid him down two flights of stairs and outside into the rain. Putting one of Raffie's arms around his own neck he dragged him across the muddy ground, through the gates to the car where he bundled him, like a dead man, into the rear seat.

As he pulled away and drove off down the road he caught just a blurred glimpse in his rain-spattered wing mirror of something flickering red in the darkness. An instinct told him he should stop and investigate. But something else told him him he had enough on his plate.

'A verdict of Accidental Death was recorded at the inquest on the death of Abdul Gilani, of Pendragon Court, St. Austell. A fire which broke out in the sitting room of his one-bedroom flat, gutted the flat along with most of the second floor of the building. The cause of the blaze was thought to be a silver oil lamp, of a type often used by members of the Hindu faith as a domestic shrine, and which was found among the debris. It was possible that Mr Gilani, who had a very high level of alcohol in his blood, met with some minor accident which knocked over the lamp which then set fire to papers or soft furnishings. A post-mortem revealed a blow to the side of the skull, compatible with the head hitting a hard object such as a piece of furniture as a result of a fall. Such a blow would almost certainly have concussed him. Given his blood alcohol level, it is unlikely he would have recovered consciousness, being suffocated before that by the smoke which would very soon have filled the room. Two friends had visited him earlier that evening. They reported that throughout their time with him, although he had been slightly inebriated, he had been in excellent spirits. Colleagues of Mr Gilani at the restaurant in St Austell where he worked in the kitchens confirmed his reputation as a heavy drinker. He was known to have financial problems. There was no suggestion of foul play.'

Barney and Raffie tried to carry on as though the Abdul incident had been just a tragic accident, a malign concurrence of events which they had simply to try and put behind them. But it was not to be. Raffie was wracked with shame. By accepting and drinking alcohol, he had let down himself, his family, his whole culture. Furthermore, had he not thus fallen victim to his own weakness, Abdul, his treasured friend and mentor, would almost certainly be alive now. Within a couple of weeks, he had left Saint Mawgan and returned to Leeds.

Barney too was mortified by his own actions. He had allowed the cowboy in himself, the tosspot, the delinquent – of whose existence he was only too well aware – to call the shots. He had all but forced alcohol down Raffie's throat. Without that, Raffie would surely never have accepted beer from Abdul, would not have fallen into the stupor which set off the tragedy's final act. But most disturbing to him personally was that he, and only he, knew of the shove he had given Abdul in order to get him away from the door. It's force, fuelled by alcohol and panic, had been unwarranted. A firm nudge would have been enough to move anyone so drunk. The image of that big man trying, against the odds, to keep his ponderous body upright as he staggered backwards, was one which would remain with him.

With Raffie gone, he wanted no more of St Mawgan and its memories. He resigned from his job at the 'Ring O Bells' and gave notice to Davina Cassells. He took a barman's job in 'The Fountain' pub in Newquay. Accommodation on one of the upper floors came with it. He mourned Raffie. The relationship with that gentle, open, kind young man was a sad and painful reminder of that with his own baby son. And like that, it had meant much more to him than he'd ever suspected at the time.

52.

The door was flung open with such force that I started back.

"Yes?" A woman with the face of an eagle stood looking at me. She filled the narrow doorway. She was probably in her fifties. She wore a full length real fur coat which was either too small or wrapped too tightly around her ample body. Everything about her seemed tight – even the skin of her face from which her slightly prominent eyes bulged. I got the unsettling impression that her skin was only just containing what was inside. She was heavily made-up, had dyed blonde hair and wore spectacles with jewelled frames. Her hands were red like they had been scrubbing floors. Her long fingernails were painted orange. The effect was, for an instant, terrifying. Was this McDonald's woman – the one Celeste had told me about? I hoped I'd knocked on the wrong door.

I hadn't.

"Yes?" she said again, as to an annoying child.

I cleared my throat. "I'm sorry to bother you," I said, "but I'm looking for a Mister Giles McDonald. Have I got the right address?"

"Might I ask," she said, "who wants him?" Her upper class accent was laid on with a trowel, and whoever I was it was clear I was entirely unwelcome.

"My name," I replied, "is Marshal. Barnaby Marshal."

"Do you have an appointment, Mister Marshal? If so, would you mind going via the shop which is - " - and she pointed a talon-like finger along the side of the building - " - just on the corner there."

"I don't have an appointment," I said, happy to be able to contradict her. "It's not business. It's a – somewhat personal matter."

Her eyes narrowed.

"If you wouldn't mind just giving Mister McDonald my name, I think he'll see me."

She eyed me with grave suspicion. "You'd better step inside then." With which, she invited me into a small, cramped hallway. Stairs led up to what I presumed was a flat above the shop. "Whether or not he'll see you," she said, "I couldn't, of course, say." She opened an inner door. A current of cool air wafted out a cocktail of seeds, dog biscuits, insect repellents. She went through and I started to follow her. But she turned, held up before me a hand like a traffic policeman. I stopped. She went in and closed the door behind her.

I shrugged. I tried putting out of my mind any thought of how he may react. I looked around. On the wall, in an elaborate gilt frame more interesting than the picture, was a water colour – a small lake bordered by winter trees. Underneath the one handwritten word, 'Ogston'. Wherever that was. Or was it the artist? How was that shambling scarecrow going to react to the news his stepson's father had come a-calling? Calmly? With curiosity? Anger? Would he start up in a fury from his chair and come loping through the shop to get at me?

Where was she? I looked at my watch. Three minutes. On the opposite wall a document framed in black. Giles William McDonald, it declared, had met some required standard in bookkeeping, August 1975. Between the glass and the paper, in a corner to which it had retreated in a doomed attempt to escape, the desiccated remnants of a bug.

Suddenly the door was thrown open, and she stood there, eyeing me now with an intense and disapproving curiosity. She pointed into the shop and announced in regal tones, "The office at the far end."

"Thank you." I went through. Low-ceilinged, with a plain concrete floor. Shafts of sunlight through small windows high up in the walls lighting up a dusty interior. I'd stepped back into the 'fifties. Among the open grain sacks, displays of pet foods, cat and dog toys, rubber bones, budgerigar mirrors, bird feeders etc., two grey-haired, middle-aged men in brown overalls stood waiting for customers. I could see no office. I approached one of the men, told him I'd come to see Mr McDonald and could he tell me where I might find him. At the mention of McDonald's name, the man pulled himself just a little more upright and pointed towards the rear wall. "Over there, sir. Just by the display."

The display was a huge placard promoting a fur ball treatment for cats. A few metres back from it, the office was little more than a corner of the shop separated from the main body by glass partitioning. Inside was a desk, telephone, metal shelving, posters on the walls. And seated at the desk with his back to the door and to me, apparently poring over some papers, the strange man with the dishevelled hair I'd last seen retreating up Celeste's garden path. I became seriously uneasy.

I knocked. The man looked up very quickly from his papers but avoided turning my way. He took a second or two to gather himself together. Then stood up and walked briskly towards me. He opened the door.

It was a strange moment. We looked at each other. There was no expression on his face, or on mine either probably. How, after all, would your inner self know in such circumstances what face to put on display? This untidy, ageing scarecrow of a human being had been father to my son. I felt painfully ill at ease. But that was shot through with some irrational anger that he should have seized from me my function, along with a completely rational anger with my own self for ever having let it happen in the first place. And what was he feeling - anger, resentment, a sense of moral superiority? All three, probably. He could hardly be pleased to see me.

"Good morning," I said, my voice faltering despite myself.

His nod was almost imperceptible. His pale blue, bird-like eyes flicked all over me.

I put out a hand. "Barnaby Marshal. I'm Matthew's father." It was such a peculiar sentence to mouth, I heard it like it came out of a machine.

He shook my hand. But said nothing.

"You," I said, "must be Giles McDonald."

"I am," he said. His voice was quite fragile, like that of a much older man. It lessened my nervousness just a little.

I forced a smile. "It's good to meet you."

"What can I do for you?"

Had I asked the price of the furball treatment, he could hardly have shown less apparent interest. "Well," I said, trying to strike a balance between a reasonable self-confidence and an appropriate humility, "first off, I apologize for just dropping in on the off chance like this."

He shrugged.

"I've been staying in the area – as I think you're aware. And I wanted to take the opportunity of meeting you and thanking you. If thanks are anywhere near enough for what you did."

He just looked at me.

"And I'd also like to ask a favour of you – if you don't think that's presumptuous." I cleared my throat. "Given the circumstances."

He said nothing.

My mind went blank.

"Long time," he said, looking down his nose at me.

"Excuse me?"

"It's been a long time." He flicked a few grey hairs out of his eyes.

"What has? I'm sorry but I'm not quite sure - "

"You can't do much of a job with only half the tools."

I couldn't figure that out and didn't try. "I have no illusions about this," I said. "I fully realize what you did - and what I did not do. I'm doing my best now to try and set some of that right - if it's possible after all this time. And I've come here to ask for your help."

Still he stood and simply looked at me. There was an hauteur in his manner which I had, reluctantly, to grant him. But he was a strange creature. His skin was pallid, flaky-looking, like a man who eats a poor diet. His straggly grey hair fell almost to his shoulders. He wore an ancient, brown leather jacket, the substance of which had all but disappeared and which hung about him like sackcloth. Beneath that, an open-neck shirt, and grey trousers, the turnups of which finished a good two inches above his ankles. Then those sandals with white socks.

One of the brown-clad assistants was standing within earshot. "Could we," I said to McDonald, "perhaps go into your office?"

He turned away and headed back inside. I followed, closing the door behind me. He sat down at his desk and pointed to a grubby tubular chair in a corner. I dragged it out and sat opposite him. Then again he just looked at me. I took it as a ploy. One which he perhaps used on the brown-overalled assistants out there. On my way here from Celeste's, I'd bought a local newspaper. I made a meal of folding it very carefully and laying it neatly in my lap. Then I took a breath and looked up. My mouth was just about to form my first word when he said, in his odd, fragile voice, "Read all that stuff, did you?"

It took me a second or two to catch up. "I did," I said. "Yes. Thank you. I'm much indebted to you for everything you did."

He reached to one side and dug around in an overflowing desk tidy.

"I'll be frank Mister McDonald. I'm not proud of that period of my life. Things like that come back to haunt you."

From the desk tidy he delicately extracted, between finger and thumb, a paper clip.

I struggled on. "It led me in the end to put aside everything else in my life in order to try and find him. I realize I'm hoping to mend something which may not, in the end, be mendable. But that's why I'm here now."

"You gave up everything?" he said. "Does that include your job?"

"It does."

"You remarried, didn't you?"

"That too, I'm afraid, is over."

"Two marriages down the drain then, eh?"

I wasn't sure if he was trying to anger me, but if he was he would have to try harder than that. "So," I said, "I'm here to ask for your help."

"You must be pretty flush to be able to give up your job just like that."

I wasn't going there. "I've been trying to contact Matthew, but I've had little luck. It's been a very long time. And he seems quite elusive into the bargain. If you agree to help me, I realize you'll want to contact him first to ask him if he wants to hear from me."

He fiddled with the paper clip, bending and twisting it.

"Have you," I said, "any objection to that?"

"Nope." He flicked the paper clip away across the room where it hit a metal shelf unit and rattled to the floor. "Except I can't."

"Oh?" Had Celeste been right and he didn't know where Matthew was. Or was just he being tricky? "Can I ask why not?"

"You can ask. And I can answer. Which is I don't know. I don't know where he is. Simple as that." He flicked the hair from his eyes. "Nor does anyone else."

"That sounds," I said, "quite dramatic."

"Dramatic was Matthew." He fished out another paper clip and began fiddling with that one. Perhaps it was something old men did in this part of the country.

"I'd heard," I said, "from someone – though I don't know how much they knew about it – that he went to London."

"Ha! We all know that bit. Never heard much from him though. Came back here for a weekend once to pick his stuff up. That was about all."

"What about his mother?"

He looked away.

"Surely she knows - no?"

"If she does, she keeps it to herself." He considered the floor for a few seconds. Then looked up. "All I can tell you is he went to London. But he moved. Strangers answered his phone." He put the paper clip down and with a great sigh, closed his eyes and fell back in his chair. "That's about it. It would have been nice to have had a postcard once in a while. I was fond of him. Just a line. 'How are you, Dad?'" That sort of thing."

A spike of anger rose up in me. "Is that what he called you?"

"What?"

"'Dad' - is that what he called you?" But already I was regretting it.

"What else would he call me?"

I back-tracked. "I'm sorry. I'm finding it hard to - "

"If you'd wanted him to call you 'Dad', you should have been here, shouldn't you!"

"Can we just forget that?"

We sat in an awkward silence. There didn't seem much else to say. I'd gleaned nothing from him, and I sensed it unlikely I was going to. All I could say was I'd met Matt's stepfather and knew now what he looked like. Short interview.

But then my mind went to Stella. I couldn't rely simply on his assumption that she knew no more than he did. I broke the silence. "I'm aware," I said, "that Stella might not want to see me. Even so, if you'd agree to giving me - "

"Ha! She'll see you alright!"

I looked oddly at him.

"Got children of your own, have you?"

What sort of question was that? "Yes," I said, trying not to show my confusion. "Matthew."

"He the only one?"

"Yes. So - as I was saying, I'd be really grateful if you could give me - "

"Like you - I had only the one." He reached out to a small silver photo frame on his desk and turned it to me. A delicate boy of about ten, attractive-looking with fair hair and eyes like his father's, stood smiling into the camera. "Died at fourteen. I took flowers for a while." He turned the photograph back again. He looked at it with an expression I couldn't fathom. Then pushed it to one side, shrugged. "What's the point? He couldn't see them and I couldn't see him. I gave it up."

Somewhere a phone rang. He snapped into high alert. His eyes raked the shop checking that somebody would answer it. It stopped. He relaxed. Then looked at me with a quite unexpectedly accusatory eye. "He carried a photograph of you around with him."

I really hadn't expected that. "Yes," I said, "I'd heard."

"Everywhere he went. Probably took it to the toilet with him. You should have thought what it was you were starting, you know."

I frowned. "I'm not quite sure what you mean."

"We ended up living in the dark."

"Who did? I'm sorry."

"Matthew was off the wall. Philip was dying. Stella fought me, I fought her. The business had gone." He paused. "People lose their way. When you walked away from Endell Street, you left behind a ticking bomb. It went off in my house fifteen years later."

On the drive there I had made a resolution. Getting into any sort of confrontation with him would do me no good. However he might choose to behave, in this matter he would always hold the moral high ground. All I said in reply - with a certain sincerity - was, "I'm really sorry. If I could do more about it than I'm doing now, I assure you I would."

His demeanour softened again. A wry smile came to his lips. "I'll tell you a story." He folded his arms and settled himself back in his chair. "It was April."

Like it or not, it seemed I was about to hear a story. I was intrigued. I too sat back.

"Early April. I remember thinking how nice the daffs were that spring. I went down to Peterborough one morning. It's not far to Peterborough. Fifty miles maybe. The business was in trouble. I was doing everything I could to keep it afloat. As it turned out I could have saved myself the trouble. But this bloke in Peterborough had showed some interest in coming in with me and trying to build things back up again, so - nothing ventured, I thought. Anyway, he had to cancel at the last minute. His wife had been taken ill or something. We didn't have mobile phones in those days and I didn't find out till I was there, and one of his men told me. So I had a sandwich and a cup of tea, and turned round and came back."

He was silent for a few seconds, as though checking what he was about to say. "So - I get back in the house. I call out that I'm back – like I do. There's no answer. So I call out again. Still no answer, so I think, 'Oh, well, she's out.' But then I think, 'Wait a minute – her car was outside'. So I thought that was odd – unless she's just gone out for a walk. Though Stella was no walker. Anyway, I'm hanging my coat up and I – er - hear things upstairs. Like – footsteps and running around. People, you know? And well, then I – er - " - but his voice started to crack. "You've probably heard anyway." He turned away, shaking his head.

We sat there like that – me, in some shock, looking at him, and him with his eyes on some distant point way beyond the shop. I felt profoundly sorry for him. He looked lost, even more fragile, more bony. He reminded me of a bundle of sticks. What could I say to him? I could be no help. He needed to be left alone. I was about to break the silence and ask him once again if, before I left, he'd mind giving me Stella's address when, with a sudden flick of the head, he turned to me. There was an ominously purposeful look in his eyes.

Instinctively I sat further back in my chair. Then started, as he shot out an arm and grabbed a heavy glass paperweight from the desk in front of him. I was convinced he was going to hit me with it. I ducked. As I did so, he swung his arm around in a great arc, and with a strange, guttural exclamation, hurled the paperweight off to one side. With a thunderous crash, it ploughed through the glass wall of the office. A web of fractures shot instantly outwards from the hole and the complete two-metre square pane of glass slid out of its frame to the concrete floor where it exploded. Showers of glass flew across the office and out into the shop. I vaguely remember covering my head with my arms.

For some moments after the glass had stopped falling around us, there was a total silence. McDonald was staring at me over the debris. He looked as shocked as I was. Then men in brown were running across the shop and peering anxiously through the now windowless frame of the partitioning.

He waved them away. He turned to me, pulled himself upright and cleared his throat. "I apologize." He said it like he'd done no more than sneeze. "What else did she tell you - the Celeste woman? I presume it was her gave you this address?"

I was struggling to get my head back together. "What else did she tell me about what?"

"Keeps her fingers in a few pies, does Celeste." He picked up a pen and jotted something down on a notepad. "Needs watching." He tore the page out and with the one word, "Stella," passed it to me. On it was an address in Skegness. "Listen, Matt's Dad," he said, sitting back, "now I'll tell you something else."

'Matt's Dad' - was I hearing aright? Suddenly the door burst open and in scuttled a grey-haired woman in an apron and armed with dustpan and brush who, with a nod from McDonald, began feverishly to clean up around us. Out in the shop, men with brooms were appearing, filling the air with a sound like that of breakers on a shingle beach, as an ocean of broken glass was swept and shovelled up. I wondered at the lunatic surrealism.

"Matt – poor lad," said McDonald, "and it'll help you to know this – never could settle. He was a trial as he got older. Never at rest, forever searching. Women came, women went. Like - whatever he was looking for he'd find like that. Perhaps his mother was somewhere at the root of it. Or maybe - who knows - he was looking for you, eh? I guess you'll need to find out."

It was another half an hour before I made it outside again. He had a deceptively persuasive way with him. And in any case, I owed him. He insisted I join him in a glass of sherry – a drink I've never warmed to - while he went over in minute detail the setting up and early success of 'Jordan Florist'. He was at pains to make sure I understood they'd used Stella's maiden name rather than 'McDonald' because the latter, being Scottish, could have emphasized their 'foreignness' in a part of the country seldom comfortable with outsiders. I had the feeling nevertheless that his primary concern was to kill off any suspicion I might have that 'our Stella', as he'd taken to calling her, had worn the trousers in their marriage.

When he had finished and I stood up to leave, he lay a hand on my arm. "By the way," he said, quietly, "I admire you. You need courage to do what you're doing. And a proper sense of what's right."

He stunned me. I could say nothing in reply.

"And if you find the boy, ask him to give a thought to me, would you? Just once in a while. Tell him I'm still here."

When I made it out into the street again it was raining. I hurried to the car and sat for a while, listening to it pattering on the roof, watching it ripple down the windscreen. I took from my pocket and looked at properly for the first time, the piece of notepaper on which McDonald had written the address in Skegness. His handwriting was beautiful – flowing, elegant and verging on copperplate. What an enigma he was.

And I wondered if he, like me, was aware of the relationship he and I now had - and, unbeknown to us, had always had. We were two men with a joint son. What did that make us - uncles-in-law? What a very strange feeling. If I found Matt, one of the first things I'd do was ask him to say hello again to his stepfather.

I'd intended driving to Skegness as soon as he and I had finished. But after an experience like that, did I really want to drive twenty-five miles in the rain? Then buy a street map and cruise the rain-swept streets of an unknown town, one eye on the road ahead and the other trying to peer at the map and read street names at the same time?

And just turning up on Stella's doorstep – how sensible an idea was it? But what were the alternatives? Ring her? Write? Do either and she could just refuse to have anything to do with me. But if I'm standing in front of her, she can't ignore me - even if all she does is throw something. Though that odd exclamation from McDonald - 'Ha! She'll see you alright' - made me wonder if yet again there were signs I was not reading well.

But not today. It could wait till tomorrow. So I would need a bed for the night. Indeed the idea of a warm, comfortable bed, preceded by a good dinner sounded delightful. Celeste had one day taken me to lunch at an excellent hotel. It was one of those country house hotels you very occasionally stumble across in the UK, right off the beaten track, yet an oasis of excellent food and hospitality. They're often housed in rather beautiful old buildings. You've never heard of them and you wonder who on earth patronizes them. Yet it's clear from the Jaguars and BMW's parked outside, that plenty do. Some rural cognoscenti? Insiders from big cities on secret assignations? This particular hotel, inexplicably saddled with the name of 'The Gables', was in an elegant 18th century Palladian mansion approached through half a kilometre or so of rolling parkland.

It took me a few U-turns, a bit of backtracking and a lot of page-turning of the road map to find it. But eventually, under clearing skies, I was sweeping through the long access drive which curved gently between lines of tall trees, almost leafless now. In my advertising days I worked occasionally with a man who would have looked at these trees and said, 'Ah – those are beeches. And those over there are elms. And the flowers you see over there are – ' - well, whatever they were he would have known. Me - I don't know an oak from an ash, a beech from a hole in the ground. I'd recognize a daffodil. A tulip. And a bluebell, I guess.

I could have taken my boy to look at trees. Flowers. I could have learned about things like that with him. When I was at school, I listened with a puzzled longing when I heard other boys talking about how their fathers, in the vacations, sometimes took them fishing, swimming, kicked a ball around with them. Their fathers held their sons' hands, taught them about life and helped them grow into men. Like McDonald probably did with my Matt. My Dad was too busy. He ran a business. Instead of his time he gave me his money.

53.

They had a room. I registered and was led upstairs by a polite young woman to an attractive wood-panelled room. It was flooded with late afternoon light from a large window of beautifully simple proportions. In the air hung the fragrance of a herbal potpourri. The crisp white sheets on the bed were already turned down. I was instantly at home. And the young woman left the room without hanging around in the hope of embarrassing me into giving her a pourboire for doing no more than she was paid to do. Churlish that may sound, but the business of tips in hotels and restaurants is beyond a joke these days. I made a mental note to give her something when I left.

I went to the window. It looked out over a narrow valley along the bottom of which ran a small, fast-flowing river. Low shafts of lemon-pale sunlight swept the darkening hillsides, springing slivers of silver from the waters of the running river. A large bird, black against the sky, tumbled joyfully in the wind. Fluffy white sheep dotted a distant slope. I felt tears coming. I turned quickly away and collapsed onto the bed where I fell into a disturbed half-sleep. I came round at about six o'clock feeling a little brighter.

I was determined to enjoy my dinner. I took time over it. Although the dining room was almost full, conversation was pleasantly subdued. From where I sat I could hear the river bubbling happily away in the bottom of the valley. The food was good, the staff attentive. I ate an excellent rack of lamb which I washed down with half a bottle of Chilean red wine made with a grape with which I was quite unfamiliar - Carmenere. It was first class and I made a point of remembering the name.

At around ten o'clock I went back up to my room feeling reasonably confident of a good night's sleep. If my hope of meeting the following morning with my ex-wife were to materialize, I was going to need it. I undressed, climbed into bed, lay down and composed myself for sleep.

But I drifted back and forth, half-in, half-out. My whole body did a convulsion as that paperweight shattered the office windows once again. Then I was standing on Stella's doorstep – a palace of a house with Doric pillars, behind iron gates overgrown with weeds. I am before a door five times my own height. I am reaching above my head to the huge brass knocker when the door flies open – there she is! Gulliver in Lilliput, towering above me, cigarette between her fingers. And peering fearfully out of the pitch darkness behind her, clutching at her skirts, is the very young Matt, and in his big, brown eyes, apprehension at the sight of his own father.

I was fully awake again, and in a troubled state. I needed something to take my mind off things.

There was a radio by the bed. But if I turned that on, although it would probably lull me to sleep, I didn't want it on all night. It was likely it had a snooze feature, but my mind was in no shape to try working out the snooze feature on an unfamiliar radio. The only reading I had was that useless computer book I'd bought in Boston. Ah! – I did however still have the newspaper I'd bought on my way to see McDonald. I got out of bed again, pulled it from my briefcase and took it back with me.

I ploughed doggedly through conflict and bloodshed, scandal and corruption. What a pig's ear we're making of things. But it had its effect - as much as anything because there's a limit to how much of that you can take. Quite soon my eyelids were drooping. Then - just as I was folding the newspaper up, a photograph caught my eye. Frowning, I held it under the bedside light. Ellen?? I stared at it. Ellen - Christ, it was her - coming down the steps of some dark, neo-classical building on the arm of a tall man in military dress uniform, weighed down under medals, coloured braids, even a sword, for God's sake, at his side. In Edinburgh. Edinburgh? And she in a long dress and a hat which would have turned heads at Ascot. Frantically, I sought the text at its foot. But my mind was spinning so much I didn't, couldn't take it in. I plunged into a hail-storm of assumptions. She'd married again - had she? As I'd thought – she'd soon find someone, the ex – being me - presumed dead. But no, that has to be seven years, doesn't it? Ah! - maybe not quite married, just engaged? Who the hell gets engaged these days? And why would anyone anyway want to know if Ellen had got engaged? Or married? Ah – now my mind calms a little and I catch up with the text and it's nothing, nothing like that at all – she just happened to be there on the arm of this over-decorated bigwig when the photographer caught him exiting from some ceremony. But clearly they're an item. The way she's looking at him! Brigadier or General or something - Randolph Mortimer - a man, it seems, of monumental military import.

What Ellen, have you done?

I read it again, slowly this time, trying to take it all in. Is that how he likes her to dress? Doesn't suit her, doesn't work. Look at it! A fit of fury was about to descend on me and my arm was flexed prior to hurling the paper from me. But I saw McDonald with the paperweight in his hand, and caught myself. I sat back, closed my eyes and took a deep breath.

It hurt.

I folded the newspaper and put it carefully to one side. I got out of bed. I went to the same window I'd looked out from before dinner, and drew back the curtains. I looked out again over the valley, lit now by stars and a half moon in a mostly clear sky. I was a hundred years old. Was it this clear over Edinburgh? I could pick out the soft curves of the low hills. A twisting, white ribbon of road. The silver, moon-tinged edging to one small cloud. I raised the lower panel of the sash window. A wedge of clean, cold air hit me, along with the teeming smell of the still-damp earth. I heard the night wind through bare branches, the tinkling trilling of the river down below.

Ellen lies in Edinburgh beside a new man.

McDonald struggles to comprehend the life that got away.

Stella is an orphan-shadow in a wasteland.

And I despair of what I have become.

In the dark space between the moonlit hills and me, I see the face of Matt. I'm sorry, dearest Matty. So very sorry. I have turned your world, my world and that of too many others upside down. None of it can I undo. But I can leave you in peace. Perhaps that, above all else, is what I owe you now and what I can best do for you. 'What about him,' Licia had said, 'will he want to be found?' I have no way of knowing. But everyone has a right to their own life. It's the only one any of us has.

I was up early the following morning. By half-eight I had breakfasted, left a generous tip for the girl, and checked out. By lunchtime I was back in my shuddering cell in Kilburn. The sight of it, the smell of it, the sense of pointlessness it exuded overwhelmed me. What on earth had I brought upon myself?

54.

'Dearest Frank,

I am so sorry. I need to go. You were the love of my life. You have been a good father to our children. But I can no longer be to you what I have wanted to be. You have borne it with your usual fortitude but it has been a great sadness to me. That sadness has weighed heavier with each passing day. This thing comes and goes but the only certainty, as you know, is that it will get worse. I want to go with dignity while I am still able.

You have the rest of your life to lead. I am not afraid and I have no regrets. I take with me some lovely memories. Please let the children know that I love them very much and have always done so, and that we will all meet again. This is not all there is.

Frank, I know about you and Ellen. I only tell you that in case you think this action of mine is anything to do with it. You are not a young man and for the time you have left you deserve a true companion and no doubt, a lover. I wish you happiness.

I go now, taking with me the memories we shared.

I have loved you Frank. God bless.

Only adieu.

Your Martha xxx'

With trembling hands, Ellen set the letter slowly back down on the table. How on earth had she found out? They'd been so very careful. Nobody outside could possibly have known. But to be so sure as to refer to it in a suicide note must mean she had information beyond hearsay. Had she seen things? A careless look, some surreptitious touching of a hand? For God's sake, had she somehow been able to hear any of their whispered conversations?

However she got to know, it's clear that on the many occasions when they had met at Frank's house to discuss the book, she must have been looking at them in the full knowledge of what was going on behind her back. When she went out to the kitchen to make a cup of tea or fetch a plate of her damn cakes did she wonder while she was out of the room if they were holding hands beneath the table? Snatching a quick touch of a knee - or worse? How bloody, goddam dreadful.

She made herself read it again. She frowned. Not 'I love you, Frank', but past tense – 'I have loved you'. Was that a touch odd? Perhaps there's something a touch odd about all suicide notes.

She turned the paper over. Scribbled diagonally across the back in pencil was, 'Eggs – 1 doz. Cauliflower'. Christ! Why on earth had Frank sent the original? He surely must want it back. Do people hang on to suicide notes? Like you would a love letter? The whole thing was too awful. She'd have to send it back to him. And that contact could, of course, be just what he was angling for. Once again, she picked up his letter.

'My darling Ellen,

I enclose here Martha's note. I will explain. It's heart-rendingly sad I know, but in its own way, rather beautiful. She's gone out of her way to make it clear to both of us that you and I had no part in what she did. I fully understand that, for that was Martha. Although it's unlikely MS in itself would have been the end of her, it nevertheless made her acutely aware of her mortality. That in turn prevented her from ever equivocating in matters of conscience. So to hers, I can confidently add my own assurance that she would say nothing which she did not entirely mean.'

Oh, Frank.

'Ellen, I'm still with the children - who were utterly devastated by the news of their mother - in Melbourne. I miss you just as much. Since that dreadful day I have thought of little else. Despite Martha's kind words and indeed my own inner convictions, I have struggled with a mountain of guilt. But I can only look back on what we had, you and I, with the utmost fondness. I hope beyond all hope that you will see your way to changing your mind. You brought to my life real companionship, a zest for the ordinary everyday things and something I had never before had - a genuine joy in intimacy.

I shall be back in England very soon now - when I feel we have all adjusted as much as we're ever going to. I hope then you will find it in you to come back to me. We could have such a life together. But tempus fugit.

All my love,

Frank.'

Ellen put that letter slowly down beside the first. Poor, muddled Frank. She still felt bad about ending it. But it had no future. He would come to terms with things. One does. Martha's suicide had saved her an unenviable task.

She pushed the two letters away and looked up towards the french windows. Dusk was settling across the countryside. The lights of Ludlow twinkled in the distance. A car passed in the lane. Its headlights swung the black shadows of the bare trees across the curtainless window like grasping, grappling hands. Tomorrow she would be gone. The agent would come and supervise the emptying of the house, the clearing out of everything that remained. And what would they do with the house, those who would come after, with their new feet tramping the floors and the lawns?

She made her way between the few remnants of dustsheet-shrouded furniture to the kitchen. Her footsteps on bare floorboards echoed around the walls. She placed her train ticket, along with two twenty-pound notes, by her handbag on the end of the table. Her mobile phone beeped. A text. 'Checking you're OK for tomorrow. Any probs, ring me. Otherwise see you Haymarket Stn - NOT Waverley - half-four. R.'. She texted back, 'No probs. Looking forward to seeing you. Just want to go now. Lots of love. xxx'.

She ate her salad meal, accompanied by the last glass from a bottle of Chardonnay.

55.

I gave my landlord notice and paid him a month's rent, cash. I bought a roof rack for Fido. The following day I loaded that and the interior of the car with all my belongings which, though they took up every inch of space, didn't seem to amount to very much – then drove away from Kilburn. It was to be the last time.

I headed north for Newcastle upon Tyne. I like Newcastle. In my advertising days my main client had been based there. That had necessitated many overnight stays, so I knew the town reasonably well. One senses there a beating heart. And the countryside around, especially to the north, is wild, open and unspoiled. The sea is just a short drive away with sand beaches as wide and as empty as those of Lincolnshire. Press on just a little further north and you cross the border into Scotland with all that exquisite Borders scenery.

Arriving in the late afternoon, I based myself in a small, boutique hotel in the affluent district of Jesmond. Within a week, I had taken a year's lease on a roomy, elegant, first floor apartment in a large Edwardian house in a street with the delightful name of 'Rainbow Street'.

It was a pretty cul-de-sac, narrow and cobbled. Low, red-brick walls separated the pavement from the attractive front gardens. There were flower beds and flowering shrubs, some of which looked, to my untutored eye, quite exotic. My landlady, a Mrs Ida Bullen - a one-time air hostess, it turned out - assured me that come May through July and August the street would be ablaze with colour, and heady with the scent of flowers. It sounded idyllic.

I wanted to get on with Ida. I liked her and I hoped she would come to like me. I was in danger of seeing myself as an old man with nothing and nobody, a mendicant turning up out of the blue seeking affection and sanctuary. I needed to work that out of myself. Hence the new start. Another! Goodness, I was becoming master of the new start.

And with a new start, I felt – with a touch of sadness – a change of image was called for. Trim the hair and the now quite bushy beard right back. Do away with the shades. They, along with the black leather cap, black leather jacket, jeans and trainers were the mark of a brasher man than I intended henceforth to be, and out of place in middle-class Jesmond. It would have been wrong to have gone back to the Savile Row days, but something in between seemed appropriate.

I spent a pleasant half day shopping in and around Grey Street in the centre of the city. What a very impressive street that is. As impressive in its own way, as Edinburgh's Princes Street. I was pleased with my purchases. Clutching bags full of new clothes and a box containing a pair of excellent brogues, I caught the Metro back to West Jesmond. I'd gone for a more laid back look. Light colours, pastels almost. I hadn't, however, bought a jacket. In the end, I had not been able to forego my lovely black Italian one. But that, in any case, would go well enough with – and indeed, quite set off – the other lighter colours.

Back in my new apartment I tried on the whole ensemble and stood with a frisson of anticipation before the mirror. My initial response, if I'm to be honest, was a touch of disappointment. I'm not sure what I'd expected. Despite the black leather jacket, it all looked a touch bland. The short hair and stubbly beard would take some getting used to as well. But giving it some thought, I felt the blandness was primarily in contrast with my previous rather creative and self-assertive image. It was a question of getting used to it. No more than that.

Jesmond was a lively area of the city. There were interesting shops, cafés, restaurants. Lots of young people around - students, I was told, from the university which was only a few minutes walk away. I like university districts. I love to see the young people frantically pedalling their rusting bicycles, late for lectures, their backpacks stuffed with books. Or sitting outside the cafés and pubs talking, chattering, laughing, men and women together enjoying a communal freedom – a far cry from my own student days when the uptight sanctimony pervading society in those days turned the mildest of my sexual encounters into a guilt trip.

One day, in my general meanderings around the area, tucked away down a narrow side street, I came across a nursery selling plants, flowers, shrubs, earthenware pots. It made me think that a few houseplants would look good in my spacious new sitting room. With all the light that came in through the large windows, they would probably do well. With the help and advice of a charming young nurserywoman I bought half a dozen assorted pot plants. I felt quite proud of myself as I carried these earthy creatures from the car to my apartment. They would look good and give me pleasure when the spring and summer suns filled my sitting room. I just hoped I would be able to care for and look after them adequately.

I passed those Jesmond days doing whatever took my fancy. Most of the summer I spent touring in faithful Fido the moorlands and the Borders to the north. I sat in the inglenooks of isolated pubs that rubbed shoulders with the land itself. I sat alone on the endless, empty sands and watched that cold northern sea licking and lap-lapping at the shore as if tasting before eating – as it did all along that eastern coast, tempting the uncertain land, bit by bit, into its maw.

The only contact I had now with the things that had been was the very occasional phone conversation with Martin when, as we had agreed, we briefly touched base with each other. Still I gave him no idea why I had wanted the money, and he – ever discreet and dependable – never asked. Though after that phone conversation in the Newark car park, I'm sure he had a fair idea.

To be free, at long last, was a rebirth. No past, no future – just present reality in which I saw, heard and felt with a wonderful, reassuring clarity. I wondered occasionally if Celeste – a hundred miles to the south, were still sitting on her beach in her hidey-hole, thinking her thoughts, watching the gulls. In those moments I felt her arms around me once again. I tasted her lips. I saw the morning sun as it glinted through the diamond panes of her kitchen window. But there were no regrets. I'd discarded my baggage, and I was me – here - in my own time. A time to be. A time in which, like the plants that stood now in my sitting room window, I could sit in the sun and grow.

It was not to last. Nothing does. I heard his voice again. Saw his face as he stood on the lawn in that photograph. Did he, even as it was taken, have the picture of me in a pocket of that suit? I dreamed again of the figure in the garden with the black coat and the red scarf, his face turned ever away from me. I heard the wheels of the pushchair on the pavements of Endell Street. I clamped my hands to my ears but you can't keep out what's already in. The countryside, the sea, the wide skies, the pine forests and the rolling moorlands began to lose their edge. The days came to lack purpose and I struggled to impart meaning to them.

I sold Fido the Sierra. He was spending so much of his time these days parked in front of the house. He deserved better. Aged and worn though he was, like a well-loved cuddly toy, there was life in him still. When I was past this temporary hiatus, perhaps I would buy a new car. I'd treat myself - BMW, Audi, Jaguar. I sold Fido to a young couple who turned up one evening having answered my advert in a local newsagent's window. With their chatter and their youthful enthusiasm they so much reminded me of the early days in Endell Street that I was glad to see them leave. Fido disappeared round the corner into the main road with a final 'Goodbye' to me from his right rear winker. I was sad to see the last of him.

I took a job. Bit of a desperate measure, but I was in need of something to occupy my mind. There are few jobs for men in their sixties. But the people who owned and ran Jenkinsons were the old fashioned sort - 'Jenkinson Bros.', long-established family firm, timber merchants in Jesmond since the 1920's. And only a ten minute walk from Rainbow Street.

The Jenkinsons had just the one shop – or whatever you'd call it – 'outlet'? They were friendly people. I'd seen the notice in their window as I'd passed one day - 'Man wanted for general duties. Any age. Apply within.' (I thought they might be taking a chance. Wasn't it sexism - whatever that is - to show a preference these days for one gender over the other?) They wanted someone to help carry cut timber to customers' cars, move it around the yard, tidy things up after the weekend rush – things like that. 'Just light duties,' they told me. That suited. I wanted nothing that was going to demand anything of me. Or remind me of anything.

The two Jenkinsons were Geordies through and through. In my cursory interview I did my best to curb the excesses of my southern accent. It seemed a courtesy. Even so, they looked at me a little oddly. I didn't fit the stereotype of a man employed to do little more than odd jobs about the place – I could see it in their faces. But we got on. I told them I was recently divorced and had moved far away from my former home in order to put the past behind me. They nodded with understanding and asked no questions.

Apart from Mondays, weekdays in the timber yard were busy. At weekends we were run off our feet. DIY was king. It was heavier work than I'd anticipated or they'd given me to understand. At the end of each day every joint and every muscle ached. Really, I was too old. Or perhaps just too unfit. Maybe I should sign on at a gym. But I really couldn't cope with the idea of cycling on the spot while watching some amateur video of the countryside going by. Perhaps a bit like having sex with a prostitute. I decided the job itself would soon enough have me fit.

I got used to the routine and to my new colleagues, who came to regard me as an eccentric trophy won from the southerners. I had never in my life worked as hard in such a purely physical way. Beyond that, the job made no demands whatever. But I was so exhausted at the end of every day that my mind switched off along with my body and I slept at nights like a baby. I started to feel settled once again. I saw no more of the man in the garden.

If however, you position yourself with your back to the ocean, you don't see the tide coming in.

In my very early days as an Account Executive in my first London advertising agency, one of my assignments had been to go along and keep an eye on the shooting of a TV commercial for some now long-forgotten breakfast cereal. I knew nothing about shooting commercials and despite my ill-fated flirtation with it in Bristol, pretty little about advertising altogether. But it was common practice for a token account exec. to be present on a shoot. The official line was that this was to ensure the agreed and often painstakingly crafted script was being adhered to by the creative people. My unofficial reading of it was if things went wrong, I carried the can.

The main character in this commercial was played by a famous Scottish actor, now deceased, and to whom I'll refer as Alex. Most actors and actresses I was subsequently to meet were characterised by a seemingly pathological need to be the epicentre of all things. Not so this man. Despite being recognized as one of the finest actors of his generation, his humility was captivating and refreshing.

Over lunch in a pub close to Shepperton Studios where the commercial was being shot, four of us - Alex, the film director, my colleague the agency TV Producer and myself were chatting more or less casually about things in general. The conversation drifted to the stresses of modern life. This in turn led to a lot of talk about anxiety – a subject close to the hearts, it seemed, of just about everyone round the table. It was then that Alex said something which was to resonate profoundly with me in the Jesmond days so many years later.

This all took place at a time when Eastern thought was beginning to make a popular impact in the UK. The word 'guru' was becoming part of the common vocabulary. In cities, towns and villages, yoga classes were being held. Across the country, a significant spiritual wind seemed to be springing up. It became acceptable – even fashionable - to speak openly about 'depression', 'stress', 'anxiety' - problems little understood, but now being acknowledged as widespread. The talk around the table that day moved on to question to what extent – if at all – this 'stress', this 'anxiety' could be controlled and ameliorated by the mind.

Alex, on the subject, kept silent. The rest of us showed no restraint. The mind was capable of virtually limitless wonders - modern man was only just beginning to comprehend its potential. Look, we said to each other in a sort of mutual admiration by proxy, at the recent advances in electronics, in medicine, in air transport, space travel - it was virtually certain the Americans would even have a man on the moon within a year or two. So sure, it has to be possible for the mind to control anxiety - what is the mind of mid-20th century man not capable of?

Having arrived at this rather lofty conclusion, we returned to our food. It was only then that Alex, in his gently modulated Highland accent, said, "Anxiety is of the mind. It is the mind itself that is stressed and anxious. How would you use the mind as a tool to control its own self?"

We all looked up at him, mouths full, eyes wide.

"The mind is not you," he went on. "It is your servant. Use it well, it is a wonderful one." He paused. "It is however, a most terrible master."

Those words and the quiet intensity with which he had uttered them held us silent. Until I cleared my throat rather nervously and said, "But short of some form of insanity, how would you get to a situation where the mind was master over you?"

He shrugged. "There's really no difficulty. Just steer your life with unwavering commitment along a course upon which you've determined, but which nevertheless flies in the face of who you really are." And he smiled at me.

I was about to be in over my head, but I had no option. "But wouldn't that," I persisted, "be a peculiarly perverse thing to do?"

"Indeed it would," he replied, "if, at the same time, you knew who you were." And he looked around the table at every one of us. "But isn't that the difficulty we all have – knowing who we really are?"

He stunned me into silence. But I was too young. Unwise and headstrong. His words sank out of sight. Until in Jesmond thirty years later, like corks, they bobbed back to the surface. But the tide, as they did so, was already licking at my feet.

The restorative effects of my job at Jenkinsons had worn off. Once again, I was not sleeping. My son was ever at my shoulder. I'd indulged in a silver BMW drophead and had tried to relive my earlier carefree Newcastle days. Psychologists call it 'transference'. What it amounts to is attempting to solve a problem by turning your back on it.

On my weekends off, I toured again the wild countryside around, and north into the Borders. I sat, as I had done once before, on the wide beaches, and in the inglenooks of country pubs. One weekend, walking on that cold, windy beach by Bamburgh Castle, I met Barbara. We talked about the same things. We ate lunch in the Lord Crewe Arms, and laughed a lot. We seemed good together. The following day we met again. There was a gentleness, a quiet joy about it. I said I would take the following Sunday off and maybe we would go to Lindisfarne. She was pleased, and said she would look forward to that. But I had to ring her. My son got in the way. I could see nothing the other side of him.

When I closed my eyes at night, my mind, like some destructive troll from the shadows, set about me. Endlessly, pointlessly reworking, revisiting stuff, places, people, events of my life, calling up dire projections into a future dark with threats – round and round, half-dream, half-waking. Matt, Stella, Mother, Dad, Miriam on the carpet, naked below the waist, Mother's hand clawing out from beneath the duvet like Nosferatu's from the coffin, the wheels of the pushchair over pavements uneven as a range of hills, on and on - until the early hours when I'm suddenly wide awake once again, and my mind like a clockwork thing whose cogs I feel grinding out the inside of my head. Dawn comes, the singing of birds outside, and with it a delirious sense of peace. On good days I might then get a brief sleep. But when I get out of my bed, I am wrung out and exhausted. And another day to get through.

'The mind is a wonderful servant.' I hear his voice again and again. 'But it is a most terrible master'.

One evening in the week, driving home from Jenkinsons, I stopped off at an off-licence. I searched the shelves and was surprised and delighted to find there a bottle of red wine made from the lovely Chilean grape I'd come across at the Gables – the Carmenere. I bought a crate of it. The man who served me was so surprised he gave me a quite ridiculous discount. I stowed it lovingly in the boot of the BMW and drove back to my apartment.

That evening, with my dinner – a ready meal bought from the local Waitrose supermarket - I drank a whole bottle. Not a lot to some, and not to me in my drinking days long past. But more than enough these days. I did the same the following evening. And the next.

And so the bottle of Carmenere red became a routine. Like all routines, eventually it palled. It needed a jolt. A shot of malt whisky - The Macallan, for example, before eating would probably do the trick. It did. The one became two. The two became three. After three of those on an empty stomach, each poured with only a cursory eye on the level in the glass, eating lacks urgency. As often as not I didn't. The demons would come for me in the night and take me to hell. On waking, the first crack of light through the eyelids was a scimitar into the frontal lobe. Then there's the hangover until, by late morning if your luck holds, you're back to as near normal as you're going to get that day or any other day. In the evening after work you need a drink. And once again you climb aboard the merry-go-round where the monkey turns the handle and you dance to the Devil's tunes.

And so it goes. The Jenkinsons were nice about it. They warned me. I promised. But broke it. You do. You mean it at the time, but something gets in the way. They were gentlemen about it when they told me they no longer needed me. Apologized. I shrugged. OK. I don't need the money. I've never done the job for the money. I had plenty. "My time's my own now," I said. "I'm headed for the stars."

"This name's a mouthful – 'Mr. Bernat Gyorgy Horvat-Marshal'." The Police Constable looked up. "What's that – Russian? Polish?" She handed the credit card to the Sergeant who glanced at it and held it up to Ida Bullen. "Is this the name he gave you, Mrs Bullen?"

A white-faced Ida Bullen shook her head. "No," she said. "He told me his name was just 'Bernard Marshal'." Her fingers trembled as she tightened the belt on her dressing gown. "I suppose it's close."

The Sergeant gave the card back to the Constable. "Eastern European of some sort."

Ida Bullen frowned. "But he speaks absolutely perfect English."

A female paramedic appeared by her side in the doorway. "Has this man got family, d'you know?"

Ida Bullen shrugged. "He's from London – that's all I know."

"Compos mentis yet, is he?" said the Sergeant, thumbing through the contents of a leather wallet.

"No. We'll stretcher him." The paramedic withdrew.

Ida Bullen bit her lip.

The Sergeant scrutinized a driving licence he pulled from the wallet. "Does he have a car, Mrs Bullen?"

Ida Bullen pointed to the window. "The silver one outside. He only bought it a few weeks ago."

The Sergeant and the Constable peered out of the window. "Nice one," commented the Sergeant.

The Constable made for the door. "Can't make out the reg. I'll go down." She left the kitchen.

The Sergeant said to Ida Bullen, "Done anything like this before, has he?"

Ida Bullen shook her head.

"Problems with rent? Anything like that?"

"He paid a full year in advance. He's been a model tenant."

"Has he now? So what do you know about him? How's he been spending his time up here?"

"Until a few weeks ago, he was working at a timber yard."

"Timber yard?" He frowned. "You certain of that?"

"I've no reason to disbelieve him."

"Not many of them left - Jenkinsons?'

"I've no idea." She watched in dismay as the paramedics carried a loaded stretcher past the door.

"So he left the timber yard. D'you know why?"

She shook her head. "That's none of my business."

"Right. But do you have any idea?"

"No. But - " - she took a deep breath - " - well, he hasn't perhaps seemed himself recently."

"Uh-huh. In what way?"

"Funny things really. Once or twice his television's been on all night. I could hear it - my apartment's directly below. The light in his sitting room would sometimes be on during the day with all his curtains closed. Odd stuff, like that. Then I wouldn't see him for two or three days on the trot, although I knew he was in. And he didn't look well. Though he said he was fine. It was very unlike him."

"Since when was this?"

"Probably since he left that job."

The Sergeant's radio crackled. He listened, spoke into it. "OK. Ta. Stay down there, I'm pretty-well done here." He looked at Ida Bullen. "But nothing – you know – suspicious?"

She shook her head.

"OK." He closed his notebook. "That'll do for now. He'll be a day or two in detox."

Ida Bullen followed him from the kitchen. As he made his way to the front door of the apartment, he indicated the open door of the sitting room. "Left you a bit to sort out in there, hasn't he?"

"So what happens now?"

"When he comes out it'll be up to him. But I imagine he'll come back here. If you'll have him. But if he does and he gives you any trouble - you let us know, eh?"

"But what has he actually done?"

"Drunk himself unconscious, by the look of it. And had a fight with the furniture on the way - given himself a few cuts and bruises."

She put a hand to her mouth.

"Got a few problems, I guess." He said it like he understood that sort of thing. He carried on down the stairs. "Take care. I'll let myself out."

In the sitting room of Barney's apartment, Ida Bullen shook her head in confused despair. It was like it had been ransacked - papers, folders, clothes, cushions, personal belongings all over the floor. One of her high-back leather armchairs was on its side. She tried lifting it but it was too heavy. Mister Calloway would have to do it when he came in the morning to cut the grass. And oh dear, her little oak tea table was actually upside down with its lovely barley-sugar legs sticking rather inelegantly up in the air. With great care, she set it upright. It seemed unharmed. In fact she could see nothing broken or damaged. But then there was such a mess she could hardly be sure.

In righting her table, she caught sight, among the papers at her feet, of a small black and white photograph. She couldn't restrain her curiosity. A young man in a suit stood on a lawn in the rear of an old house. Nearby, a woman leaned against a wall. But none of this was hers to look at. Carefully, she placed the photograph, face down, on the mantelshelf.

She switched out the light as she left the room. Something, it was clear, had gone badly wrong in the life of poor Mister Marshal.

56.

Ellen wiped clear a small area of condensation from the bedroom window. She stood looking up and down the street. Edinburgh in the rain was, if anything, even less prepossessing than London in the rain. The Georgian terraces, their stone façades so imposing in the sun, were dismal now and depressing. She was looking forward to getting away. She needed a break. Randolph had made Hong Kong sound wonderful. Hot. By the sea. Oriental and obliging. Colonial, almost.

He had been a rock. She had not been easy. He was some years older than Barney. The army, she felt sure, conditioned a man to acceptance of duty and of responsibility. With Barney, she had had to accustom herself to an intermittent hurly-burly, an often live-by-and-for-the-minute confusion. There would be little of that around Randolph. It felt appropriate for this time of their lives.

The fact that for the time being at least, they couldn't marry, had not prevented their making known their intentions to friends and relatives. No-one would have Randolph down as a great creative thinker, but he had recently had a flash of genius. "Let's go to dear old HK," he had said, "and have ourselves 'un mariage faux'." The plan – which he had dreamed up on his own, saying nothing to Ellen until he had it clear in his own mind - was to stay with some ex-military friends of his who had settled there in what used to be called the New Territories. "In the old days," he told her, "you used to get the old Star Ferry across Victoria Harbour from Hong Kong Island. That was quite a trip with the mountains on the Chinese mainland in the distance. With the new airport, that's all a thing of the past. But it's still a splendid location, HK. You'll love it."

And there, they would go through a freelance, unofficial wedding ceremony, based loosely on that of the Church of England, and taken by his friend, an ex-Lieutenant-General. Ellen would be known thereafter as Ellen Mortimer. There would be champagne, food, music and dancing. And that simple ceremony, though not legally binding of course, would, in the eyes of the world, seal their commitment to each other as firmly as though it were.

It was a spirited idea. She had warmed to it. It was maybe a tad unusual in that she and Randolph were already, here in Edinburgh, sharing a bed. It was something she would not have wanted the whole wide world to know, but it's what people do these days. And it would not, in any way, take from the significance of the occasion in Hong Kong.

She checked her appearance in her dressing table mirror. Looked at her watch. Breakfast would soon be ready. Randolph was probably back even now with his daily newspaper. As she went from the room, she felt a gentle, butterfly nervousness. A rather nice feeling.

"Good morning, my Eastern Rose." Randolph smiled and put his coffee cup down.

She blushed. She did rather more of that these days than she liked. She returned his greeting and kissed him briefly. Then in some confusion, sat down at the table and arranged herself. She hoped she gave the impression of taking the compliment with the same easy grace with which it had been given. She was not convinced. She seemed prone these days to a certain fluttery femininity she had never associated with her own self. But the feeling wasn't entirely unpleasant.

He picked up the cafetiere and poured her coffee. "Only ten days now to 'Mrs Ellen Mortimer'!"

"I do hope," she said, "that 'Ellen Mortimer' is going to be able to handle the heat out there."

"It's not Africa, my darling, or the Middle East." He sat back. "It's not the heat, it's the humidity. That's the killer in HK. But I'm sure you'll handle it all perfectly well."

"I warn you, I've never been anywhere that exotic."

"Exotic, noisy, exciting." He rubbed his hands. "You'll love it. I've often said, one could take old Doctor Johnson's dictum re London and apply it just as easily to HK."

Help! The only thing she knew – or perhaps only thought she knew – about Doctor Johnson was what he's reputed to have said about –

But Randolph rescued her. "'If a man be tired of Hong Kong'," he said, with a twinkle in his eye, "'he is tired of life.'"

She laughed, mostly with relief.

The door opened. Emma wheeled in the breakfast trolley. "Good morning, Ellen," she said, brightly,

The girl's Glaswegian twang irritated Ellen just a little. But she guessed she'd get used to it. "Morning, Emma."

Emma set a plate before each of them, then lifted off the silver covers.

The aroma of scrambled eggs and bacon mingled with that of the freshly-ground coffee. This was Edinburgh, this was Randolph, this was them now. She felt a sudden delightful warmth inside. This was as things should be.

"The post's here," said Emma. Then making conscious eye-contact with each in turn, "Would you like it now? Or should I just put it to one side?"

Randolph looked at Ellen, referring the question to her.

Despite the fact that Ellen could give Emma – at a guess – the best part of forty years, she still felt a little like the new Mrs de Winter in the presence of Mrs. Danvers. "Er – " - she dithered. But then suddenly went for informality and affability - " - if it looks interesting we'll have it now, Emma. Otherwise, it can wait."

Randolph smiled to himself.

"Then I'll bring it now," said Emma. "'Cause there's one for you actually – redirected from Ludlow."

Ellen frowned.

Emma left the room.

They started eating.

"Who's still sending stuff to Ludlow then?" said Randolph, casually.

She shrugged. "The London estate agent, I expect. Though what he might want now I can't imagine. And in any case, he had this address."

The telephone rang.

Randolph dabbed his lips with his napkin. "'Scuse me, my darling. Julia, probably. About the flight." He got up from the table. "She said she'd ring earlyish this morning." He took the phone from its base and left the room to take the call.

Ellen smiled to herself. Barney would have clamped the telephone to his ear and chattered away at the table like a chimpanzee, eating at the same time.

She sipped her coffee. Then almost spilled it as a sudden hot flush went through her. Frank! Another letter from Frank? Please no. Surely by now he's come to terms with things.

She forced her thoughts onto the day ahead. There was still an awful lot of shopping to do for their trip. She hoped the rain would ease off - she loathed having to climb in and out of taxis in the rain, laden with bags and packages.

Emma reappeared and lay the mail in a little pile on the table along with a paper knife. Then with a discreet, "Thank you," left the room again.

Ellen sifted rather nervously through the envelopes. The majority was army and business stuff, all for Randolph. But there was indeed one for her, redirected as Emma had said, from Ludlow. She picked it up. Peered curiously at it. Both addresses – to Ludlow and the redirection to

Edinburgh – were handwritten. Neither was in Frank's hand.

She should have been relieved. But an unease, the origin of which she couldn't discern, was creeping up on her. She slit the envelope open and drew from it a sheet of paper, also handwritten. She adjusted her spectacles. At the head of the paper, an attractive graphic of a large country house set among trees. And beneath that, 'The Gables, Country House Hotel'. She frowned.

'Dear Mrs. Ellen Marechal' – who the hell is this? 'We are at present in the process of having the bedrooms on the first floor refurbished. The accompanying enclosure was discovered by a workman' - what accompanying enclosure? - ' - who was removing some of the old floorboards. It seems almost certainly to have fallen on the floor, then slipped through a gap in the boards. How long ago this happened I'm afraid we have no means of knowing as the rooms in that wing have not been upgraded for quite a few years. Even so, as it's addressed to yourself, I'm taking the liberty of - '

Her heart was thumping as she thrust her hand into the envelope and drew from it a second, smaller envelope. Tattered and dirty, but still sealed, it bore no stamp and was addressed to the Ludlow house. The address was handwritten. It was Barney.

She grabbed the edge of the table. Then with fingers she struggled to control, tore open the envelope and pulled from it yet another handwritten sheet.

'Darling Ellen,

Hello. First off – I am well.'

The world went dark.

'Nothing bad has happened to me. I haven't been kidnapped or taken hostage or in any way hurt.'

She tried to control her breathing.

'...... try and remember that however hard it may be to believe it at this moment, I love you.'

Oh, Jesus.

'One day, I wonder if you remember this......on the way back to the house in Turney Road .....plans for the wedding.....the time had come when I really had to tell you.'

She went on like someone in a hurricane trying to make sense of the chaos taking place around them. She wanted to scream.

'...when I finally managed to open my mouth to tell...you said, "No, my Barney...I don't want you to tell me anything. Just marry me."

Ellen, I have a son.'

I know you have a son, you stupid bloody man! It was left to others to tell me! Where the fuck are you??

'He meant more to me ……...part of me is missing. Please try and.......'

She crumpled the letter in her fist and sat staring straight ahead.

"Top-notch flight. Cathay Pacific." Randolph appeared in the doorway. "Gets us into HK in time for - " - but his words tailed off.

Ellen was very slowly getting up from the table. Her face was white. With the hand still clutching the crumpled letter pressed to her mouth, she made her way towards him.

"Ellen?"

She went straight past him.

"For God's sake, what - ?" He gazed emptily at her retreating back. Her footsteps started up the stairs. He came round and set off after her.

"For goodness' sake, you don't still love him though. Or do you?" Randolph, standing militarily upright beside the bed, was trying to look masterful. He looked instead uncomfortable and rather ridiculous. How on earth did one deal with this type of thing? He tried to strike a moderate tone. "The man writes a letter from some third rate hotel, God knows how long ago – more like an apologia for his actions, if you ask me – didn't even post it and perhaps never would have done. And it sends you into a state of collapse. What is this all about?"

"I don't know, Randolph. I don't know." Ellen turned over and buried her face in the pillow, then pulled the ends of the pillow up over her ears.

It was childish and irritating. It reminded him of his sister when they were children. He bent down towards her. "What, Ellen, is it you don't know?"

"I don't know. If I did, I'd tell you."

He stood back, dug both hands into the pockets of his trousers and gazed down at her. "So we don't even know what we don't know."

She flipped over onto her back. "Not 'we' Randolph - 'me'." She pointed a finger at her own chest. "I'm not a 'we'!"

He blanched.

"I'm sorry. I didn't mean to be rude."

His world was under attack. There came a rumble of thunder. Storms outside as well as in. What should one say or do?

She pulled a used tissue from under the pillow, sat up and noisily blew her nose. "I can't expect you to understand."

"Even so, my darling," he said, "I'm trying."

"Randy, I know you are. And I'm sorry."

He needed, he guessed, to be kind. But, at the same time, determined. "I might find it easier," he said, "if you – actually told me everything."

"If I what?"

"If you told me everything. I said I might understand if - "

"You think I'm keeping things from you? Randolph, I'm confused. The man I lived with and loved for sixteen years disappeared overnight off the face of the earth. He might have had a heart attack and fallen in a ditch. He might have been murdered. He might have been abducted by bloody aliens for all I know. For months I couldn't sleep at nights. Then years later, out of the blue, I get a letter from him saying he was fine and I should never have worried anyway."

He had no idea how to respond.

"Can you not see," she said, taking it very gently, "that that might confuse one just a fraction?"

He tried to match her tone. "But what I also see, my darling, is you can't love both him and me at the same time."

"It's not a question of loving him, Randolph."

"But how, in any case I now wonder, could you ever have loved a bounder who takes his responsibilities so lightly that - ?"

"Barney is not a 'bounder' as you put it! He's a lovely man."

"Who ups and leaves you without so much as a by your leave or any sort of explanation? What sort of 'lovely man' does that?"

"People are people. Maybe in the army they're not. Maybe in the army they're just numbers you can order about as you like and tell them how to behave and what to do. Barney was wounded by a lot of things in his past, but that didn't stop him being a lovely man most of the time."

"Ah. Right." Randolph stood back, adopted a tone of quiet superiority. "Well, I'm afraid I don't subscribe to the liberal-left view that one's unethical actions today are excusable on the grounds of an unhappy childhood!"

She turned her back on him.

"One's actions have consequences."

"You're pissing on me from a great height Randolph! - and I don't like it."

The blood drained from Randolph's face.

Thunder rumbled gently across the hills to the north.

He made his way to the door. "I think," he said, opening it, "I shall leave you to calm down. Then we must see what we must see." He went out, closing it quietly behind him.

Ellen fell back on the bed. "Fuck. Just fuck!" What the hell have we all come to? Martha's dead – her own hand doing the work of others, if we're to be horribly honest. Frank's a jobless widower, adrift in the world. I'm in danger of trashing the sort of life I filled my salad days dreaming of. What have we all come to at the hands of Barnaby Marechal? And Barney himself? – obviously alive and well and doing whatever the hell he likes!

She turned towards the window. What little sunlight was in the sky kicked a reflection off the wet rooftops opposite. A spindly television aerial waved back and forth in a sudden gust of wind.

"What on earth, Barnaby Marechal, you fool, did you think I was made of that I would not understand?"

57.

My fall from grace had not come as a complete surprise. In the few weeks leading up to it after losing my job, I had sometimes drunk so much during the day that at some point in the evening I'd fallen asleep wherever I happened to be. I'd wake up around midnight with my head on the table and whatever ready-cooked meal I'd warmed up, cold and half-eaten right in front of me. More than once I'd woken around dawn to find myself lying fully clothed on top of the bed, on the sofa, even in a foetal position in one of the high back chairs, freezing cold and feeling more ill than I have words for. On one occasion, I woke up in the early hours to find myself sitting on the toilet, naked.

In my peripatetic process to Cornwall, after the breakup with Stella, I had done things I have no pleasure recalling. But nothing was as self-demeaning as my elderly trashing of Ida Bullen's lovely apartment. I was mortified. I was also scared – the whole evening was a blank. I could remember nothing of it.

I would have to move on, it seemed, yet again. There was no way I could carry on living there and look Ida Bullen in the eye. Not that I imagined Ida Bullen would want me. I'd be surprised if she even allowed me through her front door to collect my belongings.

When I turned up on her doorstep again however, her reaction both to me personally and to my announcement that I intended leaving, astonished me. She invited me into her sitting room on the ground floor, handed me a cup of tea, and having delivered a very soft-edged remonstrance, said how nice it was to have me back. Was I recovered, she asked, and what was all this about leaving?

I had no interest in dissembling. "I have let you down," I said, "I have let myself down. I'm seriously embarrassed and not sure how to look you in the eye."

"My dear Mister Marshal, those are not, in themselves, reasons to give up your home. And what about the lease? You've paid it all and there's still months to run."

"Please accept that money," I said. "I owe it to you."

She shook her head. "You owe me nothing."

"Then I must at least pay for the damage."

"There was no damage."

I looked askance at her.

Again she shook her head.

"Then there must have been a pretty dreadful mess to clean up."

"Mister Calloway is paid to do that sort of thing." She then set about trying, in a rather roundabout, middle-class way, to persuade me to stay. She said that leaving aside this 'unfortunate lapse', it had been so nice having me around. There were, she said, few men of my age (which was her age) who showed 'an interest in things' and with whom one could hold a 'real conversation'. And as she said it, there was something in her eyes I had never before noticed. Or maybe it had never before been there. Either way, it came as a shock – though not an unpleasant one. To that point I had regarded our relationship as purely that of landlady and tenant. But perhaps it had never been quite that simple.

"I don't think for one minute,"she said quietly, looking down into her teacup, "that it was intentional."

I must have looked surprised, for she went quickly on, "I don't mean one could call it accidental. Clearly it wasn't." She paused. "I hope you won't think me prying, but when it came to clearing up, I couldn't help but be aware of the personal nature of some of what was on the floor."

I waited.

"That, along with my knowing you as I've come to do, suggested to me that you had probably been overtaken by some – well - personal crisis?"

"Possibly."

"I'm so sorry."

She'd meant it. She smiled a rather nervous smile. Then lowering her voice, said with an almost playful shake of the head, "I know about crises."

There was a weight behind her words the levity had not concealed. Was she inviting me to question her about her own problems? Was it an offer of support? Both, even? I was tempted. I could have done with talking with someone. But it was neither the place nor the time, nor was Ida Bullen the person. If her interest in me were more than simple concern for my well-being, the intimacy that sort of exchange inevitably engenders would get us both into trouble.

So once more, and yet again, I was on the move. I told Ida I would be out within a couple of weeks. That, she said, was quite unnecessary and unrealistic. She was right. But if only for my own self-respect I needed to be out as soon as possible. What made me drag my heels was the fact that every one of my 'new starts' had ended in calamity of one sort or another. Did I think this one would be different? Not only that - this is a small island, and I was surely running out of bolt-holes. So I hesitated. And I drifted. Then one morning, woke up to the realization that my lease had only a month to run. And still, I had no plan.

The answer dropped into my lap - they say the devil looks after his own. On my way back from a cashpoint in a row of shops a few minutes' walk away, I noticed, parked in the drive of a large detached house, a motorhome. It must have been six metres in length. It was a handsome beast, white and gleaming, polished chrome bumpers and window-surrounds. It was for sale. I had never in my life taken the slightest interest in such things. But projecting out over the cab, with a small curtained window in its side, was what I took to be an upper sleeping area. A sudden excitement gripped me.

I slipped surreptitiously in through the open gates to the drive. Shielding my eyes from the morning sun, I peered furtively in the side windows. Goodness! Gas cooker, sink, fridge, kitchen units. A wraparound sofa, table, cupboards, TV. And if I craned my neck right around, I could just make out on a door, the word 'Bathroom'. A self-contained, travelling palace! Selling the BMW would fund two thirds of the price.

I rang the house doorbell. A patronizing middle-aged lady with oddly untidy hair and whose lipstick could have been better applied, informed me that 'the man of the house is at present away at the office' and could I return that evening after six. I did. With the man of the house in the passenger seat, I took the beast for a test drive. I was beside myself - sitting in its lofty command module I could see over the tops of cars. I was master of all I surveyed. And it drove like a dream. The man of the house and I shook hands. The deal was done. The world was my playground.

The days spent preparing for my departure were idyllic. I don't think that's too strong a word. I hadn't experienced simple happiness like that since I was a child. The days were timeless and the sun always shone - or so it seemed. I came and went in a spirit of quite innocent enjoyment. My new prize and I were to be as self-contained as possible, able to go long periods without fresh supplies of food or water. I christened it, 'The Camel'. I was a medieval adventurer, about to set forth for distant lands unknown, with no idea when – or even if – I'd return to civilisation.

Most of my possessions had to go. During my time in Jesmond I had acquired more than even the capacious cupboards in The Camel could accommodate. I packed boxes with magazines, books, clothes and distributed their contents among the local charity shops: I gave a few things to Ida, including – with some sadness – my pot plants to which I'd become seriously attached. She, in turn, gave me a book – a curious little paperback novel entitled, 'At Swim-Two-Birds'. Her previous tenant, a woman who worked in the Engineering Faculty in the university had given it to her because, she'd said, she really had no idea what it was about. Nor, admitted Ida after reading a quarter of it, had she. But she'd thought that I, being 'an Oxford man' as she put it, might understand it. Feeling oddly flattered, I set it on a small secure wooden bookshelf, alongside Graham Greene's 'The End of the Affair', Ray Bradbury's 'The Silver Locusts', a little book of Chinese poetry which I'd dipped into from time to time and found strangely powerful. And something I'd spotted the day before in a secondhand bookshop - 'The Rubaiyat of Omar Khayyam' - one of the few literary delights of my early adulthood.

I arranged things inside The Camel exactly as I wanted them. It was to be my home, and I couldn't wait to be on the road. I had made a decision - I would tour the western Scottish Highlands right up to Cape Wrath. To see the grey Atlantic battering that most northerly point of the UK mainland had been an ambition since when, as a boy, I'd first seen it on a map. I would have no schedule. I would just leave and head northwest. It would take as long as it took and fate alone would be my guide.

Ida watched my preparations from the sidelines with what I took to be a certain sadness. I wondered if she had visions of my inviting her into my travelling palace and whisking her off to the end of the rainbow. I doubt such a thought ever entered her head, but it was a notion I quite enjoyed toying with.

It was a Monday evening and I was all set to go. The BMW was sold. The Camel was packed. Food filled its cupboards, my clothes filled its wardrobe. Its fuel tank was topped right up, its freshwater tank likewise, complete with water purification tablets. Ida had given me a supply of pleasantly perfumed soaps for the bathroom, along with new face flannels and towels. I had bought a new duvet and pillows for the upstairs sleeping area. The duvet was a double one – I might meet another Barbara. Coloured cushions were scattered over its sofa and chairs. Four glasses – two wine, two spirit – were secured in a special holder on the wall. (Ida asked me who I thought might be drinking from the second glasses). It looked wonderful. It looked like home. It stood outside, washed, polished, gleaming and ready. As a final touch, I'd had decals depicting an affectionate, bright yellow, cartoon camel applied to the bonnet and to the rear.

Ida invited me to join her that evening for a farewell dinner in her ground floor apartment. Although she herself was teetotal, she had, to my surprise, bought a half-bottle of very passable French red wine. She said, with something of a twinkle in her eye, "You'll have to drink that all on your own. Just so long," she added, "as you don't throw all my furniture out into the street when you've done."

I just about managed a smile.

We had an evening, she and I, on which I was to look back with affection and a confused nostalgia. The food she provided, all of which she had cooked herself, astonished me – gazpacho – not an easy thing to get right - followed by a delicious boeuf en croute. I was not a little flattered. Bless her heart, she had gone to town.

At the end of the meal I sat back with the last glass of wine. I told her how much I'd enjoyed it and how unexpected it had been.

"So, tell me," she said, "once you've gone, if I should need to contact you, how would I do that?"

I replied that as I'd taken care of just about everything I could think of, I couldn't imagine what she would want to contact me for.

"Things happen," she replied, and sipped whatever clear liquid it was in her glass. "And anyway, you can't just disappear into nowhere with nobody knowing where you've gone."

I guess I'd become so used to being on my own, doing everything alone and for my own self that it had not occurred to me that another person could be concerned for me or have part in what I was doing. "Well," I said, feeling more touched than I found comfortable, "I've got an old mobile phone. One I haven't used since I've been here. I suppose I could charge that up and give you the number."

"Lovely. I mean, if you were to break down in some remote part of the Highlands at night in the pouring rain, wouldn't it be nice just to hear a friendly voice on the phone?"

It would indeed. I just sat looking at her.

"And I've got a computer. I could even look up a garage for you on the internet." She smiled.

I didn't want to prick her balloon and tell her I'd joined one of the road rescue services. So I thanked her, and gave her the number of mobile number two – the one I'd bought when I'd started my search for Licia. Arriving in Newcastle, I'd switched it off, removed the battery and put it away in a drawer. All I would have to do was put the battery back in and charge it up overnight.

It was with obvious pleasure that she wrote the number down in her diary. She closed it, then looked up at me. "All I ask in return is that you send me a postcard from time to time. Would you do that?"

"Only," I replied, "if, also in return, you'll humour my curiosity and tell me what it is you've got in that glass." And I pointed to her wineglass.

Puzzled, she looked from me to the glass then back again. Then broke into a sudden, girlish laugh. "Elderflower cordial!"

"My!" I said. "Racy stuff."

"Ah," she said wryly, tapping the now empty bottle on the table, "like you however, I've had my moments."

There was more to Ida Bullen than met the eye. What a shame she wasn't my type. Or was she? I'd lost any ability to know any longer who was and who wasn't.

We had coffee. Dallied over it a little. Exchanging views and comments on this and that. Eventually we fell silent. "What time," she asked after a while, "will you be away in the morning?"

"Early. Sixish."

"Oh. I see."

I stood up from the table.

"You will," she said, "take care. Won't you?"

"I promise. And you please do the same." I took her by the shoulders and kissed her on both cheeks. We said goodbye. She watched from her doorway as I made my way back upstairs. I went slowly along my landing. Arriving at my front door, I stopped. Listened. I could sense her presence down below, still outside her own door. I waited. After a few more seconds, I heard her door close. Then her key turn in the lock.

My apartment, denuded now of my things, was bleak. I was of the past and it had no further business with me. I was very tired. I dug out the old mobile and set it to charge. I looked out of the window. The sky was clear with stars. I hoped that presaged sun for the morning. Down there, its gleaming white paint an odd, sickly hue in the orange light from the street-lamps, The Camel waited. I bade it goodnight. Then, with a flutter of nervous excitement, climbed into my bed.

The following morning, a few minutes after six o'clock and carrying only my small overnight bag, I tiptoed down the stairs. I slipped my key in through Ida's letter box. I closed the heavy street door behind me as quietly as I could, then walked away from the house for the last time. The Camel, waiting for me at the roadside, was resplendent in the sun. It was with a huge sense of pride and anticipation that I unlocked the door of the cab, threw my bag in before me, then climbed in and sat in that high-up throne of a driving seat. The Camel and I had, to date, only planned and played. This was the real thing. I took the newly-charged mobile from the pocket of my leather jacket, switched it on and lay it carefully in a depression in the dash which looked like it had been made for it. That would henceforth be its home while I was driving. I turned and looked back into the body of the vehicle. My sitting room, my kitchen, above me my bedroom. My home. This was where I was meant to be.

I started the engine and was about to put it in gear when there came a sudden short burst of musical chimes. At the same time, the display on the mobile in front of me lit up. Ida? So soon? She'd probably heard the engine starting. A surge of slightly uncomfortable excitement went through me as I reached for it and pressed the button. A woman's voice told me I had a voicemail. I pressed the button again. The same woman told me I had one new message. And that it was sent weeks back.

"Hello. My name is Katalin Varga. Minxie Charing gave me your number. I think I know where your son might be. Please ring me. Thank you."

A bomb had gone off. I stared sightlessly out of the front windscreen. The early morning traffic on the main road at the end went by in silence.

It was a short drive to the sea. I parked by the dunes. I was stung with betrayal. On my son's behalf, I'd poured away my life to date. He'd had his chance. Now was for me and whatever future I had. 'Ah, make the most of what we yet may spend,' I'd read in 'The Rubaiyat', 'before we too into the dust descend'.

I made a cup of coffee on the gas range in my new kitchen – my new kitchen. I drank it looking out over the sea. It should have been a glass of Laphroaig and I should have been gazing out over a loch enfolded among the misty slopes of the Highlands. Along the shoreline a woman and man walked together, holding hands.

I lay down on the wraparound sofa to wait for nine o'clock. That seemed a reasonable enough time in the morning to ring anyone.

By her voice she was a young woman. "Minxie and me talked about this." She spoke with some sort of foreign accent. "I meet her on the set of a TV commercial."

"Is that where you met this man?" I asked. "The man you think may be my son?"

"He was one of the film crew."

"What name did you know him by - 'Gaston'? 'Matt'?"

She hesitated. I sensed other people with her. "If that's an awkward question at the moment," I said, "it doesn't - "

"I cannot say right now because I - "

"Listen Katalin, I'm a long way out of London at the moment. But if I put my foot down I can be with you by early this evening. Then if you're free, perhaps we - "

"No, no. I have to leave for the airport in a few minutes. But when I am back can we please meet?"

"Do you actually know where he is?"

"I must talk to you when I am back." Voices were hustling her in the background. "Now I have to hurry. Sorry. In only a few days. OK? Thank you so much for calling me. Thank you." And that was where it was left.

I put the mobile down. Sat once more looking out at the sea. Two young boys in swimming trunks scampered down the beach and threw themselves like excited dogs into the breakers. The wind whipped the heads of the grasses on the dunes.

Travels with The Camel would have been a disaster. It was only a few weeks ago that I'd drunk myself to the brink of insanity attempting to drown out his voice.

I drove south, going nowhere in particular, but keeping to the coast as far as the road permitted. I tried to keep my son out of my mind. And Katalin Varga - whoever she turned out to be. When I heard from her again, then I'd head back to London. If I heard from her again.

I wandered around, stopping here and there. Eating a sandwich in a pub, coffee in a seaside café. Sitting on a beach, throwing pebbles into the sea. Bed and breakfast – I could summon up neither the will nor the energy to look after myself in The Camel - in a scruffy village plagued with motorbikes in the night. Cheap hotels in cheap towns, shops boarded up, their gimcrack shopping centres half-empty. And every now and then, scattered around their peripheries like wounds left undressed, swathes of rough ground gone wild, where rusted railway tracks go from nowhere to nowhere, where crumbling red-brick buildings, their windows smashed and doors broken into, drown amid a jungle of nettles, brambles and loosestrife. Places that were once the spokes in the industrial hub of half the world.

A week or so into these wanderings, I passed a sign by the side of the road telling me I was five miles from Skegness. It was not intentional. I seem to have just drifted there, like a balloon loose on the wind. Folded away in my wallet I still had the scrap of paper on which McDonald had written Stella's address. I stopped by a corner newsagent's and bought a local street map. It wasn't a thick one. Skegness does not have many streets.

58.

Had I passed her in the street I doubt I would have recognized her. But the voice, when she opened the door with a curiously unsurprised, "Oh. Hello," was as familiar had I last heard it the previous day. "Hello," I replied. And just stood there. The fleck of green in her left eye was still shockingly familiar. As was the tiny mole, just above her wrist on the right arm.

She said nothing.

"You don't seem surprised," I said.

"You've grown a beard."

It took me aback. Her unquestioning assumption, that after all these years, she could step uninvited, back into my space, infuriated me. I swallowed hard. "I've had it many years now," I said. I hadn't. But I needed to keep hold of my own separate existence.

Her smile was one of amused tolerance. Or was I being defensive? This wasn't going well. I cleared my throat. "I was passing through," I said brightly, "on my way to London. You don't seem surprised to see me."

"I guessed you'd turn up. Sometime."

"Oh? Why?"

"McDonald. You asked him for this address."

"That was a long time ago. Did you mind?"

She shook her head.

"You still keep in touch with him, then?"

She gave a non-commital shrug. We stood looking at each other. Cars passed in the street behind me.

"You look well," she said.

"Really?" Given my recent traumas, I was surprised.

"What's that down to then – clean living?"

I took that as friendly raillery. "That, and a clear conscience," I replied.

She smiled, took a step back into the hallway. "Come in, Barney."

My name on her voice after all these years threatened the release of a lot of stuff.

She gathered together something inside herself. "Nobody hears from him. Friends nor family. I really don't know what help I can be. I know no more than you do."

"Is he still in London?"

"As far as we know. But who knows?"

We sat in rattan chairs in a tiny, sunny conservatory. It overlooked a small rear garden. There was a neat lawn surrounded by flowers. Two black and white collie dogs slept in the sun on a concrete path. Around us, indoors on windowsills and on shelves, houseplants in colourful ceramic pots. I felt tense, uneasy. There was music from a radio somewhere.

"The last I heard of him was from a friend of mine who bumped into him when she was in London for the day. In John Lewis's in Oxford Street, of all places."

"And?"

"He didn't stop to talk apparently. Just said hello. He seemed nervous. Anxious to get away." She hesitated. "And he was dressed - well - funnily, apparently."

"What sort of 'funnily'?"

"Leather stuff." She pulled a face. "A pendant round his neck." She sighed. "Who knows - maybe he's gay now."

"With his reputation with women? I doubt."

"Maybe you can be both these days." She looked out of the window at the dogs. "It's like he's erased all of us from his life, Barney. Why would he do that?"

"How would I know?"

"You're his father."

My cheeks burned. "Yes, I'm sorry. Really sorry."

"Are you? What for?"

So many things. She knew. I shook my head. It was a door better left shut.

In a show of assumed casualness, she extracted from the earth in one of the pots an embryonic weed. "So now," she said, "you've given your life over to finding him."

She'd made it sound more facile even than Licia.

"Yes. Basically," I said. "I see things now, Stell, that I didn't in those years."

She tapped the tiny root so that the few fragments of earth still clinging to it fell back into the pot. "It's a shame," she said, "you didn't see them slightly earlier."

I took a deep breath. "I hope," I said, "I can put at least some part of it right."

She toyed with a corner of the tablecloth. "We all played a part – me, McDonald. But that built on damage already done."

I said, warily, "And what damage was that?"

"Endell Street, Barney. He adored you."

"'Adored's a powerful word."

"And it's the right word. A three-year old little boy lost the father he adored."

"Though, as you say, there were other factors."

"Which came much later. Anyway, what happened to you? You played with him. You made him laugh. You took him places in his pushchair. Then one day you weren't there. You'd gone from his life, and his world fell apart."

"I didn't just go away from him, Stell. It was a bit more complex than that. I - "

"'Complex'? What's 'complex' to a three year-old? You'd gone. If you'd wanted him, you would have stayed."

I couldn't allow myself to get pushed into that corner. "You can't have that, Stell. You've just said - "

"Don't tell me what I can and can't have, Barney!" Angrily, she tapped her own chest. "I was the one who - " - but she stopped, and looked for a second or two out of the window. She turned back to me. "Look, it's a long time ago now, and I don't want a slanging match. Just I think you ought to know that every night for weeks afterwards I sat on his bed making up stories about why his Daddy wasn't around. I had to hope that as time went by I'd be able to concoct some half-plausible one about your never coming back that wouldn't completely break his heart." She turned away again. "You need to know that."

I looked at a tiny insect, on a plant by my shoulder, scurrying across a leaf on its minuscule legs. Out in the garden the dogs slept. White clouds meandered across a blue sky.

She went on. "As he got a bit older, he decided he wasn't, after all, the problem – I was. You'd left because of me."

I didn't want to get pulled into this. I had no answers. But she sat looking silently at me. "How did he work that out?" I asked.

"He didn't 'work it out'. He went with the only version of events he could handle. The poor boy was in trouble, Barney." She took a tissue from her sleeve and blew her nose.

Sunlight played in the shallows of her hair. Here in this small suburban space, the wound occasioned by my years of absence was weeping in my sight, as it had wept for so long out of it. But what could I do, or say? "I know how you must feel," I said. It was meaningless, and I instantly regretted it. She jumped on it. "Oh? And how do you manage that?"

"Well - I – "

"You know how I felt when you walked out on us?"

"You kicked me out. Stell."

"In a fit of rage I told you to eff off. But - "

"Look - "

"No – you look, Barney! You walk out and then your father pays me off and kicks me and his grandson into the long grass - you know how that felt?"

"You took the money."

"You bet I took the money! And the house. That way I could look after that little boy without you bringing your women home and screwing them on the living room floor." Tears of anger stood in her eyes.

"There were not 'women'. There was one."

"So one's alright, is it?"

"Stell," I said, "look - I'm really sorry."

"So why weren't you sorry years ago?"

"Christ – I don't know! Look, if I knew that I wouldn't have left in the first place, would I?"

She did a sudden switch of tone to one of ominous calm. "Tell me," she said, leaning forward on her elbows, "did anybody know?"

"Know what?"

"That you had a son? Did you tell anybody about him? Your friends, the people you work with?"

I didn't answer.

"Your new wife? Did you tell her?"

I shook my head.

"So - in over thirty fucking years you never told anyone you were a father and that you even had a son? Is that right?"

"I'm afraid that's about it."

"How, Barney, could you not?" She gave her eyes a savage wipe. "You say you know how I feel. Well - do you know how it feels when another man – not the best or the brightest in the world but my God at least he did what he saw as his duty – when another man looks after, brings up, takes all the swipes your son aimed at him along with his own natural son dying and generally behaves like a hero - do you know how that feels?" She glared at me like she would drill holes in me.

"And you fuck his best friend."

Silence.

I was as shocked as she was.

The colour drained from her face. "What did you say?"

"I'm so sorry." I half expected her to get up and hit me. But she didn't move. I said again, "I'm so sorry, Stell."

She turned towards the window. Sat silent for some seconds. Dabbed at her nose. Then shrugged. She said, very quietly, "Don't be. It's the truth."

We said no more for a long time.

"Would you like a cup of tea?" eventually she asked.

I nodded. "That would be nice."

She stood up. "The beard suits you, by the way."

She was starting to look old. So, I'm sure, was I. She was overweight. Her brown hair showed grey at the roots - 'a suicide brunette', Mother would have been pleased to call her. She stirred her tea. One of the dogs came to the window wagging his tail. She mouthed to him an affectionate, 'What d'you want, then?' She tapped the window by his glistening wet nose. "That," she said, "is 'Benbow'. The other one's 'Nelson'."

"Admirals," I said "Why?"

"I live by the sea. It seemed fitting."

This might have been us. In our house, our life. In Skegness or wherever. Looking out over a postage-stamp garden which I tend with the intensity of one fending off thoughts of death. "How long," I said, "have you had dogs?"

"A while. They're company." She took a sip of her tea. "I got them originally so I didn't have to come home to an empty house."

"You work?" I was surprised.

"I've no option. 'Jordan Florist' gobbled up all my money. I got nothing from the divorce. And have you tried living on the pension they give you in this country?"

"Does McDonald give you anything?"

"Why would he? He's kind enough anyway in his own funny way."

"What work do you do?"

"I work," she said, turning on a smile of comic pride, "in 'Paradise'."

"So that's where it is - Skegness!"

It pleased me to see her laugh.

"It's a warehouse full of one-arm bandits just by the pier. I change their money for tokens. In the summer it's a madhouse. This time of year it's pretty dead. So I read. Or sometimes knit." She turned away, looked out of the window. "It's easy. It pays. It's only three days a week."

Stella, with her Oxford education, handing out tokens to the hoi polloi in a seaside arcade! But she seemed at ease with it. And what was it to do with me these days, anyway?

"So," she said, putting her cup and saucer down on the table with a purposeful clunk, "this woman in London – does she actually know Matt?"

"She knows a man who – it's possible, I think – could be him."

"And does she actually know where he is?

"She thinks she knows where he was when she left the voicemail on my phone. Which was some weeks ago – though don't ask why."

"So where was that?"

"Till I meet her I don't know."

"Are they – were they - a couple?"

"She didn't say, but it sounds like it. And incidentally - " - I took out my wallet and drew from it the battered black and white photograph Celeste had given me - " - can you let me have a more recent photograph?" I handed it to her. "That's the only one I've got."

She studied it, smiling. "I haven't seen this in years. Where did you get it?"

Some weird, residual feeling of infidelity rose up and confused me. I cleared my throat. "I - er - I'm not sure. Perhaps McDonald - I think." I went quickly on. "Who took it?"

"Giles went through a brief photographic period." She grinned. "He wasn't a natural." She peered closely at the little print. "I doubt," she observed wistfully, "our boy looks much like that now."

"You doubt? You must have more recent ones."

"Must I?" She handed it back. "I've got one taken with a woman who used to help with flower deliveries in the early days. And one taken on the water splash thing at Thorpe Park. In the first he's standing behind her and pulling a silly face over her shoulder with a flower in his teeth!" She tried, without success, to avoid a smile. "Matty and photographs didn't mix. And in the second we're all of us covered in so much spray you can see almost nothing of us." She pointed to the photo in my hand. "If you want to see what he looks like, that's still the best."

I looked bleakly down at the little print. I ran a hand through my hair.

"So." She took a deep breath and drew herself upright. "When are you seeing this woman?"

"Very soon." I took out a pen. "Give me your number. I'll ring you afterwards."

I wrote down her landline and mobile numbers on the back of the photograph. She said, rather tentatively, "So where are you living, these days?"

I pointed in the general direction of the road outside. "In the motorhome."

"So the world's your oyster."

"It will be - if I ever get to use it in the manner I'd intended." I slid the photograph back into my wallet. We looked at each other. A clock struck the hour. I checked my watch.

"Do you have to go?" she said.

I shrugged. "Whenever."

"Do you want to stop and have something to eat?"

I was taken aback. "Yes," I said. "I'd like that."

"It'll have to be a takeaway. I'm not into cooking this evening."

"Any decent Indian round here?"

"Not bad. Chicken Vindaloo?"

"Crikey - you remember."

"It's all you ever ordered."

"I've gone off the chillies a bit. Age, or something. But a chicken or lamb bhuna – something like that would go down a treat."

I stayed that night. Until Katalin Varga was back in the country I was in no hurry to get back to London. Stella's house had a small spare bedroom. She moved boxes and plastic bags off the bed, then put a hot water bottle in it. "Just to make sure it's properly aired. It's a long time since I had a visitor."

Eating with her, talking to her, watching her go about things in the house, then lying in bed that night knowing she too was in bed just a few metres away in the next room was a strange experience. For both of us and for Matt, I felt a sadness for what might have been. But at the same time, I had a reassuring, settled feeling. A sense almost of closure. I was soon asleep, and slept well.

The following morning, before I left, we took a walk on the beach with the dogs. It was cold, with an icy wind knifing in off the North Sea. There were few people about. In the distance, the fairground's big wheel and roller coaster were bleak skeletons against the grey overcast.

It was a good time. We were easy together. "Did Matt," I asked her, "talk about me?"

"In the early days, he talked about little else. But as reality set in he hardly ever did. He tried to blank you. I never told him who you were."

"Why not?"

"In case he contacted you and was rejected again. I'd no idea how you might react. Looking back though, I think I should have done. Particularly when he grew into his teens. He kept it all to himself, but I know he needed you."

We came to a wooden groyne that ran down to the sea. We sat on it side by side. One of the dogs – I couldn't tell one from the other - came bustling up to us. I think he was just letting us know he'd registered our slight change of circumstance. It made me think perhaps I'd like a dog. Could I have a dog with me in the Camel?

"What about McDonald?" I asked. "Were you happy with him?"

"Mostly." She kicked the sand at her feet. "He was - is - a good man."

"I liked him. Once I'd got used to him."

She chuckled. "Not everybody's cup of tea, is he?"

"Nor's that woman of his."

"Belle, you mean?"

"'Belle'? Is that her name, for Christ's sake?"

"It's what she calls herself. Behind her back, everybody else calls her, 'Liberty'." She laughed. "It suits her - she has more than just an eye for the men. She throws his money around, drinks like a fish. One way or another she's going to ruin him. This time he won't be able to blame you."

"He left me in no doubt I'd been a thorn in his side."

"Poor man. He really thought one day you were going to show up again."

"On a white charger? And carry you and Matt off into the sunset?"

She turned away and retired into her own thoughts. Then looked round at him. "Barney?"

"Stella?"

"I need to ask you something."

"OK. Ask."

"Our splitting up was one thing. But your staying away all those years – why?"

Out on the horizon, a triangular white sail dipped and swung in a flash of sudden sunlight amid the waves. I watched it till the sun had gone in again.

"Barney?"

"Oh, Stell - I had so little idea what relationships were about. What life was about. You know what a train wreck Mother and Dad were together. After you and I split, I got involved in stuff I don't even want to remember. Then one day I looked in a mirror. I didn't like what I saw. So I put together a human being - like you would a do-it-yourself bed from IKEA. He would be all the things I had never been – solid, personable, successful, popular with all and sundry. And being born at the age of about 30, he didn't have a past. He'd never been married, he had no children. Endell Street had never been. He wasn't staying away - there was nothing to stay away from."

Stella grimaced. "That's scary."

"And I made a good job of it. Trouble was, it wasn't me."

"So is 'me'," she said, running a finger gently along the wood of the groyne, "the man I'm sitting here with now?"

I thought about it. "Maybe. Ask me again when I've found the boy."

"Do you ever wish you'd known at twenty-five or thirty what you know now?"

"Doesn't work that way though. Does it?"

She shook her head. "It's easier for women."

"What is?"

"Children. Families. Life, in a way."

"That's not what my feminist friends tell me."

"No. It's a view I keep mostly to myself. Though I did upset poor Giles once telling him."

"What exactly did you tell him?"

"That little girls are born with an insight into life. They have a primitive sense of purpose. Women are part of the earth, Barney. We're in no doubt of our place in it. I know that goes against everything you read and hear these days, but most of that stuff is sexism in one form or another."

I was intrigued. "Go on."

"You men don't have that. You have to find your place. Some do. An awful lot don't. It accounts for a lot."

"A lot of what?"

"Women's behaviour. And men's."

I thought about it. "The years haven't blunted your edge, Stell."

She leaned down and picked up from the sand a small piece of driftwood. "It's been in mothballs a while though." She called out to the dogs. "Nelson! Benbow!"

They scampered towards us, scattering sand. She threw the driftwood over their heads towards the sea. They spun around again and raced off after it.

We both sat in silence, looking down at our feet and the sand. She had on a pair of red, canvas shoes. As she sensed me looking at them, she playfully waggled them. I waggled my brogues in reply.

"You know something?" she said. "It'd be really nice to think this is the real 'you'." Then as though she needed to change the subject quickly, pointed suddenly to the top of my head. "You've still got a surprising amount of hair, haven't you?"

I felt the top of my head. "What's 'surprising' about it?"

"That it's lasted so well. You were already losing it when we were in Endell Street."

"That's what marriage did for me."

She smiled. We fell silent. The dogs came back, one with the piece of wood in its mouth. I looked at my watch. "I guess," I said, "it's time to go."

She took a tissue from her coat pocket. She seemed about to do something with it. Changed her mind, and put it back. She dithered. Went to say something, but checked herself.

"What?" I said.

She shook her head.

"Stell? What were you going to say?"

She took a deep breath. "That photograph - Matty and me in the garden. Where did you get it?"

Awkwardness threatened me again. This time I coped. "A - er - woman I met. A one-time friend of Matt's."

"Celeste Johansson?"

"'Johansson'? I wasn't aware of her surname. But – yes. Why?"

"Did she tell you about her and Matty?"

"Yes."

"What exactly did she tell you?"

"Why?"

"Please - tell me what she told you."

"OK. Well, she was quite open with me. She told me she'd had the hots for him when he was in his twenties but had kept her distance. She didn't want to be just another notch on his bedpost. Or to be seen as a baby snatcher - she was quite a lot older than him. And that they'd gone on and become just friends. Is that not true?"

"Basically."

"So what's the mystery?"

"You know Matty left Skegness and went to work in London?"

"She told me that too. In advertising. So did McDonald."

"And did she also tell you that a few years after that he came back to pick up some of his stuff which was still in the old house at Marsh Enderby?"

"McDonald mumbled something about it."

"He came up for a weekend. He stayed with his stepfather in Boston. Celeste knew from McDonald that Matty was coming back. And that he'd be going to the empty house." She stopped, like she was reluctant to go on.

"And?"

"And – they met up at the house that Saturday afternoon."

If this were going where it seemed it could be going I might have to accept the slightly unpalatable fact that my son had been where I'd been some years earlier. But so be it. That aside, I couldn't see a problem. "So," I said, "she went to the house. Maybe they had a bit of slap and tickle among the dust sheets and the - "

"You have a granddaughter, Barney."

The breath went out of me. "I what?"

"You have a granddaughter. She'll be about twelve now."

The sound of one of the dogs barking was mixed with the pounding of the blood in my temples. I saw again Celeste turning to me from the foot of the stairs in Christmas Cottage with that hitherto unfathomable look on her face.

I turned off the motorway. I needed a quiet place where I could stop, make myself something to eat, and confront this latest twist. I came across a large area of green on the edge of a village. I parked under a tree. Made a cup of tea and a sandwich. I sat at my table right by the window. I looked out on pretty thatched cottages, and beyond them, on rising ground, a church with a spire. Beyond that, a hillside with sheep grazing.

A granddaughter. Celeste's daughter. My son's daughter. There was not the space in my head. "I am a grandfather," I said out loud. "I-am-a-grandfather." It wouldn't have meant less had I said, "I am Attila the Hun," or "Coco the Clown." I had to forget about it. Christ, I had more than enough to handle. Katalin Varga had rung as I'd left Skegness. I was meeting her at eleven the next morning. Sufficient unto the day. And anyway, the chance of my ever meeting the girl seemed impossibly remote.

The story was that Celeste had not wanted the child. At the same time, she was fervently anti-abortion. She had therefore determined to have it, but arranged for its adoption at birth. This took place in a private nursing home hundreds of miles away, somewhere in the West Country. Where, I wondered, had she found the money for that?

According to her, Matt had refused to accept responsibility. Despite assuring him he was the only man she'd slept with in the relevant time frame, he had been adamant. To some extent, I sympathize – he knew her as well as anyone and probably better than most. Some said she'd asked him to have a DNA test and he'd refused. Others that he'd demanded one and she'd refused. I have to say that if she were going to have the child adopted at birth I couldn't see how she was going to arrange any DNA test - or what the point would be anyway. It was even rumoured that her refusal to have the test which Matt is supposed to have asked for was because she didn't know for certain who the father was but had seen this as a heaven-sent, last ditch opportunity to land a man she'd coveted for years. Neither Stella nor I thought even Celeste capable of that. But who would know? The whole thing was so mired in tale and counter-tale, supposition and invention - out of which the truth was never likely to emerge - that I wanted nothing of it. The only thing I wanted was to get down to London and find out what Katalin Varga had to say.

Before I left Skegness, Stella had suggested I stay that night at what she'd referred to as the Caravan Club's campsite at Crystal Palace in South London. "It'll cost you peanuts compared with any hotel. No parking problems. And you'll be able to sleep in your lovely mobile home. And it's right on a bus route to the West End." I'd been curious to know how she knew about such things. "I had, not so long ago," she told me, "a rather jolly liaison with a nice chap from the continent who was seriously into all things camping." I'd like to have known more, but that was all she was saying.

I'd rung the site and booked, for the following seven nights, what the woman who answered the phone referred to as 'a pitch with hardstanding and electric hook-up'. I knew nothing about campsites, camping, hook-up or pitches. I'd have to find out when I got there.

59.

My first encounter with sand dunes had been via a few smudgy black and white photographs in a school geography book. They did not excite much interest in any of us. We knew about sand – it was for kids. They dug holes in it on seaside holidays, filled little buckets with it and made sandcastles out of it. And maybe the man next door, constructing a garden path one weekend, would use sand in mixing his cement. And sand was a major component in the manufacture of glass. How that could be I could never grasp, but it's a fact. Sand was a common, simple, naturally occurring substance to which you would not give a second glance.

But the sand I saw in the desert struck awe in me. The dunes – vast, sleekly undulating mountain ranges of it - rise sharply up out of the desert floor like alien beings. Their colour, texture and form is quite different from the dark brown and broken rubble out of which, from a distance, they appear to arise. A closer look reveals they are indeed quite separate from the ground beneath them. They have a life of their own. They move, and have made their way here, driven by the endless, whispering wind. They flow, expand and engulf, advancing the desert into areas where once men grew crops and fed families. In the low sun of dawn or twilight they have a tantalising, mesmeric beauty. Treat them with anything less than meticulous respect, and they will ingest and annihilate you.

On our journey to Iferouane, we passed extensive areas of dunes. I watched them as they slid slowly past in the distance, like monsters from prehistory snoozing in the heat. I peered at them at close range through the vehicle's open window as we rocked and swayed past them, up their smooth yellow flanks towards their summits and their ridged, dinosaur backs.

We stopped one day by a lone thorn tree. The sun was at its zenith. In the tree's threadbare shade we stretched out on mattresses thrown down on the sand waiting for the worst of the heat to pass. A short distance away an area of dunes shimmered in the heat.

I couldn't rest. There was no breeze and the heat was suffocating. It would be the same in all directions for a thousand kilometres. I stood up. I pointed to the dunes and said to Youssef, "Can I walk to the top of those dunes? Will the sand take my weight?"

"It will," he said. "But take water with you."

"Why," I asked, "would I need to take water when we have so much with us?"

"The dunes are two kilometres away."

I looked at him in disbelief.

"When you get there it will be maybe an hour to the top. They are three hundred metres high."

Open-mouthed, I looked again at the dunes. Sand, piled one thousand feet high. But you can't judge distance, you can't judge size. The sun's overhead and there are no shadows. I lay slowly back down under the thorn tree with the others. I did not take my walk.

It was around mid-afternoon of the third day, half-asleep with my head hanging on my chest, that I felt a sharp tap on my shoulder. Startled, I look up. Youssef was pointing out of the windscreen towards the distant horizon. Right across it, from one side to the other, shimmering so much in the afternoon heat that it seemed to be trying to break free of the earth, stretched an undulating yellow line. The sands of the Tenere. That word echoed ominously through the corridors of my mind. I sat up, and remained with my eyes glued to it as we approached. Slowly, slowly it grew in height. We were here.

We drew up within a few kilometres of the dunes. I say 'a few kilometres', but really I'd given up guessing distances. But however far away they were, they dominated the landscape, exuding a tense, mysterious power. I looked at them the way I imagine primitive man looked at the moon and the stars, on the approach of a storm, how he watched the evening sun's demise in the face of night - all the works of some unimaginable entity before which he stood in awe. Those dunes are the guardians of my secret. Somewhere, up there on their hidden summits, baking in that terrible sun, lies the karma that has shadowed me for forty years. I hope against all hope that I will acquit myself with some dignity.

The second Land Cruiser came to a halt beside us. The doors of both vehicles sprang open and a spate of activity broke out. The cook climbed up onto the roof of his vehicle and threw to the ground a couple of large branches from the stock of dead wood he had collected on the journey. He dragged them to one side and with an ancient sand shovel, set about digging a large round hole in the sand. Whatever he was up to was a welcome diversion. But he spoke no English, so I asked Youssef what the cook was doing. Youssef was poring over one of his maps spread out on the bonnet of our Land Cruiser. He said simply that we had run out of bread.

I wasn't sure if that related in any way to my question. I stood around, watching what was going on. I wanted to do something; I wanted to help. But it was all so well scripted and rehearsed that I would have got in the way. I looked around for the European man. Perhaps it was time I tried to get to know him. But he was nowhere to be seen.

I wandered away and sat down in the sand. In the far distance, I could just make out the irregular line of the same dark mountains which had been with us almost since the start. I pulled my knees up, and as Celeste had done that first day as we'd talked by the sea, clasped my arms around them. How, now, was Celeste? Where was she? With someone else? Breaking out the champagne again, telling him tales among those other dunes, watching the small birds scatter across the breakers?

I watched the activity around the vehicles. The cook, to my continued puzzlement, appeared to be lighting a fire in the hole he had dug. Sam had his head under the bonnet of the second Land Cruiser. Youssef was still studying his map. And then, in the rear seat of our vehicle I could just make out the motionless head-and-shoulders silhouette of the European man.

I was a one-person audience for a play enacted on a stage of stupefying size. No-one however will review their efforts or share moments from it with others. When it's over it will be gone. Mist burned off by the sun. But that's the way with all things.

In my pocket is the black and white photograph. I take it yet again, from its crumpled brown envelope and look at it. I avoid looking towards the dunes.

With our dinner we had the luxury of fresh-baked bread. It smelled and tasted wonderful. Baked in a desert oven. So that's what the cook had been up to. I'd heard of such things – a hole dug in the sand, a fire made from foraged wood, and home-made dough. In western supermarkets, gleaming metal baking machines the size of Centurion tanks grind and groan; the 'baker' in smart white coat and supermarket-issue, hygiene-aware white hat stands, arms folded, scrutinizing dials. You can't bake bread for civilization's millions in an earth oven, I know – but something's awry with us. And already we're on our reserve tank.

We ate. Drank water. Always at mealtimes I gave thanks for the water. We finished, pushed our plates to one side, sat back. The sun was low now, the heat fast escaping into the empty sky. I stood up, excused myself and wandered away into the fading light. I needed to be alone.

I sat down on a low ridge of sand. I was surprised at the distance I had put between myself and the others. In the twilight, the vehicles were just two angular black blocks. Shadowy figures were hauling mattresses off the roof of one of them. The last of a red sun was dropping slowly behind the dunes turning them a fabulous, deep black, shadow-striped orange-yellow. I sat very still, trying to quieten the clamour in my head.

From time to time, voices floated to me on the still air. In between, there was silence. Until my time in the desert, I had never experienced silence. Not the real thing. In what we are pleased to call the 'developed countries' it doesn't exist. But out here, in a thousand kilometres there is no traffic; no sound from next door's TV; no birdsong; no footsteps along the floor; the wind sighs through the branches of no tree, rustles no leaf. You come to hear your own breathing; the blood moving through your veins. Thus exposed to your own organism, you recognize its perilous fragility, teetering as you do on some razor-thin and entirely mysterious dividing line between the bit we think we know, and the infinite vastness we know we don't. Alone here I would fear for my sanity.

As I considered the morrow, I could see no option from which I might realistically expect any joy. If my son were in the red pickup, then either he was alive or he was dead. If alive, he'd be in a parlous state. And out here in no-man's land, getting medical help in time would likely prove impossible. If he were not in the pickup, then he'd walked out into the desert in the hope of finding water or human habitation – both vain hopes. Or, like Captain Oates, he'd walked out into the desert in order to end things and stave off insanity. Either of those options means that what's left of him could be under the sand anywhere within a mile or so's radius of the vehicle depending on how far he managed to stagger in 50C. I had once asked Youssef how long a Westerner might expect to survive alone on the dunes without water. "One hour," had been his reply. "Maybe less."

I must have looked incredulous, for he went on, "You walk. Maybe half an hour - you dehydrate. You sit down." He shook his head. "You not get up." I don't remember John Mills and Sylvia Syms having that problem. As I remember it, they staggered on under blazing skies for a lot longer than that. I guess they had plenty of water.

Or had Matt stuck to the rules? Had he remained with his vehicle?

There comes a grotesque vision. I am struggling through the sand to the Suzuki and Matt is in the driving seat wearing the black coat and that same long red scarf and slowly he turns to me - I can't recognize him from that photograph and he doesn't know me from Adam so when he calls out to me for help and I call back and tell him I'm the father he hasn't heard from since he was three years old come to rescue him he thinks I'm an apparition born out of his own desert-crazed madness.

I pull myself together. I sit in silence.

The only thought that could offer me any comfort was that perhaps this whole venture was based on a fundamental error - my son was not in the red Suzuki pickup because I'd got the whole thing wrong and he'd never, ever been out here in this country in the first place.

I must have been there a long time, for it suddenly struck me that dusk had turned to darkness – or at least as near darkness as there ever is in the desert. A vast, overarching canopy of stars twinkled above me so bright it felt I could touch them. But I had to go. I needed sleep. I stood up, and was brushing the sand from my jeans when, from somewhere behind me, there came a sound. I spun round, froze, staring into the darkness. It came again. An animal? The movement of a snake through sand? Do I stay or run? A black shape detaches itself from the gloom, and my heart is pounding.

"I am sorry," said a voice. "I startle you."

That accent. The European man. And that sound, his wheezing breath. The relief that flooded over me was straight away replaced by the vague apprehension I always felt in his presence.

"Forgive me," he said. "I should not come upon you like that." He was quite out of breath. I think it was the first time I'd heard him utter a complete sentence. "That's alright," I said. "Have you been for a walk?" It was a line straight out of middle-class, Sunday afternoon England, embarrassing and meaningless. It had also been my nervous overlay on a troubling suspicion I had that he might have been out there using, under the cover of darkness, some advanced IT device to communicate with a foreign government or terrorist cell.

"I will tell you," he replied. "I have been – how do you call it? - relieving myself." He chuckled. "That is the expression, is it not?"

I guffawed, partly with relief and partly with surprise at his unexpected affability.

We set off together towards the camp. To my surprise I was feeling quite at ease with him. I wanted to ask him about his part in this expedition. It had, after all, been put together at my behest and on my behalf, yet I had no idea what he was doing in it. Having some insight however into the half-truths that characterize so much of what goes on between governments and their agents of one sort or another, I struggled to find an opening line.

He forestalled me. "I hope," he said, "that tomorrow for you will be a good day."

He'd meant it. A wave of gratitude washed over me. For all the affability and general good humour from the other members of this expedition, not even Youssef had openly expressed concern for my situation. "Thank you," I replied. "So much."

As we continued on together he said, "I imagine you know that things recently have not been good in this country."

"I do, yes."

"You should be prepared. It would be prudent."

Though I appreciated his bluntness, it still unnerved me. "I feel," I said, "that I'm as prepared as I'm ever going to be. But the omens are not good. Are they?"

"Who knows?" He shrugged. "People can – and do - survive. As long as they have water. And they stay with their vehicle."

"It must be tempting though," I replied, "even if you do obey the rules, to think that if you just walk over the next ridge or two there's got to be a village. Or a camel train or something. The thought of sitting alone in your vehicle and never seeing another human being ever again must be - I don't know - " - I shook my head rather than contemplate it.

"Yes," he said, quietly and with a wry smile, "the desert will undo a man's mind."

We walked the rest of the way back to the camp in silence. Sam and the cook were playing cards by the light of an oil lamp. Youssef was already stretched out on his mattress and appeared to be asleep.

We walked to where our two little orange-coloured tents had been pitched, side by side, three or four metres apart. "Listen," I said. "I'm afraid I don't know your name. We've never even spoken properly before. But I appreciate your concern. And your frankness."

I expected him simply to acknowledge my thanks and say goodnight. Maybe to first tell me his name. But instead he stopped and looked directly at me. He stood so still that for a moment or two I saw the night sky reflected in his eyes. I felt awkward – an odd pressure to say something. All I could do was repeat myself. "The omens," I said, "are not good. Are they?"

He took a deep and rather noisy breath. "We insist on conclusions, don't we?"

It seemed an odd response. "A successful conclusion tomorrow," I replied, "would be one of the high points of my life."

All he did was smile.

"Do you mind my asking," I said, "what your function is in this group? No-one has ever told me."

"My sole purpose here," he said, brightly, "is to ensure that these boys - " - he indicated the card-players and the sleeping Youssef - " - do nothing which would be considered inappropriate."

It posed more questions than it answered. But I had to go. Tiredness was overwhelming me. I put out my hand. We shook, then bade each other a very good night. He turned towards his tent. But as he walked from me, despite my fatigue, I felt a strange reluctance to let him go. But under what pretext could I detain him?

He must have read my thoughts. As he undid the ties on his tent, he looked back at me. "We read the signpost - we take the road." Then did a slightly comedic Gallic shrug. "Our part in it then is over." And slipping with surprising agility into his tent, he wished me a final goodnight.

I was perplexed. Also slightly irritated. The light came on in his tent, converting it into a big orange lantern. I turned away and walked slowly towards my own tent. Unlike him, I scrambled awkwardly and inexpertly into it. I was shamefully unfit. Then the nightly pantomime of undressing in that cramped space and inserting my protesting body into a sleeping bag. The sores in my groin hurt. I was not meant for this sort of life. I did not put my tent light on. I baulked at the idea of the card players seeing my elderly contortions shadowed on the walls. I settled myself in, then lay looking up through the thin fabric at the vaulting roof of stars. Silence eventually from the card-players. Someone snored.

I couldn't sleep. Who the hell was he, that European man? Some colonial civil servant giving me life lessons in the bloody desert? I was angry, confused. And in the darkness outside, tomorrow lay in wait.

60.

Whatever business Katalin Varga was in, it paid well. The lobby of Empress Court seemed to Barney not a lot smaller or less opulent than that of the Empire State Building in New York. He waited for the lift. The floor at his feet was black marble. Hand-carved oak panels decorated the walls. Art deco mirrors reflected bas-relief copper murals. Chandeliers hung from a stuccoed ceiling. What did this girl do?

He went to the top floor. The door of number 32 had been left ajar – a nice touch, he felt. Inside he could hear music – jazz or rock - he was never very clear on the difference. Given that the door had been left open, he felt it inappropriate to use the heavy brass knocker. He rapped discreetly with his knuckles.

The music stopped. He half-expected the appearance of a liveried flunky. Instead, it was a woman. Slight, quite short, fragile, her short fair hair stylishly cropped. She was probably around thirty, with rather striking eyes of an intense, greenish-blue. A plain, off-white, smock-like garment reached to her knees. She had no stockings or tights, and was barefoot. She smiled and said, in a voice so soft he only just caught it, "Hi."

And he knew her. Knew the face, but couldn't place it. "Good afternoon," he replied. "Katalin Varga?"

"Mister Peters?"

He nodded. "Not my real name, I'm sure you guessed. But if we can let it go at that for the moment."

She smiled archly, as to a fellow conspirator. "Come in, please." They shook hands. Her grip was surprisingly firm.

Again that suggestion of an accent. As he followed her along a hallway lined with photographs of her under stage lights with a microphone in her hand he realized, with a jolt, that she was the singer, Dione.

"We were filming a video. You know the sort of thing – you sing and dance to playback."

"Is that where you met the man - Gaston - who you spoke about?"

"The first time, yes."

They sat at a table in a kitchen big enough to have catered for an army, yet oddly devoid of character. A window looked out over the whole extent of Regents Park. Beyond that, the buildings of central London and in the far distance, bled of colour by the haze, the towers of Canary Wharf.

She was attractive. Though nervy and a touch curt, she seemed generally open and unpretentious. Barney had been under the impression that unpretentiousness and the music business were mutually exclusive. Perhaps - and he hoped - he'd been wrong.

From a small, plain glass she sipped what looked like water. "We shot all night - on and on, over and over again. In Docklands. It was weird. There was no traffic but the traffic lights are changing - red, green, yellow. I was cold. I don't like night shoots. I didn't want to do it, but my agent bullies me. I guess he's right. They soon forget you."

"And what was Gaston's part in this?"

"He assist the director. The director was nervous man. That gives everybody jitters. Gaston brought me a blanket for my shoulders. He was nice. I like him." She sipped again. "I expect it's funny to you that we call him that."

Barney was already getting a tiny frisson of excitement. Some sixth sense was telling him he could trust this woman, and that sitting here with her, he might have stumbled across the first genuinely fresh footprint left by his son. "Before we go any further," he said, "I assume you know that whatever you and I talk about in this room is between you and me and no-one else. Absolutely nobody."

She nodded. "Minxie said." She placed a playful finger on her lips and whispered, "Mum's the word."

The colloquialism, delivered in her accent, was deliciously cute. He reached into his inside pocket and pulled from its brown envelope the black and white photograph."Is this your man?" he asked, handing it to her. "Is that Gaston?"

"Great! Let me see!" She took it, looked at it. Then frowned.

Barney bit his lip.

She looked up at him. "This guy is so young."

"Er - yes. It was taken quite a long time ago."

She scratched her head. "Well - maybe he is the same height. But short hair - Gaston's hair was long to his shoulders. And a suit and a tie. I never see Gaston wear these things." She peered hard again at the photograph. "His eyes are a little bit the same. But - no, I dunno." She shook her head. "I am so sorry. But I can't tell." She handed the photograph back.

"OK. Well, it was something of a long shot. He was only about twenty then. And unfortunately, it's the only one I have." He slipped the photograph back into its envelope. "I don't suppose there's any point asking if you have a recent good one - is there?"

She took up her mobile phone, pressed a button and passed it to him. "I have that."

"Ah, great!" He took it. "Thank you." He looked eagerly at the photograph. Then sagged. Two wide-open eyes, presumably male, their colour obscured by red-eye, looked out over the top of what appeared to be a tea-towel held up in front of the face. A few brownish-grey locks of hair sprouted from beneath a small upturned saucepan on his head.

Barney was not amused. "Mmm," he muttered. "Right." He handed back the phone.

She pulled a face. "He think that is funny. He thinks photographs steal your soul. Like tribes in the jungle. I say that to him once but he gets angry with me."

Barney put the envelope back in his pocket. He felt let down. "So really," he said, letting his irritability get the better of him, "whether your

Gaston could be my son or not, hinges an awful lot on whether the man you had a relationship with was the same one Minxie had a relationship with. Don't you think?"

She frowned. "Why you say that? Of course he is the same man."

"Did you ever see him with Minxie?"

"No, But - "

"Did Minxie ever see him with you?"

"No. But they - "

"So how can you be absolutely, one hundred percent certain you're talking about the same man?"

"Of course it is!" She was offended. "Gaston Vincent is Gaston Vincent. He is the same, same man!"

"OK, OK. I'm sorry, Katalin. Really. I'm getting rattled by all this. I've been searching for this boy for a long time now and every single trail has fizzled out. I don't want it to happen to this one."

She smiled. "I understand. And they both wear big silver rings on their fingers and don't like photographs."

"OK. Got it." He took a second or two to gather himself back together. "So," he said, "that message you left on my phone. You said you thought you knew where he might be."

A shadow crossed her face. She took another sip of her drink. "That was a few weeks ago. I had talked with him on the telephone. He said he would ring me when he got to Agadez. But - "

"Agadez?" Barney frowned. "Where's that?"

"Africa somewhere. He rang me from - "

"Big country, Katalin."

"I know. I'm sorry - I don't know geography. He was at the airport and he said he was going to go to Agadez. But first he needed a vehicle." She topped up her drink from a plain, unlabelled bottle. From the way the liquid poured it looked suspiciously thicker than water.

"Did he say what sort of vehicle?"

She sipped, nervously. "No."

"Or what he wanted it for?"

"He said it was – 'a tool of the trade' - is that an expression?"

"It's an expression. What 'trade' was he talking about? I guess he didn't say."

She shook her head. "He just said it was hot there. Lots of flies. He would get a mosquito net. And he would ring me from Agadez."

"And did he?"

"No. He rang me. But he was in a car with some men. He was scared, you know. Really scared. It was horrible."

"What was he scared of?"

"I dunno. His voice was shaking. I could hear the men. They were talking and laughing - in a rough way." Her hand shook as she picked up her glass again.

"What language were they speaking – could you tell?"

"Very loud. I dunno what it was." She drank. Liquid spilled on the table. She wiped it up with a tissue she took from the pocket of her smock. "I say to him what is going on. He said to tell them he was in a red Suzuki pickup. And he was on 'AF something'."

Barney's eyes narrowed. "'AF something'?"

"Yes. Then a number. Like '123' – except it was something else, not '123'."

"Sounds like a flight number. Air France."

"'What do you mean?' I say to him. "Who you want me to tell? Why?' But then the phone is dead."

"And was that the last you heard from him?"

She nodded.

"And you've no idea where in Africa this place is – Agadez?"

She thought hard, screwing her face up. "Is there some place called - Niger?"

"Niger?" Barney's heart missed a beat. "What on earth had he gone there for?"

"He said to make lots of money."

"In a dirt-poor country like that?"

She shrugged, looked helplessly at him. But then, remembering something, she reached into her handbag, took out a little purse, and drew from it a piece of paper. She handed it to Barney. "He tell me I can get in touch with him on that number."

"Ah!" He looked at it. Then up at her. "But - this is a London number."

"Yes. He say the man would know where he was and what he was doing."

"What man?"

"The man at that number there. He said his name is Rik."

"And have you rung Rik?"

"Yes. Never anybody answers."

"And you've left messages?"

"Yes! They don't call back. It's one of those robot things. Not a person."

Barney ran a hand through his hair.

"Oh - and, yes - and he knew someone else who had done it."

"Christ Katalin! – someone else?? Who? And had done what?"

"No!" She shook her head. "Don't be angry with me! Please." She indicated the piece of paper in Barney's hand. "He say that man there did the same thing."

Barney looked again at the number, written in a hand which might just be that of his son. It stared blankly back at him. He cursed himself for the months in Newcastle.

Katalin meantime, with tears now in her eyes, drew from her handbag a tiny, embroidered white handkerchief, shook it open, dabbed at her cheeks. "I grew up without my father too," she said.

"Did you?" he said, absently.

"My mother never speak to me about him. She say it upset her." With her thumb and index finger, pushed the handkerchief gently back into the bag. "One time I say to myself I will pay someone to find him."

He looked up. "And did you?"

She shook her head. "I was scared they might find out he is dead." She sipped her drink.

He pointed to her glass as it went back down on the table. "D'you mind my asking - is that water?"

She looked like a child caught cheating. Slowly, she shook her head. "Gin?"

"Vodka." Then with a hesitant, placatory smile. "But with lots and lots of lime. And I only sip it."

"Don't."

"Why not? Look!" She held a hand out over the table, palm down, fingers spread wide. It trembled like a leaf in the wind. "It's the fucking music business that does - !" She clapped the same hand to her mouth. "Sorry! I'm sorry."

He pointed to the glass. "I've been there. You'll lose everything you think you're gaining - and then more."

She pushed the glass away out of reach. She said, very quietly, "It's nice that you care." She stood up and walked over to the window on the opposite side of the kitchen. She looked out across Primrose Hill, through the zigzag rooftops of St. Johns Wood and on up towards Hampstead Heath. "I like London," she said, vaguely, as though to no-one in particular. "When I was little I want always to live here."

Barney wasn't listening. A nasty thought had lodged in his mind. At least one way in which a man might earn 'lots of money' in a country like Niger had occurred to him. "Listen," he said, standing up and flourishing the piece of paper, "I'm going to get hold of this man ASAP."

She turned from the window. "Is there a child?"

He stopped. His mind blanked out. "Pardon?"

"A child. There was a rumour."

He sat heavily down again. "What sort of rumour?"

She made her way back to the table. "He tells Minxie the same thing - he is going to go away abroad to earn lots of money. But when I meet him – he has not gone away." She sat down opposite him.

"Child, you said - what about it?"

"That he had one."

"What - Matt? Gaston?" He hoped he sounded utterly incredulous.

"A long time ago."

"How long?"

"I dunno. Years. Maybe ten."

"Who told you that?"

"Minxie. She wondered. Some woman in advertising had told her."

"What woman? And what, in any case, has that to do with his going to Niger?"

"My friends say maybe the mother found out where he was living. So then he - "

"'Friends', Katalin? What friends?"

"My style director, my hairdresser. There would be lots of money to pay."

"What - and he's gone to Niger to avoid paying a load of back-maintenance on the off chance the mother turns up after ten years?? Is that what they're saying?"

"No, no." The tears were back in her eyes. "I dunno! Maybe he's just gone. Not to Niger. Not anywhere. Just gone." She shook her head slightly distractedly from side to side. "I just dunno." She pointed to herself. "Me?? Has he dumped me? Is that what it is? I am so, so confused."

An aircraft droning low overhead on its way into Heathrow forced them into silence for a few seconds. When it had passed, Katalin had calmed a little. She dabbed at her eyes with her handkerchief. "He did the same with Minxie. Went. She did not know where except abroad."

"But you do know where he went."

She shook her head very slowly. "I know where he told me he went."

"Phone calls purporting to be from Niger, AF 123 or whatever it was, travelling in a red Suzuki pickup with men he's supposed to be frightened of – don't you think it's a rather involved way of just dumping someone?" But Barney was not as sure of himself as he hoped he sounded.

With the backs of her hands, she wiped her eyes. "I'm sorry. I am just so unhappy with all this. I dunno where he is, what's happened." She put her head in her hands.

Barney lay a hand gently on her shoulder. She was shockingly thin, and seemed all of a sudden hardly out of her teens. "Katalin," he said, gently, "if Gaston is Matt - then you are the only person he has stayed in touch with. No-one else. I've just returned from seeing his mother."

She looked up, took the hair out of her eyes.

"She hasn't heard from him for very much longer than you. Nor has his stepfather."

"I am sorry for them. Say 'Hi' to them for me."

"I will. And take some advice from one who's been around the block a few times - don't listen to people who don't know what they're talking about." He tapped the left side of his chest. "Listen to that."

"I try. I try."

"Now - I really have to go." He stood up. "Somehow or other I'm going to get hold of this Rik character. Don't worry - we'll sort this out."

"You never told me your real name."

"No. Perhaps one day, eh?"

She smiled. "You're a kind man. People say my Dad was kind."

Barney sat down on a bench by the boating lake in Regents Park. Ran his hands through his hair. A pair of ducks - man and wife, he presumed - cruised around in the sunshine, in and out among the reeds. Slowly, serenely. At peace.

He looked down at the ground. Time for a decision. Was 'Gaston' Matthew? Was Matthew 'Gaston'? Or had Katalin put him onto another trail that would just fizzle out - this time after the expenditure of huge amounts of time and money? But as he couldn't possibly answer yes or no to that, he asked himself a different question; should he trust his instinct and go with his feeling that it was at least possible - perhaps bordering on the 'probable' - that the two men were one and the same?

Or should I wait?

Wait for what?

To be more sure.

How will you get more sure by waiting? You were going to read life's runes.

That's right.

So what are they telling you now?

I don't know.

But you do. Just get on with it.

It scares the hell out of me. People have been taken hostage there. Had their throats cut. What sort of place is it for a middle-class, English, ex-public schoolboy - a one-time luminary of Her Britannic Majesty's government, for Chrissake? Or for my son?

Your son's already there.

Or was. Or may have been. Or may not have been. Oh, Christ - to be a duck! If one of them had soon to go to the wildfowl equivalent of Niger, it would in no way disturb its present tranquillity. When the moment was on it - and not until then - that duck would deal with it. Something has to be deeply amiss with the mind of man that he so vexes his present moments with fears of a future in which he can discern with certainty absolutely nothing.

He stood up. He needed to get hold of 'Rik'. Even though no-one had responded to Katalin's calls, someone was surely monitoring that phone. He thanked the ducks for the advice, bade them adieu and made his way out of the park. At Oxford Circus he boarded a number three bus to Crystal Palace. He would ring Rik from the comfort and privacy of the Camel.

61.

I am in the 'Intrepid Fox'. It is a pub in Soho and I am out of my depth. It's around nine-thirty in the evening. It is smoky and noisy. People have had a lot to drink. I remember Soho, many years back, as the haunt of prostitutes in dark doorways. They are long-gone now, replaced by 'new young models' who wait in seedy rooms on dim-lit staircases. It is a part of town of which, in present circumstances and given a choice, I would keep well clear - there are those in Westminster who frequent it – for the many excellent restaurants and maybe even for more venal things.

I am very nervous. The man opposite me is younger than I'd expected. Why I'd expected any one age rather than another I've no idea. His name turns out not to be 'Rik' as Katalin had told me, but Kit. I try hard to control the tremor in my voice. "So - what exactly did you do?" I ask.

He looks at me. He is trying to make sense of me. Probably in his late thirties and almost completely bald. Wiry, with unhealthy skin and tiny, sparkly eyes. His jeans trousers and jacket are scruffy, torn in places. He sips with hummingbird-like darts at his beer. As he finishes one cigarette he lights another. His hands shake. How did my son come to know such a person?

"So this Gaston," he says, "is your son?"

"He is," I say. "Yes. Where did you meet him?"

"On a job."

"What sort of job?"

"Commercial. TV commercial."

"Are you in films too?"

"I'm in whatever."

Something tells me to take that no further. "So," I say, "he talked to you about going out to the Niger?"

He nods, draws on his cigarette. "I told him – fucking madness. Stay out of it." He knocks the ash from his cigarette with a self-conscious flick of the index finger of the other hand. "Sounds like he took no notice."

He is hardly well-spoken. Yet he is far from the lout I'd expected. "I've been told," I say, "that he wanted to do the same as you did. So what did you do?"

"No." he shakes his head. "That's wrong. He said he was going to do what I wouldn't do. What I refused to do."

"How," I venture tentatively, "do you mean?"

He looks me in the eye. Then says very quietly, "You sure you want to get into this?"

"No. But I've no choice."

"OK." He draws with tensed, string-thin lips on his cigarette. "He was looking for some action."

"'Action'? What did he mean by that?"

He studies the lit end of the cigarette. Then even though it is no more than halfway burned down, extinguishes it by ramming it into a battered tin ashtray. Immediately ejects another from a flip-top pack. "So I'm in Algeria – right?"

"No. Matt – Gaston – has not gone to Algeria. He's in - "

He puts up a hand to silence me. "I'm in Algeria. A US airhead - all money and fuck-all sense - has this clapped-out Pontiac Firebird. Christ knows where he picked it up in Algeria. Anyway, he bets me I can't drive it solo across the desert."

I am looking aghast.

"'Why?'" he says. Then answers his own question. "Because it's there."

I'm totally adrift. "The Sahara, you mean?"

"Did you ever read, 'Fear and Loathing in Las Vegas'?"

I shake my head.

"Or see 'Vanishing Point'?"

Again, I shake my head.

"Seminal. You should."

I surrender to my confusion. He is party to some unthinkable parallel world. The only thing I can think of to say is to ask how he knew the way. And I recognize the crushing stupidity of that even before he throws back his head and laughs.

"Set off south from Algiers," he says, "and you got to hit the Big S. It's like that." And he spreads his arms wide and looks from one hand to the other. "All across Africa. Then keep on south till the sand runs out.

Simple."

I feel like Oliver in the presence of Fagin.

He inhales, then ejects an aggressive plume of smoke. Watches it swirl around in the air. Switches his glance straight to me. "Look - " - do I detect a note of concern in his voice? - " - I can't tell you what your Gaston is doing out there. All I can tell you is what he kept pumping me about."

"Please. If you would."

"OK. More by luck than judgment I hit a town – if you can call Agadez a town. Two thousand kilometres south, in the Niger. If I'd aimed myself a few miles to one side or the other I'd have missed it and gone on for another eight hundred. Except I wouldn't 'cos I was nearly out of fuel. I hadn't eaten for a week and I couldn't see straight. There's supposed to be a road – the Trans-Sahara Highway." He gives a humourless laugh. "A lot of it's caved in, parts don't exist at all – so you're wandering about in the sand with the temperature up beyond the forties. You gotta expect anything - brigands, bandits, masked men on camels with rifles."

I am stunned, horrified. "Did you tell all this to Gaston?"

He takes a long draw on his cigarette. Shakes his head. "No."

"Why ever not?"

He shrugs. "The man was set on going to some sort of edge. I gave him a couple of contact numbers. Then told him to go home and forget about it. Anyway – that's not the point of the story. The point is, I meet this guy – South American, Brazilian - in Agadez, who pressurizes me – real, heavy pressure – to do the journey again, only in the opposite direction."

I am hanging now on his every word.

He pinches the end of his cigarette to extinguish it. "And drop off something 'very important' - " - and he mimes the quotation marks in the air - " - in some desert place called Iferouane. For a lot of money. I mean - a lot." He shakes his head. "I'll do a lot of things, but not that. In a place like that, on your own? You might as well dig a hole and jump in it."

I am staring back at him with my mouth open. I see Matt in the vehicle with men he was scared of, hear the fear in his voice. "And is that," I say, "what Matt intended doing?"

He shrugs. "Maybe just bravado. Bullshit. I didn't know the guy enough to know."

This is one of the worst days of my life.

He sits back. Looks at me. Then smiles a faint and - it seems to me – understanding smile. "I dunno what you can do, you know, even if you go out there."

"I can't just sit here on my own fat arse though, can I?"

"Probably not." He sits up. "Listen - I'll give you those same two numbers. It's all I can do." He takes from a pocket what looks like a business card. Turns it over, and with an expensive ballpoint, writes on the back of it, talking as he does so. "You fly to Niamey. That's the capital. Whatever you need, you'll get it there. A couple of four-by-fours. A driver. Someone who can cook. A guide. Make sure he's kosher - Tuareg preferably. There's monkeys out there who'll dump you and leave you to the vultures. And if he's as good as he should be, he'll act as fixer as well. Water. Food. Fuel. It's going to cost."

He slides the card to me across the table and points to the first of the telephone numbers. "Ring that guy - he'll get it together for you. Tell him you talked to me. The other one's backup just in case. And be careful, eh?"

I thank him. I turn the card over to see what sort of business he claims to be in. But the only thing printed on the other side is a large, yellow Smiley and that London phone number.

Perhaps he is more than the scurrilous rogue I first took him for. Yet how can I judge? He is off my map, and I would never want part of his world. Yet I share a planet with him. Living, as I've done for so long, at such a disconnect from him and his kind, seems an evasion of some common destiny. But now, it appears I may be about to share in that destiny. And like poor Matt in the car with those men, I'm scared.

I stepped out of The Intrepid Fox into a cold night wreathed in that sort of damp, clinging mist which gets to your bones. In Regent Street I caught a number three bus and sat on the top deck. It was late. People were spilling out of the pubs, laughing, shouting. They drink a lot in this country. The bus took me right past the Palace of Westminster. Lights were on in all the windows. For the first time since jumping off that train in Wigan, I envied those of my former colleagues ensconced right now inside that run-down Gothic labyrinth, engaged in a business with which they were comfortable and familiar.

I pulled Kit's business card out of my pocket and gazed at its big, yellow smiley. To what world is it the key? Are its people my son's people? I'd spent so much time fantasizing about the times we'd have together, Matt and I - the laughter we'd share, the trips, expeditions we'd go on together – making up for the lost years. What if it turned out we had little in common? That his friends were the Kits of this world? As Licia had said as we lunched by the river, what if Matt had no desire to be found by me? Old man, who are you, and what do you want?

I got off the bus at the stop just by the BBC's Crystal Palace television transmitter. It was a five minute walk from there to the Camel. I climbed thankfully back inside and closed the door on a very uncomfortable evening. I turned the heating on, poured myself a generous Laphroaig, and settled myself down on my lovely wraparound sofa. I had some thinking to do. If I were going to get this expedition – for it looked like it would be no lesser thing – off the ground, I would need help way beyond that of a telephone contact best part of five thousand kilometres away. Serious preparation would be necessary at this end. Then while I'm away I'll need a base here, a reference point, someone who will keep track of my movements, to whom I can relay information, questions, ask for help, discuss progress or lack of it. And as dear Ida Bullen had pointed out in a different context, I couldn't just disappear with only two chance acquaintances - Katalin and Kit - knowing where I was and what I was up to. But who else did I have?

There was one - and only one. Martin. Retired now and hopefully with time on his hands, with influential contacts amassed over the years, he could be the answer. His organizational skills along with his acute understanding of what had to be done had been apparent from the day I first rang him from Liverpool. That, along with his apparent penchant for the spicy and stimulating, suggested he might be not only interested, but intrigued - even eager. I would contact him in the morning.

I settled back into the cushions on my sofa. I was warm now, and the whisky was taking the edge off things. My eyelids drooped. I drifted. By my side I saw Stella. We hadn't been married long. She was wearing her slightly-the-worse-for-wear plum-coloured coat and that pretty white silk scarf. She turned to me, slowly, very slowly. Her eyes were sad. I jolted awake again, and sat up.

I sipped my Laphroaig. I'd bought it while imagining myself savouring it as I gazed out from the Camel on a blood red sun setting across some placid Scottish loch in whose millpond waters were reflected the silhouettes of brooding mountains and the rose-tinged clouds of evening. 'If you want to make God laugh,' a colleague had once said to me, 'tell Him your plans.'

I rang Katalin to report the details of my interview with Kit, and to assure her I would contact her again when I returned from Niger with whatever news I had of Matt/Gaston. Politely, and with obvious sadness, she thanked me, but asked me not to do so. She told me why, though she had no need - I'd guessed. From what I had pieced together over all these months, it was clear my son had been less than straightforward in his relationships with a number of women. Katalin had decided it wasn't worth it; she had chosen to put herself and her career first. I understood. I thanked her for her help, wished her all happiness in the future. As she put the phone down she wished my mission well. She was on the verge of tears, and my heart went out to her.

62.

Ellen quite liked flying – in a nervy sort of way. Floating through the air. Fluffy white clouds way down below. Like puffs of steam from those old trains of long ago. And a blue, blue sea, its surface shimmering gold in the sidelong sun. A tiny shard of glass – a ship? - cutting a long, white scar across its surface. A little green island drifts past, white water nudging at its shores. No buildings on it, no roads. Maybe there were parrots. Coconuts. Monkeys. Her new life.

Randolph, by her side, read his book, sipped a gin and tonic. His shoulder touching hers should have been more reassuring than it was. The aircraft banked slightly and the sun glinted off the glass in his hand. Ten hours out of Heathrow and the only sleep she'd managed was the odd catnap. Not so, Randolph. He had snored all across the Middle East.

She had tried reading. But lines of that letter kept floating across the page. Stuffed away in one of his pockets - like that pebble he'd picked up off the beach. Then one day in that hotel, getting undressed – no doubt in order to clamber into bed alongside some vapid, adoring woman – it falls to the floor. Panicking, he kicks it away where it slips into the shadows and down a gap between floorboards. There was no date on it, but something told her it had been written not long after he'd disappeared. If so, he'd had ample time to change his mind about everything he'd said in it.

She took a swig of Randolphs' gin. She closed her eyes. And there was Frank. Nice-but-simple Frank. His life had been ransacked and burned. Was what she and he together had done so wrong? Wandering the same wasteland it was inevitable they would stumble across each other. It had been short. And until that dreadful day, quite sweet.

Barnaby Marechal – bringer of chaos. There were times she almost wished she'd never met him, wished she had never accepted the fondly-remembered Toby's invite to a funeral.

"More?"

She started.

Randolph, eyebrows raised, was holding up his glass.

She placed a hand on his arm. "Order me one please would you?"

He reached up and pressed the call button. Then patted her hand as one would in leaving a young child to sleep, and returned to his book.

She looked out of the window again. The puffy white clouds were thinning out, leaving longer, wider stretches of sparkling ocean. The ship had gone. The gin and tonic would soon be here. She felt easier. Calling this off would have been a terrible thing to do. There would not be another Randolph.

63.

The first light of dawn was a faint smudge on the orange fabric of my tent. It was here - the day I dreaded and longed for. I had not slept. I was ragged. The electric high that had shot through me on first opening my eyes had been superseded by a gut-wrenching apprehension and an overwhelming sense of the pointlessness of just about everything. Matt's early childhood jostled around in my brain. The pushchair clattering over uneven pavements; Matt crying and struggling in Stella's arms as she flings open the living room door; his hand slips from mine and he runs, as fast as his little legs will carry him, towards the slide; I hear his voice calling to me. I need this day to be over. A day, I remind myself, is finite and can be only as long as a day can be. But this one stretches before me like an added lifetime.

How it might end, and how I might feel were I really to discover, out there on those dunes, my only child not seen since infancy, I did not have the imagination or stomach to speculate. Nor, were he there, did I dare wonder what condition he might be in.

Only with aching slowness did the light outside intensify. Voices came as a blessed relief - the cook, Youssef. We breakfasted. I don't remember eating. Perhaps I didn't. It was vital we were up and away. Things were taking a long time. I was irritable and increasingly nervous. By the time we were ready to move, the sun was climbing the sky. I'd hoped to be away in the brief cool of the early morning.

Only one vehicle was to go up onto the dunes – that containing Youssef, Sam, the European man and myself. The cook was to stay behind with the other vehicle as a backup in case of emergency. Youssef broke out a set of two-way radios and gave him one of the handsets.

By the time we moved off it was already hot. The dunes, at their closest point, turned out to be over four kilometres away. We advanced on them so very slowly. That undulating yellow strip, stretching from one side to the other of my vision, grew in height, encroaching bit by bit on the pale blue band of sky above. Then quite suddenly it seemed, yellow sand was filling the windscreen. The front wheels of the vehicle lifted and we were on them.

We climb a wall of sand. Only by getting my head down almost on a level with the dashboard and peering upwards do I see a ribbon of sky. Bit by bit that ribbon broadens until, after climbing for an interminable time, we breast a sort of crest like a small boat in a rough sea. The nose of the vehicle tilts gently back down to level, revealing in that one movement, an empty yellow sandscape stretching ahead and on all sides to infinity, with the sun positioned directly above. All thought goes from my head. It is hauntingly, terrifyingly beautiful.

We set off. I sit back. Some measure of calm settles over me. All will be well. All manner of thing shall be well. Where did that come from?

The heat builds up. We drive. The air conditioning gives up - par for the course. The windows are wound down and the furnace blast resumes, whipping us with grains of sand, drying our throats, burning skin left uncovered. The rise and fall of the vehicle over the humpbacks of sand brings on a leaden nausea like that of seasickness. Wind-sculpted swirls on the dunes' ridges lead the eye nowhere except to more of the same. The sun has bled from the sky all but a pallid remnant of blue. Its scorching heat penetrates the metal roof of the Landcruiser. The sores in my groin hurt. In a magazine a thousand years back in the past, there was a cartoon - man in Panama hat and full desert outfit struggles across the Sahara and meets, going the other way, cheery-countenanced chap in bathing trunks with towel over his shoulder. "Where on earth," asks first man, "d'you think you're going - to the sea?" "That's right," replies second man. "Wide beach, isn't it?"

I sit up, straighten my back. Something unsettling is going on. Through the front windscreen, the top half of my vision - the sky - is a featureless wash of almost grey blue. The lower half - the surface of the dunes - an almost featureless wash of pale yellow. A more or less flat horizon divides it from the grey-blue above. Like an abstract painting. The ones you see in exhibitions hanging on the walls and you think to yourself - 'Really? Are they serious?' And it's moving - the painting's moving vertically up, then down, then back up again. Like there's someone the other side, raising and lowering it. And we are going nowhere -we have no forward motion. Yet I hear the Land Cruiser's engine and sense the suspension responding to the terrain. We are floating up and down, like a balloon, in the middle of the desert. With the engine running. I am sick, dizzy.

"Look!"

I started wildly. Youssef was pointing ahead through the front windscreen.

Adrenalin thumped through me. The Suzuki?

"Look. There."

But when I looked, the only thing I could pick out in the sea of sand ahead of us was a very small black object which had appeared at some indeterminate distance directly ahead. "That?" I said.

He smiled. "Keep watching."

I did. What was he smiling about? I frowned. Whatever it was seemed to be getting bigger. Now floating above the ground. A mirage? It continued to grow in size and at an increasing speed – a speed which very soon seemed out of all proportion to the speed with which we appeared to be approaching it. Was it also on the move and accelerating towards us? It had no recognizable outline – just an irregular black chunk. But then it was the size of an articulated truck and coming straight at us. "Jesus Christ," I said. "What the fuck is it?"

But still he just smiled and pointed. And as he pointed, his pointing finger swung with it as we and the object were about to pass each other. Now it was shrinking again. With my eyes riveted to it, it was collapsing in on itself. As we passed it I found myself staring down on a black rock no more than a metre high. I gasped. We left it behind. Open-mouthed, I turned to Youssef who was now smiling the smile of one who knows. He was tickled pink with himself. With a twinkle in his eye, he said, "The desert, " then went to say more.

But I had switched off and retired to a quiet corner of the riverside bar. Amid the hum of conversation, glasses clink. The pleasure boats go gently by on the river in the sun, their flags fluttering in the breeze. The 'Eye' turns majestically, its elegant pods brimming with eager sightseers. A red, double-decker bus crosses Westminster Bridge but there's so much perspiration running down my forehead and into my eyes I really can't see it clearly. The European man is tapping me on the shoulder. Passes me a water bottle and indicates for me to drink. Does he think, for Christ's sake, I'm incapable of looking after myself? Even so, I drink. "How much longer now?" I demand of Youssef.

Calmly, he shrugs. "Not long."

The Land Cruiser gave a sudden lurch and came to a dead stop. As it did so, the engine wound instantly up to a high-pitched whine. I sat upright and looked around. We were rocking violently from side to side. Youssef put out a hand and switched the engine off. The vehicle came to rest. I looked at him. He looked at me. "Stuck in sand," he said.

"Problem?"

Shaking his head, he jumped out. As he did so I saw we were pointing up the rising side of a dune at almost 45 degrees. Sam followed him and the pair of them set about pulling tools of some sort from the rear of the vehicle.

I turned around and looked at the European man in the rear seat. Again we were alone together. He looked at me, and smiled. What is it about this man? I feel like a student in the presence of my tutor. I resent it. I resent him. I resent this fucking country.

"How are you?" he asked, adopting an infuriating bedside manner.

I blanked him, looked the other way. I'm not handling this well. In the absence now of the hot wind through open windows, I could actually feel the air temperature rising around me. We were stationary directly under the sun. How much hotter could it get?

He said, very quietly, "I think you find we are now nearly there."

I spun round to face him once again, my pulse quickening. "How do you know?"

"Youssef and Sam speaking together just now."

"You understand their language?" I was shocked.

He nodded.

Of course he did. He probably understood every language on the bloody planet. I fought to control a fury bordering on tears. "How long," I barked, "will it take them to dig us out?"

"I do not know. But there is no problem. They have done it many times."

"I think," I said, "I need some space. Some air. Please excuse me." With which I opened my door and was about to step out onto the sand when he lay a hand on my arm. "Fifteen minutes," he said. "No longer."

"Yes," I replied, unable to control the anger in my voice. "I know. Thank you so much."

I stepped outside. The sun hit me with an alien ferocity. I gathered myself together.

"No, no!!" Youssef, who seemed to be pushing some sort of short ladder beneath one of the rear wheels, shouted to me. He pointed to his own head. "Hat! Put hat on."

"I haven't got a hat!"

"Then put something – anything – on your head. Out here it is fifty!"

In a fury, I flung the door open again. On the floor by my seat was a French newspaper. On seaside holidays of my childhood I'd honed a skill of which, in those days, I was proud – I could fashion, from any old newspaper, a hat with a pointed top. My 'admiral's hat' I used to call it. Wearing it back then, I looked the bee's knees. Now, as I put the selfsame thing on my head out here on the dunes of the Tenere, it's likely I looked demented. And maybe I was. What the hell.

Fuelled by fear, self-loathing and a tentative scrap of hope, I set off up the incline. I went at it like a man thirty years my junior. It was steeper even than it had looked and when finally I made the crest I was gulping in great gobs of hot air and my heart was hammering against the wall of my chest. I looked around at a mercilessly identical landscape – sand. Sand. Sand. Perspiration was pouring down my body, front and back. The perpendicular sun was burning through the newspaper hat onto my balding head and the heat from the sand hurt my feet through my sandals. This was no place to be. I felt fear. I have to get back to the vehicle.

But then, over to my right, through the perspiration which was stinging my eyes and half obscuring my vision, there was something. Something red. I dragged my hands across my eyes, clearing them for a second. My stomach lurched. It seemed all cockeyed as though it might be half buried in sand. And so small. Like a wind-up toy given to me one Christmas. It might have been a long way away, but you can't tell, you see. You can't judge. Clutching my newspaper admiral's hat to my head, I set off in that direction like a man on Clacton beach in August heading for the sea, all warnings, all caution gone.

The European man clambered out of the Land Cruiser, went to the rear of the vehicle and spoke with Youssef. He tapped the watch on his wrist then pointed towards the crest of the dune. Youssef exchanged a few hurried words with Sam who was on his knees by one of the rear wheels. Then Youssef and the European man set off quickly up the slope. At the summit, they stood looking around. Youssef pointed away to their right. The European man set off in that direction, disappearing over the crest. Youssef ran back down towards Sam and the Land Cruiser.

The red Suzuki pickup was a speck, lost in the vastness like a spot of blood on the surface of the moon. The driver's side was up to its wheel arches in the sand, its door immovable. The other side was angled at forty-five degrees to the sky, its door jammed wide open by something caught in its hinges. It gaped at the sun like an abandoned nestling. The European man half ran, half tumbled down the steep slope of the dune. With a snatched glance at the truck's rear cargo area, empty apart from a single fuel can on its side with its cap hanging off, he shoved his head in through the driver's window. The tiny cab was half a metre deep in sand which had, within the last few minutes, been disturbed and scattered around. A blue jean jacket had been pulled out of it and thrown to one side, the contents of its pockets turned out. Rotted banana skins lay around, discarded sweet and biscuit wrappers, a half-empty pack of Gauloises, a small backpack, its compartments open and empty; a French cinema magazine; plastic water bottles, all empty. And curiously, on the dashboard, the metal casing of a lipstick, the contents of which had melted away, staining a packet of tissues and the area all around a dull crimson. The European man took a quick, practised look around, then withdrew his head and hurried round to the other side of the vehicle.

The Land Cruiser pulled up in a flurry of sand. Youssef and Sam jumped out and joined the European man who was standing by the gaping passenger door. He pointed to the ground at his feet, then to a ridge of sand some hundred metres away. A line of fresh footprints left the vehicle and disappeared over the ridge which shimmered in the heat. Fluttering on its rim in the current of air across the dunes were the torn fragments of a newspaper.

Each man looked at the others. With a sweep of his arm, Youssef motioned them back to the Land Cruiser. Then took from his pocket a two-way radio and pressed the 'Call' button.

In the distance, silhouetted high against the washed-out blue of the sky, a large bird on widespread wings rode the thermals.

64.

Ida Bullen, doing a final check of the newly refurbished apartment, stopped in her tracks halfway across the sitting room. She didn't really know why. It was quite involuntary - like she'd walked into an invisible wall. And there came over her a most uncomfortable sensation. Like time had stumbled, missing out a second or two. It was rather like a car she once had in which the engine would occasionally misfire, sending a shudder through the whole frame. She put a hand to her mouth. Sat herself quickly down in an armchair.

She closed her eyes. She sensed her heart beating just a little faster than usual. Even though there was no history of cardiac problems in the family it was a little concerning. She took a deep breath and tried to put all thoughts out of her mind.

She waited what she thought was about two minutes, then opened her eyes again. Checked her pulse. It was back to normal. Firmly grasping the arms of the chair, she raised herself carefully to her feet. Turned her head this way, then that. The world remained steady. A little warily at first, she returned to what she'd been doing. She moved around carefully. One gets older. Is that was this was - age? Probably. Even so.....

65.

The Land Cruiser, its engine racing, screamed down the plumb line of a road at the head of a spiralling cloud of dust.

Youssef, stooped in the rear of the vehicle, braced himself. Then lifted to shoulder height one of the large plastic water containers. With as much care as he could, given the vehicle's violent movements, he poured the contents from one end to the other of the blanket which covered from the neck down, Barney's naked body stretched out across the rear seats.

The European man, kneeling in the water swilling around on the floor, patted the soaking blanket closer to Barney's burning skin. He peered at his closed eyes. His face was bloated, red, dry. His breathing deep and rapid.

Youssef pulled a small section of the blanket away from Barney's shoulder, and drew from his armpit a thermometer. He studied it.

The European man watched his reaction.

His expression gave nothing away. "Forty-two, five." He shook the thermometer and replaced it.

The European man turned away.

The vehicle swerved, its horn blaring. Water washed over the floor as Youssef was thrown against the side of the vehicle.

I didn't know what I was doing, you see – I didn't know. Well, I did but it meant nothing. I had a compulsion. It shot up from somewhere inside me like a striking snake. Nothing else mattered. I was going to walk - I was going to walk just as far as the next ridge. No further. But that was all that was necessary because, you see, I knew he was over there and only just out of sight. Indeed, were I a tiny bit taller I could probably have seen his head from where I stood. Seen the red scarf around his neck and the collar of the black overcoat. He'd got out and walked, that's what he'd done. It's against all the rules, I know, and I'm sure he did too. But who of us is that level-headed? The boy panicked. Silent, alone in that suffocating cab that could turn out to be his tomb - who wouldn't panic? It would send Christ himself off his head. So what d'you do - stay there going mad while you wait for rescue you know's never coming because nobody knows you're there? Or take a walk thinking, in your innocence, you'll find a man on a camel – or if you're not so innocent, knowing you're likely dead inside an hour? Poor, poor lad. I shall go to him, put my arms around him and tell him it's all over now. I'm sorry Matt, so very, very sorry. I'm back. For keeps. So, I too step out into the wilderness. I might burn up in this sun. Burn up and die. Merge with him that way, if that's the only way left to me. He deserves that of me. I gave him life once. Now maybe I give him mine. That's all I have left to give. I hope that will be enough, lad. I hope so much that will be enough.

"Turn his head," said Youssef. "Right over to the side. Pull his tongue forward – or he will choke on it. With your finger."

The European man did so.

Youssef looked at his watch, shrugged.

The Land Cruiser, its windows all down, its horn blaring, careered through the village. It swerved wildly to avoid a cyclist who came out from a passage between mud walls. It sped on in a cloud of dust, scattering people, chickens, dogs and anything else in its way.

66.

The last customer left the shop. She checked the clock. One minute to closing time. She hurried to the door to forestall any last-minute chancers. She locked up, turned the 'Closed' sign outwards to the street. On her way back to the counter she heard a vehicle draw up outside. She turned. It was white and so large it blocked most of the light. How inconsiderate. They really ought not to allow vehicles that big down these little narrow streets.

The clock on the village church chimed wheezily. She opened the till. Scrutinized the day's takings. This is no way to get rich. It's the weather - yet again, no summer to speak of. A movement caught her eye and she looked up.

A man, quite elderly, thin, balding, wearing jeans and an open-neck shirt was standing at the locked door. His face was right up to the glass, peering in. He caught her eye. She shook her head and mouthed, 'Closed!'

He looked for a moment as though he might try to dissuade her. She was preparing to stand her ground when he mouthed in return, 'OK', shrugged and turned away.

She felt sorry for him. She hurried across the shop, unlocked and threw open the door. "Hello!"

He was about the climb into the cab of the white vehicle. He turned to her. What hair he had was almost white. He was quite nice-looking.

"If," she said, "it's just a couple of things you want."

"Pint of milk and a loaf of bread. That's all."

"The only bread I've left is rye."

He smiled. "No problem."

She beckoned him in.

He closed the door of the vehicle. "Thank you. You're very kind."
Together they went into the shop.
Close up, he was frail and underweight.

She locked the door again. Stood and watched the large white vehicle drive away. On the rear was a little coloured picture of some animal. She was pulling down the blind this time to make sure nobody else was tempted even to look through the window, when her friend who ran the tourist shop across the road appeared the other side of the glass. Once more she unlocked and opened the door.

Her friend came in. "Fancy coming over to mine for a glass? I've called it a day, too. Dead as the dodo, isn't it?"

"Listen," she said, "do you remember – some years ago now – some politician disappearing? Just – vanished overnight and no-one ever knew what had happened to him?"

"'Lord Something or other, wasn't it?"

"No, no – much more recent than that." They walked back to the counter. "A politician. Not a celebrity. But still quite well-known. Disappeared off a train down south somewhere."

"Oh - and they found his phone in a skip or something. In London?"

"That's him."

"What about him?"

She said, quietly confidential, "I think it might have been him in that white motorhome that's just driven away."

"Get away!"

"Seriously."

"You sure?"

"Sort of. He bought a loaf of bread and a pint of milk. He looked a lot older – well, I suppose he would anyway. And not very well actually."

"Ooer. You going to tell the police?"

"Police?" She frowned. "Why?"

"I'm sure they'd like to know."

"What's it to do with them - after all this time? He seemed a nice chap."

"What makes you think it was him?"

"I said it might be. I don't know - he just looked a bit like him, from what I can remember. But it was something he said. I asked him if he was here on holiday - like you do. He said no, but he had just come back from abroad. 'Oh, somewhere nice?' I said. And he had to think a bit before he gave a funny little smile then said, ever so quietly, 'Not really.' Just like that. I didn't know what to say, so I just said, 'Oh dear,' smiled a bit awkwardly and handed him his goods. But he kept looking at me with this - well - kind and almost sad look. 'It's sometimes the way of things, isn't it?' he said. 'You just have to do what you have to do.'"

"So - what's that supposed to mean?"

"Don't know." She shrugged. "But he said it like it was important. And anyway, I just got the feeling that that's who he was. That's all."

"Where's he off to now then in his motorhome? With his loaf of bread and pint of milk."

"The Caravan Club site up at Kinlochewe? Maybe."

"What d'you think makes someone do that? Leave their wife, family, friends – throw away their career and everything they have, and just disappear like that?"

She shrugged. "I guess he had his reasons."

"Whatever they were, I hope it was all worth it."

67.

The water is red with the sun's reflection, and still, like glass. A few thin, high clouds straggle the sky's margins. A single large bird moves with slow wing beats in silhouette across what remains of the sun. I sip my Laphroaig. I watch the slow ripples that fan out across the surface of the loch from a point just out of my sight on the shore. A duck, probably, dabbling – or whatever it is they do. The ripples sparkle orange in the sun as they run outwards, slowly fade then become one with the water which, as the last little arc of the sun dips out of sight, turns a massive, jet black. The scent of gorse through the open window of the Camel mixes with the smoky fumes of my whisky.

'We read the signposts,' he said. 'We take the road,' he said. 'Our part in it then is over.' That's the hard bit. We want endings, and I don't have one. I have instead a silver pendant. It is inset with a ruby, and hangs here against the glass of the window. It catches the sun, the light, raindrops. I treasure it.

I came within an ace of doing away with my own self. Were it not for the simple humanity and selfless risk-taking of four men, strangers from other lands, who came so much by chance into my life, my bones would now be beneath the sands of the Tenere. As it is, my bones and me are here in this deepening dusk by these serene and beautiful waters. I will get well again. I owe those men my life. I must use the years they have given me. For I see now that what has gone before was stuff I had to move aside in order to get a clear sight of the road ahead. With that view now more clearly open to me, once my health has recovered, I can begin again.

So now? No immediate course of action jumps up waving its hands at me. I sense a need - for the moment at least and until my health recovers - simply to experience my own self in this place. A voice in my head reprimands me. 'Nothing will come of nothing.' That, in a sense is clearly so. But then there is another voice, from a deeper, silent place. 'Do nothing,' it says. 'Bide your time. Be. And be ready. The time, in its time, will come.'

The light is now mostly gone. I detect a movement by the loch. Those ripples again spreading out over the surface. And then a figure, like that of a man, climbing the rising ground from the water and stopping on a slight ridge, standing still, mostly hidden in deep shadow.

I set down my glass. I step out of the Camel and hurriedly make my way across the rough ground through the gorse and the heather. The air already has the edge of night about it. Who is he, that man? Walking silently in the dark? I wonder, would he like to join me in a glass, a dram?

I pass behind a granite outcrop and emerging on the other side, I am virtually on the shore. The first stars are in the black water. I look around. The man has gone. I scan the outline of the near hills, still just discernible against the purple sky. There is no-one.

I make my way back to the Camel. I will look for you again. I will see you again. 'Let me go down next year with the spring waters, And search for you to the end of the white clouds in the East.'